LINDBERGH, CONDON & HAUPTMANN, 1932

- DIGGING DEEPER -

by

John Allison, Ph.D.

With commentary from Mark Falzini and The A. Wiskowski Photograph Collection

ISBN 978-1-961017-77-1 (Paperback)

Inquiries and Book Orders should be addressed to:

Leavitt Peak Press
17901 Pioneer Blvd Ste L #298, Artesia, California 90701
Phone #: 2092191548

Dedication

This book is dedicated to my parents, John and Florence Allison, and to my Aunt and Uncle, Helen and Haskel Winslow, my constant sources of support and encouragement.

Acknowledgments

Special thanks to Fred Wish and Loretta Bolger-Wish for advice and editing, for their authentic interest in the project, and for their endless musical talents. Also, there were TCNJ students, too many to mention, who made creative contributions in my Forensic Chemistry courses and in Undergraduate Research. Finally, I appreciate those people who are passionate about anything Lindbergh, and just enjoy talking about it. Thanks to Mark Falzini, who always makes time to help, and to Barbara Wiskowski who found and shares here a set of photos from her father, Alphonse, a fan of Charles Lindbergh and the early days of aviation.

About the Author

Dr. John Allison received his Ph.D. from the University of Delaware in Physical Chemistry. He was a National Science Foundation Post-Doctoral Fellow at Stanford University. He joined the faculty at Michigan State University (MSU) where he taught, did research, and was co-director of the MSU Mass Spectrometry Facility – a research and service lab on campus. He rose through the ranks from the level of Assistant Professor to Full Professor. After 25 years at MSU, he moved back to the East Coast (having been born and raised in Philadelphia) and joined the faculty at The College of New Jersey (TCNJ), formerly Trenton State Teacher's College. He had spent the last six years of his career at MSU pursuing forensic applications of the instrumental technique known as mass spectrometry. His primary interest is in the area of Questioned Document Analysis. Dr. Allison has published more than 100 research papers in refereed journals such as *The Journal of Forensic Sciences*, the *Journal of the American Chemical Society*, the *International Journal of Mass Spectrometry*, *Inorganic Chemistry*, and the *Journal of Chemical Education*. He's also made over 275 presentations at local, national, and international scientific meetings. His published papers have been cited more than 3,500 times to date.

At TCNJ, he taught courses in Forensic Chemistry and a First Seminar Program course on the Lindbergh Baby Kidnapping. In his 15 years back on the East Coast, you could find him on the sailing vessel "Alice" on the Barnegat Bay, or playing with Fred and Loretta, his three-piece band, "Rising Smoke."

After 15 years at TCNJ as the Premiere Director and creator of the Forensic Chemistry Specialization, part of the Chemistry Program, he retired at the end of the 2018 calendar year.

CONTENTS

PART I

BACKGROUND INFORMATION YOU'LL NEED

CHAPTER 1
INTRODUCTION

Since you enjoy investigating the most perplexing criminal cases, we're going to take a fresh look at one of the most challenging – referred to by many as the *Crime of the Century*, and *One of the most Famous Cases in the History of American Law Enforcement*. First, I want you to imagine something. Imagine!

You've been having a good life lately, an exciting one. You're in your new house on a mountain top. Your first child is 20 months old. It's about 10 p.m. and you learn that your child is gone, and there is now an envelope in the room. It contains the following letter:

> ***Hey Chuckk!***
>
> ***Yess, we gots your kidd. Do NOTcall the cops! That will piss us off.***
> ***Wheel give him back for 50 thousand bucks. You got the mony, we know.***
> ***We want it in $1 bills.***
> ***Your kidd is doing oK, butt. Is annoing but get the cash asa.p., oK??***
> ***To Help u out, I gonna put my seal on every letr from me. [Symbol to right]***
> ***and tare off 2 corners. Gott it!***

Perhaps you scratch your head for a second, finding the letter to be such an odd document, but the important fact quickly hits you. Your child is gone. Stolen! Who is holding him now? You feel so helpless. You have in your hand a letter from the kidnappers, and they will write an unprecedented 14 more. Will you ever know who was just in your home? Will you see your baby again? Imagine how you would feel. Now imagine sharing every intimate fact and feeling with the entire planet. Would you feel satisfied when one person is found guilty and the investigation is closed, when the kidnappers had identified themselves as a gang of five years earlier?

I've written this book for multiple audiences. First, this will serve as a summary for those who are not familiar with the 1932 kidnapping of Charles Lindbergh's baby. This is very much a New Jersey story, although some may feel it takes place in the Bronx. Other states claim Charles Lindbergh as their own. Michigan! Lindbergh was born in Detroit where his mother taught chemistry at the Cass Technical High School. As he was growing up he spent time with his mother in Detroit and with his father, a politician, in Washington, D.C. Minnesota claims Lindbergh – he spent some of his young life in a house, now maintained as a historical landmark, in Little Falls. Wisconsin also claims him since he (briefly) attended The University of Wisconsin - Madison. The national and international interest in the Lindbergh family has been with us since the 1920s.

I've written this book as a workbook for readers who would like to develop their critical thinking skills. The book is an interactive document. It is unique, informally evaluating information through the eyes of a scientist (chemist). It is unlike other "Lindbergh books", examining the challenging case through a scientific lens, not a book that suggests one more possible explanation of events based on a few new "facts."

Together the reader and I evaluate evidence and make measurements. One goal is to teach you about some of the tools available, and how to think with those tools as a context. I am fortunate, having completed a graduate program. I was trained in how to perform meaningful experiments (and understand how and why they work). Advanced graduate work can also hone your ability to question and thoroughly consider more, and to be prepared to take that next step. Ideas can be proposed based on evidence. If an idea seems to stand up to criticism, it might become a theory. Perhaps you will be able to show logically that it is sound because it stands on known facts. Often the last step is physically testing your theory. Perhaps you will be the first to go back to the drawing board when you try to do what you and others had theorized. Often this last step is the hardest for an investigator to take. You will be looking at this case through my eyes, understanding that "experts" always consider new topics in terms of what they know best. We have had newspaper reporters, talented seasoned and first-time writers, smart people, and experts in fields such as forestry, law enforcement, and handwriting analysis write books on this case, but I believe this is the first time a traditional scientist will be beginning your education in making measurements and evaluating evidence.

Also, I've written this book to provide some new information for the people who have been continuously working on this puzzling case since 1932 - a few more contributions for the Lindbergh hobbyists. Hobbyists continue to discuss and debate the crime and the trial on web sites, in chat rooms, and discussion blogs. They are very active and always come up with many theories. Occasionally they snipe at each other as well. Actually, they snipe at each other quite a bit, and I'm sure they'll find many things to criticize in this book. They add to the body of knowledge by using old "facts" to create new facts, but unfortunately, they do not always document their sources, so we cannot evaluate how they reached their conclusions. A. Scott Berg, in his book *Lindbergh* (Berg, 1998), opens Chapter 14 with the line: "Much of yesterday's hearsay became today's history." This is a good summary of where we are today in this case. For just about every fact in the story, there is at least one other version. Often, neither seems to make sense. But this is what we must work with.

As you will quickly detect, I am writing this book for you as my student, my trainee. My goal is not to write a stuffy text, but to informally share with you things that I have learned. One thing I've learned from a teaching career is that students won't have fun unless I have fun, so I intend to. I also think you should learn about some side topics related to the main subjects. I promise you, one can never know too much.

When I was looking for a job a few centuries ago, I found myself at Michigan State University (MSU), interviewing for a faculty position. A Dean started to tell me about how MSU was one of the first land-grant institutions (and what that meant). I nodded and said, "Yes, 1855. You've come a long way." He must have thought I was showing off because he started to question me.

"We weren't the first. There were two schools that started in the same month in 1855 as land grant colleges."

"Yes, I know," I replied.

He stared at me for a while, then blurted out, "Well, so what was the other school?"

I could detect his desire to finish that question with "wise guy," but he controlled himself. I sat there and tried to look like I was thinking before I said, "Penn State."

He laughed. "So, you did your homework before coming here, eh?"

Actually, no, I didn't. But when I was young, I collected everything – stamps, coins, baseball cards, etc. and I enjoyed my mostly filled book of U.S. stamps. I admired every one of them, got to know them all. I just happened to remember there was a green three-cent commemorative stamp honoring the First Land Grant Colleges. It was a 1955 stamp commemorating their beginnings in 1855. The stamp showed "Michigan State College" on one side and "Pennsylvania State University" on the other side. It may have seemed when I was ten years old that my head was needlessly filling with useless information too quickly, but here I was in my late 20's, realizing that a stamp from my collection was making me look like I knew something! It was a good thing. Keep learning. Stay curious.

CHAPTER 2
ABOUT THE BOOK/SOME ADVICE

2A. An Investigative Workbook

One challenge of the Lindbergh kidnapping story is that it is a cold case. You and I will be reviewing the "facts," researching various aspects of the story, using a bit of common sense, and thinking deeply about the evidence. Since I am a scientist, I naturally look at the evidence and think about what more I can do with it, so a variety of measurements – physical and spectroscopic – will be presented, the methods will be explained, and the experience will be an interactive one. Through the workbook aspect of this text, all readers will have an opportunity to learn new things and participate in the discovery process.

Analysis of the 15 letters from the kidnappers is the largest single topic in the book.

2B. A Cold Case

The complication of discussing a cold case is that we will need to deal with the fact that Lindbergh's son was kidnapped in 1932. It is vital to understand what life was like in the 1930s. If you don't know how people lived back then, you will jump to many incorrect conclusions. We will go back in time to understand relevant aspects of the 1930s.

Fortunately for me, most of the evidence associated with the case is in the New Jersey State Police Museum, which is about ten minutes from my home. Mr. Mark Falzini, the Museum Curator, is one of the world's experts on the topic and has been very cooperative in providing me and many others with access to museum items. Mark will have something to say about my ruminations, and I'm happy to share his comments, which will appear as boxes containing *Mark Falzini comments* and *Author comments.*

2C. Things to Do

I have integrated some questions and assignments throughout this book to keep you involved. Of course, you can ignore all of the questions and just read, but the experience will be less satisfying. Are you willing to do some extra work, and learn a little more? I want your answer to be 'yes.'

2D. Some Advice - Making Measurements

Science has at its disposal hundreds of different types of instruments that could be used to investigate various aspects of physical evidence; these can be very helpful if used correctly, and if you question your results to decide if they could be correct. Even if you are using an accepted technique, question your work.

For example, it would seem relatively simple to use a scientific balance to measure masses/weights. I have a small pocket balance that I bought in a store in Times Square, which will weigh items up to 100 grams. (The small balance is perhaps purchased mostly by drug dealers). Suppose five rocks are thrown through my windows. I'm curious if they came from the neighbor's rock garden. (I know that he spent several weeks trying to find a supplier of rocks that were all of similar weight, in the range of 70-150 grams.) I weighed each of the five rocks with my pocket balance and wrote down the results, listed in Table 2E.1.

Table 2E.1: Weighing some Rocks

Rock No.	Measured weight
1	75 grams
2	92 grams
3	100 grams
4	100 grams
5	100 grams

I recommend that after you finish gathering data, even such simple data, take a step back and look at the big picture. Ask yourself, could this data possibly be correct?

Q 2E.1: What do you think?

A 2E.1: ____

The odds of having three stones weigh exactly 100 grams is unlikely, but I did say the rock garden is composed of rocks in the 70-150-gram range. What else do we know? We know the scale only gives useful numbers if the sample is in the 0-100 gram range. Stones #3-5 likely weighed more than 100 grams, but 100 is the highest number the scale can report, so it does. The manufacturer did warn us. The last three will need to be weighed on a balance that has a larger range.

Conclusion: *It's easier to do an experiment than to do a meaningful experiment.* Make sure you understand what your "instrument" can and cannot do.

2E. Best Advice

In terms of investigating this case, the best advice I have found is in:

Studying the Lindbergh Case: A Guide to the Files and Resources Available at the New Jersey State Police Museum written by Mark Falzini in 2007. https://dspace.njstatelib.org/xmlui/bitstream/handle/10929/22290/c9292006.pdf?sequence=1&isAllowed=y

If you want to develop your critical thinking skills, you can't be lazy. I've given you a reference. Now it's your job to find it and read it.

I've learned many things from Mark Falzini, and perhaps the most important thing is that the path to being an expert in a field is field-dependent. As a Chemist, if I need the atomic weight of rubidium, or an explanation of how gases differ from solids, or how water can be a liquid and also a solid, I can grab just about any Chemistry book off my bookcase and find the answers.

If I'm someone like Mark, and he wants to find the names of the Lindberghs' two dogs that they had in 1932, scores of books could be consulted, and Mark has likely read them all. He's read each one critically and has a sense of which would most reliably provide the correct names. I think he ranks available books/authors by researching facts they provide, deciding who is most dependable.

Consider just a few of the points Mark Falzini makes in his very useful *Studying the Lindbergh Case:*

- "The Lindbergh Case is riddled with contradictions and unanswered questions. It is truly America's "soap opera" … It is almost too over the top for television!"

- "Once the researcher has gained a general overview of the case, s/he should then pick a specific aspect or area of the case on which to focus."

- "The researcher does not necessarily need to try to prove Hauptmann's innocence or guilt. Nor does the researcher need to find out what "really" happened. Rather more is to be gained by digging deeper into the case."

In some ways, Chemistry books are generally reliable; Lindbergh books are not. In part this may be because there are Lindbergh books from the 1930s and books from the 1990s. In the 30s your source of information was newspapers and reporters. Over time we've come to learn that reporters would fabricate information on slow news days. And then there were players like John Condon who was the sole source for so many pieces of information; how do we know if any/all of them are true?

Your only choice here is to work with the information I've given you - all things that I've found in the books that I've read. For the training you'll get here, you have to work with what you get. After this you can always read more and develop your own truth.

2F. How to Use This Book

You can just read the book and find the things that may be most interesting to you, but I have provided the opportunity for you to participate, to feel what it's like to investigate this case. If you're new to the case, you may not know who everyone is (although you need to). In the beginning, I certainly had to do some research to understand who's who. To allow you to follow in the steps that I've taken, I've provided a small hard copy internet for you at the back of this book, so that you can look some things up. It's called ALLISONweb. Feel free to surf ALLISONweb at any time, so you'll know what it contains. I'll also be giving you opportunities to express your opinions as we move through the information. I will again encourage you to participate, to take notes or at least highlight as you read, because I may challenge you with an occasional quiz, to make sure you're paying attention.

You may feel that the labels that I use seem a bit excessive, but I want you to always know where you are and always be able to find sections when you want them. Suppose we have CHAPTER 100, which covers seven topics. These Sections would be labeled as 100A through 100G. In Section 100A, there may be questions (and answers). The first you encounter would be labeled as Q 100A.1: and A 100A.1: The first Table you would see in this section would be Table 100A.1: and the first Figure you would encounter would be labeled as Figure 100A.1: If I feel it is essential for you to know where a fact came from, there is a list of the references in Appendix II. If I give you the names of the authors and the date of publication, that should be all you need to find the complete citation in the References. So, if you see (A. Smith & D. Jones 1945), the references are in alphabetical order, so find the authors first. The date will confirm that you have the correct source.

2G. A final FYI

Newspapers called Charles Lindbergh "The Lone Eagle" and his son became the "Eaglet." For this book, I'll try to consistently call Charles Lindbergh the aviator "Lindbergh" and his first son, also Charles Lindbergh, I'll call "Little Charlie." "Anne" refers to Anne Lindbergh, wife of Charles and mother to Little Charlie.

In the next chapter, we will meet young Charles Lindbergh, and those around him, even before he became the world's hero and crush. So, "Hang onto your hat," as people said back when they wore hats.

Chapter 3

CHARLES LINDBERGH THE AVIATOR – THE EARLY YEARS

Front Page Headline, The New York Times, Sunday, May 22, 1927:

LINDBERGH DOES IT! TO PARIS IN 33 ½ HOURS; FLIES 1,000 MILES THROUGH SNOW AND SLEET; CHEERING FRENCH CARRY HIM OFF THE FIELD

CROWD ROARS THUNDEROUS WELCOME

BREAKS THROUGH LINES OF SOLDIERS AND POLICE AND SURGING TO PLANE LIFTS WEARY FLIER FROM HIS COCKPIT

AVIATORS SAVE HIM FROM FRENZIED MOB OF 100,000

Paris Boulevards Ring with Celebration After Day and Night Watch – American Flag is Called for and Wildly Acclaimed.

Charles Lindbergh's (1902-1974) parents didn't get along and usually resided apart. Lindbergh would often shuttle back and forth between the two. He did not learn much from the problems between them. He didn't integrate into society but isolated himself. He had no friends his age and was very self-absorbed. Perhaps the person of most interest to young Lindbergh was his Grandfather Land, his mother's father, a pioneering dentist.

Lindbergh's early schooling was only occasional, but he did graduate from Little Falls High School in 1918. Perhaps Lindbergh was not interested in college, but since he was encouraged to go, he did. He enrolled at the University of Wisconsin in 1921. He began as a Mechanical Engineering Major. During his first semester, he was put on probation for low grades in chemistry and mathematics, and he failed his engineering course. Still, his early passion was for using and understanding mechanical devices. One machine that got his attention was the automobile. When he was twelve years old, he drove his mother from Minnesota to Los Angeles in her car. While classwork bored him, he did excel in other activities. He was outstanding when it came to firearms, and he joined The University of Wisconsin's Marksman Club. The team finished the 1921 season as the best in the country with Lindbergh recognized as the best marksman among college teams. This may explain why he had a Winchester .30 caliber –'06 bolt action rifle in his closet at the time of the kidnapping (1932). By 1935 he had purchased two more weapons, a Colt revolver and a Fitz snub nose .38 with a 2" barrel.

Lindbergh left college while still in his early 20s to pursue another interest – flying. He enrolled in a six-month flying school in Lincoln, Nebraska. His father contributed so he could buy his first plane. Lindbergh found someone who was selling surplus World War I airplanes for $1,000 each. Lindbergh talked the owner into selling him one for $500. Lindbergh learned everything he could about airplanes, and to make some money, he became a barnstormer – doing dangerous stunts at county fairs. He also became a wing walker, and, at times, he would even parachute off his airplane.

For his first 20 years, he was known to everyone as "Slim"- a 6 foot, 2 ½ inch tall, 150-pound flyer and entertainer.

Two years after leaving the University of Wisconsin, he enlisted in the Army to learn more by joining their flight training school, where he became the best student pilot in his class. He was hired by Robertson Aircraft Corporation of St. Louis to fly U.S. Mail between St. Louis and Chicago. Lindbergh lore reports that, on two occasions flying the U.S. Mail on days with very low visibility because of blizzards, he grabbed the bag of mail and parachuted out of the plane, leaving it to crash wherever it might go. When he hit the ground, he would catch a train and finish his mail delivery run.

Lindbergh's lack of focus changed when he first heard of the Orteig Prize, a $25,000 prize to the first person who could fly between New York and Paris nonstop. There were trained pilots who responded to this challenge. All had failed. Some had even died trying. Lindbergh started to raise money from investors in St. Louis and the Midwest. He named the plane he was building *The Spirit of St. Louis.* He creatively made the plane as lightweight as possible. He developed new ways to fly to increase mileage, reducing diesel fuel consumption. While most competitors started with larger, more powerful planes, Lindbergh started with a much lighter single-engine aircraft.

On a foggy, rainy morning on May 20, 1927, 25-year-old Lindbergh took off from Roosevelt Field (in Long Island, New York) hours before others who wanted to participate. He flew for 33.5 hours and landed in Paris. He instantly became the world's darling at a time when America and many other countries needed a hero. Lindbergh spent the next month with world leaders throughout Europe, being wined and dined, and being presented with many awards. He received cash, and cars, and overnight became a rich man with many job offers. He was hired, when he returned home, to tour the country in his plane while giving talks on the future of air travel and the possible uses of airplanes. He visited all 48 states. For this three-month tour he received $50,000 from the Guggenheim family. Through them, he met several important people including Henry Breckenridge, the attorney to the Guggenheims (who eventually became a very close friend), and Dwight Morrow. Lindbergh flew over 260 hours for this tour, delivered 147 speeches, and he was in parades for over 1285 miles. Thirty million people – a quarter of the nation, had an opportunity to see him.

In addition to the gifts he received after crossing the Atlantic, he was offered movie work, vaudeville engagements and corporate positions. Often monetary gifts had no single donor; he would use them to make donations to organizations such as the Red Cross. He was made a Colonel in the Army Air Corps Reserve by President Coolidge. After his successful flight, he received 3,500,000 letters, 100,000 telegrams, and more than 14,000 packages. He was hired to serve as a technical advisor for many upcoming airlines and earned more than a million dollars in 18-months. As he toured the country discussing the future of aviation, he also talked about a pet project - creating a National Meteorological Organization.

The *Spirit of St. Louis* was a unique airplane, as was Lindbergh's approach to flying to save fuel. Once he returned to the U.S. after his flight to Paris, he continued to meet the most influential men in Aeronautics in the world. They all wanted to benefit from his expertise and his celebrity. He spent time with Transcontinental Air Transport, a Canadian Group. They believed that they could offer 48-hour coast-to-coast flights in the summer of 1929. Lindbergh worked to reduce that time by 12 hours. Transcontinental had a fleet of five airplanes, which, they hoped, with Lindbergh's help, could each travel at 105 miles per hour. He defined a new goal of flying 32 passengers at a time, with their planes flying at 130 mph. He received $10,000 a year for chairing their Technical Committee, plus a $250,000 signing bonus that he could use to purchase 25,000 shares of their stock. Lindbergh also let them use his name. Their premiere flight was called "The Lindbergh Line."

On a trip to Cuba, Lindbergh met Juan Terry Trippe, who owned Eastern Air Transport. Trippe had purchased two small competing airlines, Pan American Airlines and Floriday Airways. Once again, Lindbergh became a technical advisor (for $10,000) with the right to purchase company shares at 1/10th the price. Lindbergh worked with them for the next ten years.

Offers to endorse products and appear in movies continued, but Lindbergh was not interested. Within two years after his famous flight, he had earned more than $1,000,000 advising the Pennsylvania Railroad. With J.P. Morgan and Company investing his money, by the age of 26, he had become independently wealthy. His only real expense was to send his mother $3,000 two times a year.

While on a trip to South America, Lindbergh again met the U.S. ambassador to Mexico, Dwight Morrow Sr., and his family. Morrow was concerned over tensions between Mexico and the U.S., so Lindbergh agreed to fly south of the border, to spend some time in Mexico. He often stayed at the Embassy with the Morrows, including Constance, their 14 -year-old daughter, and Dwight Jr., their 19-year-old son. They also had two older daughters – Elizabeth, the older, beautiful girl, and Anne, the shy and quiet 21-year-old. The family was surprised when Lindbergh called, hoping to return and take their daughter out on a date. The family and even the paparazzi assumed he would begin courting Elizabeth, but Anne was the one who interested him.

A loner for all his life, he had finally decided that it was time for him to marry. Less than a month after their first date, Charles proposed to Anne, and she accepted. He often took Anne flying with him and taught her to fly as she studied navigation. With many common interests, they were always together. On a trip to California, they took up gliding, and Anne became the first licensed female glider pilot in the U.S. The couple was constantly in the news. Flying throughout North and South America, every trip offered something new. While flying over Mexico, they once discovered an ancient temple deep in the jungle and reported it to the Secretary of the Smithsonian. It was the Temple of the Warriors. Equipped with cameras they would locate ruins no one could see from the ground. They recorded the locations with such accuracy that exploration teams were able to study parts of Mexico and South America at a rate that had never been possible before. The Lindberghs explored land in a few hours that would take months otherwise. They thrilled the archaeological community and attracted extensive coverage by the press.

In 1930, Lindbergh and Anne purchased a new plane from Lockheed for $18,000 (with dual controls). They flew it from LA back to New York in 14 hours, setting a new transcontinental speed record.

Lindbergh met Robert H. Goddard and instantly developed an interest in rocketry. The Lindberghs built a small house /lab in Roswell, NM, close to where Goddard was building a rocket launching tower. Goddard successfully developed the world's first liquid-fueled rocket, launching it in 1926. The work was not cheap, and Lindbergh approached several possible donors for Goddard. He convinced Daniel Guggenheim to support Goddard's work with a donation of $100,000. Because of the many activities the Lindberghs were involved in, they didn't get many chances to settle down. Between projects, they would live with Anne's parents in Englewood, NJ, in their home, *Next Day Hill.* Even though years had passed since his flight across the Atlantic, the paparazzi was still eager to get photos of the couple – a constant irritation to the Lindberghs. When Anne learned that she was pregnant with their first child, they decided to settle down and build a house. Their top concern was privacy, although they also wanted a place to build a landing strip and hangar. Of course, the best way to shop for real estate was, for them, by air. They found themselves in the hills of central New Jersey, over the Sourland mountains. They identified vacant land on the highest point in the area, which was difficult to find by car. It was wooded and was substantial enough to allow them to build a large comfortable home, which they did. The land spanned two counties but was usually considered to be in Hopewell, NJ.

I want to stop here and ask a simple question because this is just so typical of what we know about the people and the case. The Lindberghs bought land on a mountain top. *How much land did they buy?* They purchased, according to one online forum (LKH, *lindberghkidnapping hoax.com*), 400 acres of land. But is that correct? The original floor plan and description of the house that they were building (*Highfields Estate*) indicated that the house would sit on 700 acres of land, almost twice as much. I doubt that it will change the story, but just as an example of how difficult it is to determine *anything* at all from the available literature, here's what I found on the size of the land they purchased, the *Highfields Estate:*

Table 3.1: Size of the Highfields Estate in Hopewell, NJ

Size (acres)	Source
400	(web, LKH)
425	(Berg, 1998)
550	(Brant & Renaud, 1932)
500	(O'Brien,1935)
425	(Fensch, 2001)
360	(Greary, 2008)
500	(Fensch, 2001)
425	(Falzini 2008)
500	(Falzini 2008)
700	House Plans
400	(web,LKH)
Avg. = 471 acres	**range 400-700**

One might assume that facts in publications are verified. This is not the case, but, of course, writers try to get the correct information. For the numbers 400, 425 and 500 acres, they all appeared at least twice (what one would expect if a writer reported information from an older source.) The numbers 360, 550, and 700 appeared once (in my search).

Chapter 4

ATTAINING TOTAL ENLIGHTENMENT ON THE SUBJECT

Your immersion into the topic now must seriously begin. There is no single, consistent story that describes the kidnapping and evidence. There are often multiple versions of every small fact. I've taken two good summaries of the story and added to them different versions of "known facts." These should get you started. I want you to willingly, and with an eager, open mind, become familiar with the information that is out there. In the 1930s, people went to the movies not only to be entertained but to catch up on the news. Short newsreels on current news topics, often about this case, were popular. You can find dozens on *YouTube*. Check out the following at a minimum:

1. *World Shocked by Kidnapping of Lindbergh Baby 1932.* British Movietone (2:11)
2. *Newsreel Nation Aroused at Revolting Kidnapping of Lindbergh Baby*, Hopewell NJ (2:22)
3. *The Lindbergh Kidnapping – What the World is Saying!* (3:30)
4. *1932 Lindbergh Baby Kidnapping* (silent) (0:35)
5. *America. Where Baby Lindbergh was Found.* British Pathe (0:55)

Just look up *Lindbergh Kidnapping* on *YouTube,* and you will find dozens of presentations. The more you learn, the more wisely you can reach your own conclusions (or suggest new ones). I'd also recommend:

6. *Who Killed Lindbergh's Baby – A PBS Nova Program* (52:21)
7. *How They Caught the Lindbergh Baby's Kidnapper* – Smithsonian Channel (3:29)
8. *Who Killed Lindbergh's Baby Documentary – Unsolved Mystery* (1:18:09)
9. *The Lindbergh Baby Kidnapping – Was It a Hoax?* (54:02)
10. *The Lindbergh Baby Kidnapping* – Reel 1 (5:30)
11. *The Lindbergh Baby Kidnapping* – Reel 2 (10:06)
12. *In Search Of – The Lindbergh Baby Kidnapping* (Part 1 of 2) (11:00)
13. *Charles Lindbergh Jr. Lives – Amazing!* (10:18)

I've listed the titles as well as run times. The Nova program (6.), for example, is 52 minutes and 21 seconds long. The Unsolved Mystery Documentary is more than an hour long, and the one listing from the Smithsonian Channel is only 3 minutes and 29 seconds long. Occasionally, in the discussion of a video, I may refer to a specific item in it by the time in which it occurs. So, if someone wants you to "look for the collection of dogs (21:34)", this likely means that the dogs will appear at 21 minutes and 34 seconds into the video.

There are also the web sites where hobbyists continue to debate various aspects of the kidnapping. Some of them contain many hundreds of pages and are constantly growing, with the contributors often disagreeing with each other to the point where it isn't very pretty. Some contain reams of information. I'm content to be a fly on the wall for now and watch their creative moments (and their cranky ones). Here are a few worth following:

1. Jim Fisher The Official Web Site (JF)
   URL: Jimfisher.edinboro.edu/Lindbergh/a1988_1.html

2. The Lindbergh Kidnapping Hoax (LKH)
   URL: linderghkidnappinghoax.com/lindy.html

3. Lindbergh Kidnapping Discussion Board (LKDB)
   URL: Lindberghkidnap.proboards.com

4. Falzini, M.W. Archival Ramblings. (FMAR)
   URL: njspmuseum.blogspot.com/2008/02/one-of-the-most-facinating-areas-of-study.html

No, you don't need to complete this assignment by nightfall, but you can start today. Every version of the story will make you appreciate the others more and help you to decide what is true and what is not.

(Since this is not a book on the history of the kidnapping case and the many questions that continue to swirl around it, I offer here two short versions of the case for you (Chapters 5 and 6). I didn't make up any "facts" in these two chapters. You can find them all in the references that I used.)

Here we go. Front Page of The New York Times, Wednesday, March 2, 1932,
Late City Edition:

LINDBERGH BABY KIDNAPPED FROM HOME OF PARENTS ON FARM NEAR PRINCETON; TAKEN FROM HIS CRIB; WIDE SEARCH ON

FOUR STATES JOIN HUNT

CHILD STOLEN IN EVENING

Parents Distraught, Guarded in Home – Police Deny Report of Ransom Note.

CHAPTER 5

THE LINDBERGH KIDNAPPING AND TRIAL - A SUMMARY

At 7:30 p.m. on March 1, 1932, family nurse Betty Gow put 20-month-old Little Charlie in his crib. She promptly washed (in the bathroom) the baby's clothes, after putting him down, and, at approximately 8:10 p.m., went to the cellar to hang them up to dry. It was a dark and stormy night. Around 9:30 p.m., Lindbergh, who was in the library just below the baby's room, heard a noise which he imagined to be slats breaking off a full crate of oranges in the kitchen as it fell (it was *that* close). He did not investigate. At 10:00 p.m., Betty discovered the baby's crib was empty. Finding that the baby was not with his mother, Anne, Betty alerted Lindbergh, who immediately ran upstairs to the child's nursery, where he found an empty crib and a note in an envelope on the windowsill. He then got his gun and went around the house and grounds with butler Ollie Whateley. They found impressions (ladder impressions, and footprints of a man, a woman, and a dog) in the ground under the window of the child's second-floor room and, nearby, pieces of an oddly designed wooden ladder. Anne said the woman's footprints were hers, and some who saw the ladder impressions in the ground reported that they were far too shallow to have been used. Anne ran from the nursery to her bedroom, opened the window and leaned out. She thought she heard a cry from the woods. Mrs. Whateley assured her it was just a cat. Whateley telephoned the Hopewell Police Department to inform them of the missing child. Lindbergh then contacted his attorney, Henry Breckinridge and the New Jersey State Police.

Hopewell Borough Police and New Jersey State Police officers arrived first. They searched the home and the surrounding area for miles and began to question members of the family and staff. When the police arrived, they found Lindbergh searching the grounds by flashlight.

After midnight, a fingerprint expert arrived and examined the ransom note, the nursery and eventually the ladder; no usable fingerprints or footprints were found, leading experts to conclude that the kidnapper(s) wore gloves and had cloth on the soles of their shoes. No adult fingerprints were found in the baby's room, including in areas that family and staff admitted to touching, such as the window. The baby's fingerprints *were* found.

The brief, handwritten ransom letter was filled with spelling errors and grammatical irregularities. (It may look familiar.) It read something like this:

Dear Sir!

Have 50.000$ redy 25 000$ in 20$ bills
15000$ in 10$ bills and 10000$ in 5$ bills After 2–4 days
we will inform you were to deliver the mony.

We warn you for making anyding public or for notify the Police
The child is in gut care.
Indication for all letters are Singnature [Symbol to right]
and 3 hohls.

News of the kidnapping spread quickly. Hundreds of people converged on the estate, destroying any footprint evidence. Along with police, the well-intentioned continued to flood onto the Lindbergh estate. Military colonels were offering their aid, including Herbert Norman Schwarzkopf, superintendent of the New Jersey State Police. Lindbergh and others believed that organized crime members perpetrated the kidnapping. The letter, they thought, seemed written by someone who spoke German as his native language. Lindbergh, at this time, used his influence to control the direction of the investigation.

Several organized crime figures –Al Capone, Willie Moretti, Joe Adonis, and Abner Zwillman – spoke from prison, offering to help to get the child returned in exchange for money or for legal favors. Capone offered to help in return for being released from prison suggesting that that his assistance would be more effective if he was free to move about. This request was denied.

The morning after the kidnapping, U.S. President Herbert Hoover was notified of the crime. At the time, kidnapping was classified as a local crime and the case did not seem to have any grounds for federal involvement. However, Hoover and Attorney General William D. Mitchell offered the assistance of the Department of Justice to the New Jersey authorities.

Within a few days, a new ransom letter arrived by mail at the Lindbergh home. Postmarked March 4 in Brooklyn, the letter carried the perforated red and blue "singnature" marks, just like the first letter. The kidnappers used this special symbol on (almost) all their letters that followed, so Lindbergh would know each letter was from them. The ransom had been raised from $50,000 to $70,000. A third ransom letter postmarked from Brooklyn, and including the "singnature," arrived in Breckenridge's mail. The note told the Lindberghs that John Condon should be the intermediary between the Lindberghs and the kidnapper(s). It requested notification via newspaper that the third note had been received. Instructions also specified the size of the box the money should be delivered in and warned the family not to contact the police.

During this time, John F. Condon, a well-known Bronx personality and retired schoolteacher, wrote a letter for the *Bronx Home News*, a local paper, offering $1,000 of his own savings if the kidnappers would turn the child over to a Catholic priest and if he could serve to assist in information flow between them and Lindbergh (whom he had never met). Condon received a letter reportedly written by the kidnappers. It authorized him to be their intermediary with Lindbergh. Lindbergh accepted the letter as genuine and Condon as an intermediary, no questions asked.

Following that letter's instructions, Condon placed a classified ad in the *New York American* which said: "Money is ready. Jafsie". Jafsie is a code name Lindbergh suggested for Condon, based on his initials, JFC. Condon then waited for further instructions from the gang.

A meeting between Condon and a representative of the group that claimed to be the kidnappers was eventually scheduled for late one evening at Woodlawn Cemetery in the Bronx. According to Condon, the man he met sounded foreign but stayed in the shadows during the conversation, and Condon was unable to get a close look at his face. The man said his name was John. He was a Scandinavian sailor, part of a gang of three men and two women. The baby was being held on a boat by the name of Sally, unharmed, but would be returned only when they paid the ransom.

On March 16, Condon received a child's sleeping suit by mail, a Dr. Denton's one-piece suit with feet in the bottom, and a seventh ransom note. Lindbergh identified the sleeping suit as his son's. Condon placed a new ad in the *Home News*: "Money is ready. No cops. No Secret Service. I come alone, like last time." One month after the kidnapping, Condon received a letter saying it was time for the ransom to be delivered.

The ransom was packaged in a wooden box that was custom-made of several different woods in the hope that it could later be identified. The ransom money included many gold certificates – gold certificates, a type of US paper currency, were about to be withdrawn from circulation (see ALLISONweb), and hopes that they would draw attention to anyone spending them. The bills were not marked but their serial numbers were recorded.

The next day, Condon was given a written message by an unknown cab driver. Following instructions, Condon met John, this time in St. Raymond's Cemetery in the Bronx and told him they had been able to raise only $50,000. The man accepted the money and gave Condon a note indicating that the child was in the care of two innocent women on a boat called Nelly, off the coast near Block Island.

On May 12, trucker William Allen pulled to the side of a road about 4.5 miles south of the Lindbergh home near Mount Rose in neighboring Hopewell Township. Going into a grove of trees to relieve himself, he discovered the body of a young child. Allen notified the police, who took the body to the morgue in Trenton, New Jersey. The skull was badly fractured, and the body decomposed, having been chewed on by animals; it was apparently a quick burial. Betty Gow identified the baby as the missing infant from the overlapping toes of the right foot and a shirt that she had made for him the night of the kidnapping. It appeared that a blow to the head killed the child. Lindbergh insisted on an immediate cremation.

By June 1932, officials began to suspect an "inside job" perpetrated by someone the Lindberghs most trusted. Police considered Violet Sharp, a British household maid at the Morrow home, as a suspect. She had given contradictory testimony to the police regarding her whereabouts on the night of the kidnapping. Police reported that she seemed to be nervous and suspicious when questioned. She committed suicide on June 10, 1932, by drinking a silver polish that contained potassium cyanide just before what would have been her fourth interview with the police. After her alibi was confirmed, it was later determined that the possible threat of losing her job and the intense questioning had driven her to kill herself. She may have been trying to hide details of a love triangle that she found herself in. At the time, the police investigators were criticized for their handling of Violet.

Following the death of Violet Sharp, police also questioned John Condon. They searched Condon's home, but nothing was found that connected him to the crime. Charles Lindbergh supported Condon during this time.

Investigation of the case soon stopped. There were no new developments and little new evidence, so police turned their attention to finding the ransom payment. A pamphlet was prepared with the serial numbers on the ransom bills, and 250,000 copies were distributed to businesses, mostly in New York City. A few of the ransom bills appeared in scattered locations, some as far away as Chicago, Minneapolis and Tokyo, but those spending the bills were never found.

Following a presidential order, all gold certificates were to be exchanged for other bills by May 1, 1933. A few days before the deadline, a man brought $2,980 to Manhattan Bank for exchange; the bills were from the ransom. He had given his name as J. J. Faulkner of 537 West 149th Street. No one named Faulkner lived at that address. A Jane Faulkner who had lived there 20 years earlier denied involvement. (so, someone named Faulkner HAD lived at that address.)

For a period of 30 months, a number of the ransom bills were used throughout New York City; detectives realized that many of the bills were spent along the route of the Lexington Avenue subway, which connected the East Bronx with the east side of Manhattan, including the German-Austrian neighborhood of Yorkville.

On September 18, 1934, a Manhattan bank teller noticed a gold certificate from the ransom; a New York license plate number (4U-13-41-N.Y.) was written in the bill's margin allowing it to be traced to a nearby gas station. The station manager had written down the license number because a customer was acting "suspicious" and was "possibly a counterfeiter." The license plate belonged to a sedan owned by Richard Hauptmann of the Bronx, an immigrant with a criminal record in Germany. When Hauptmann was arrested, he was carrying a 20-dollar gold certificate; over $14,000 of the ransom money was found in his garage.

Hauptmann was arrested and interrogated – and beaten by the police – throughout the following day and night. The money, Hauptmann stated, along with other items, had been left with him by a friend and former business partner, Isidor Fisch. Fisch had died on March 29, 1934, shortly after returning to Germany. Only following Fisch's death, Hauptmann stated, did he learn that the shoebox left with him contained money. He took the money because he claimed that Fisch owed it to him from a business deal that he and Fisch had made. Hauptmann denied any connection to the crime or knowledge that the money was in his house, in a box given to him by Fisch for safe-keeping, and that the money was from the Lindbergh ransom. He only discovered the shoebox's contents after a bad rainstorm caused leaks in the house, getting Fisch's box wet.

In the search of Hauptmann's apartment by police, a considerable amount of possible evidence was found. One item was a notebook that contained a sketch for the construction of a ladder like what was found at the Lindbergh home in March 1932. A key piece of evidence was a section of wood used to make the ladder. After being examined by an expert, it was determined to be an exact match to the wood used in Hauptmann's attic, where a floorboard had been removed.

Hauptmann was indicted in the Bronx on September 24, 1934, for extorting the $50,000 ransom from Charles Lindbergh. Two weeks later, Hauptmann was indicted in New Jersey for the murder of Charles Lindbergh Jr. He was handed over to New Jersey authorities by New York Governor Herbert H. Lehman to face charges directly related to the kidnapping and murder of the child. Hauptmann was moved to the Hunterdon County Jail in Flemington, New Jersey, on October 19, 1934.

Hauptmann was charged with capital murder, meaning that conviction could result in the death penalty. The trial was labeled as the "Trial of the Century"; reporters swarmed into the town, booking every hotel room. The presiding judge was Thomas Whitaker Trenchard.

In exchange for rights to publish Hauptmann's story in their newspaper, Edward J. Reilly was hired by the *Daily Mirror* to serve as Hauptmann's attorney. David T. Wilentz, Attorney General of New Jersey, led the prosecution.

Evidence against Hauptmann included $20,000 of the ransom money found in his garage and testimony alleging handwriting and spelling similarities between his writing and writing found in the 15 ransom letters. Eight handwriting experts (including Albert S. Osborn) pointed out similarities between the ransom notes and Hauptmann's writing specimens. The defense called an expert to refute this evidence, while two others refused to testify. The latter two demanded $500 before looking at the letters and were dismissed when Lloyd Fisher (the Assisting Attorney for the Defense) declined. Other experts hired by the defense were never called to testify.

Based on the work of Arthur Koehler from the Forest Products Laboratory, the State introduced photographs demonstrating that part of the wood from the ladder matched a plank from the floor of Hauptmann's attic: the type of wood, the direction of tree growth, the milling pattern, the inside and outside surface of the wood, and the grain on both sides were identical, and four oddly placed nail holes lined up with nail holes in joists in Hauptmann's attic. Additionally, Condon's address and telephone number were found written in pencil on a closet door jam in Hauptmann's home.

Hauptmann admitted to police that he had written Condon's address. He testified:

> "I must have read it in the paper about the story. I was a little bit interested and keep a little bit of a record of it, and maybe I was just in the closet, and was reading the paper and put down the address [...] I can't give you any explanation about the telephone number."

Despite not having an obvious source of income, he had enough money to purchase a large $400 radio (nearly $7,000 today) and to send his wife on a trip to Germany. The purpose of the trip was to see whether Hauptmann, if he returned, would be arrested for having committed earlier crimes there.

Hauptmann was positively identified as the man to whom Jafsie delivered the ransom money. Other witnesses testified that it was Hauptmann who had spent some of the Lindbergh gold certificates, that he had been seen in the area of the estate in East Amwell, New Jersey near Hopewell on the day of the kidnapping, and that he had been absent from work on the day of the ransom payment (and quit his job two days later). Hauptmann never tried to find another job after that yet continued to live well.

I should note that through the entire trial, neither side offered the German Hauptmann an interpreter.

When the prosecution rested, the defense began their case with an examination of Hauptmann himself. In his testimony, Hauptmann denied being guilty, insisting that the box found to contain the gold certificates had been left in his garage by Isidor Fisch, who had returned to Germany in December 1933 and died there in March 1934.

The defense called Hauptmann's wife Anna to corroborate the Fisch story. But upon cross-examination, she had to admit that while she hung her apron every day on a hook higher than the closet top shelf, she could not remember seeing any shoe box there. Later, rebuttal witnesses testified that Fisch could not have been at the scene of the crime and that he had no money for medical treatments when he died of tuberculosis. Fisch's landlady testified that he could barely afford his $3.50-a-week room rent. Various witnesses called by the defense to put Fisch near the Lindbergh house on the night of the kidnapping were discredited in cross-examination with incidents from their pasts, which included criminal records and mental instability.

In his closing, Reilly proposed that the evidence against Hauptmann was all circumstantial, as no reliable witness had placed Hauptmann at the scene of the crime, nor were his fingerprints found on the ladder, the ransom letter, or anywhere in the nursery.

Hauptmann was convicted and immediately sentenced to death. His attorneys appealed to the New Jersey Court of Errors and Appeals, then the state's highest court; the appeal was argued shortly after that.

New Jersey Governor Harold G. Hoffman secretly visited Hauptmann in his cell in October 1935, accompanied by a stenographer who spoke German fluently. Hoffman urged members of the Court of Errors and Appeals to visit Hauptmann.

Early in 1936, still insisting that he held no opinion on the guilt or innocence of Hauptmann, Hoffman cited evidence that the crime was not a "one person" job and directed Schwarzkopf to continue a thorough and impartial investigation to bring all parties involved to justice.

In March 1936, Hauptmann's second and final appeal asking for clemency from the New Jersey Board of Pardons was denied. Hoffman later announced that this decision would be the last legal action in the case and that he would not grant another reprieve.

Hauptmann turned down a large offer from a Hearst newspaper for a confession and refused a last-minute offer to change his execution to a life sentence in exchange for "the truth." He was electrocuted on April 3, 1936, just over four years after the kidnapping.

Following Hauptmann's death, some reporters and independent investigators came up with questions regarding the way the court ran the investigation, and the fairness of the trial. Many raised questions on issues ranging from witness tampering to the planting of evidence. Twice during the 1980s, Anna Hauptmann sued the state of New Jersey for the unjust execution of her husband. Both times the cases were dismissed. She continued fighting to clear his name until her death in 1994.

Chapter 6

THE LINDBERGH KIDNAPPING AND TRIAL - A SECOND SUMMARY OF THE STORY

It was unusual for Little Charlie to be kidnapped on a Tuesday evening because the family was never at their unfinished home on a Tuesday. Construction of their new house was continuing, so the Lindberghs would come on weekends and leave on Mondays. Their schedule for the week was changed because Little Charlie was sick, and a cold rain was falling. So how did the kidnappers know to come and get Little Charlie at that location on that day? The police believed it must have been an inside job because no one except family and staff would have known the Lindberghs would be there. Some contractors were likely there, so they knew. The house was on a hilltop, and they had no curtains, so locals knew when they were and were not home. Perhaps whoever came to the house wasn't there to kidnap anyone at all. Perhaps they were just simple crooks.

The newspapers asked: "How would anyone know where the baby's room was? Where would they put up the ladder that they had brought with them?" Ollie Whateley, Lindbergh's driver and servant, with his wife, Elsie, had been living in the house as it neared completion, and would occasionally, for a small fee, take strangers who appeared there for a tour of the house – so any of them could have learned the layout of the building. It had also appeared in several magazines.

Just before that fateful night, on the morning of Monday, Feb. 29, 1932, Charles called Anne from his office and instructed her not to return to Englewood that day. All three of them had colds, but he was concerned about Little Charlie. That night Lindbergh didn't return to Hopewell. He spent Monday night at *Next Day Hill,* Anne's parents' home, which was close to New York City.

At 8:00 p.m. on March 1, 1932, family nurse Betty Gow reported to Anne in the living room that the baby had gone to sleep already, although they had yet to tuck him in at his usual 8:30 bedtime, so Betty quickly went to the kitchen to eat dinner with the Whateleys. When did Lindbergh arrive home? Anne reported that she thought she heard car wheels on the gravel driveway, but it was 15 minutes after that when she heard Lindbergh's car horn indicating that he had arrived. He put the car in the garage, and came into the house through the garage, through the back hallway and the kitchen. It was also a memorable evening because Charles was home. He was supposed to have been giving a talk at an NYU Alumni Centennial Dinner that evening at the Waldorf Astoria in New York City, but he forgot about the commitment, so he just went home after work. It was a 2-hour drive from New York to the house, following Route 1 through New Brunswick and on to Princeton.

Lindbergh would often get lost in his work. He had become involved in a project at the Rockefeller Institute in New York, developing a machine for "washing corpuscles" (red blood cells). He was home by 8:30 p.m. when Betty and Anne were putting little Charlie into his crib. Part of putting Little Charlie to bed often involved wrapping a metal cylinder over each thumb, which was then pinned to his clothes, to discourage thumb sucking.

Betty and Anne closed all the shutters. The set of shutters on the east side of the room were warped, and although they did swing shut, they would not latch, so Betty opened a south window a crack behind its shutters to let in some fresh air. After dinner, Lindbergh and Anne went upstairs to draw baths. Elsie Whateley and Betty talked about Elsie's new dress in the Whateley bedroom. Ollie sat alone reading in the servant's sitting room on the first floor, with Lindbergh's dog Trixie keeping him company. Around 9:30 p.m. Lindbergh, who had gone back downstairs to do some work in the library, just below Little Charlie's bedroom, heard a noise which he thought could be a breaking tree branch, possibly, on that windy night. He didn't get up and look. Anne didn't hear it. Many believe that Lindbergh had lost some of his hearing through long-term exposure to airplane noise and years later Anne's daughter Reeve wrote that Anne had a bit of a hearing problem as well.

Charles had established some house rules; one was that if Little Charlie cried, no one was to go to him, and he wasn't to be "looked in on" until 10 p.m. so he wouldn't expect someone to come running every time he cried. So, it was not until 10 p.m. when Betty entered the baby's room and found the crib empty.

She ran downstairs to the living room and informed Lindbergh and Anne that the baby was gone. Betty said to Lindbergh, "Colonel Lindbergh, have you got the baby? Please don't fool with me!" Why would she have said that? Well, two months earlier, Lindbergh hid the baby in a second-floor closet and let Anne and the staff panic for about 20 minutes before he told them it was a joke.

Mark Falzini comments

It had to be more than two months earlier because Marie Cummings, Betty Gow's predecessor, was still there.

Author comments

OK, interesting. For the real kidnapping, the Eaglet was 20 months old. He was born on June 22, 1930. Marie left on July 30, 1930, so he must have only been a month old when Charles hid him in a closet.

This time, Lindbergh denied it. They immediately ran upstairs. The baby was not in his crib, and an envelope was on the windowsill, but only Lindbergh had noticed it. Betty later reported that she looked out her bedroom window and saw the ladder still up against the house. Lindbergh turned to Anne and said, "Anne, they have stolen our baby."

Whateley called the Hopewell Police to inform them of the missing child. Lindbergh called his friend and lawyer Henry Breckinridge and the New Jersey State Police. There were no bloodstains found anywhere, nor were there any fingerprints. Their dog was known to bark at strangers (and Charlie wasn't very comfortable with them either), but they heard no barking or crying that night. We understand a part of this because we know the dog slept with Ollie that night. If you're in a house with 24 rooms and 23-inch-thick walls, you might miss a lot of audio warnings.

Lindbergh got his gun and went outside with butler Whateley. They found shoe impressions of a man and a woman, and dog prints in the soft wet dirt around the ladder impressions.

Ollie and Lindbergh drove up and down the dirt road, shining headlights on either side, searching for anything. Then Lindbergh told Whatley to go into town and get some flashlight batteries. Whatley took Lindbergh's car and drove off towards town, but met police cars, and escorted them back to the house.

Hopewell Police and the New Jersey State Police arrived quickly and searched the area. Police questioned Ollie first, then Betty. After midnight, a State Police fingerprint expert arrived and examined the ransom letter and envelope, as well as the room. He found no usable fingerprints of any kind, so the kidnapper must have worn gloves and perhaps had socks over his shoes. No adult fingerprints were found anywhere in the nursery. By this we mean that he found no complete fingerprints. Many incomplete, smeared, fragmented prints were found, which is typical.

While the ransom letter remained undetected until Lindbergh's return, it was opened as soon as the writing expert arrived, for all to see.

The brief handwritten ransom letter was a poorly written oddity. The kidnappers should have been embarrassed. The salutation was on the right. It read:

> **Dear Sir!**
>
> **Have 50.000$ redy 25 000$ in 20$ bills 15000$ in 10$ bills and 10000$ in 5$ bills After 2–4 days we will inform you were to deliver the mony.**
> **We warn you for making anyding public**
> **The child is in gut care.**
> **Indication for all letters are Singnature [Symbol to right] and 3 hohls.**

There was a cryptic symbol on the lower right corner of the page that the kidnappers called their "singnature." The symbol was two interlocking circles, whose overlap comprised an oval. The oval was colored red and the remainder of the circles blue. At the center of each geometric shape was a square hole.

Lindbergh trusted his staff and didn't feel they needed to be interviewed by police, but they were, not only by the local police but by representatives of many government organizations. For example, Murray Garsson, from the Labor Department arrived and "vigorously questioned everyone in the house until dawn." He even had Anne show him the basement. She watched as he poked through the furnace ashes looking for skeletal remains.

Soon, a second ransom note arrived. Unlike the first, this one was typed. There were more to come.

The news spread through the area; hundreds of locals converged on Lindbergh's home. Many believed that the kidnapping was the work of organized crime members.

The next morning, the FBI was notified of the crime by President Hoover. Hoover immediately initiated a law defining kidnapping as, now, a federal crime.

Anne put a large ad in the local papers, writing that Little Charlie had some medical problems and required a special diet, and explained what it was. The kidnappers agreed to follow it in a subsequent letter.

A few days after, a ransom letter arrived at the Lindbergh home. The ransom rose to $70,000. A third ransom note from Brooklyn arrived in Breckenridge's mail. The letter told the Lindberghs that Dr. John Condon, who had volunteered, was acceptable as their go-between. Lindbergh suggested that he go by the name Jafsie, because of his initials – JFC.

Condon (who lived in the Bronx, 1279 E. 222nd St.) followed instructions on a subsequent ransom letter and wrote a note to the *Bronx Home News*, offering an extra $1,000 of his own money if the kidnappers would turn the child over to a priest. They refused. Some question how Condon could get messages put into local papers so quickly. The editors of newspapers such as the *Bronx Home News* often contacted Dr. Condon when they needed an outside opinion on some topic (they would send a reporter to Condon). The Doctor would always come up with some quotes on any topic. He loved to see his name in print and believed he was an expert on everything.

Eventually Condon (who lived in the Bronx – 2074 Decatur St.) put a classified ad in the *New York American*, saying "Money is Ready. Jafsie." Condon than waited for their response.

A meeting between Condon and a representative of the kidnapping group was scheduled for an evening at the Woodlawn Cemetery in the Bronx (517 E. 233rd Street). The man he met sounded foreign. Condon asked him if he had a name, but he didn't answer, so Condon said, "I will call you John." John told his story, of how he was part of a gang of three men and two women. Condon learned that Little Charlie was being held on a boat named Nellie, unharmed, but they would only return him after the ransom was delivered. Condon tried to speak to John in German, but he did not reply. John told Condon that Red and Betty, two of the Lindbergh staff, were not part of the gang. The police were considering them for a while as possible suspects.

Within two weeks, Condon received the seventh ransom letter. Condon responded in the *Home News*, with "Money is ready. No cops. No Secret Service. I come alone, like last time."

They delivered the ransom in a wooden box, and most of the bills were gold certificates. Their serial numbers had been recorded by the Treasury Department, against Lindbergh's wishes.

Condon and John had some interesting discussions during their two cemetery visits. Condon wanted to see the baby before he handed over the ransom. John said that would be impossible, "My father wouldn't let me." No one further questioned this comment. Was his actual father the head of the gang? Is "father" a gang term for leader? (There is a dinner theatre called Capone's. They have a web page that includes a gang slang dictionary (from the 1920s). There is no "father" in it. Does this mean Cemetery John's father really was involved?). Also, during one of their conversations, Condon casually asked "Bist du Deutsch?" (Are you German?). John answered the question – "No, I am Scandinavian," in German.

They also talked about safety pins, according to Condon. The night of the kidnapping, Anne and Betty were worried about sick Little Charlie getting sicker. Betty made a little flannel shirt for him as they were putting him to bed. They even pinned down his blanket with two big safety pins so he could not get out from underneath the warm blanket. Condon borrowed those two big safety pins for just this moment. He showed them to Cemetery John and asked him if he knew what they were. John, who strongly resembled Hauptmann according to Jafsie, correctly identified them. This proved that Hauptmann had been in the nursery. He also said he left a ransom note in the baby's crib.

It was May 12 when a delivery truck driver, William Allen, pulled to the side of the road a few miles from the Lindbergh estate. He went into a grove of trees about 45 feet from the road and discovered a decomposing child's body. The body lay in a shallow depression; the remains were covered with vermin [sic.] and leaves. There was only one building near this field: St. Michaels, a Catholic Orphanage.

Lindbergh took the body to the morgue in Trenton, NJ. Betty Gow identified the child. It was concluded that a blow to the head resulted in death. Lindbergh identified the body as that of his son, by counting the number of teeth. The next day, Lindbergh had the body cremated and sprinkled the ashes over the Atlantic Ocean, just as Little Charlie would surely have wanted.

There are photographs of the dead baby. A photographer reportedly broke a window in the morgue so he could get in and photograph the decaying remains.

In June 1932, officials focused on Violet Sharp, one of the Morrow family's servants. They were not happy with her testimony on where she was the night of the kidnapping. They never found anything to connect Violet to the crime. On 10 June 1932 she committed suicide by drinking a silver polish that contained Cyanide Chloride. The Police were criticized locally and internationally for their interrogation methods.

Investigation of the case eventually stopped. By presidential order, all gold certificates had to be exchanged for new bills by May 1, 1933. One man brought a fairly large sum, $2,980, to a Manhattan bank for exchange. They were bills from the ransom. He listed himself on the deposit slip as J.J. Faulkner, 537 West 149th Street, New York. No one named J.J. Faulkner lived at that address.

Many believed that the NJ State Police altered evidence, suppressed information, and did whatever they could to get Hauptmann convicted. At times it seemed like the State Police were everywhere with their fingers in the evidence. Consider this: there was a group of people who always knew when the Lindberghs were in their new house as it was being completed – the contractors of course. Michael Hullfish of Hopewell gave the police the names of all the men employed on this construction site, all of whom were questioned. The problem I have with this is that while he was part of the construction gang when the house was being built, he had moved to a new job – as a State Trooper.

Mid-year 1934, a bank teller in Manhattan realized that a gold certificate had been turned in with a NY license plate number written on it (4U-13-41-N.Y.). The bank determined that it had come from the Warner-Quinlan gas station on the corner of Lexington and 127th Street in Manhattan. John Lyons, an employee who was on the job at the time, described to police how a customer with a thick German accent purchased

5 gallons of ethyl, with a $10 gold certificate, for his blue Dodge (a 1930-31 model). As the stranger pulled away, John wrote the license plate number down, wondering if the man with the accent was a counterfeiter. The plate belonged to a sedan owned by Richard Hauptmann (1279 East 222nd St, Bronx, NY) who was German. When Hauptmann was arrested, they found $14,000 of the ransom money in his garage.

Hauptmann was interrogated – and beaten at least once – in the following day and night, when the police forced him to provide many writing samples for comparison with the 15 ransom letters. He explained how he had taken the money that he found in a box given to him by a business associate named Fisch, who left for Germany and died there.

Within a few weeks Hauptmann was indicted in the Bronx and moved to New Jersey to be tried for Little Charlie's death. He was moved to the Hunterdon County jail in Flemington, New Jersey.

Some evidence never was brought to the trial. For example, Condon, with the help of the FBI, made a transcript of all his conversations with Cemetery John, and made phonograph recordings of the transcripts, imitating the pronunciation and dialect, to more clearly define the kidnapper. These were never used in the trial.

Hauptmann's "Fisch Story" was also questioned. Did Isador Fisch really leave a shoebox full of money with Hauptmann for safe keeping? Hauptmann did have a going-away party for Fisch, and this was where Fisch brought some things that he wanted Hauptmann to hold for him. One of Bruno's best friends, Hans Kloppenberg, saw Fisch give Bruno a shoe box. Hans was going to testify on this point, until Attorney General David Wilentz threatened to make Hans an accessory in the crime if he testified about that box. (Many believe the police and the lawyers planted and hid evidence.)

While the evidence was only circumstantial, Hauptmann was convicted and sentenced to death. Numerous issues related to witness tampering and planting of evidence were never brought up.

Again, to give you some idea of the variation in information related to the case, it is easy to evaluate numerical facts. As I read books and summaries written about this subject, many give specific values concerning, for example, finding Little Charlie's body. Many report how far his body was found from the road and how far away his remains were dumped relative to his home, *Highfields*. Here is what I found:

Table 6.1: The distance x from the road where Little Charlie's body was found, and the distance y miles from his Highfields home

Feet from Road where Body Found (x)	Source
75	Fensch, T. 2001
75	Cahill, R. 2014
45	Web, FBIH
45	Web, LIK, (Did the Lilliput Kill Charlie?)
60 ft. (20 meters)	Web, FERA

Distance in miles (y)	Source
"Several Miles"	Fensch, T. 2001
7 kilometers (~4 miles)	Web, FERA
4.5	Web, FBIH
4.5	Fensch, T. 2001
4	Condon, J. 1936
2	Web, WENC
4.5	Web, LKI
1	Web, WENC

I continue to find it interesting that numerical values often occur twice, which one would see if one writer copied from another source, rather than independently discovering it from a primary source of the information. Also note the range of the data. The baby's body was 45-75 feet from the nearest road and was one to several miles from home.

Side note: Anna Hauptmann was surprised when her husband was called Bruno Richard Hauptmann in court. She had only known him as Richard. The lawyers decided to use his first name, Bruno, because they thought it sounded more dangerous than Richard.

QUIZ

Answer the following questions in the spaces provided. I prefer to call tests of knowledge quizzes rather than tests or exams, because quiz is more of a fun word. No, you can't look back while you're taking the quiz. How much information that you read do you retain?

1. Point out at least one curious part of the story.

2. *True or False*. After the kidnappers took the baby and the fingerprint expert arrived at the Lindbergh house, no fingerprints were found on the ransom letter, or anywhere in the nursery, including the window.

3. List at least two words that the ransom letter's author misspelled.

4. At the time of the kidnapping, how much was the ransom?

5. John F. Condon decided to go by the name Jafsie, when acting as an intermediary. Why Jafsie?

6. How many people were in the "gang" that was responsible for kidnapping Little Charlie?

7. Condon met a kidnapper in two different cemeteries. His name was John. How did Condon know this?

8. What chemical compound, a component of silver polish, presumably poisoned/killed young Violet Sharp?

9. Did Condon speak German? Did Hauptmann speak German?

10. Police arrested Hauptmann on several charges, but not for kidnapping. Why?

11. Who identified the child's body that was found as that of Little Charlie?

12. *TRUE/FALSE* Once the ransom was paid, ransom bills (currency) started to appear in circulation, mostly along one subway line in New York City.

13. *TRUE/FALSE* JJ Faulkner lived at 536 West 149th Street in New York.

14. *TRUE/FALSE* Hauptmann's license plate number was NJ 44-13-41.

Answer Key to Your Fun Quiz on Chapters 5 & 6

1. Curious is a subjective kind of thing, so whatever you answered is probably acceptable.

2. Well, technically, TRUE. There were no useful fingerprints found. There were partial or smudged fingerprint fragments found, but no complete, useable ones.

3. In the first ransom letter, words such as where (were), money (mony) and anything (anyding) were misspelled. You must be careful. Some references don't report what the actual ransom notes said, but the "cleaned up" version with all the misspellings corrected.

4. In the first ransom letter, it was $50,000.

5. Depending on who you ask, Jafsie was either a code name selected by Lindbergh based on Condon's initials, JFC, or it was a shorthand version of his name that he occasionally used, even when he was teaching (according to his former students).

> Mark Falzini Comments
> The Jafsie code name was not selected by Lindbergh but by Condon himself.
>
> Author Comments
> Both Condon and Lindbergh contributed to the decision. Condon often wrote articles for local newspapers under names such as P.A.Triot and J.U.Stice. Lindbergh felt he couldn't use his real name when communicating with kidnappers. Condon suggested that if you quickly say his initials, J.F.C., it sounds like Jafsie. According to Condon's book *Jafsie tells All*, when Lindbergh heard it he said, "Use that one," approving that pen name.

6. Five – three men and two women.

7. Many facts obtained from Condon frequently changed. At one point, Condon and a kidnapper were in a cemetery and Condon asked what his name was. The kidnapper responded, "John." Or perhaps, Condon asked his name, and he did not reply, so Condon said, "then I will call you John."

8. The poison present in silver polish is a toxic cyanide salt, potassium cyanide. The chemical formula is KCN(s). The pure solid can react with moisture (water vapor) to release toxic HCN gas. CNCl, cyanogen chloride, has also been identified as the poison. It is also a highly toxic compound that is used in chemical warfare, but CNCl is a gas, so probably couldn't be part of a cleaning material.

9. Condon reported that, in one of his meetings with "John," he attempted to begin a conversation in German, but John did not seem to understand. Condon may have been required to learn German in college or may have just picked it up from his environment (living in a German area of New York). Part of his environment includes the German man who his daughter married.

Mark Falzini Comments

No she didn't. He was born in Iowa.

Author Comments

The FBI Files, p. 211, suggests that Myra Condon's husband was of "alleged German extraction."

While it was reported that John did not understand German, Condon said that he visited with Hauptmann in prison and spent time speaking with him in German. Perhaps Hauptmann is not Cemetery John.

10. Kidnapping was not a serious crime at the time, only a misdemeanor.

11. Some reports focus on Lindbergh as identifying the body, however Betty Gow also went to see the body, and made a positive identification, because Little Charlie was still wearing a little flannel shirt that Betty had made for him the night of the kidnapping.

12. While this is mostly *TRUE*, some bills appeared as far away as Chicago, Minneapolis, and Japan. This is probably not surprising – it is what money in circulation does.

13. *FALSE* There was a woman with the last name of Faulkner who had lived at that exact address, and the police tracked her down, but when she said she had nothing to do with the kidnapping, they did not investigate her. Does that sound plausible to you? It is also *False* because the address was 537 West 149th Street. (Sorry. I won't do that to you again.)

Mark Falzini Comments

They did investigate!

Allison Comments

Mark is correct. The police found Jane Faulkner Geissler and her family. They collected writing samples from the family members to compare to the writing on the Faulkner deposit slip. They found no matches.

14. There are multiple reports of Hauptmann's license plate number, including NY 44-1341 and 4U-13-41-N.Y. There are some photographs of Hauptmann's car in the Lindbergh exhibit at the New Jersey State Police Museum, and the license plate number is 4U13-41. They were New York tags, not New Jersey tags.

CHAPTER 7
GOING BACK IN TIME (BIT)

Before we discuss the evidence, we must put it into the appropriate context. It was a different world in the 1930s and there are certain things we need to know. For example, we will be discussing the ransom letters and the unusual "singnature" that most of them contain. I'm interested in the possibility that they were made not with conventional ink, but with other blue and red liquids. What colored liquids were in people's homes in the 1930s? Also consider that almost all the "characters" in the story live in New York, while the crime itself took place in New Jersey. What was travel like in the 1930s? Were there decent roads for making that trip? Answers to such questions are very important. So, come back with me, (and Mr. Peabody and Sherman), to look around. If you don't know Peabody, the most famous time traveler, please consult ALLISONweb. Also, I have a special treat for you – some photos of historical/aeronautical interest from the 1930s that we may be seeing for the first time.

7A. The Dismal 1930s

The northeastern coast of the U.S. was particularly complicated. After the fun and excitement of the roaring 20s, the country moved into the depressing 30s. Prohibition had been in place since 1920. Many of the immigrants from Europe came here and established parts of cities that were theirs. There was often, especially in larger cities, an Irish Town, a German Town, an Italian Town, Chinatown, etc. Immigrants could stay surrounded by people and stores that spoke their language, slowing down their integration into the culture of the United States. Many continued to live as they had in their former countries where, if you needed a driver's license, for instance, you might take a bottle of whiskey to the DMV, assuming that a bribe was necessary. They often continued to follow the standards of their own culture. Even though alcohol was illegal, many routinely sought out bootleggers and speakeasies. Laws were not what people followed; laws were what people found ways to circumvent. In some places, there were active gangs, who may have controlled entire neighborhoods.

The 1930s saw the first substantial wave of immigrants as the Irish flooded into New York and led to a criminal underworld that laid the groundwork for New York City to become "the battleground of today's democracy." As gangs faded away, much more legitimate, and ruthless political parties took their place. It was a dangerous time, that ultimately resulted in a nationwide depression.

Fortunately, the state and federal governments were able to start bringing the country back to life, by getting rid of the ban on alcohol, and by introducing several anti-stock market crash plans to create jobs and stimulate new construction.

7B. Money

$100 in 1930 would be equivalent to $1204 in 2018. You could buy a new car for under $700; steak was 20 cents a pound, and a 5-tube bedroom radio sold for $9.95. Gas was 10 cents a gallon.

Did you get that last one? Gas was 10 cents a gallon. When Hauptmann made the mistake of buying gasoline for his car with a gold certificate, he reportedly purchased 5 gallons of "ethyl" for 98 cents. (Why does so little information regarding this case ever match up?)

As an economic move, and in an attempt to assist Lindbergh, President Roosevelt declared that the U.S. would abandon the gold standard as the value of the dollar. He called in all gold certificates, which meant no one was supposed to keep theirs. (O'Brien, 1935).

7C. The Government Responds to the Depression

In the early 1930s, almost 25% of Americans were not working. The stock market crashed on October 29, 1929. Possibly a result of World War I, within a few years nearly 10,000 of this country's banks closed. Herbert Hoover didn't do much about this crisis, but after Franklin D. Roosevelt was elected in 1932, he used the power of the federal government by establishing his New Deal that immediately began to bring back the confidence of Americans. He introduced the *Works Progress Administration* to build bridges, schools, highways, and parks. *The Wagner Act* gave workers the right to form unions. *The National Labor Relations Act* gave workers the right to participate in collective bargaining. Also, in 1935, *The Social Security Act* created a kind of unemployment insurance for older Americans. By the end of the decade the war stimulated the economy, as wars usually do, ending the Great Depression.

7D. Changing Lifestyles

Prohibition of the sale of alcoholic products ended in 1933. This was monumental!

While families suffered, lifestyles had to change and did. People learned how to sew their own clothes, how to stretch meals, shop for clothes in second-hand shops, do home maintenance, and start small gardens. As servants such as cooks became a luxury, more housewives learned to cook.

People worked to change their lives while maintaining a sense of normalcy. Vacations became more modest, possibly morphing from a hotel stay to a camping trip. While some movie houses closed, some were converted to Bingo parlors. Home board games became a common purchase.

Oh, yes, and everyone smoked.

7E. Automobiles

Even during the worst years of the 1930s, most families owned a car or truck; some vehicles were very impressive by today's standards. For example, 1930 Buick Touring Cars (Figures 7E.1-2:), purchased by the New Jersey State Police were assigned to troopers on patrol that year; these beautiful four-door vehicles, purchased for $1350, were traded in the next year.

The New Jersey State Police had a real friend in Peter Ranere of Hammonton, NJ who sold them the cars. When they were traded in, the Ranere family kept one, and recently Dominick, Peter's son, completely restored it. In 1990 the family returned the car to the New Jersey State Police. While this is a convertible, and the top of Buick's line is a Touring Car, it is in many ways like Bruno Hauptmann's car, so take a good look at it.

Figure 7E.1: 1930 Buick

Figure 7E.2: 1930 Buick

Cars became flashier and more exciting in the 1930s. Standard Oil, one of the companies that maintained gas stations, had twelve stations in 1920. A decade later, that number had changed to 1,000.

7F. Houses/Homes

Most middle-class families in the 1930s owned their own homes. Homes built in the 1930s were typically bungalow styles with two bedrooms, one living room, one bath, one dining room, and a kitchen. Most homes had electric service. Usually, garages were added later when the family could afford one. Garages were usually disconnected from the house. Homes were going through changes inside as well. Furniture might consist of older hand-me-downs or more modern chrome-framed items in the newer art-deco styles. Kitchens were also changing quickly. Iceboxes were replaced by refrigerators, and many new appliances such as toasters and coffee makers began to appear. Pastel colors were becoming more popular as wall paints, moving homes away from the dark walls/heavy curtains look of pre-depression days.

7G. Communicating – Radios, Newspapers, Newsreels

People continued to buy radios, and often multiple families would get together daily to listen to certain programs. Unfortunately, radios cost about $700 (in today's dollars) and not all families could afford one. Newspapers also became important. The New York Times cost two cents. For families that could afford an occasional trip to the movie theatres, short movies called Newsreels kept them informed about current events and became a primary news source. By the end of the decade, almost 90% of American households owned a radio. This decade ended up being the golden age for radio and film. Since it was a substantial expense, not all households had telephones in the 1930s; families who couldn't afford one would go to someone else's house if they needed to make a phone call. The rotary dial phone was developed in the 1930s.

If one could purchase a radio, families listened to the news and variety shows for 4-5 hours a day. Radios brought families and neighbors together. Often while they listened to the radio, they would play board games on the dining room table. Those who had radios usually listened to President Roosevelt's *Fireside Chats*, and comedy programs such as *Amos 'n' Andy* and *the Ozzie and Harriet Show.*

People enjoyed shopping (whether they made purchases or not), and chain stores were quickly spreading across the country. Woolworth had a thousand stores in 1930 and had two thousand ten years later. This has been attributed, in part, due to an explosion in commercial (color) advertising (newspapers and magazines.)

7H. Fashion

Most women wore simple print dresses, which were inexpensive. Women often wore hats and carried a pocketbook and wore jewelry to change their look rather than buy new clothes. Women's clothes were occasionally in the style of uniforms, such as a pilot's uniform (even the hats!), a fashion trend in part stimulated by the obsession with Lindbergh. Women started to have waists again, created by belts – sometimes wide flashy belts.

7I. Writing

Handwriting letters to friends was a popular pastime. In 1932, the cost of a regular postage stamp was 2-3 cents.

7J. Fountain Pens

In the 1930s, most people wrote with a fountain pen.

The ballpoint pen is now the most used writing instrument, but they did not become available until after World War II.

Fountain Pens are nib pens, which contain internal reservoirs of ink.

Figure 7J.1: A common kind of fountain pen. Note reservoir.

The pen ink flows from a reservoir through a channel to the nib, shown in Fig. 7J.2, due to gravity and capillary action. The reservoir can be filled/refilled with ink in several ways, such as using a syringe.

Figure 7J.2: The Nib (tip) of a Fountain Pen

From the 1880s through the 1920s, Waterman was the leader in fountain pen construction.

These pens often leaked, until Schaeffer introduced a "level filler" in 1912. Cheaper pen inks began to appear. The ink often had the potential for skipping or creating uneven color on the page. If the pen produces a heavy ink flow, the ink on paper dries very slowly. To collect excess ink, blotting papers or blotters were used, such as this example, a rocker style blotter, which holds blotter paper; the user rocks it over fresh writing to absorb excess ink. Do you think the ransom letter writer used a blotter?

Figure 7J.3: Using a blotter with fountain pen ink

Perhaps the first ransom letter shows fountain pen writing at its worst, with extensive smearing and variations in ink intensity. Perhaps someone wrote the ransom letters in a moving car, or more likely they were written by a right-hander with his/her left hand. (More on this later.) Some claim that the State Police did extensive modification of Hauptmann's writing exemplars and on the ransom letters so that his writing would look more like the ransom notes, by shaping specific letters, for example.

Mark Falzini Comments

The State Police were never accused of modifying the ransom notes.

Author Comments

In my copy of *Scapegoat.* I found a newspaper clipping. The newspaper from which it was extracted wasn't clear. The story was: "Lindbergh Kidnap Ransom. Notes were Forgeries, Expert Asserts." It reports the opinion of a handwriting expert, Hilda Braunlich, who said some of the original ransom notes were over-written. She told Edward Reilly, and he said she couldn't testify. His reason? "He really didn't want the truth to come out." According to Ms. Braunlich, the ransom notes were originally written smoothly, but if you magnify the words, you can see that many letters were modified, with a slightly different color of blue ink, to look more like Hauptmann's handwriting. The modified letters are thus considered as forgeries. I found the identical story in the New York Times under the title "Forgery is charged in Hauptmann Case" (Peter Kihss, April 4, 1977).

7K. Shopping – Chains, Convenience Stores, Bodegas

If you had a sudden need for bread, or batteries for your flashlight, you would head for a store depending on where you lived. In cities, there was always something, of course. Even in less populated areas, there was something like a small convenience store not far away. Some suggest it began with J.J. Lawson, who had a dairy facility in Ohio, and decided to open a small store attached to it, which eventually led to a chain in the area. They were not supermarkets, more like a 7-Eleven kind of store, and in the 1930s, they almost always carried:

milk	bread	soft drinks	cigarettes
condoms	coffee	candy bars	Twinkies
Slim Jims	hot dogs	ice cream	candy
gum	lip balm	chips	pretzels
popcorn	beef jerky	donuts	maps
magazines	newspapers	small toys	cat food
dog food	toilet paper		

There is no specific mention of batteries or flashlights. Such small stores often sprang up in the U.S. next to a gas station, at major highway exits, etc.

Modern convenience stores began in the 1920s in the Dallas, TX area. At the time, if you had a refrigerator, it was an air-tight icebox, in which you kept things cold using large blocks of ice. There were many places where people bought large blocks of ice. One was the Southland Ice Dock in Dallas. They decided in 1927 to go from being open 7 a.m.-11 p.m., seven days a week, to 24 hours a day, and since they were always open, why not try to sell some other things like milk and eggs? Eventually, the stores were called 7-Eleven stores. Corner convenience stores in New York City were often called bodegas. A bodega was a cross between a 7-Eleven store and a liquor store. In Canada, and New York City, a bodega sold at least cigarettes, beer, candy bars, and magazines, but they were often just a front for racketeering. They were known for front aisles full of "liquidation items," which were there just to give the store a "store look," while most who entered did so to complete an illegal alcohol purchase or place a bet.

Still, where would one (i.e., Ollie Whateley) go to buy batteries or flashlights in Hopewell, NJ, at 10 p.m. in 1932? There could have been a "Bob's Photon Shop" boutique nearby, but I find none on record. The closest "city" was probably Princeton. One way to quickly learn about the environs are from the local papers of the 1930s, which include the *Local Express*, *Nassau Lit*, Princeton University's weekly paper *The Daily Princetonian*, *Town Topics* (often a 2–4-page publication printed once a week), and the *Princeton News* (largely providing college-town news, and information on campus talks and presentations). I'm also looking for red/blue liquids.

In the December 1, 1931, issue of *The Daily Princetonian*, there were 12 ads. One was from *The Princeton University Store* ("Everything the College Man Needs"), citing typewriters, fountain pens, and stationery. No hours were listed. Surprisingly, not all the ads came from stores in Princeton; some were from as far away as Trenton, Philadelphia, and New York City.

I read an issue of *The Local Express* (November 7,1935), which included eight ads from food stores and two others of note. *Quality Meat Market's* ad mentioned Cape Cod cranberries for 17 cents a pound, and sweet juicy red yams. *The Grippens Market's* ad highlighted specials on red pitted cherries, strawberries, fancy red raspberries, and cranberries. Alcoholic beverages were available at the *Princeton Wine and Liqueur Store*. Hinkson's listed specials such as white paper – folded sheets, single sheets, and envelopes, all made by Highland Linen. *The Milton C. Latta Store* ("Everything in paper for the home") also specialized in household products.

According to the *FBI Files* (Fensch, T. 2001):

> "The Lindberghs only contact with anyone in the vicinity of their home was with merchants in Hopewell in the purchase of groceries, meats, etc. Mostly they were indirect contacts, with servants ordering over the phone."

7L. Kidnapping

In the 1920s and 30s, kidnappings, often performed by gangs, were common. They could involve extravagant ransoms ($100,000+). Usually, the kidnapped person would be returned (kidnapping usually did not equal murder). Corruption in local politics often complicated kidnapping cases. In 1932 Congress passed the Federal Kidnapping Act (also known as the Lindbergh Law), making kidnappings across state lines a federal felony, with serious penalties. The Hauptmann case was initially considered as a robbery – clothes were stolen (since Little Charlie was wearing clothes).

When Police took Hauptmann's garage apart, they found medical-grade ether there. It was called the "anesthetic of choice for 1930s kidnappers." They assumed that the Hauptmann gang was already planning their next kidnapping (Why didn't they assume the ether was used for *this* kidnapping?)

7M. Big News

The 1930s were difficult times for the planet, and the U.S. came out of it all remarkably well. There were incredible technical breakthroughs such as aviation and radio and the movies. The Nazi Party (and Hitler) came into power in Germany in 1933. Roosevelt's New Deal created many big and small public works projects (such as the Hoover Dam.)

Frozen foods were introduced. Nazi Germany started the production of the VW Beetle in the 1930s. Construction of the Empire State Building was completed.

7N. The Chemistry of the 1930s

7N.1. Pen Inks

While not many people still use fountain pens in the present, they are still available and some inks for them are of the same formulation as was used 100 years ago. Advances in both fountain pens and their inks were made in the 1900s.

Fountain pen inks are usually water-based. In theory, dyes or pigments can be used as the colorant. The water is referred to as the vehicle because it transfers the colorant from the pen to the page. Dyes are chemical compounds that dissolve in water, while pigments usually do not dissolve in water (such as pigments used in house paint). Pigments exist as a suspension of very small particles of color, which can easily clog up a fountain pen tip, so they are not often used.

Many of the dyes are aniline dyes, made by chemically linking together various forms of aniline. The building block, the aniline molecule, is shown here.

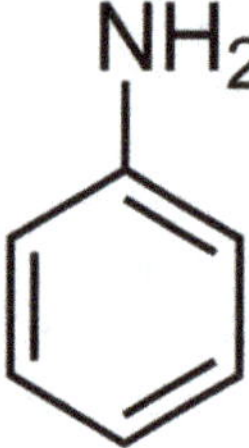

Figure 7N.1.1: The aniline molecule

Of the many aniline dyes, Mauveine is the oldest. William Henry Perkin tried to make the molecule quinine, which was essential for the treatment of malaria. He was unsuccessful in synthesizing quinine from aniline, but the compound he made had a deep purple color and became one of the first man-made dyes for fabrics, fuschin.

Chemists developed a reaction to couple two molecules that are aniline-like together. The reaction is called an azo coupling reaction and yields a product molecule that has an azo (-N=N-) bond. Figure 7N.1.2 shows an example:

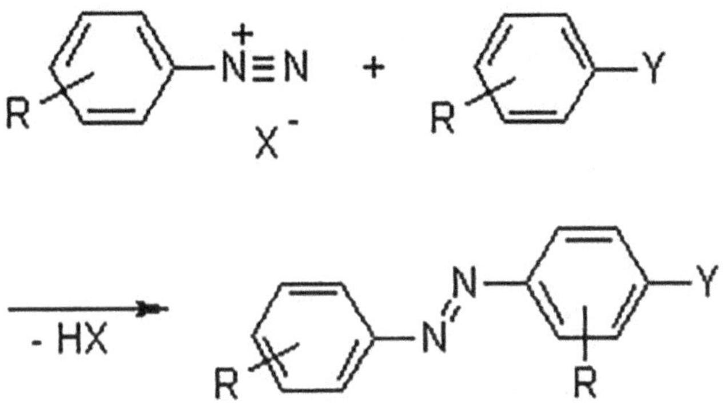

Figure 7N.1.2: Azo Coupling Reaction

If R = H, X^- = Cl^-, and Y = NH_2, the azo dye that is formed in this reaction is called aniline yellow. (The other product, HX, is hydrogen chloride gas, HCl). Oh, do you think I'm wrong? I thought I heard you say that the product is hydrochloric acid and if you said or thought that you would be incorrect. Hydrochloric acid is a solution of hydrogen chloride gas in water.

Since we understand the chemical aspects of pen inks much better today, their components tend to be more common. Glycerine is now a common thickening agent used to control the viscosity of the ink, to allow it to flow at a certain rate from a specific pen. Glycerine is also used by fast food chains to make milkshakes thicker. Surfactants are added to reduce the surface tension of an ink, decreasing the chance of it clumping up and not flowing. Detergents are also added to assist the ink in better wetting the surface, allowing for a smooth, uniform flow. Fungicides are common as well now to keep mold from growing inside the pen. There are also chemical buffers to control the acidity of the ink, so it will not slowly dissolve metallic parts such as the pen tip.

Many of the dyes used in pens were initially developed in Germany, not for pens but for dying fabrics.

Some fountain pen inks available today may be labeled as washable or permanent (found more often on inks made decades ago). It would be ideal to have a permanent ink which, even if it gets wet, the ink on the paper will not run, but the labels are a bit misleading. If your pen leaks in your pocket, you can probably wash it off your shirt with some hot water. These are the washable inks. The permanence of an ink indicates that you could hang a handwritten document on the wall or outside and it will not fade, even when exposed to light for a long time. In some cases, this is a property of the ink. In other cases, chemical compounds are added to the ink that act as a sunscreen to protect the colorants from fading.

To learn more about the chemistry of pen inks, see "Chemical Composition of a Fountain Pen Ink" (Martin-Gil, J. *et al.* 1906) in the *Journal of Chemical Education.*

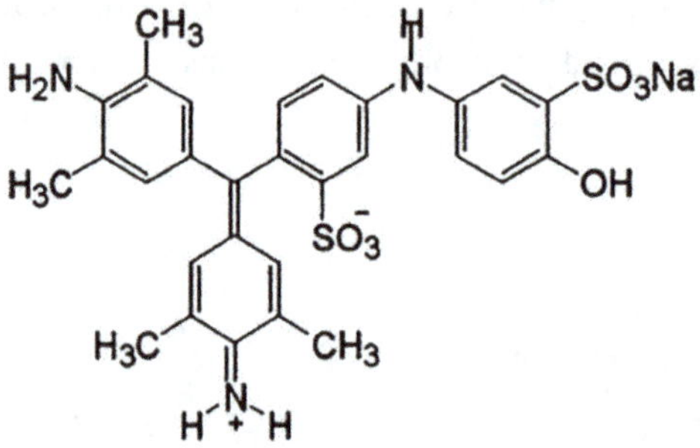

Figure 7N.1.3: A Typical Dye Molecule

7N.2. Back in Time – More Chemistry

There is some chemistry in this book, and unfortunately, if I explained all you needed to know, we would pass the 1000-page mark. We do need to explore compounds that have color. I am very curious about how the signatures were created and whether the inks used were just pen inks or something different. Perhaps they used some food colorings. They would be easy to use. If you go into your kitchen, you will probably find many of the FDA approved food colors. They are:

FD&C Blue No. 1 – Brilliant Blue FCF, E133 (blue shade). It is a powder that is soluble in water. You can find it used in ice creams, mouthwash, and shampoos. It is consumed primarily by Americans since who else would look at a blue and white birthday cake and assume it is edible?

FD&C Blue No. 2 – Indigotine, E132 (indigo shade)

FD&C Green No. 3 – Fast Green FCF, E143 (turquoise shade)

FD&C Red No. 3 – Erythrosine, E127 (pink shade, commonly used in glacé cherries)

FD&C Red No. 40 – Allura Red AC, E129 (red shade)

FD&C Yellow No. 5 – Tartrazine, E102 (yellow shade)

FD&C Yellow No. 6 – Sunset Yellow FCF, E110 (orange shade) It is used in foods, cosmetics, drugs, candies, and sauces.

Before there were government-approved, safe food colorants, housewives would have to be practical and creative. If they wanted to make a red cake, they might put some beet juice in it, for example. However, the list of food colorants outlined here would not be useful for our work because they are the artificial colorings generally permitted for use in food as of 2016. What you want is the list of synthetic colors that were selected by the Pure Food and Drug Act of 1906. They are:

Ponceau 3R (FD&C Red No. 1) – This was initially on the acceptable list, but eventually replaced with something safer, see above. This was used in the 1930s.

Amaranth (FD&C Red No. 2), - This was used when synthetic food dyes were first introduced, and it is still used today.

Erythrosine (FD&C Red No. 3), has remained on the acceptable dye list since 1906.

Indigotine (FD&C Blue No. 2), has been on the acceptable food colorants list since the FDA started identifying acceptable food dyes.

Light Green SF (FD&C Green No. 2).

Naphthol yellow 1 (FD&C Yellow No. 1), a popular food colorant in the US until 1959.

and **Orange 1 (FD&C Orange No. 1)**.

One must never assume that what is true today was true in the past.

7N.3. BIT – Chemistry – Other Red Stuff

When I'm BIT, I particularly want to look for red liquids. You will probably find some in the kitchen, the medicine cabinet, and even in the garage. I'm interested in red because, looking at the "singnatures," the red spot is very uneven. It doesn't look like it is a red ink because ink naturally adheres to paper. This red liquid does not seem to "stick" very well. So, apart from food colorings, we might also find beets, cherries, and other natural items that have a red juice. Blood is, of course, very red, and it would be appropriate for a kidnapper to pick such an intriguing liquid, but while fresh blood is red, it quickly turns a very unimpressive brown when it oxidizes.

We'll begin in the medicine cabinet. I wouldn't be surprised if everything in the medicine cabinet is either a red liquid or a white solid. Here are some examples from the 1930s.

Mercurochrome – a typical bottle of the red liquid is shown here along with the molecular structure.

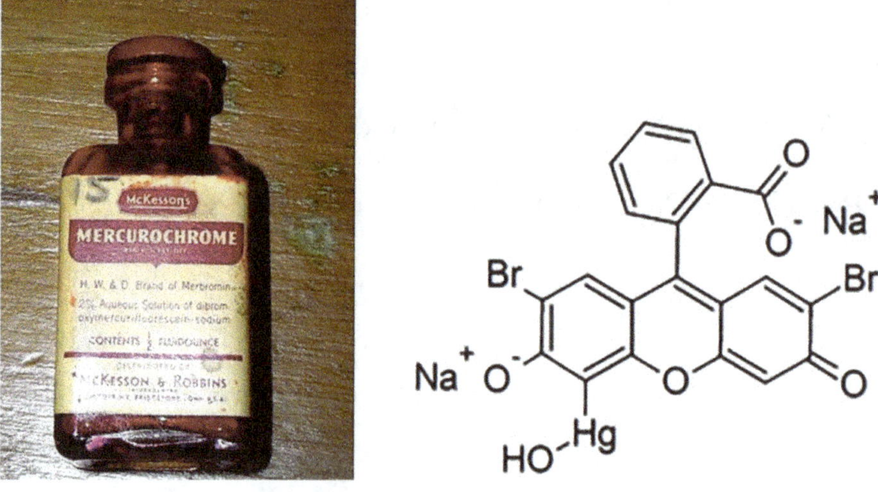

Figure 7N.3.1: Mercurochrome and it's Chemical Structure

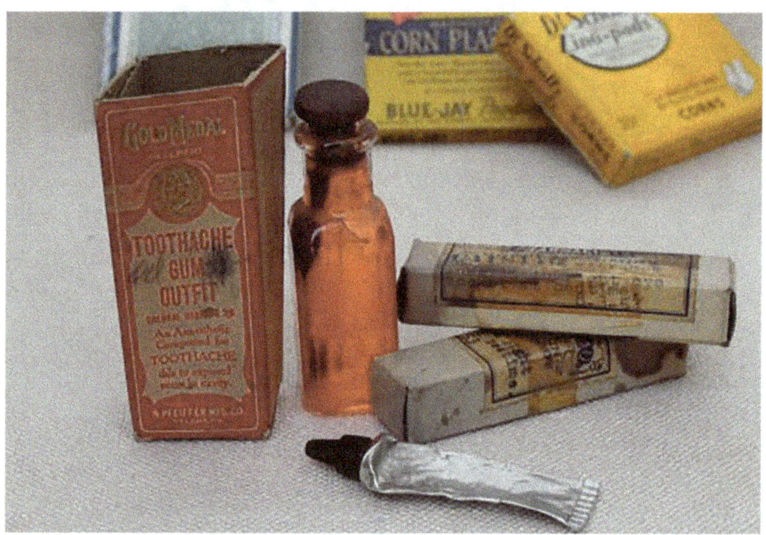

Figure 7N.3.2: Toothache Gum Outfit

I'm not sure what a **toothache gum outfit** is, but it came in a stoppered bottle and was red.

There were several **soft drinks/pops/sodas** at the time, that came in many colors, including red ones. NEHI soft drinks came out in 1924 and came in many flavors.

Figure 7N.3.3: Snake Oil

Snake Oils such as the one in Figure 7N.3.3 were reported to cure all kinds of illnesses and were found in medicine cabinets, due to the promises they made. They are often red to brown liquids.

Figure 7N.3.4: Sloan's Liniment

Shown here is another famous and popular addition to the medicine cabinet – Sloan's Liniment - again a red to brown liquid. A liniment is a lotion, often made with oil, that one can rub on his or her body with the promise of relieving pain.

As we move to the garage, there are also many red liquids we could find, such as these poisons, used to get rid of varmints or kill unwanted plants. As the stains on the label show, these were other brown-to-reddish liquids.

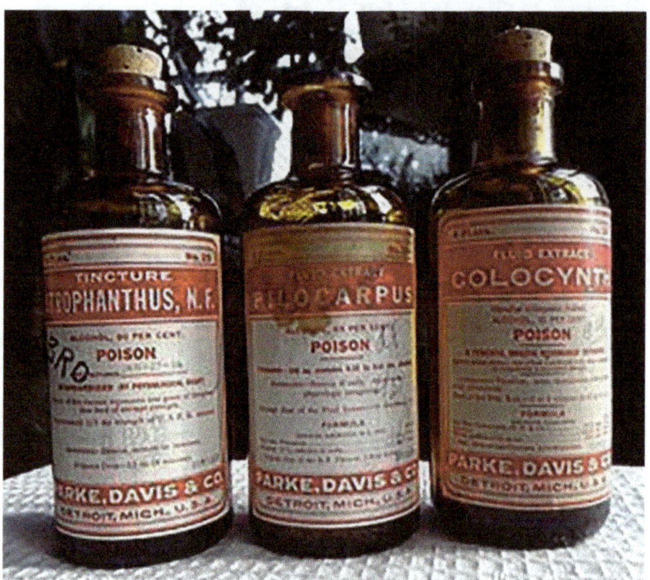

Figure 7N.3.5: Household Poisons

Many of the drugs/medications from the 1930s are no longer used but can still be purchased on-line.

7O. Roads in the US – 1930s

I was thinking about Lindbergh having to travel from his little mountain top to New York City, to his office, and wondered about what the roads were like back then. I was surprised at how far back the topic of roads went. There were public road acts that the East and West Jersey assemblies passed to build public roads and to fund them by county taxes. This began in the 1600s in this state. To connect farms and plantations, roads opened in all directions. In 1768, William Franklin (Ben's son), the last NJ "royal governor," referred to road travel between New York and Philadelphia as "jarring" because of the bad roads that were "seldom passable without danger or difficulty." In the 1800s, it was clear that roads were needed, but the issues and solutions were complex. For example, labor was an issue. For a time in the 1800s, road work by residents was compulsory for 6-8 days a year. (It was an interesting but insufficient idea.) Roads were terrible because they were usually made of dirt, so they were typically soft and uneven.

New Jersey had Turnpikes, which were toll roads. They had movable barriers at certain places to block cars from passing until the driver paid a toll. The Morris Turnpike (1861) was NJ's first turnpike.

Some New Jersey roads became Plank Roads in the 1800s. They were made from three-inch x six-inch hemlock planks, laid six inches apart, filled in with dirt, and topped with a three-inch-thick wooden floor. Some NJ roads were made with macadam. At times it was a mixture of stones, held together with water, asphalt or tar, or a cement and sand mixture.

Stagecoaches began to be available for public use in the 1770s. You could travel by stagecoach from Philadelphia to New York through Bristol, Trenton, Elizabeth, and Newark. It was a two-day trip and cost the equivalent of $60. The Stagecoaches seated eight. Today the trip takes less than two hours, and a one-way train ticket cost less than $50. The highway effort in New Jersey began in 1917 – it laid out a network of 15 highways that could serve the state. Updated versions of these 15 are still in use today. For example, Lindbergh probably drove on Route 1 – Elizabeth to Trenton via Rahway, Metuchen, New Brunswick, and Hightstown.

In the 1920s, New Jersey had two transportation problems on the roads – safety and traffic "management." One solution was the circle. One opened in Camden in 1925, allowing traffic from several directions to cross paths safely without stopping. Projects such as the Garden State Parkway did not begin until after World War II.

Both cars and roadways here underwent substantial technological changes from the time Ford started mass producing cars in 1903 to the growth of good roads in the years just before World War I. Let me tell you why road technology developed so quickly in the state. New Jersey's location between New York and Philadelphia, two population centers, was good news for the state. As people moved into New Jersey, good roads became something that attracted them. It was the congestion around the Port of New York during World War I that increased the need for roadway improvements. Also, trucks began appearing on the roads, which rapidly degraded existing roadways.

The roads were so bad in 1913 that the speed limit was 25 mph. By 1930 the state was building 3- and 4-lane roadways. The Lincoln Highway, the primary route between New York City and Trenton was dedicated in 1913. Lindbergh also briefly used the Pulaski Skyway, which was completed in 1932. It was 3.5 miles long, an elevated roadway that went over Jersey City to Kearney, over the Hancock and Passaic Rivers, and was high enough to allow warships to pass under it. It connected to the Holland Tunnel. It was an extension of Routes 1 & 9 from Newark and Jersey City.

The drive from New York or the Bronx to mid-New Jersey could be completed in a few hours in the 1930s. The cars were impressive, dirt roads were disappearing for main thoroughfares, and legal speed limits were increasing.

So, next question:

Q7O.1: What was Lindbergh's NYC address?
A7O.1: I looked on Google, but with no luck. Google images had an interesting collection of Lindbergh signatures, some on letters, but with very non-traditional headers. For example, he "won" a Bulova Watch for making his non-stop flight from New York to Paris. He wrote them a thank-you letter which said at the top, "Charles A. Lindbergh/" Spirit of St. Louis"/ New York. Paris Flight." My search ended on eBay, where there was a typed letter signed by Lindbergh on 7.11.1930, to a Dr. Burton R. Charles in Los Angeles. The stationery read:
Charles A. Lindbergh
25 Broadway
New York City

13-27 Broadway in New York is the Cunard building in the Bowery, almost across from the Bull in the lower Manhattan's financial district. It is an impressive 22-story office building, opened in 1921, that was the home of the Cunard Line, Anchor Lines, and had other tenants, notably Lindbergh's lawyer and friend, Col. Breckenridge.

7P. Highfields -The Lindbergh House

You should get to know your way around the house since this is where the Lindbergh baby was last seen before he was found dead in a nearby field. I have never found any of the floor plans sufficiently detailed to answer all my questions, but perhaps you will have more luck.

My apologies for making you wait so long for this. The house is essential to understand. In Mark Falzini's *Their Fifteen Minutes*, in which he introduces all the members of this story, one of the "people" he includes is the house. It's a crucial part of the story.

Highfields was the name the Lindberghs gave to their new home. It was in East Amwell, NJ – near the town of Hopewell. After the kidnapping and death of their first child, the Lindberghs never lived in the house.

We appear to have the house to ourselves for the moment, so let's walk through. Yes, it is big! There are 23 rooms in here. Did I mention that the walls are 28 inches thick? That's 28 inches of stone! It's my understanding from most reports that by March 1932, most of the construction had been finished although the family only spent weekends there. However, the book *Hauptmann's Ladder* (Cahill, R.T. 2014) reported that house construction was completed in 1931. Two aspects that I'm very interested in are the attic and basement. While most narratives of the kidnapping assume a ladder was put up on the SE corner where there was a nursery window shutter that needed to be replaced; some think the kidnappers came in and out the front door or perhaps came in the west end of the house and walked to the east end using either the attic or basement. There is little specific information on either, although the house is described as a 2 ½ story dwelling.

Let's look at the floor plan. The nursery is on the corner of the second floor. There appears to be a hallway the length of the house, from the Lindbergh rooms at the east end to the servant's quarters at the other end. Outside of the nursery, a bathroom, and Betty Gow's bedroom, there is a staircase. Either the drawing represents stairs down to the first floor and stairs up to the attic, or stairs up to a landing a few steps below the second floor, where one would turn to take the last few steps to the second floor.

The drawings seem to also show stairs going up and down outside the nursery, and at the opposite end of the hallway. Note that at the west end, first floor, there is access to the garage – an easy in/out far from the living room.

If you locate the stairs in the drawings, there appears to be stairs coming up from the basement at both ends of the hallway. It is not exactly clear if they're meant to indicate first-to-second floor steps, but at least one suggests steps down from the first floor (I believe).

Anne supposedly went to her bedroom after dinner and a shower, but never reported hearing anything. So perhaps the kidnapping occurred while they ate in the dining room.

The National Park Service lists the property as spanning two counties, Hunterdon and Mercer. After the kidnapping, the property was given to the State of New Jersey and was/is used as a residential youth correctional facility.

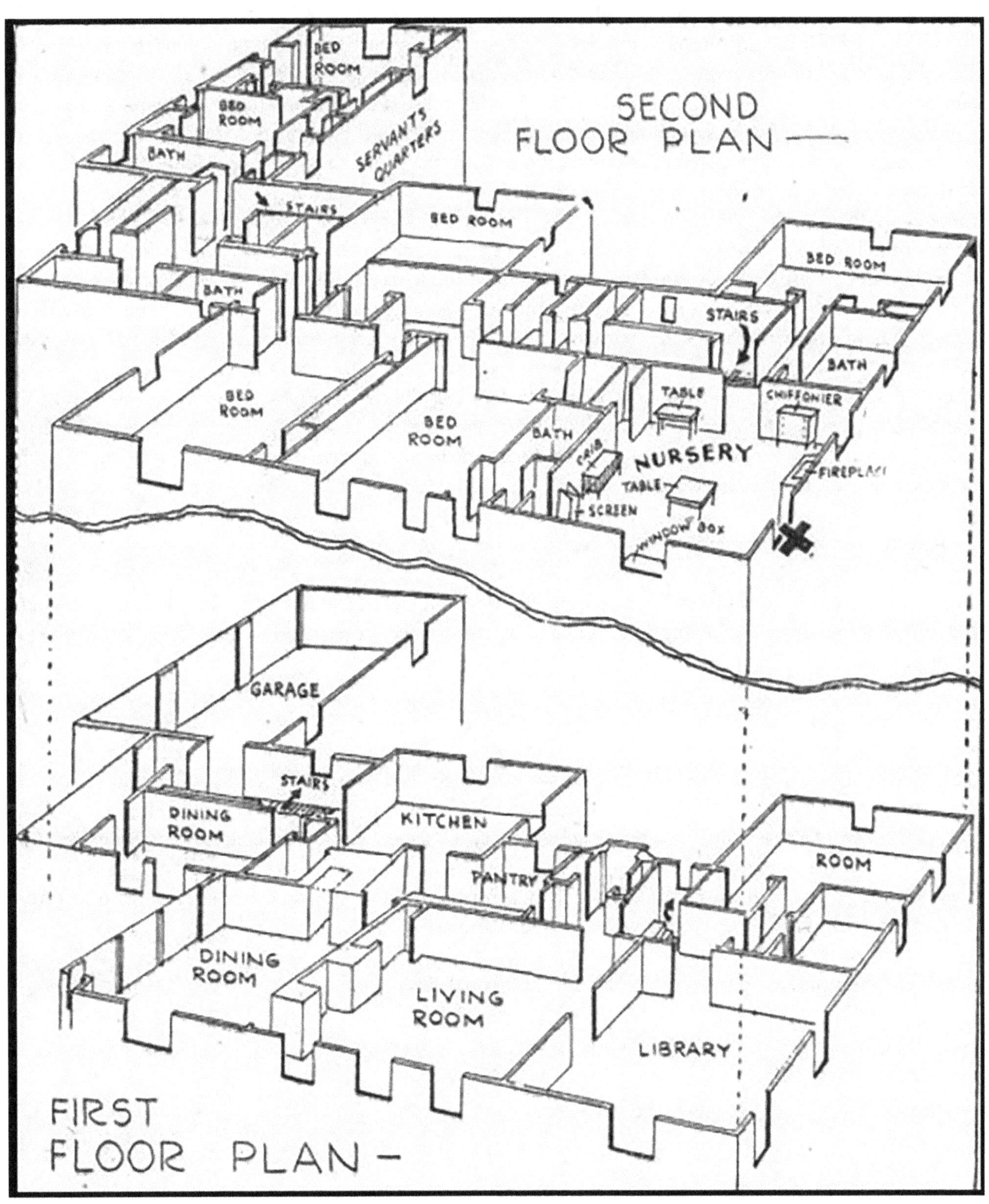

The Lindbergh House – My personal questions: It has been suggested that the kidnapper(s) may have come in the front door and gone up the stairs to grab little Charlie. From there, they could have handed him out the window, thrown him out the window, walked back down the steps and out the front door with him, or, walked the length of the house and exited out a window over the garage, or down and out the garage. They could have walked the length of the house down the first-floor hallway, or the second-floor hallway. What are the other options? They could have carried Little Charlie up to the attic and walked the length of the house that way as well if it had an entrance at one end and exit at the other end. I could never make out for sure if there was an attic (There are windows above the second-floor windows, so I assume so) or a basement. I have seen one comment on the attic, that it was an unfinished space. I've also read that Betty would often wash Little Charlie's clothes on the second floor and hang them to dry in the basement. Also, at one point early in the investigation, Anne was asked to show an officer where the furnace was, and they looked inside it to see if any bones were in it. So again, the basement could have been used by kidnappers to move the length of the house and out the back door, if the basement had access doors at opposite ends. I'd been planning to take a tour of the Lindbergh home, which is now a Treatment Center for Adjudicated Females under the care of the NJ Juvenile Justice Commission, Department of Law and Safety. It is very important that no one touring the house has contact with any of the females living there, so no pocketbooks, cameras, cell phones, etc. are allowed. Those who work there take their jobs, including the protection of the juvenile residents, seriously.

I'd been dragging my feet on arranging a tour, and when I finally called in November, Vanessa informed me that tours were over since October and wouldn't start again until probably April. I told her I didn't need a tour, I just had a few personal questions for my book, so she would have to answer them for me. She very kindly did so, and I appreciate her assistance.

"Is there an attic and how many points of access are there?"

"Yes, there is an attic, and I know that occasionally when an electrician has to go up there, he pulls stairs down from the second-floor ceiling to go up and come down the same way since there is only one place to get in/out."

"Same question for the basement."

"Yes, we have a basement, and there is a door to get down there. There's no other door, just one."

So, cancel my visit for now! Thank you very much, Vanessa, "Designee" for the Lindbergh home in Hopewell, NJ.

I would urge you to read through the extensive description of The National Register of Historic Places' Description of the Lindbergh House, which can be found at:

https://npgallery.nps.gov/pdfhost/docs/NRHP/Text/94001096.pdf

7Q. THE ALPHONSE WISKOWSKI PHOTOGRAPH COLLECTION

I have a treat for you that will surely make the early 1930's on the Northeastern Coast of the United States come alive for you, and to help you appreciate just how quickly aeronautics was changing from an interesting possibility to something that would be impacting our future. I present here the Alphonse Wiskowski Collection. Alphonse Wiskowski was born in 1918 and grew up fascinated by flying and the Lindberghs. He even built an early "kit plane" and became an airplane mechanic. He fostered his interest and excitement in his family. After he passed away in 1998, one of his daughters, Barbara, discovered a set of photographs. While Alphonse was also a photographer, these were probably not taken by him, since many of them depict events occurring in 1931-32, when Alphonse was a 13-14-year-old boy. Nonetheless, I have been unable to find any of them on the internet, and possibly this is the first time they have been seen. So, if you are a fan of the early days of commercial aviation and the famous flying characters of the time, you should enjoy these. I am very grateful to Barbara Wiskowski and her family for allowing me to share with you this collection. I believe you can feel the excitement of the times through them. I have scanned the original sepia prints and have made small changes in the contrast to enhance them a bit. The photos shown here are the full pictures, all originally 9 ¾" x 8" on relatively thick photographic paper. Most of them have either holes in the corners or corners torn off, suggesting that at one time they may have been posted on a cork board with thumb tacks. Some have a few words written on the reverse side, lightly, in pencil.

On the next page is the first photograph, Figure W1 of the collection, showing Roscoe Turner. Turner (1895-1970) was born in Mississippi. He was known for his racing and barnstorming. He was also known for Gilmore, his pet lion. Roscoe held the Transcontinental Air Speed Record (New York to Los Angeles) (1930 and 1932). He established the Roscoe Turner Airways Corporation, which had a single biplane built to hold up to 16 passengers. Turner was known as an aviator, a movie star, and as a spokesperson for Camel Cigarettes, United Airlines, and Heinz Foods. He even had a daily NBC radio show in 1936 called *Flying Time* (Wikipedia, Roscoe Turner).

Photo W1. "Roscoe Turner (center)"

Photo W2. A pilot, waving

No description is given. I'm going to suggest that it was taken at the Newark Airport in 1931, only because some of the photographers seem to be the same in another photograph. Note the Shell Oil truck, carrying drums of what are likely fuel oil for airplanes.

According to a Shell website, Shell Aviation serves 850 airports, refueling an aircraft every 14 seconds. (https://www.shell.com/business-customers/aviation/aviation-fuel.html)

Photo W3. Unidentified smiling pilot in a biplane

While I have not been able to identify the pilot, the side of the plane indicates that it is from the Great Lakes Aircraft Corporation (GLAC). The specs are listed on the side such as the wingspan (26 ft.), length (20 ft.), useful load (578 lbs.) and gasoline capacity (26 gallons). The Great Lakes Aircraft Company began in Cleveland in 1929. The specifications match their famous 2T biplane. The plane sold for $4,990 but when the Depression hit GLAC lowered the price to $3,985. Even that could not help, and the Depression put them out of business in 1936. (Wikipedia, Great Lakes Aircraft Company)

Photo W4. Willie

The backdrop for the picture is a plane from NAT, the National Air Transport (airlines) (1925-1934). They were the first airline to provide cross-country service. NAT was purchased by Boeing in 1930. Boeing split into three smaller companies in 1930, and the part that had been NAT became United Airlines.

NAT began carrying U.S. Airmail in 1927 and had passenger flights in 1930 between New York (actually Newark) and Chicago. (Wikipedia, National Air Transport)

Also, I should probably acknowledge the robot in the room. Willie Vocalite was a robot built by Westinghouse (as you can read on his chest). Willie is shown here attending the Ford trimotor National Air Transport opening ceremony at the Newark Airport in 1931. If you want to know more about the amazing Willie, check out the following Smithsonian website:

https://blog.library.si.edu/blog/2017/08/04/21005/#.XDpN8i2ZOA8

Look closely and you can see a photographer with a still camera, one with a movie camera, and one using his iPad.

Photo W5. United Airlines. (no additional information)

Photo W6. Written on the back side of the photo: Governor Hoffman (not)

I'm not sure what the rules were for holding the position of governor of the state of New Jersey, but A. Harry Moore served as governor three times: 1/26 – 1/29; 1/32 – 1/35; and 1/38-1/41. He was governor during the kidnapping of Little Charlie. Harold G. Hoffman was governor for one term, 1/35-1/38, and was the governor during the trial of Hauptmann. Photo W6 is identified as that of Governor Hoffman, but in fact, it is of Governor Moore.

Photo W7. Amelia in Newark

The scene matches, even down to the number of steps, the entrance to the Administration Building of the Art-Deco Newark Airport. Amelia Earhart, shown here, was present at the dedication ceremonies in 1934. *Decopix*, the Art Deco Architecture web site, provides some information if you'd like to know more:

http://www.decopix.com/newark-airport-fabulous-building-one/

Photo W8. Amelia and friends

Photo W8 shows Amelia dressed to relax while posing for the camera. There is a haze/glare in the photo that could have been created during the printing of the photo or could perhaps suggest that the picture was taken through a vehicle window.

Photo W9. R. N. Buck

The photo is of Robert N. Buck, a famous pilot. In 1930 he got his pilot's license. He was 16. Lindbergh was known for his aerial archaeology however Buck was the first to photograph ancient ruins from his plane. "Red-haired and apple cheeked, the young Mr. Buck was known in the newspapers as 'the schoolboy pilot'" [The New York Times, "Robert N. Buck dies at 93; was record-setting aviator' by Margalit Fox, May 20,2007] He was born in 1914 in Elizabethport, New Jersey. I believe this is a photo of Buck in his Pitcairn Mailwing the 'Yankee Clipper'.

Photo W10. Charles Lindbergh and an unidentified man walking in an unidentified location, probably an airfield

What I liked best about the photo is the young man on the left. Mounted on the front of his bicycle is what looks like a small replica of an airplane engine, complete with a propeller, which likely spins as he rides.

Photo W11. Two gentlemen flirting with Anne Lindbergh while she's at work

Again, there is a possible reflection from shooting through a window, or evidence for a damaged negative.

Photo W12. Anne and Charles

This last photo of the collection that I've selected appears to be Anne and Charles in their Lockheed Sirius monoplane which they flew from New York to Tokyo in 1931.

(http://www.charleslindbergh.com/history/orient.asp)

Anne also documented their trip in her book *North to the Orient*, published in 1935.

Photo W13. Alphonse Wiskowski, Aviator

Again, many thanks to Alphonse Wiskowski for saving these photographs for his family. He is shown here in a 1945 photo and a second photo taken 46 years later, with one of his favorite airplanes, the Martin B-26 Marauder Bomber. I sincerely appreciate having an opportunity to present this collection of photos. On E-bay, there are several collections like these, usually smaller sets (3-4 photos, often 5"x7"). I have not found these photos elsewhere (except for a similar one of Willie Vocalite's airport visit), so I am very pleased to be able to share them with you.

SUMMARY OF PART I.

My goals were to make this a brief historical introduction, a workbook for students interested in digging deeper, to share new ideas, and to help you immerse yourself in the topic as much as you can, using information in the many media options on the internet. I've tried to introduce you to the Lindbergh story, how he quickly rose to stardom, at the same time outlining the confusion concerning the facts of the kidnapping case. We took a trip back in time to understand the physical and emotional environment of the 1930s and its impact on how facts and new ideas are evaluated. Question everything and don't hesitate to learn more. These are important concepts in such investigations, and in life.

PART II

EVIDENCE AND SHOULD-BE EVIDENCE

CHAPTER 8
WHAT IS EVIDENCE?

See: Ho, Hock Lai, The Legal Concept of Evidence 2015.URL = plato.stanford.edu/archives/win2015/entries/evidence-legal/ for a serious discussion. Also, Max M. Houck and Jay A. Siegel did an excellent job of discussing the concept of evidence in their book *Fundamentals of Forensic Science* (Houck, MM & Siegel, JA, 2010). They state:

> "Evidence can be defined as information, whether personal testimony, documents or material objects, that is given in a legal investigation to make a fact or proposition more or less likely ... Physical evidence {refers to} things evolved in the commission of the crime under investigation."

So, facts and information, not just a smoking gun, are evidence, in addition to smoking guns.

Obviously, you need to know something about the story before you can start to recreate the crime scene(s). Many books have been written on the Lindbergh case, and they offer an interesting perspective since some were written immediately after the trial, and some were written recently. Opinions and "facts" have changed over this period. First, some relatively small "facts" have been presented that conflict with other facts. I'm glad you're here so we can think about these together. Then we will get into the significant items associated with the crime.

So far, you should have read the first seven chapters, and used the ALLISONweb to look up any relevant information, such as who the characters are in this story. You should have taken the quiz at the end of Chapters 5 and 6 and read the answer key. Part II will begin with some things that I find interesting/curious that may or may not be evidence. We will have to evaluate the partially relevant information that we have.

Assignment: Write down as many questions as you have so far related to this case if you're trying to get to the Truth.

CHAPTER 9

THE RANSOM MONEY – MEASURE TWICE, COUNT ONCE; THE BOX; CHECKING FACTS BY RECREATING THEM; HOW BIG IS MONEY?

Question everything! As in real life, you may never get information when you *need* it, but I suggest you get used to *finding* what you need. When considering evidence, you never know when even small things may come together and explain something big. We should do some arithmetic together because some things about the case don't add up. Look at a few of the ransom letters in Chapter 16 to understand what money the kidnappers were asking for.

Q9.1: Did the kidnappers ask for $50,000 and then for $20,000 more? And do the dimensions of the box in which the ransom was to be delivered make sense?
A9.1: The kidnapper(s) was(were) very specific about how they wanted to receive the $50,000 they requested. If you read carefully, you'll realize the kidnappers didn't want the money in a box. They were asking for a package, but Team Lindbergh took it to mean a box. Let's look at the money requested first. The ransom letter asked for $50,000 in a very particular way. It was to be delivered as 2000 $5 bills, 1500 $10 bills, and 1250 $20 bills.

Q9.2: (Sorry but we must check.) Does the amount requested here add up to $50,000?
A9.2: Your answer ____

(no peeking)

A9.2: My Answer
(2000 x $5) + (1500 x $10) + (1250 x $20) = $10,000 + 15,000 + 25,000 = $50,000

Q9.3: How many total bills is this?
A9.3: Your answer____________________________________
A9.3: My Answer
2000 + 1500 + 1250 = 4,750 bills

Lindbergh was told that $50,000 was to be hand-delivered in a packet. The ransom letter illustrated a package 9 x 6 x 14 inches. It was assumed, from the language of the ransom letters, that the author was German. (The money would occupy a volume. of 328 cu.in.; the volume of the. packet is 756 cu. in. Does this make any sense?)

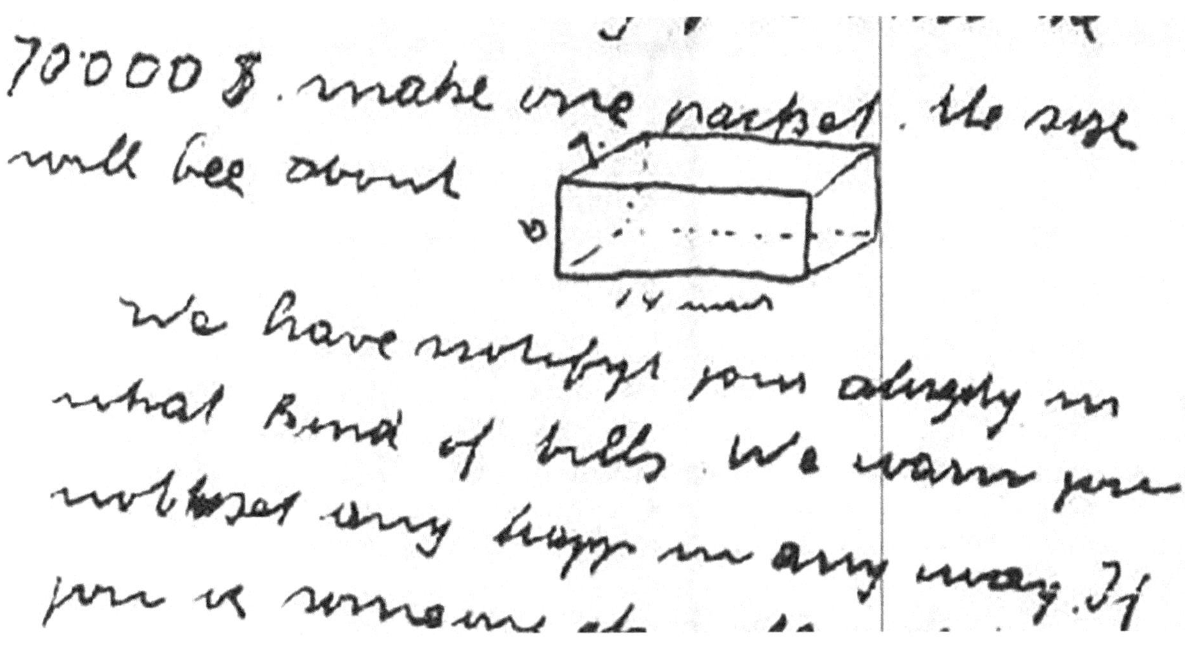

70000 $. make one packet. the size
will bee about

14

We have
what kind of bills. We warn you
any way. If

Figure 9.1: The Ransom Package Dimensions

Soon after, the kidnappers asked for an additional $20,000 because of delays, for taking care of the baby. In one ransom note, they described the $70,000 as follows: $20,000 in $50 bills, $25,000 in $25 bills, $15,000 in $10 bills and $10,000 in $5 bills.

Let's check the arithmetic again. The total is

$20,000 + $25,000 + $15,000 + $10,000 = $70,000

We're still good. In a following letter, they asked for the ransom differently. They wanted $20,000 in $50 bills, $25,000 in $20 bills, $15,000 in $10 bills and $10,000 in $5 bills.

We'll have to check again.

$20,000 + $25,000 + $15,000 + $10,000 = $70,000

Q9.4: They twice explained in the Ransom Letters how they wanted the $70,000. Why would they have changed their minds? Is it really important?

A9.4: Did you figure it out? There are many possible reasons. Maybe the total number of bills in their first version of $70,000 would no longer fit in the package, so they had to do some recalculations. That is plausible and easy enough to check. But I'm sure you know by now. The first time they indicated how they wanted the $70,000, part of the ransom was in $25 bills. Oops.

Q9.5: Let's revisit how big this box is supposed to be?

A9.5: The drawing indicates that it should be 6 x 9 x 14. It is unclear (at least to me) what the units are. What are our choices? Perhaps you would say inches if you are an American. But if the author of the letter was from just about any other country, the natural units for them would likely be metric – millimeters (mm) or centimeters (cm). There are 2.54 cm in an inch, and 10 mm in 1 cm. Let's consider the one side that is six somethings long. If it is cm, that would be equal to

6 cm/2.54 cm per inch = 2.3 inches

If the unit is mm, the box would have one dimension of less than an inch. Both seem unreasonable, so we will assume the units are all in inches, even though that is a surprising choice for a German/Scandinavian.

The ransom letter never demanded a 'box', only to have the money in one bundle of certain dimensions. A bundle is defined as a group of things fastened (tied or wrapped) together for convenient handling; a package wrapped for carrying.

We can determine if the money requested would actually fit in the dimensions indicated, but we need to understand a few things. The country was in the process of changing the size of our paper currency, from large bills to smaller. Also, the government decided to no longer use gold certificates, paper currency based on a gold standard. The decision was made to pay the ransom with all gold certificates to hopefully facilitate the capture of the kidnappers. This is not exactly true, so I will provide the details here.

I will assume in my calculations that follow, that all bills were of the newer small size. In 1929, all U.S. currency had been changed to its current modern size.

The $50,000 ransom was paid as follows: $10k in $5 bills, $15k in $10 bills, $25k in $20 bills.

In 1928, small gold certificates were first printed, distributed in 1929. No $5 gold certificates were printed in that series, so all the $5 bills had red seals and red ink serial numbers, all with serial numbers beginning with an A. Five dollar bills of this kind were printed in 1928, 1953 and 1963 so these had to be 1928 series. In the ransom, all the $10 bills were gold certificates. Of the 1250 $20 bills, 1000 were gold certificates and 250 were federal reserve notes. Series 1928 $20 gold certificates were the first small size gold certificates issued.

The new smaller size paper currency that we still use today is 2 5/8 in. by 6 1/8 in., but how thick? The new size was printed on the <u>same</u> rag paper, so I assume it was the same thickness as the larger bills, 0.0043 in. Again, all the bills used to pay the ransom were small size bills.

So, the new paper currency in circulation in 1932 was 6.14 in. by 2.61 in. by 0.0043 in. If you piled 4750 bills (the $50,000 total) into one stack, it would be 6.14 in. by 2.61 in. by (0.0043 in. x 4750 =) 20.43 inches - a pile more than a foot tall. If a box were 6 x 9 inches at the base, you could start one pile of bills, the length of 6.14" could sit along the 9-inch axis, take up 2.6 inches of the 6-inch axis. This would allow a second pile beside it, using up 2.6 + 2.6 of that footprint (=5.2 in). There is not enough room to make a third pile (going up), but bills set on their edge could fill up the remainder of the 6 in. axis as well. If the box is 14 inches high, and we put two equal stacks of money in it, each stack would be (20.4 in/2) = 10.2 inches high. The 14-inch box would be almost full but would have plenty of room to put additional bills in it around the two 10.2 inch piles. Supposedly there was so much currency in the box that Lindbergh pressed on the box to close it and cracked it. It may have been wrapped up with paper and string, and then put in the box, but there was no reason for additional wrapping. No one needed a small create. The dimensions don't make much sense.

If you understand the above discussion, make a drawing here, of the box with the money in it.

Supposedly Jafsie convinced John to accept the original ransom request of $50,000, so we never need to know if $70,000 will fit in the dimensions the kidnappers indicated. Still, I can summarize my calculations for you. The requested $70,000 would contain 5150 bills, 400 more than what we had in the $50,000 piles. 400 additional bills would be 400 x 0.0043 in = 1.72 inches high. We had two piles of money each 10.2 in. high in a box 14 in. high, so we can easily fit an additional stack, 1.72 in. high, in the box.

There are versions of the story where, when it was time to pay the ransom, Lindbergh asked Breckenridge to tell Jafsie to get the box built. Jafsie obtained some different pieces of wood, so the box would be unique, asked his son-in-law to draw up a design for its construction, and took it to someone to get it built. The price tag was less than $4 but Jafsie considered it excessive, located a family heirloom, an old ballot box, and used that as a model. Voting ballot boxes used by state and federal agencies are of a similar shape, but they must be large to hold many ballots, or they would constantly have to be emptied. As the history of the story progresses, it seems like the ballot box story has been dropped.

Since we're stacking up money, supposedly Fisch did leave Hauptmann a shoebox that that contained up to $16,000 (or, if there were five in the gang, Fisch and everyone else would have received $10,000, so that might be the more likely contents of his shoebox) in ransom bills, although we don't know the distribution of denominations. According to the Fisch Story, a shoebox containing roughly $20,000 was given to Hauptmann before Fisch left his going-away party at Hauptmann's home. To be more precise, he left a trunk, two suitcases, and a shoebox tied with a string for Hauptmann to hold for him.

Q9.6: How big is a shoebox? (estimate)
(Don't forget units.)
A9.6: (estimate. Don't forget units.)
Perhaps the obvious answer is, it depends on the shoe and the size! There is no one standard shoebox size. *The U.S. Post Office* has a priority mailing box that they call their "shoebox," which is 7 ½ x 5 1/8 x 14 3/8 inches. Also, a place called *The Container Store* sells a "man's shoebox" that is 10 1/8 x 5 5/8 x 14 ¾ inches. If the original $50,000 dollars was divided into five piles (one for each kidnapper), and the original stack of bills was 20.4 inches tall, then one person's portion would be roughly 20.4 in./5 = 4.1 inches high. It appears that a shoebox could easily hold $10,000. Let's consider, for example, the Post Office shoebox. If we lay a pile of bills along the 7 ½ inch axis and make two piles side by side, the total width would be 6.22 inches, which is larger than the P.O. shoe box. We could have a single 4.1 inch high pile; that would fit. We could stand the bills up on their edges; they would easily fit in the box, with much room to spare.

From our simple calculations here, we should comment:

1. If Fisch left a shoebox, it could have easily held 1/5th of the $50,000 ransom money (his share if he was one of five) or even $20,000.
2. Over the years, the drawing and dimensions in the ransom letter seem to have been interpreted as requiring a box to deliver the money in, but the note specifies a package. They could have wrapped some paper around the money and tied it or taped it. It would be unlikely that one could make a

package with those dimensions with either the $50,000 or $70,000; the package size would not have prohibited Jafsie from giving them $70K, but he chose not to. He seemed to want to help Lindbergh by not paying what he didn't have to. Or maybe he wanted to make sure there was money left so he would be paid when this ordeal ended.

3. It seems like people are making up a lot of "facts" surrounding this concept of a ransom payoff "package."
4. Counting paper currency and making piles in a box is not a very challenging exercise, but the result makes you question just about every aspect. Why did the kidnappers put the dimensions they did on the original drawing? Why did they think they had to specify dimensions at all? This is not a large number of bills, and if they had to be wrapped up, there aren't many practical options.
5. Why didn't the police arrest Jafsie? When they questioned him about the box, he said he had it made by a guy he knew. Jafsie said he knew where the man's business was, but the police could not find the business at the location he gave. What law enforcement officer would find this acceptable? Then he said he used a box he had in the family - a completely different story, and the police accepted it. At times like this it feels like everyone was working together, and you and I are the only two who aren't in on the plan.
6. I don't know if the volume of this pile of money has been calculated before, but this should have been verified long ago to check every part of the testimony.
7. Keep in mind that nobody really saw Cemetery John except for Jafsie. (A cemetery guard and Al Reich both saw him briefly, but not long enough to provide a useful description.) For all we know, Jafsie took a box with $50,000 inside, hid it in the cemetery, and came back for it later.

Q9.7: Are you convinced there was a Cemetery John, since everything we know comes from Jafsie?
A9.7: Your Answer: ______________________________
We would certainly hope so because Jafsie is supposedly one of the good guys in this story.

Q9.8: What did I do wrong in these calculations? ______________________________
A9.8: Nothing. Hopefully, you feel confident that you can do simple calculations like this when you want to verify a "fact." I always do them at least twice.

One small concern of mine is that a new bill, never in circulation, is 0.0043 inches thick. We calculated how tall these piles of money would be according to that thickness. If they were all new bills, never in circulation, our calculations would be pretty good, but, if they were bills that have been in circulation, folded and handled, this might make the pile a little higher than we originally calculated.

As you go through this book, what we do constantly changes, and we are now going to move into more substantive investigations of some aspects of the evidence. Specifically, we are going to attempt to think deeply about a few key components of, and related to, this case. They are topics that have been extensively studied in the past, but we will try to look at them with the fresh and curious eyes of a scientist (and his assistant). Hold onto your hat!

PROJECT: Get some cardboard or cardstock and make a "shoebox" using the information provided in this chapter. Cut at least 20 pieces of paper to the size of the currency as listed. If you kept the bills in neat piles or all standing up on their sides, how many bills do you think you could put in a shoebox?

Drawing of your experiment:

CHAPTER 10

QUESTIONS, INFORMATION AND MORE QUESTIONS

John A. Condon. Where do we begin? Condon is a critical figure in the Lindbergh Kidnapping Case. He was a nobody with a history of writing patriotic stories for small newspapers in the Bronx. Condon had a Ph.D. with some local notoriety. The first time he met with a member of the kidnapping gang, eventually known as Cemetery John, he gathered lots of information such as John's description and the location of Little Charlie. (FYI: One Cemetery was St. Raymond's Cemetery in the Bronx (2600 Lafayette Ave.), the borough's only Catholic Cemetery and one of the busiest in the U.S., handling roughly 4000 burials a year.)

Q10.1: Did Condon speak German?
He claimed to have tried to speak German to Cemetery John in the cemetery, but got no response, suggesting John wasn't German. However, after the trial, Condon claimed to have gone to the jail, and spoken to Hauptmann for almost an hour in German.
A10.1: Well, he did live near a mostly German part of the Bronx, but this may be irrelevant. I tried to research his education. Condon received a B.A. degree from the City College of New York in 1882. He received a second B.A. from St. John's College (now Fordham University), an M.A. from Fordham University in 1902, and a Ph.D. in Pedagogy in 1904 from NYU. Fordham/St. John's has a useful website which contains many of their old General Catalogs and Publications. The 1902/03 General Catalog states that the admission language requirement was French or German. Also, students should know some Latin and Greek (syntax, etc.) and have a complete knowledge of French or German, including an ability to translate simple prose at sight. Students could take courses, as needed, in French, German or Spanish (2 hours/week for two terms). So, it is likely that Jafsie could speak German, from all the schooling he had. Perhaps.

Q10.2: How do we explain the day of the week that the kidnapping took place? Why Tuesday? The Lindberghs only came to the house on weekends, then always returned to Anne's parent's home. They were never there on a Tuesday, so how would the kidnappers have known to come to the house and kidnap Little Charlie on a Tuesday? In one of the ransom letters, they claimed they had been planning the kidnapping for a year, so they likely knew the regular whereabouts of the family. How do we explain a Tuesday kidnapping? And how do we explain the time? Why not sneak in at 2 a.m. when everyone in the house is asleep, instead of before 10 p.m.?
A10.2: Some Possibilities

1. Anne called her mother to tell her they wouldn't be coming home on schedule, so family members and staff knew where they were. It could have been an inside job or a "family job." There was even a theory that Anne's older, unbalanced sister Catherine had been upset for some time because

Lindbergh chose to marry Anne instead of her; Catherine had become obsessed, and during one of her visits to the new house, she went into the nursery and threw the baby out the window. The family then staged a complicated cover-up to protect its reputation.

2. We don't even *know* that the kidnapping took place on the night they called the police. The baby could have been taken out of the house at any time, possibly days before, if it was an inside job.
3. Perhaps a group of thieves was planning on a simple breaking-and-entering (B&E) for that night. They (somehow) knew that one of the shutters in the nursery didn't latch correctly and decided to enter the house through the upstairs window of Little Charlie's room. When they realized the Lindberghs were home, they decided to make it a lucrative kidnapping instead of a B&E.
4. Presumably, that Monday and Tuesday were workdays for the carpenters and other people who were still working on finishing the house, if any, so possibly some workers knew that the family plus child were in the house on that Tuesday. Contractors knew that there was a nursery shutter that needed to be replaced because it didn't close correctly.

> Mark Falzini comments
>
> The house was complete. No workers were there.
>
> Author comments
>
> Sources do not provide clarity. Construction of Highfields began in March 1931, and was nearing completion in late summer 1931. Other sources state the house was built over the period 1931-35. 'Most' of the house was completed by March 1932, according to *Their Fifteen Minutes*. The last part of the house to be finished was landscaping.

If this began as a breaking and entering, the burglars wouldn't have carried appliances or furniture out the front door of a crowded house, when they just could have come back the next night to an empty house, so that does not seem like a reasonable explanation. The ladder could have been a prop that wasn't used or was only used to enter the house.

You've already read my BIT comments on the house. We know there was a basement and an attic, so, using the ladder for entry and get-away is not an iron-clad part of the kidnapping story.) Also, we can probably rule out Anne's sister as the killer. While some books describe her as sick and obsessed with the marriage of Anne and Charles, she was considered psychologically sound despite her physical ailments. If the baby was taken or disposed of days before it was reported, this would indicate the family and/or staff were involved.

Q10.3: How old was Little Charlie when he was Kidnapped? ______________________
A10.3: The wanted posters listed his age as 20 months. Every book I've read says 20 months. But in *Hour of Gold, Hour of Lead,* Anne stated that "our eighteen-month-old child" was kidnapped. So, which is it?

Little Charlie was born on June 22, 1930; kidnapped on March 1, 1932. June 22, 1930, to June 22, 1931, is 12 months. June 22, 1931, to Feb. 22, 1932 is another eight months, and Feb. 22, 1932, to March 1, 1932, is seven days. The total is 20 months and seven days. The poster is correct. Anne is wrong unless we don't really know when Charlie was born or when he died. There may be reasons why they might hide such information.

Q10.4: Lindbergh took over the investigation from the very beginning, frustrating the state and local police, and the FBI. One can understand how a tall, imposing figure with an international reputation might intimidate the police, to the point where they allowed him to make key decisions, but was Lindbergh the impressive hero and statesman that the public saw?
A10.4: It was clear from his early days that Lindbergh usually kept to himself and had very few social skills. There are many stories about Lindbergh's stunts that show he had a horrible sense of humor. While in the Army he filled another soldier's canteen with kerosene and let him start to drink it. (This could have killed him.) Another time, on a warm summer day, one of his fellow soldiers was asleep in his bed during the day (naked). As the story goes, Lindbergh tied a rope around the young man's penis, which Lindbergh had painted green, and took the rope outside to find someone to pull it.

When it came time for Little Charlie to start walking, Lindbergh would supposedly throw pillows at him to knock him over. Let us conclude that there were multiple sides to Charles Lindbergh.

> Mark Falzini Comments
> It (the pillow story) is not "supposedly". Will Rogers witnessed it.

Q10.5: OK, I've dangled the "gold certificate" phrase in front of you for too long and you may not know what it means. (You could have looked in ALLISONweb.) What is the gold certificate story?
A10.5: In 1900, the Gold Standard Act formally established our unit of currency as the dollar and defined its value as equal to 1.67 grams of gold. The actual system was based on gold and silver. A dollar was not only equivalent but could be traded in for 1.5 grams of gold. [FYI. The rest of the world uses the SI system (Systeme Internationale) of units. While we measure weights/masses in pounds or ounces, the rest of the world uses grams or thousands of grams (kilograms). You may not have a sense of what 1.5 grams of gold means. A paperclip weighs approximately 1 gram.]

Oh, you noticed that little inconsistency too?

Q10.6: Is it 1.67 grams or 1.5 grams?
A10.6: Well, of course, both are correct. The 1.67 grams of gold they are referring to is "gold nine-tenths fine," so it was not highly pure. Only nine parts out of 10 had to be gold. So, 1.67 grams of 90% pure gold contains 1.50 grams of actual gold. The practice of turning in paper for gold, the substance that is your financial standard, was not uncommon, but became problematic, especially during World War I. Some companies in the U.S. owed European companies and governments a lot of money. They started turning in their dollars for gold, and substantial amounts of our standard were leaving the country. In 1914 the gold standard was suspended because of this. Once we hit the Great Depression, most countries had to suspend their gold standards. By the early 1930s, people started hoarding gold coins. In early 1933, Roosevelt banned the private ownership of gold coins. He devalued the dollar in foreign exchange markets and fixed the value of gold at $35/ounce. This was an attractive exchange rate, so international buyers were suddenly eager to convert gold back into dollars. The US also moved to a silver standard, and there was currency identified as silver certificates – redeemable for silver dollar coins or silver bullion.

In 1933, there was a gold recall to change the basic system of exchanging dollars for metal. As part of this, the U.S. had to get all the gold certificates out of circulation. Citizens were given a year to take their gold certificates to banks and trade them in, or they would no longer be recognized as U.S. Currency.

The actual timing of returning gold certificates became deeply associated with the search for the Lindbergh baby kidnappers since many of the bills used in the ransom were gold certificates, which would soon lose their value if they were not exchanged.

Federal Reserve Notes featured a green Treasury Seal as of 1928. This was the only type of currency that, at first, featured the seal over the large, engraved word to the right of the portrait.

These bills also carried a seal bearing the identity of the Federal Reserve Bank from which they were issued.

Q10.7: One piece of evidence brought to the trial was the fact that Hauptmann had Jafsie's address and phone number written on a board, probably a doorframe, inside one of his closets. Why?
A10.7: This is just one of the items found at the Hauptmann house. An address and phone number had been handwritten on a door frame board. The board was brought to the trial, and Hauptmann was questioned about it. He wasn't sure, but that closet is where they put all the newspapers after reading them. He was initially keeping track of the kidnapping story, and maybe he was reading a paper as he walked into the closet, and when he saw Jafsie's address in the paper he just decided he'd jot it down somewhere. Really? John Condon's address was in the newspaper? And what about the phone number? Hauptmann didn't remember it but said he must have written it down too. No one seemed to point out that the Hauptmanns didn't even have a telephone. More importantly, I believe the board was found long before the trial, and after a short time passed, a reporter admitted that he wrote it on the board, because they were having a slow news day. So, it was known that it wasn't written by Hauptmann. Nonetheless, Bruno confessed that he probably wrote it there. Something is very wrong here. Perhaps I misunderstood the timing, and the reporter's admission was only after the trial. Nevertheless, Hauptmann had to know he didn't write it, but he lied and said he probably did.

CHAPTER 11
DEAD BABIES AND FIREARMS

Little Charlie was reported missing a little after 10 p.m. on March 1, 1932. It was a rainy, noisy evening, and the family and staff were in the house from the time he was put down in his crib, a few hours before. A ladder found near the home had one section broken. It was a strange ladder. Police assumed it was used to enter and exit the baby's nursery window. One window had a warped shutter that did not correctly lock, and had to be replaced, but had not yet been repaired. This is the window that everyone assumes the kidnapper climbed through. How many people knew about that one shutter that could not be locked? Possibly the ladder broke when the kidnapper was descending, the baby was dropped, and Little Charlie died in the fall. The baby would have introduced additional weight, perhaps exceeding the capacity of the oddly constructed ladder. If this is so, the kidnapper may not have escaped injury. Perhaps it is inexplicable that one of the Lindbergh dogs loved and protected Little Charlie but did not signal the intrusion of a stranger into the house. Ollie reported that the dog was with him in the servants' rooms that night, not on baby guard duty. Is this explanation sufficient?

11A. The Autopsy

With every suspicious death, an autopsy report is generated, and one was filed for Little Charlie. I have it, and I'd like you to read it. Before you do, I want you to look up the definitions for a few words that will help you understand it. (No, this is not an ALLISONweb assignment.)

Definition #1. Thorax: ____

Definition #2. Incisor: ____

Definition #3. Fontanel: ____

Definition #4. Bifurcate: ____

The autopsy of Little Charlie should have been performed by the county physician, Dr. Charles H. Mitchell. It was not. The actual dissection was done by the county coroner, a funeral home director, Walter Swayze. The baby's doctor, Dr. Philip Van Ingen, felt that was unthinkable. Unfortunately, he arrived too late to witness the autopsy. Mitchell was an older physician, and "used" the hands of an untrained mortician, Swayze, to carry out the autopsy of this famous child. The single-page autopsy is on the letterhead of Walter H. Swayze, Trenton, New Jersey, dated May 12, 1932. It is signed by Mitchell.

The entire autopsy report is given here:

"Report on Unknown Baby

Sex Undetermined due to marked decomposition of body

General appearance badly decomposed

Left leg from knee down missing

Left hand missing

Right forearm missing

Abdominal organs except liver missing

Thoracic organs except heart missing

Eyes softened and decomposed

Skin of head, face, portion of chest and right foot discolored and decomposed

Body shows evidence of prolonged exposure and usual decomposition that would occur in the course of approximately two to three month's time depending on climatic and other conditions that might produce such results

Special characteristics -

Unusually high and prominent forehead & cranium apparently greater in circumference than would be found in a child of this age, The first toe on the right foot completely overlaps the large toe and the second toe of the right foot partially overlaps the large toe

There are eight upper and eight lower teeth, the upper incisors are well formed, rather prominent, but do not protrude

The two lower canines tend to divert towards incisors are below the line of the adjacent teeth

Height Thirty-three and one-half inches, light curly hair about three inches in length, and section of skin on the right foot which had not become discolored indicated a child of the white race

The facial muscles the only ones of the body that had not deteriorated would indicate a well-developed child

Autopsy findings-

General decomposition of the muscles of the entire body and other soft tissues except the face but marked discoloration and some disfigurement of this part of the body existed due to softening of the eyeballs and a swollen condition of the lips and tongue.

There was also a fracture of the skull, extending from the fontanel down the left side of the skull to a point posterior to the left ear where it bifurcated into two distinct fractures.

There was also a perforated fracture about a half-inch in diameter on the right side of the skull posterior to the right ear. There was evidence of a hemorrhage on the inner surface of the left side of the skull posterior to the right ear. There was evidence of a hemorrhage on the inner surface of the left side of the skull at the point of fracture. The scalp was so badly decomposed that it was impossible to find any contusions or hemorrhaged conditions external to the skull, The fontanel was not closed, the opening in the skull at this point being about one inch in diameter. Diagnosis of the cause of death is a fractured skull due to external violence.

Signed

The corpse that was autopsied was in an advanced state of decay. Swayze found four fracture lines on the skull and a decomposed blood clot. The cause of death was listed as a blow to the head. The baby could have been murdered in his room since a baby's fractured skull does not bleed, or he could have been dropped from his Nursery room window. The fontanelle was found to be one inch in diameter. Little Charlie was 20 months old.

No photographs of the skull, the blood clot, or the small round hole were made. Swayze typed the report, and there was nothing else for investigators to use.

The biggest questions that I believe remain unanswered include:

Q11.1: How was the baby extracted from the house, how did the baby die, and why did the child have to die?

We may never have the answers to these questions.

Babies, especially those wakened from a sound sleep by a stranger, should make some noise, especially Little Charlie, who did not accept strangers well. So, it could have been an inside job. Perhaps the staff was unhappy working for the most famous Lindberghs and decided to execute the kidnapping. They knew the house best and possibly could have brought the baby through the upstairs hallway to the back of the house and made their getaway. Since they were amateurs at the kidnapping game, they asked for a relatively small amount of ransom.

However, there was no evidence of problems with the staff. They seem to have been well taken care of and were loyal to the family. Lindbergh tried to protect them every time police wanted to interview them.

When the police first arrested Bruno Hauptmann as the perpetrator of the kidnapping, they searched his home and garage. One item found in the garage was a can of ether. The police suggested that Hauptmann could have had it in preparation for his next kidnapping, but they did not suggest that it could have been used for Little Charlie's kidnapping as well. This could certainly explain how the baby was taken from his bed without crying. Whether the ether was Hauptmann's or just a police "plant," no one knows, but ether provides a non-violent way to steal a baby from a house full of people.

Mark Falzini comments

I think ether was used to start cars in cold weather.

Author comments

Yes! Diethyl ether with a little oil and a little hydrocarbon propellent has long been used to help start car engines, sold as "Starting Fluid."

Over the years, many theories have been proposed about how the kidnapping was accomplished. A kidnapper could have come in the front door or a window, or even a back door. It seems like an impossibility to take a cranky child out of his bed and home without quite a bit of screaming; however, it happened. Even a child whose mouth is taped shut. would likely make quite a bit of noise. Some suspect the baby was dead before he left the house. Death by strangling, perhaps? (Could someone be so vicious to do this to a baby?)

While the trial was about the kidnapping and murder of a little boy, he was not a major topic of discussion. Nobody had been able to prove that Hauptmann was the kidnapper or climbed a ladder. No one had seen him in the house with Little Charlie in his hands. But there was circumstantial evidence – Hauptmann had much of the ransom money in gold certificates – many of them in his garage, hidden. Jafsie claimed to have shown John the safety pins that Anne had used that night to pin Little Charlie's blanket down. When John saw them, according to Jafsie, he identified them correctly (So he must have been in the nursery.) He offered this information freely, again according to Jafsie.

Some suggest a scenario where the kidnapper came down the ladder with an unconscious baby in a sack and dropped him. The sack may have hit the ladder on the way down or fallen on something hard on the soft rain-soaked ground, but the kidnappers probably were not planning on killing the child. According to the FBI FILES, "The autopsy suggested that the body had been dead since the date of the kidnapping." Consistent with this, there was a fracture on the left side of the skull. Dr. Mitchell pointed out that such a fracture could have been the result of being hit by a car, banged against a tree, or hit by a hard item such as a baseball bat.

They also observed a "suspicious opening" about an inch posterior to the right ear, about one-half inch in diameter, somewhat rounded, and *resembling a bullet wound.* No bullet was found inside the skull, but the fracture was on the opposite side of the hole. The cracking in the skull across from the small hole did not resemble the kind of damage inflicted by a baseball bat. The cracks and the skull in that area of the brain were pushed outward from the inside of the skull. It looked as if he had been shot.

There was some discussion in the trial about the baby's kidnapping. When Mitchell was testifying, Reilly asked, "Did you not determine the cause of death the first night to be a bullet hole until you found out a policeman had accidentally poked a stick in there?"

His response: "I never determined the cause of death as a bullet wound at any time anywhere." Michell did, in fact, verbally describe the hole as resembling a bullet hole, but "That was only offered as a descriptive statement." So, the bullet theory was not considered seriously, that is, not until Hauptmann was arrested and his Lilliput discovered. Right after that, investigators reportedly were sent back to the field where Little Charlie's corpse was found in 1932, searching for a bullet.

We'll get back to this idea of a bullet hole shortly. I first want to touch on some other theories.

11B. Where Did He Go?

Perhaps someone had obtained the corpse of a child of similar size and weight from the local children's care facility. Perhaps the body was not that of Little Charlie at all. If so, **where did he go?**

There are numerous stories from adults, whose childhood memories led them to believe that they were Little Charlie. See for example the video *Charles Lindbergh Junior Lives!* on *YouTube*.

11C. The Lilliput

There is the possibility that a bullet entered the right side of the skull, crossed through the brain, and hit the other side of the skull with enough energy to induce a fracture, but not enough energy to exit out the other side. "There was no bullet found in Charlie's skull, but the bullet could have been lost in transportation of the body as the brains were exuding from the fontanelle and from the opening on the right side of the skull."

A shot to the head is unique in many ways. A bullet without sufficient energy to exit the skull may ricochet inside the skull, while a small-caliber bullet may lose nearly all its kinetic energy. In *Forensic Anthropology* by M.M. Houck, (Houck, M.M. 2017, p. 200), he discusses the possibility of a bullet with sufficient velocity perforating a part of the body such as the skull, and then being carried away in the blood circulation system; the result is a shot to the head with no bullet found inside the skull.

There are many ways to explain the fractured skull, both accidental and planned, but it is more difficult to explain a fracture on one side and a small hole, resembling the entrance of a bullet on the other side. Most bullets could easily pass through a child's soft skull and out the other side with much of its kinetic energy remaining. This bullet, if it existed, was small, as reflected by the size of the small hole, and it did not have much kinetic energy, suggesting that, if the child was shot in the head, it must have been with a very small gun indeed. Did I mention that this story does include one very small gun?

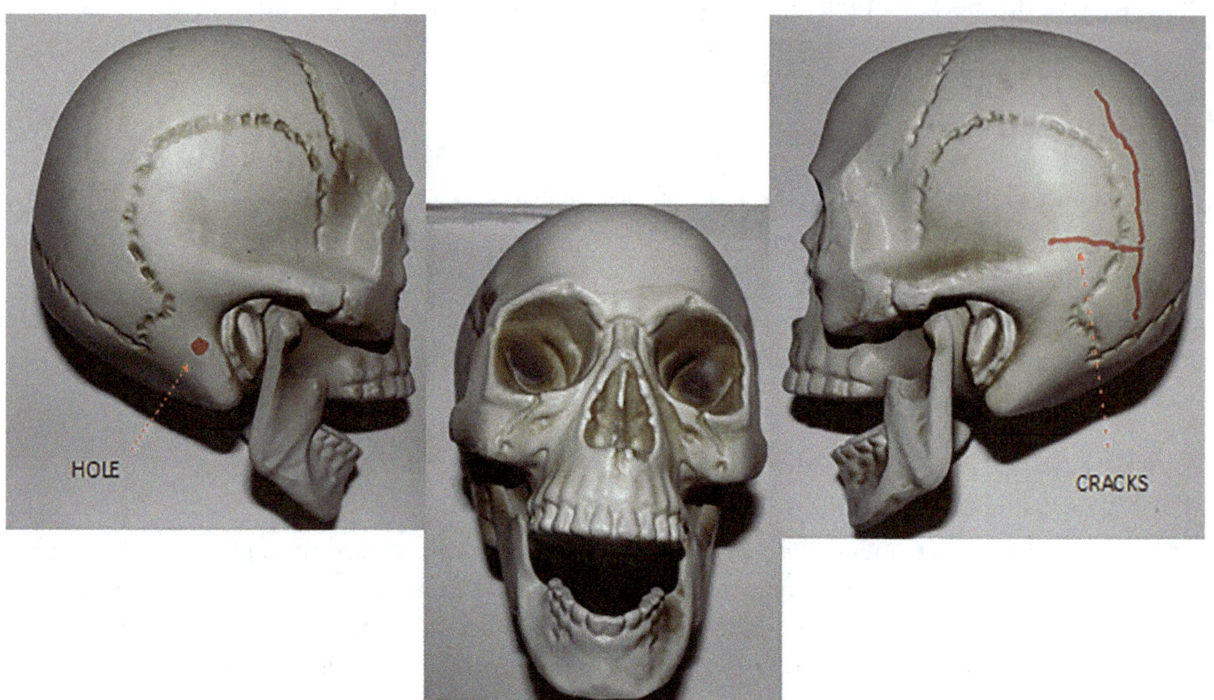

Figure 11C.1: Locations of the Hole and the Cracks in the Skull.

When the police tore apart Hauptmann's garage, they found some money hidden, which he said belonged to his friend Fisch. They found something else hidden. He had a very unique German gun. Let me tell you about it.

In 1924 the August Menz Company in Germany began manufacturing a 4.25 mm pistol, a small gun that could fit in your vest pocket, called the Lilliput. A slightly larger 6.35 mm Browning version soon followed. By 1928 a larger Lilliput pistol that held eight rounds in the magazine was manufactured. The tiny 4.25 mm Lilliput was 94 mm long, had a 44 mm barrel, was 66 mm high, and 17 mm wide. It held seven bullets. It is one of the smallest semiautomatic handguns ever made. (Take a moment and draw for yourself a square 94 mm x 66 mm.) The pistol got its name because it used 4.25 mm bullet cartridges. From what I've been able to find in the literature, the typical (if there is such a thing) bullet diameter is 0.172 cm, has a weight of 20 grains, and a muzzle velocity (the highest speed, when the bullet first exits the barrel) of 2350 feet per second (fps).

Figure 11C.2: The 6.35 mm Menz Lilliput.

Figure 11C.3: Lilliput Model I – 0.25 caliber pistol

Are these little guns dangerous? Often the effectiveness of a bullet is related to its kinetic energy (KE), which is equal to ½ times the mass (m) times the velocity (v) squared, KE = $\frac{1}{2} m v^2$

Others focus on the momentum of the bullet, which is the product of mass and velocity.
$momentum = mv$

Either way, the relevant variables are speed and mass. If you compare the Lilliput to a BB-gun, A BB is usually a steel, copper plated ball, about 4.3 mm (0.17 inches) in diameter, and 0.33-0.35 grams in weight. The Lilliput fires a bullet that has at least as much kinetic energy as a BB. Can a BB kill? If young children are the target, the answer may be yes.

> "At close range, projectiles such as those from BB and pellet guns, especially with velocities from 550 feet-per-second (fps) to 930 fps, can cause tissue damage similar to what you get from powder charged bullets fired from low velocity conventional firearms; injuries associated with … these guns can result in permanent disability or death."
> (reifflawfirm.com/pellet-bb-guns-can-kill/)

I need to put some of this information I'm giving you into perspective. I found a source that said the Lilliput bullet weighs 20 grains and has a muzzle velocity of 2350 feet/sec. With these numbers, I can calculate a kinetic energy, which is 1334 Joules (a Joule is a unit of energy). In comparison, a typical baseball has a mass of about 0.145 kg. A 100 mph (44 m/s) fastball has a kinetic energy of 140 Joules. A bullet from a .22 caliber rifle (mass, 0.003 kg; velocity 335 m/s), has a kinetic energy of 168 Joules. A bullet from a 9 mm pistol has a kinetic energy of roughly 467 Joules. OK, I've seen enough. Baseball (140 J), .22 (168 J), 9 mm (367 J), Lilliput (1334 J). I think the Lilliput velocity that I found is very wrong.

I kept looking and found that a Lilliput with a 4.25 mm cartridge generates 17 foot-pounds of muzzle kinetic energy. 17 foot-pounds is equal to 23 Joules – much more reasonable and *lower* compared to any of the other examples.

Much of the available information on bullet characteristics and the damage they can do is anecdotal. In March 2010, an 11-year-old boy, Dallas Barnes, and his 16-year-old uncle were playing with their BB guns in Kentucky. Barnes died from a single BB fired by the older boy. It pierced his chest and heart. The gun was a Daisy Pump BB Rifle. Barnes' young age contributed to his death. In an older person, the sternum would have been harder, and the chest thicker due to fat and muscle, for the BB to penetrate. For an 11-year-old, a small child, a single BB can kill.

If a BB can penetrate skin and bone and damage the heart, then conditions would be very similar for a child shot in the head, where the bullet from a gun that size would have sufficient kinetic energy to penetrate the skull, damage the brain, although perhaps not enough energy to exit out of the other side of the skull. When a bullet passes through a body, it leaves a cavity of gas, a trail of gas which pushes outward. It can be up to 40 times as large, in diameter, as the bullet itself. However, the skull is very different – a bullet passing into the skull would result in expansion of the brain, but there is little room in the skull for anything other than the brain. Of course, it also depends on where someone is shot. A shot to the frontal lobe of the brain may not be deadly, but a bullet to the base of the brain, where the skull is thinner and softer, could kill.

Figure 11C.4: Hauptmann's Lilliput

As I researched bullets and the damage they cause, I assumed that I could probably look up the specifications of the bullet that comes out of a Lilliput (mass, velocity) and find a table that would indicate if such a bullet could penetrate skin and bone and cause a fatal injury. Ballistics is a fascinating field. If you are interested in determining whether a bullet could kill, let me make some suggestions.

We will, of course, have to assume that the hole and cracked cranium could be caused by a small-caliber gun. If the baby was dropped, the cracks could have formed, but the proximity of the hole to the cracks suggests that they are connected.

The problem is, if you go into the terminal ballistics literature – which doesn't involve the firing of the bullet or its trajectory, but rather what happens where and when it stops, many articles make the reasonable distinction between low-velocity bullets (sometimes as slow as 120 meters/second) and high - velocity projectiles.

There are mathematical concepts behind understanding what bullets do – what damage they can cause. See, for example: *http://shooting the bull.net/blog/dem-bones-dem-bones/*

Here is an interesting web site on terminal ballistics:
nathcombe.net/sci-tech/ballistics/myths.html, *Shooting holes in wounding theories: The Mechanics of Terminal Ballistics (III. Myths, misconceptions and miscalculations).*

Rachael Swaby gets right to the point in *Giz Explains: What happens when you get shot in the head (2011). Kotakue.com/5798102/giz-explains-what-happens-when-you-get-shot-in-the-head.*

There is even a book – Hicks, Robert W. *Ballistics vs Lindbergh Case,* Police Research Bureau, 1954. They discuss ways in which the baby could have died before he left the house; they consider strangulation in the crib as a viable option.

Hold onto your hat! There is a website entitled "The Enigma of the Prehistoric Skulls with Bullet-Like Holes": nexusilluminati.blogspot.com/2014/09/the-enigma-of-prehistoric-skulls-with.html. They can't explain them, but they do point them out:

> "Nearly one century ago, a Swiss miner was searching for metal ore deposits in the limestone cave of Kabwe, Zambia when he found an ancient skull that dated back to between 125,000 to 300,000 years. It was the first fossil to be discovered in Africa with *Homo Sapiens* characteristics. But there was an even bigger surprise – the skull had a small circular shaped hole on the side, which forensic scientists said could only have been created by a … bullet."

The mystery continued as others found ancient skulls with the same feature – a perfectly round hole on the left side of the skull and a shattered parietal plate on the opposite side (apparently if it was a projectile, it was a high velocity projectile because it shattered the right side of the cranium).

They discuss options like having a skull pierced by a spear, an arrow, or perhaps the people were javelin catchers (joke). The report contained possibly a very useful clue –*animal* skulls with the same small hole were also found. I thought this was interesting, because a hunted animal, or a hunted human, could have been subjected to the same 'weapons.'

Back to the Dead Baby part of the story: There are, at least to me, several interesting issues that I'm uncertain about. Feel free to read on further and see what you think.

1. The baby died the day he was kidnapped, according to the autopsy. This doesn't mean that he was lying in that field since the kidnapping, but at some time he was put there and was there for long enough to be partially eaten by local wild animals. The location of Little Charlie's body was very close to where many telephone lines were run, to the Lindbergh home, as more police and newspaper reporters took up residence there. Oddly, no workers in that field noticed the body. Perhaps the body was elsewhere at the time.

> Mark Falzini comments
>
> No it's not odd. The lines were by the road. The body was in the woods.
>
> Author comments
>
> I based this on a comment from Harding's "The Hand of Hauptmann", p.77: "the baby was a few feet from the emergency phone wires."

2. Do you think the kidnappers intended to kill the child? The holes and cracks in the baby's head are consistent with being shot at point-blank range with a very small pistol, such as a Lilliput. But perhaps not.

Q11C.2: Did they need to "shoot his brains out?" Why? What possible reason could there be?

A11C.2: Your answer:____

____

3. When the body was found, Lindbergh lost no time in disposing of it. Only he and Betty, and Charlie's doctor could have identified the remains in the Trenton morgue. (Mark reminds me there were the doctors and a few police. But most of them couldn't have made a positive identification.). They identified the body based on only a few things: deformed toes, chin dimple, teeth, and a flannel shirt that Betty had made for him that night he disappeared. Pretty convincing, I suppose.
4. Lindbergh knew how many teeth his child had, counted teeth in the corpse, and was convinced that the number was correct to identify the body. Some reports are quite gruesome and suggest that Lindbergh had asked for a large set of pliers and used them to wrench the jaw off the skull to make it easier to count the teeth. After the body was identified, it was quickly sent, by Lindbergh, to be cremated.
5. When the child's body was recovered, dirt and debris around the body was collected which contained several small bones. Small bottles of the bones were on display at the New Jersey State Police Museum. Anne had expressed, to the Attorney General's Office, her wish that these remains be returned to the family, so they were. It is perhaps a little-known fact that the bones were studied, and the results published. See Bass, W.M. "Skeletal material associated with the Lindbergh kidnap case" *Amer. Jrl. Human Biology,* **3** 1991 pp 613-616.
6. Here is another interesting little tidbit of information. There was confusion over the baby's height. There was a widely distributed poster concerning missing Little Charlie. Many point to it as proof that the body found was not his. The poster reports his height as 29 inches. At the autopsy Dr. Mitchell measured the baby's length as 33 inches, so it couldn't be the missing Lindbergh baby. It turns out that the height on the poster was a typo. The poster reported height as 29 inches, but it was supposed to be 2 feet 9 inches, which is (2x12) + 9 = 33 inches, the actual measured height.

WANTED

CHAS. A. LINDBERGH, JR.
OF HOPEWELL, N. J.

DESCRIPTION:

Age, 20 months
Weight, 27 to 30 lbs.
Height, 29 inches

Hair, blond, curly
Eyes, dark blue
Complexion, light

Figure 11C.5: Parts of the Baby-Wanted Poster

CHAPTER 12
LET'S TALK ABOUT FINGERPRINTS

Lindbergh reluctantly paid the ransom mostly with gold certificate bills, and the FBI distributed a list of the serial numbers to banks and any other places that handled money. This was during a time when gold certificates had to be brought to banks and exchanged for the new U.S. currency. Were there other investigative methods they could have considered?

An interesting idea is to check any ransom bills, used after the ransom was paid, for fingerprints. In the 1930s, there were a few methods for detecting latent (invisible) fingerprints. It is useful for you to understand these, as a forensic scientist in training.

1. Dusting for fingerprints This is perhaps what most people think of when they consider detecting (visualizing) latent prints. The dusts/powders used have some affinity to the oils in fingerprints and are usually applied to a surface with a soft brush. Some fingerprint dusting brushes are made with soft squirrel (tail) hair. Prints are chemically complex mixtures. They are often thought of as oily deposits, although there is also a sweat-like component that contains many chemical compounds from salts to proteins. The skin on the palmar surface of the hands and plantar surface of the feet is specialized. It is called friction ridge skin. It is not flat and smooth like other skin. Friction ridge skin assists in gripping objects and surfaces. The first company to commercially make and sell fingerprint powders was probably Lightning Powder, which was founded in 1936, and is still in business. Before that, early versions of fingerprint powders were usually handmade, often by police crime scene technicians. Black fingerprinting powders can be as simple as fine charcoal or lampblack (which is a pigment made from soot).

I had a student point out that my description of dusting powders sounded a lot like makeup. It sticks to the oils on your face and is applied (in some cases) with a brush. We did the experiment and tried to visualize prints with a variety of makeups, and yes, they work just fine.

2. A second approach, that was still very new in 1932 was the use of a solution of **silver nitrate** ($AgNO_3(s)$). (The (s) indicates that the compound is a solid, although many solids dissolve in a solvent such as water.). It is known that silver nitrate forms ions (charged chemical species) in certain solvent.

$$AgNO_3(s) \rightarrow Ag^+(aq) + NO_3^-\ (aq)$$

where the (aq) means aqueous; the ions are dissolved in the solvent, water. Salts such as NaCl(s) are found dissolved in perspiration and can interact to form silver chloride (AgCl(s)).

$$AgNO_3 + NaCl \rightarrow AgCl(s) + NaNO_3$$

Silver chloride then decomposes in light to form elemental (black) atomic silver.

$$2AgCl \xrightarrow{\text{light}} 2Ag + Cl_2$$

Wherever salt from a fingerprint is deposited, the treatment process with silver nitrate will make those ridge lines turn black. (An aside: black and white photography is based on very similar chemistry. For those of you who remember negatives – the images are composed of atomic silver formed through a combination of photochemical and chemical processes, held in place in gelatin.)

3. Crown, (D.A. Crown, 1969) discusses that, in 1863, Professor Paul-Jean Coulier published a scientific paper on the use of exposure to **iodine** for the detection of latent fingerprints, as an alternative to dusting. Details to follow.

Do the Experiment. (seriously):

a. Make a fingerprint. I want a good one. A nice juicy oily one. You do this by rubbing a finger on the oiliest parts of your skin (your nose, forehead, in your hair). Some people make better fingerprints than others. You can wash your hands. Within five minutes, the oils reappear on the surface of your skin. Get a good, oily finger and press it down somewhere on a dollar bill.

b. If you have some silver nitrate (s), $AgNO_3$ (s), dissolve a small amount in some water (Make a 3% solution. You could do this by dissolving 3 grams in 97 grams of water.) I don't know if they used a spray bottle or a brush or dabbed it on with a wet sponge or paper towel when the technique first was developed, so be creative. You don't want to put so much on that you have to wash it off.

c. You can, if you're lucky, use a dusting powder and a nice dusting brush. (It is a delicate process.)

d. Put an oily fingerprint on a piece of glass, even on the outside of a drinking glass or a test tube. Dust it with the dusting powder. Try some makeup powders as well.

e. Put an oily print on a dollar bill. Dust it with your dusting powder.

f. Put an oily print on a dollar bill and either lightly spray silver nitrate (soln) on it or use a small artist's brush.

Molecular Iodine is a solid, with an unusual property. It sublimes. For most compounds that are a solid at room temperature, one may be able to increase the temperature until they melt. This occurs at the melting point. If you continue to heat the compound, the liquid form may go another step and convert to a gas. This occurs at the boiling point. Just think of water. If you start with solid water (ice) and heat it up, it will melt to form liquid water at 32 degrees F. If you continue to raise the temperature, you will eventually reach the boiling point and make water gas (steam) at 212 degrees F. If you understand this, you can appreciate what *sublimes* means. For compounds that sublime, the solid converts directly to a gas, without having to pass through the liquid state. If you put a small amount of iodine crystals in an empty jar and put a cap on it, some of the I_2(s) will form I_2(g) ((g) indicates the gaseous form). As the iodine slowly sublimes, you can see the air in the jar develop a slight purple tint, the color of iodine gas.

I can see you're getting a little bored over my stimulating explanation of sublimation, so perhaps I should get to the point. If you put a little iodine in a jar and let it form some gaseous iodine, then put a fingerprint on a piece of paper or something and quickly put it into the jar (get the cap back on quickly or the $I_2(g)$ will escape). Over time, iodine molecules stick to various molecules that are present in fingerprints. The iodine complexes are only formed where deposits are present, and the complexes are brown, so that a fingerprint will appear over the space of a few minutes. If you do this, you can take it out and photograph the print. Keep in mind that it will fade when it's in the air (the Iodine is lost). This method is often called iodine fuming. I am not aware of iodine fuming being used in the 1930s for latent print detection, but the element iodine was first isolated in 1811 by a French chemist.

You're probably assuming that there's a story about using invisible prints to identify the person who last handled a piece of paper currency. The police checked the nursery and other parts of the house for prints, probably with dusting powders. Someone in New York City who was developing the use of silver nitrate also attempted to find fingerprints on some of the ransom notes, including the first one, but no complete, usable prints were found. Apparently, a fingerprint expert said detecting fingerprints on paper currency was not possible.

He or she may have said this for one of three reasons:

1. He'd done the experiment and knew what he was talking about.
2. He figured that there must be thousands of prints on money, layer upon layer, so why bother?
3. He didn't want to do the analysis.

I believe that one *could* look for fingerprints on paper currency. Why people said you couldn't without trying it, I don't know. It's one of the mysteries of the case. I found the comment in (Whipple, 1935) – "impossible to find fingerprints on paper currency."

If you don't have access to any chemicals, I can share with you some of my results. I did have a black dusting powder and a squirrel-hair brush. I made an oily print and put it on a piece of paper. I picked up a small amount of the dusting powder on my brush and gently applied some of it to the area where I had placed my fingerprint. The black powder does selectively stick to the print on the paper, which is shown below in Figure 12.1:

Figure 12.1: Dusting a Fingerprint on Paper

I then put a fingerprint on a dollar bill and attempted to visualize it in the same way.

Figure 12.2: Visualization of a Fingerprint on Currency

I also found a few makeup kits and tried to dust a print with makeup.

Figure 12.3: Makeup!

Figure 12.4: Makeup Kits, Complete with Brushes

Figure 12.5: Successful Visualization of a Latent Fingerprint on Paper using Makeup.

Now, let me also show you how iodine fuming works.

I had a bottle of iodine in the lab, and, of course, beakers. I made a closed system by covering a beaker with aluminum foil.

Figure 12.6: A Small Amount of solid I_2 is Added to the Beaker

The beaker is covered, and the iodine starts to sublime, filling the beaker with iodine gas.

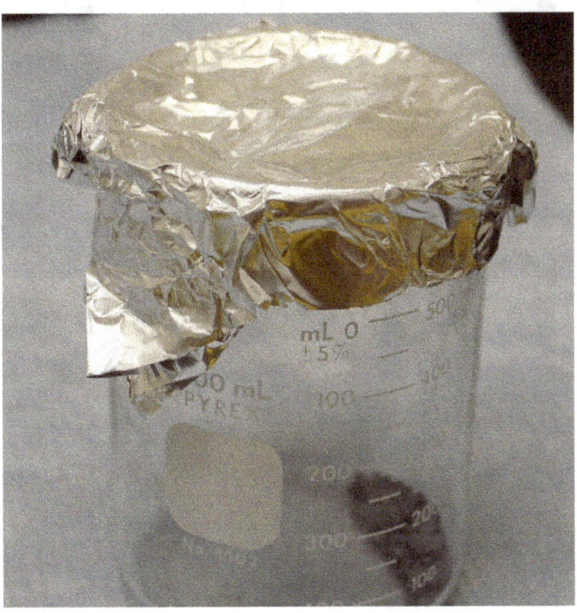

Figure 12.7: Covered Beaker containing Iodine Solid and Iodine Gas.

I then put a fingerprint on a dollar bill and put it into the beaker. Slowly, the fingerprint "develops." If you leave the dollar in there for too long, the paper starts to turn brown.

As you can see, iodine fuming does allow you to detect a fingerprint on U.S. currency.

Figure 12.8: Iodine Fuming of a Print on a Dollar Bill

Figure 12.9: Detail of the Iodine-Fumed Fingerprint

I think you can reach your own conclusions at this point. I wonder if they even tried this in 1934.

SUMMARY OF PART II

We looked at and questioned some of the evidence. I hope you learned the importance of evaluating all that you can. Don't hesitate to get out a pencil and paper and determine if accepted facts are plausible. I introduced you to the concept of evidence, and we did some simple, informative calculations. If someone states a "fact" to you, don't hesitate to test it out yourself if you can. Every time I do that, the "fact" seems to become questionable.

PART III

THE BIG STUFF – EVIDENCE AND TESTIMONY

CHAPTER 13

WE SAW HIM HERE! EYEWITNESSES

By the time of the trial, several locals were prepared to testify under oath that they had seen a car, with a driver resembling Hauptmann's description, with one or more people in the car and with a ladder inside, on the roads near Lindbergh's house. Keep in mind that Highfields could be hard to find; it wasn't even in anyone's GPS yet. This identification also required recalling someone's appearance two years later. Who can do that?

Sebastian "Ben" Lupica was a student at the Princeton Day School who claimed he saw a car with a ladder inside, around 6:00 p.m. on the night of the kidnapping, near the road leading up to Highfields. He didn't remember many details about the driver, but he did notice the car's grill. Every time the police interrogated him, his story changed to the point where they felt he was an unreliable witness. He told them that the car was probably a Dodge and had New Jersey plates. However, Hauptmann, the suspect, lived in New York City. Sixty years later, Lupica, by then a retired chemist, was tracked down. He made an additional observation that had not come out earlier. Lupica identified the car as a Dodge, because of its distinctive grille and lack of a hood ornament. He wouldn't have known, but there was one other car on the road and in the area at this time that had a very distinctive grille and no hood ornament. It was a Franklin, the car that Lindbergh drove.

There was also Amandus Hochmuth, an 84-year-old man, legally blind, who would sit on his porch and watch blurry cars go by at an intersection near the blurry road to the Lindbergh home. He didn't remember seeing anything unusual at the time of the kidnapping until he learned that he could get part of the $25,000 reward for information leading to the kidnapper(s). It was determined by the authorities that he might be eligible for perhaps $1,000 of the reward money. Suddenly his memory greatly improved. He remembered that on March 1, 1932, he saw a dirty, fast-moving green sedan driving from Hopewell. At the last minute, the driver stopped the car at the ditch in front of his house and stalled. That was when Amandus saw the ladder inside, and Hauptmann. Hochmuth identified the driver of the car at the trial, pointing to Hauptmann in a filled courthouse. A State Trooper had earlier pointed Hauptmann out to Hochmuth, who had a bad memory as well as poor eyesight.

Of course, one of the most influential "facts" for the jury, in this case, was from Lindbergh himself. He took the stand and testified that two years earlier, while he was sitting in his car and Jafsie was about to meet with Cemetery John, he heard John's voice and remembered it because it was so distinctive.

CHAPTER 14
LET'S TALK ABOUT THE LADDER

The ladder found near the house, broken, came in three parts. They nested inside each other - fit together with two wooden pegs pushed through holes in the sides to hold it all together in its extended form. When some saw it or heard about it, they were reminded of a window cleaner's ladder.

Figure 14.1: Window Cleaners

Concerning the ladder found on the Lindbergh property, the top and bottom ladder sections were each 6'8 ¾" and the middle section was 6' 8 5/8" long; we will assume that the three sections, when nested together, made a package roughly 6' 8 ¾" long. Why these dimensions? Some said the ladder was designed to reach the nursery window. Perhaps it was built for reaching a window at Next Day Hill (the Morrow home), but not at Highfields (the Lindbergh house). If the ladder broke, then possibly they were forced to use two of the sections, which would have fallen far short of the window at Highfields. If all three sections were used, the ladder would have landed on the shutter (making it impossible to open), both being less than ideal.

When the police started investigating the ladder, making exact copies, and re-enacting the kidnapping, they determined that, as-built, it could only hold 120-130 pounds; if a skinny kidnapper went up, and brought a 30-pound baby down, that would explain why the ladder broke. Perhaps the person climbing the ladder was a woman. They also concluded that it would be difficult, with either two or three sections used, to get in and out of the window quickly. Hauptmann weighed 180 pounds. How much did Lindbergh weigh? I only ask because the spacing between the ladder rungs was unusually large, suggesting that only a tall person could use it. Of the cast of characters in this story, one has to think of Lindbergh by his nickname, "Slim." I found a New York Times article, *Lindbergh, the Little Plane, the Big Atlantic* by George Waller:

http://movies2.nytimes.com/books/98/09/27/specials/lindbergh-plane.html

The article describes the day Lindbergh took off for Paris. The plane initially got stuck in the muddy runway. Waller described the events as follows:

> "He walked around the plane on a final tour of inspection. The wheels pressed deeply, tires bulging into the soft wet clay of the runway, straining beneath a heavier fuel load than the Spirit of St. Louis had ever lifted. When his lean 170 pounds was contributed, the weight of the craft would exceed two and a half tons – a thousand pounds more than the wings had carried in any of the hasty test flights."

So, when Little Charlie was kidnapped, it is likely that Lindbergh weighed about the same or more. 170 pounds. It is unlikely that Lindbergh ever climbed that ladder.

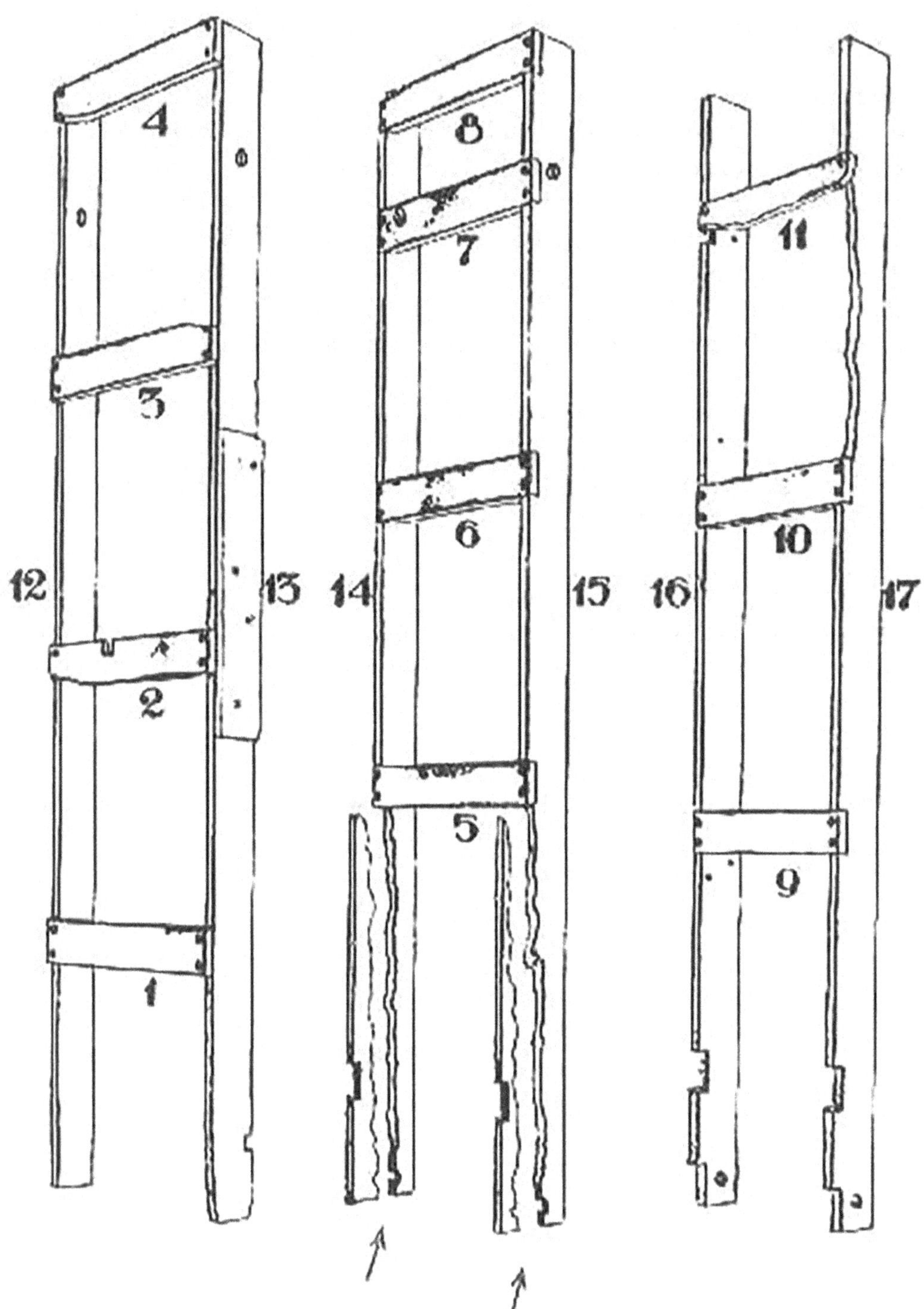

Figure 14.2: An Excellent Drawing of the Ladder

Figure 14.2 is probably the most famous drawing of the ladder, showing the bottom, middle, and top (left to right) nesting pieces. Note the holes on the side rails where birch dowels are inserted to assemble the three sections into one ladder. For the record, window washer ladders are tapered; the "Lindbergh Ladders" were nested.

Lindbergh may have been good at building odd ladders like this. While the standard dimension for ladder rung separation is 12 inches, these were 18-19 inches apart, perhaps suggesting that it was made for a very tall man to use. There are many photos of various ladder or ladder copies up against the house, although it was never actually seen there, only in a broken pile away from the house. There were, however, marks in the wet ground and marks on the upper house wall suggesting it had been put up against the house.

Lindbergh often built things for his airplane that were as light as could be. In daughter Reeve Lindbergh's memoir, *Under A Wing*, she recalls a time when she and her mother were looking at Sirius, one of the Lindbergh planes, that is in the Smithsonian. She commented to her mother on how difficult it must have been to get into the Sirius because it had pontoons to climb over (It could land on water.). Anne was a relatively short woman, and she was pregnant when they were flying the Sirius. In response, Anne said to her daughter, «But your father made me a little ladder!» It was an extremely light-weight ladder, 38 pounds. The fact that it was a telescoping ladder also was consistent with what Lindbergh would have built since it could fit into small spaces when in its collapsed form. (I have seen others refer to the three-piece ladder as a *telescoping* ladder, although I don't believe that is the correct word for a multi-section ladder such as this. Others call this construction a hinged ladder, but no hinges were used.)

Most discussions of the kidnapping put the final resting place of the ladder 50-70 feet away from the house. Some assume that the kidnappers planned to carry it back to their car, but just dropped and left it, since it was broken, and since they also had to carry Little Charlie.

If just two sections were used, there would be a sizable gap between the top rung and the window. If all three sections are used, it is also awkward.

Mark Falzini comments

I don't know how a person could put up the three section ladder. When we filmed for NOVA, three of us had a very difficult time.

Is it possible that it was brought to Highfields but not used, just a prop?

Note: The window below the nursery window was Lindbergh's office/library window. At this point in time, the house had no curtains. Lindbergh would have been in that room or an adjacent room when the kidnapping took place, and at some time during the evening he did report hearing wood break – possibly a tree branch breaking on that dark and stormy night. Wouldn't light streaming out of first-floor windows illuminate the ladder and its users for the Lindberghs to see?

Another possibility is that it was built by the construction company and was just left lying on the ground, possibly many days before. The Conover Construction Co. of Princeton, builders of the Lindbergh home, admitted the ladder was made of lumber like that used on various jobs by them -- North Carolina Pine, Douglas Fir, Ponderosa Pine, and Birch. There are aerial photos of the house taken just after the kidnapping, and there is clearly a large pile of unused lumber.

You may find this interesting ...

I'm writing this from my office in The College of New Jersey Chemistry Department. The College was recently in the process of building a new wing to the Chemistry building, and I often watched (and took photos from my window) the construction as it progressed. While the wing is finished now, they were digging a big hole and creating the foundation when I looked out one day and saw a ladder! It was a ladder made by one of the contractors. It probably served its purpose. It certainly wasn't anything fancy. Contractors *do* make their own ladders when needed. This is what I saw.

Figure 14.3: Construction Site with a Handmade Ladder

Figure 14.4: Close ups of Figure 14.3

One unusual place to get possible information about the Lindbergh case is in the book *Italian Days* (B. Harrison 1998). This is a travel book describing a trip around Italy, written in the style of a personal journal. At one point in the book, the author introduces her grandfather, who lived in the U.S. He claimed that he used to work for Hauptmann. According to Granddad, when Hauptmann was not employed, he used to make and sell ladders, and her grandfather claimed that he had one.

Of course, it seemed as though her grandfather had no shortage of stories to tell. He even claimed that he was *with* Lindbergh when he crossed the Atlantic in the Spirit of St. Louis, but he never got any credit for his participation because he was Italian.

14.A. Breaking a Ladder

I'd like to model, in some detail, the breaking of the ladder. Use the original drawing, Figure 14.2, with every rung numbered (1-11) as well as the six side pieces ("rails", numbered 12-17). The three sections of the ladder are built to nest. The ladder on the left in Fig.14.2 is the bottom section – also the widest section. At the bottom of the middle ladder section there are notches and holes. Raise that bottom of the middle ladder up to the top of the first ladder. The notches line up with rung 4, and the holes line up so that a dowel can be inserted. Figure 14A.1 shows how the two ends of the first two ladders fit together in assembling the extended ladder. There are three surfaces on each of the rails 12 and 13 that provide stability, are the surfaces in the notch marked a, b and c, and of course the dowel, d. Once we attach the bottom of the middle section to the top of the first section, to complete the ladder, we must connect the bottom of the ladder on the right to the top of the center ladder. Again, the ladder on the right is the narrowest, and its boards fit inside those of the center ladder. So, two notches and a hole in the bottom of the left ladder are lined up with the top of the center ladder, and the two fit together, we have up to five surfaces (a-e) plus the dowel, holding it together, as shown in Figure 14A.1. The top ladder-ladder union looks to be relatively stable - boards from one ladder locking around two steps on another, further stabilized by the inserted dowel. The lower union is a different matter. There is a maximum of four (3 + dowel) surfaces that touch, holding the two together. My goal is to try to understand *how* the ladder broke. It was helpful to make a model of it using balsa wood, cutting notches in it with an X-Acto knife. I was surprised by the breaks as shown in the middle ladder. I'd like to propose a few possibilities. If the full ladder was up against the wall next to the window shutters, and if the kidnapper is standing on rungs 11, 10, 9, 8, 7, 6 or 5, the situation is essentially the same – force due to the body mass points down. Each would put pressure on dowel #1. The two ladder segments lock together well around dowel #1. It does not appear that one could accidentally step on dowel #1 as you would step on a rung. However, the second joint is different. One could accidentally stand on dowel #2. This would place the entire weight onto the dowel which probably is the site of initial ladder failure. There is a very small section of wood on slats 14 and 15 below the dowel, and sufficient pressure on dowel 2 forced it through the small section below it. As 14 and 15 start to break, dowel 2 is forced down into 14 and 15; they continue to crack (up) until broken parts separate enough for dowel #2 to break through the wood below it. So, the break, up from dowel #2, is not unreasonable.

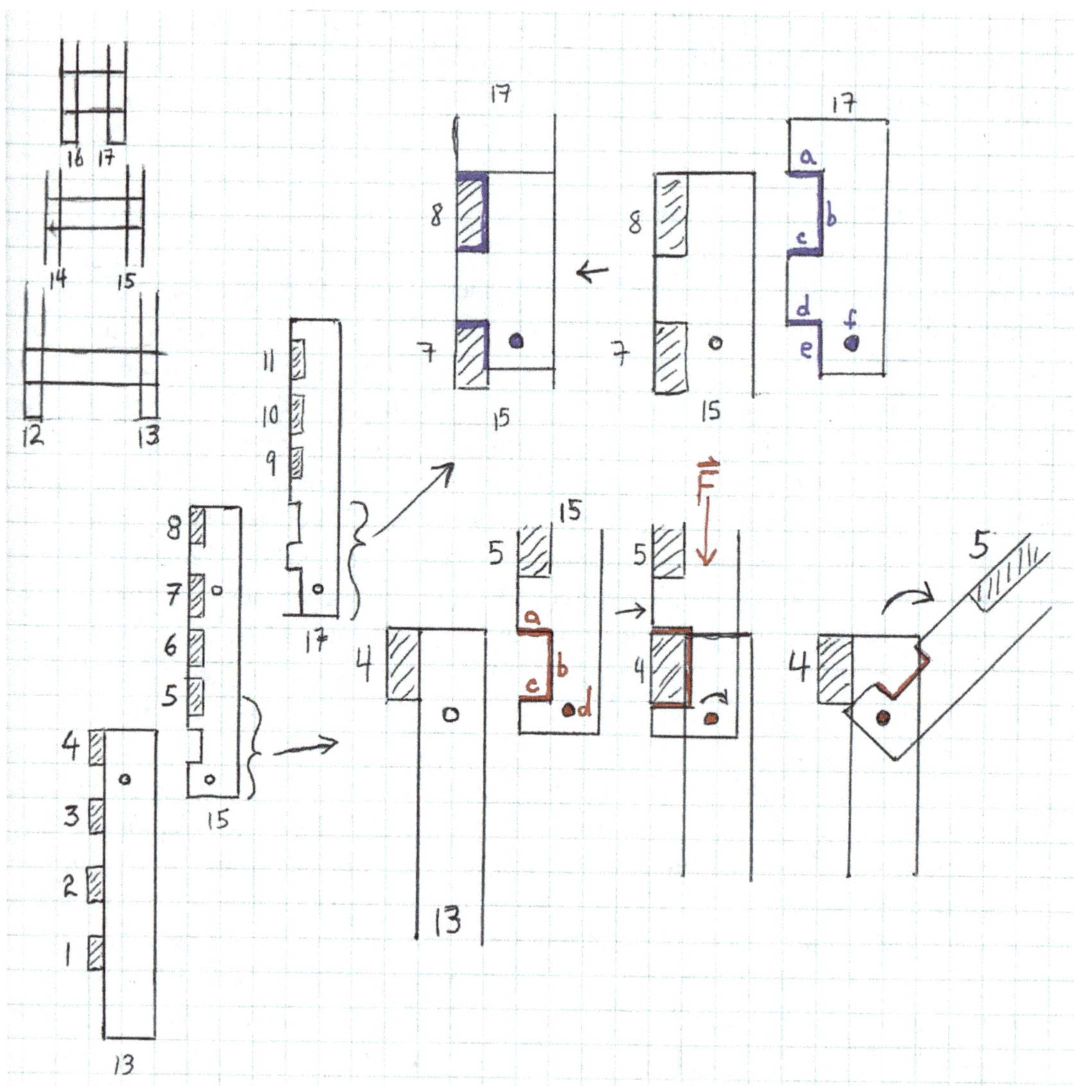

Figure 14A.1: Attachment Details

I want to propose two additional possibilities.

1. The ladder could have been used upside down. This would have certainly made it less stable as a ladder, with the narrowest section touching the ground and the widest section pointing up. If one accidentally stepped on dowel #2, it could be pushed down along the locus of the break as parts 14 and 15 split.

> Mark Falzini comments
>
> The holes found in the mud below the window match the separation of the bottom section, which had mud on them.

> Author comments
>
> Several authors feel the mud holes (1-1.5 in. deep) were too shallow for the ladder to have been actually used.

2. The widest segment containing rails 12 and 13 could be the bottom segment, as it was meant to be, but the ladder could have been put up "wrong side out," with the rungs not mounted away from the house but toward it. Again, the union between the middle and top ladder segments is the relatively stable one, but the lower one could easily slip off, leaving only dowel #2 holding them together; that could begin the splitting of rails 14 and 15.

Why are there so many possibilities worthy of consideration? Perhaps the kidnapper wasn't familiar with the ladder because some other person(s) had constructed it.

Something Else to Think About- Note that on the middle and right ladder segments, the rails are notched, with rungs inset into them, making the front surface of each smooth, except for notches that line up with rungs on the second segment. The widest segment, shown on the left side, is not built this way; the rungs are nailed to the outside edge of rails 12 and 13. The first segment is constructed differently from the other two. Some have proposed that all three ladder segments were not made by the same person. However, the overall assembly was obviously a planned part of the ladder construction, to optimize the nesting of the three segments. There was likely only one designer – probably one builder.

Still Speaking of the Ladder .... One interesting suggestion was that the ladder was built to specific dimensions so Hauptmann could transport it from his Bronx garage to central New Jersey, so it had to fit in his car. Would you like to determine if it will fit?

CHAPTER 15
CARS, LADDERS, AND LADIES

The first thing you must do is to buy a 1930 Dodge exactly like Hauptmann's car. If you are interested in the very detailed analysis of each board that made up the ladder, you might consult Adam Schrager's *The Sixteenth Rail* (2013). We're going to work on one question here. Would these three nested ladders fit into cars of the day? Richard T. Cahill Jr. reports, in *Hauptmann's Ladder* (2014), that Koehler, one of the experts who examined the ladder, tried to put it in Hauptmann's car and reportedly it fit from the back to the front seat. This was also reported by Sidney Whipple in his 1935 book, *The Lindbergh Crime*.

We don't have access to the car; as far as I know, it no longer exists. While you can find a lot of information about older cars, interior dimensions are not reported – usually, people are interested in facts about the motors and exterior dimensions.

We are going to use the simple concept of ratios. To many of you, using ratios is easy, but if not, I'll walk you through it. (There's also a tutorial in ALLISONweb.)

To warm-up, I want to consider the following:

15A. How Tall is Hillary?

While the woman (who we'll call Hillary) in Figure 15A.1 does not care to talk about her exact height, I know someone who does like to talk about his, the man in the figure (who we will call Don.) The photo is not ideal, but they are almost standing right next to each other. For this exercise, we will assume they are equally distant from my camera lens. On my computer screen, Hillary is 115 mm from head to heel. In that same photo Don is 138 mm tall. Obviously, these are not their real heights, but the proportionality of their heights, the ratio, will always be the same. Such a ratio is a unitless number, because the numbers on the top and bottom have the same units and cancel each other out.

Figure 15A.1: What is he doing?

Under these conditions, the ratio of their two heights is:

Ratio = height (Hillary)/height (Don) = 115 mm/138 mm = 0.833

If we knew their real heights, we should get that same ratio. Don told me he is six feet, two inches tall. These calculations don't work with *our* dated units of measurement, so I would need to convert two inches into a fraction of a foot. I know that, when converting into metric, 1 inch = 2.54 cm. To simplify the calculations, let's do them all in metric.

Don is 6 feet 2 inches tall = 6 ft. (12 in/1ft) + 2 in = 74 inches tall
I'll convert to centimeters. 74 in. x (2.54 cm/1 in.) = 187.96 cm = height(D)

0.833 = height(H)/height(D) = height(H)/187.96 cm
So, height(H) = 0.833 x 187.96 cm = 156.57 cm

We can convert back to our antiquated system of units if you insist.
156.57 cm x (1 in/2.54 cm) * = 61.64 in

5 feet is equal to 60 inches, so this is equal to 5 feet plus 1.64 inches which we can round to 5 feet, 2 inches. The final result should make sense to you. One inch is bigger than one centimeter, so 156 cm should be equal to a smaller number of inches.

*Note that I multiplied by a conversion factor. I know that 2.54 cm is equal to one inch so I could multiply anything by (1 in/2.54 cm) or (2.54 cm/1 in) because the top and bottom values are equal. Conversion factors essentially have a value of 1, and you can always multiply a number by 1 without changing the quantity.

Before we go any farther, if we take a step back and look at where we are, I told you Don is 72.17 inches tall, and we calculated that Hillary is 61.64 inches tall. It looks like we probably did the calculation correctly because Hillary must be shorter than Don.

What did we do? We used a value that we knew, and a relationship between two things (a ratio) to calculate a value we didn't know. For a better number I'd want a better ratio, a better photo where they were standing exactly the same distance away from the camera.

I think now you're ready to determine if this ladder will fit into Hauptmann's car.

Would the 6' 8 ¾" long ladder sections fit from the rear window to the front window (or less) of Hauptmann's car? If we can find a photo of his car, sitting at some angle, it would not be ideal, but a side view photo, with both wheels equally distant from the camera, would be a good start. What do we know about Hauptmann's car?

Here is Hauptmann's vehicle registration from 1934:

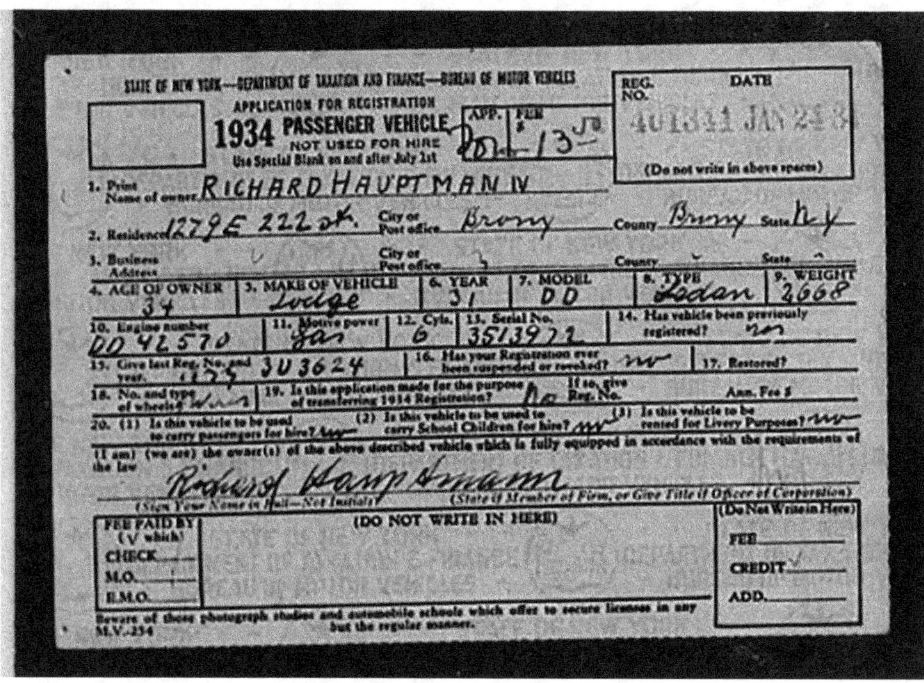

STATE OF NEW YORK—DEPARTMENT OF TAXATION AND FINANCE—BUREAU OF MOTOR VEHICLES
APPLICATION FOR REGISTRATION
1934 PASSENGER VEHICLE
NOT USED FOR HIRE
Use Special Blank on and after July 1st

APP. | FEE $ 13.50

REG. NO. 401311 DATE JAN 24 3
(Do not write in above spaces)

1. Print Name of owner RICHARD HAUPTMAN
2. Residence 1279 E 222 St. City or Post office Bronx County Bronx State N.Y.
3. Business Address City or Post office County State

4. AGE OF OWNER	5. MAKE OF VEHICLE	6. YEAR	7. MODEL	8. TYPE	9. WEIGHT
34	Dodge	31	DD	Sedan	2668

10. Engine number	11. Motive power	12. Cyls.	13. Serial No.	14. Has vehicle been previously registered?
DD 42570	Gas	6	3513972	no

15. Give last Reg. No. and year. 3U 3624 16. Has your Registration ever been suspended or revoked? no 17. Restored?
18. No. and type of wheels 19. Is this application made for the purpose of transferring 1934 Registration? no If so, give Reg. No. Ann. Fee $
20. (1) Is this vehicle to be used to carry passengers for hire? (2) Is this vehicle to be used to carry School Children for hire? no (3) Is this vehicle to be rented for Livery Purposes? no
(I am) (we are) the owner(s) of the above described vehicle which is fully equipped in accordance with the requirements of the law
Richard Hauptmann
(Sign Your Name in Full—Not Initials) (State if Member of Firm, or Give Title if Officer of Corporation)

FEE PAID BY (✓ which) CHECK M.O. E.M.O.
(DO NOT WRITE IN HERE)
(Do Not Write in Here) FEE CREDIT ✓ ADD.

Beware of those photograph studios and automobile schools which offer to secure licenses in any but the regular manner.
M.V.-234

Figure 15A.2: Hauptmann's Car Registration for 1934. Very Useful Information.

It identifies him as Richard Hauptmann, 1279 E. 222 St. Bronx, NY. His age is 34. The car is a six-cylinder 1931 Dodge DD Sedan, and the registration gives all the required numbers. The engine number was DD42570, and the serial number was 3513972. The car weighed 2668 pounds. An important discovery for me was a database on all old vehicles: Classiccardatabase.com

Hauptmann's car has an interesting history that perhaps he never knew. Hauptmann listed the car as a 1931 on his registration, but the VIN and Engine numbers tell us that it was assembled in 1930.

Do you remember Lupica, the student who claimed to have seen Hauptmann in his car with a ladder? He said the car had N.J. plates which was inconsistent since Hauptmann lived in New York. However, the license plates issued in New Jersey were yellow on black in 1932, and New York plates were white on black, so anyone might have confused them.

I found a good picture of a 1930 Dodge DD. With it we can estimate the interior size.

Figure 15A.3: A 1930 Dodge DD

Enlarge the car photo as much as you can and try to make all measurements on a flat surface. The 1930 Dodge six series DD sedan had a 109-inch wheelbase (the distance from axle to axle). When I printed the photo, the wheelbase was 178 mm and the cab was about 133 mm. We have an equation with only one unknown in it. So, the real ratio of cab length (cab) to wheelbase (wb) length is Ratio = D (cab, pic) / D (wb, pic) = 133 mm/178 mm = 0.747.

D (cab, real)/D (wb, real) = 0.747 = D (cab, real)/109 in.

D (cab, real) = 0.747 x 109 in. = 81.42 in.

The ladders were 6' 8 ¾" = 12x6 + (8.75) = 80.75 inches. Technically the ladder was short enough to fit from the front to back glass (81.4 in.), but it is very close, with less than an inch to spare.

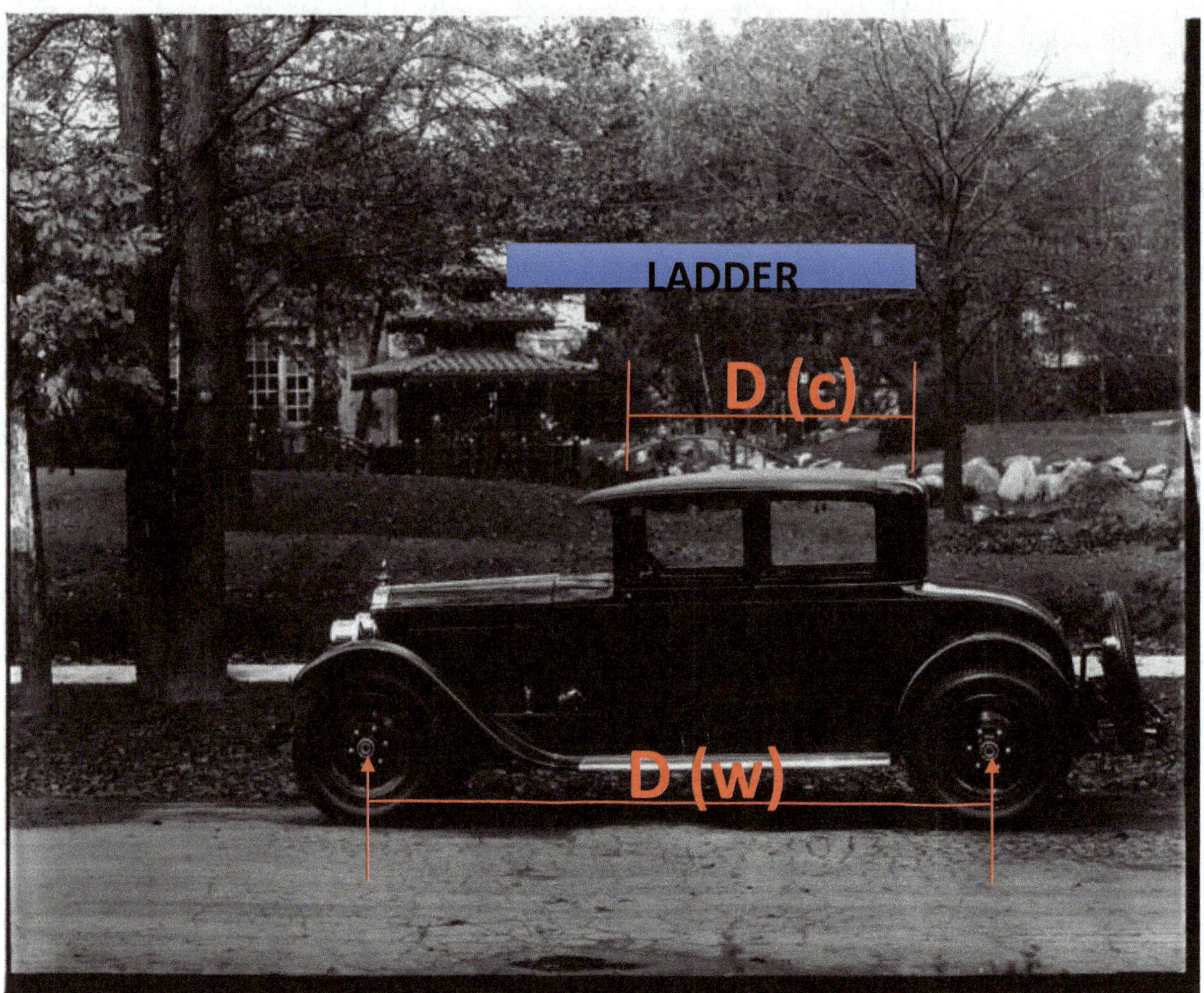

Figure 15A.4: Another Dodge of the Same Year

It is also concerning, looking at the green car with the doors open in Figure 15A.3, that the way that the doors are hinged requires a substantial part of the car frame to fall between the two doors. This would make putting a ladder inside, with only a fraction of an inch to spare, more difficult, depending on how you did it. If you attempt to put the ladders in through the front window, it wouldn't matter how the doors were mounted.

Figure 15A.4 shows a 1931 Dodge (6) DD that has a shorter cab and possibly a rumble seat in the back. There were many different models. On my photograph, D(c) is 58 mm, D(w) is 129 mm, and if the wheelbase is 133 inches, the actual space inside is 60 inches, which could not accommodate 80-inch ladders. That is,

D(c)/D(w) = 58 mm/129 mm = D(c)real/133 in. D(c)real = 59.8 inches.

Another possibility, the other car with a distinctive grille and no hood ornament was a Franklin. These were much more expensive cars than Dodges. John Rockefeller drove a 1930 Franklin. Figure 15A.5 shows his car.

Figure 15A.5: Rockefeller's 1930 Franklin

Figure 15A.6: Lindbergh's Franklin

There was another "famous" Franklin, one owned by Charles Lindbergh.

The photograph of Rockefeller's car is better for a ratio calculation, so we will use that. On my photo of the Rockefeller car the wheelbase is 110 mm and the cab is 80 mm. Covering the range of possible wheelbases from 125 to 132 inches for these cars, the cab could have been in the range of 91-96 inches. With more than 90 inches inside the cab, the 81-inch-long ladders would have fit in Rockefeller's, or Lindbergh's car.

There is just one other car I'd like to consider.

Figure 15A.7: The 1927 Pink Packard

It is unclear if this pink car in Figure 15A.7 belonged to the Lindberghs or not, but I've seen it described as the car that transported Anne to the trial. It is a 1927 Packard Open Touring Car.

Try to estimate the cab size based on measurements of the figure and using the fact that the actual wheelbase was 134.5 inches.

I think we've learned here that some simple calculations can be very powerful tools when you have access to a database of actual dimensions of cars throughout history. It would have been difficult to transport a ladder of this size in cars that were on the road in the 1930s. If the ladder(s) were built just to fit inside a car, and all three ladder sections were going to be used, then perhaps the builder should have considered making a four-section ladder, with each piece shorter, so the ladder could have easily fit inside any car of that era.

Some of these cars look amazing by today's standards, but they often had rather small interiors, that couldn't have accommodated a ladder. I'll end this discussion with two examples.

Figure 15A.8: Look Inside!

Figure 15A.9: Interior of a 1931 Dodge Sedan; note the lush upholstering on the seats and walls.

SUMMARY OF PART III

Here we considered some of the evidence - some that was used at the trial, some not. We considered many aspects of the ladder – critical to the case, even though no one saw it up against the house. We asked whether the ladder could have fit in any of the cars of the 1930s. This question can be answered without buying antique cars, with some good photos, digging for numerical information, and understanding the power of ratios.

PART IV

THE RANSOM LETTERS

CHAPTER 16
HOLD ONTO YOUR HAT!

16A. Collecting Exemplars of Hauptmann's Handwriting – Beat it out of Him

Bruno Richard Hauptmann had some terrible days. Once the police decided that he was involved in the kidnapping and murder of Little Charlie, they arrested him. The search for anyone as a possible suspect took a long time – it took two and a half years after the crime for the authorities to discover the Hauptmann connection. They questioned him for a good part of the day he was apprehended, and he watched them tear his apartment apart and demolish his garage, looking for evidence. For more than 13 hours, he was forced to write, to provide handwriting samples the police could compare with the ransom letters. The end of a long, exhausting day was not the best time to get an example of someone's natural writing. Some report that he was told to misspell certain words, and to copy entire paragraphs of original ransom letters exactly, including all the errors they contained. The police pushed him to write until he passed out. During this time, they didn't feed him. The stories of what happened in that cell certainly make it appear that someone was working hard to guarantee that Hauptmann's writing had much in common with that of the ransom letters.

16B. Comparing Hauptmann's Handwriting with the Ransom Letters – Who Can We Trust?

Some have gone much further than merely questioning the writing samples. In his 1976 article, *Bruno Hauptmann was Innocent* (A. Scaduto 1976), Anthony Scaduto wrote:

> "Every piece of physical evidence introduced against the accused Lindbergh kidnapper at his trial was either manufactured by the police or distorted by so-called expert witnesses"

There were few rules and procedures in place for collecting written examples from Hauptmann; beatings were probably not typically considered a part of the process, but for Hauptmann they may have made an exception.

Mark Falzini comments

Are you saying he was beaten?

Author comments.

There is a discussion of Hauptmann's beating in Richard Cahill's book, "Hauptmann's Ladder." Hauptmann claimed that he was beaten with a hammer. Two days after he was arrested, he was examined by Dr.John Garlock, who reported no evidence of abuse. Five days later, Dr. Dexter Thurston reported that Hauptmann was severely beaten. Cahill writes: "Hauptmann's claims that he was beaten with a hammer are not convincing although he was probably roughed up, punched and kicked several times... this kind of disgusting treatment was not uncommon at the time."

Also, Melsky, in "The Dark Corners", vol. 1, states that Hauptmann was beaten by a group of twelve police.

If you are interested in how to collect examples of a person's writing style (exemplars), you might consult the Forensic Document Examiners web page:

http://www.forensicdocumentexaminers.com/excerpt.html

Exemplars are standards used for determining the master pattern or habits of the writer. There are informal exemplars, which are usually previously written documents (contracts, checks) known to be authentic. A second kind is a formal exemplar, a requested writing sample. Requested writing samples may not be admissible in court for various reasons, such as if too long a period has passed since the questioned document was written. The advice provided by this web site (for lawyers) suggests that you do the best you can to duplicate the conditions. Where was the questioned document written? Was it in pencil or pen? What kind of paper was used? Was the paper lined?

Document examiners try to compare many aspects of known exemplars and the questioned documents, including line quality, pressure patterns, size and proportions of letters, spacing, slant, baseline, use of space, and pen lifts.

The FBI journal (*Forensic Science Communications*) article about collecting exemplars and comparing written samples is worth reading– *Handwriting Examination: Meeting the Challenges of Science in the Law* (D. Harrison, T.M. Burkes, D.P. Seigler, 2009). It lists 18 standard methods that the members of this discipline have agreed on, which are available from the ASTM (American Society of Testing and Materials) on several related topics such as analysis of rubber stamp impressions and examination of documents from various digital printers. This 2009 paper warns document examiners that it is best to present results as their *opinion* and let the judge and jury reach their conclusions.

> "In the Lindbergh Kidnapping Case, Albert S. Osborn testified that Hauptmann wrote every one of the ransom notes, writing that every one of the notes was irresistible, unanswered and overwhelming. He was right, no doubt, but had the case not been a *cause celebre*, words expressing such certitude might have been considered objectionable."
> (Scott 1999).

In the book *Hauptmann's Ladder* (R.T. Cahill, 2014), the author reports that Hauptmann was often instructed by police on how to write samples, and that some of the original ransom letters (*not* his writing) were modified by the State Police to match Hauptmann's handwriting more closely. He also reports that the police beat Hauptmann while he was writing examples of his handwriting. The author also contends that Hauptmann was clearly trying to alter his writing style.

In *The Ghosts of Hopewell* (J. Fisher 1999), Jim Fisher, Ph.D. writes that Hauptmann was the:

> "victim of a massive police and prosecution frame-up. (Even) Lindbergh obstructed the investigation and lied under oath to secure Hauptmann's conviction."

Testimony by several experts in handwriting analysis was an essential part of the trial. The prosecution hired John Vreeland Haring and his associate and son, J. Howard Haring, to participate in the case. John Haring wrote a book, *The Hand of Hauptmann: The handwriting expert tells the story of the Lindbergh case* (1937). Haring writes:

> "Now for the first time the attention of millions of people, debating this man's guilt or innocence, was focused upon the science of handwriting analysis."

The Harings worked on the following assumption:

> "The theory upon which these expert witnesses are permitted to testify is that handwriting is always to some degree the reflex of the nervous organization of the writer, which, independently of his will and unconsciously, causes him to stamp his individuality in his writing." (J. Haring 1937 p. 193-4).

They explain that an expert analyzes what he is given and then offers his opinion. The book is telling. I believe Haring had his mind made up before he and his son performed their analyses. He refers to Hauptmann as "obviously a guilty man" (p. 199). Further, he writes:

> "All of the sheets of requested writing were written rapidly although the police made no effort to speed him along. Did Hauptmann hope thus to conceal the slow, disguised hand that characterized the ransom notes? Or was it nervousness? It is hard to believe the latter, for while the forms of the letters were distorted, the quality of line here is as clean cut as a steel engraving and shows no trace of a tremor. It is a curious fact that Hauptmann's writing reveals less nervousness than do the signatures of the witnesses at the bottom of the sheet. Undoubtedly this speed, the rapidity with which it was executed, is one of the innumerable methods of disguise he attempted here, [or maybe he just wrote fast – JA] and is largely responsible for pictorial difference, such as it is, between this writing and that of the more slowly written ransom notes." (p. 210)

Haring shows his bias in the above passages. How would he know that someone wrote the ransom notes slowly? He assumes things he could not know concerning misspellings. He writes:

> "And would not the man who spelled promise "promice" also spell case "cace" and because "becauce" in the ransom notes?"

I certainly don't know the answer to that. Do you?

Continuing a few key excerpts from the Haring book:

> "We have abundant evidence here, then, that the requested writings are different in many ways from the normal writing of the prisoner, indicating that he attempted to alter this writing."

So, there are many differences between Hauptmann's writing and the ransom letters. Wouldn't one then conclude that the two do *not* match? Again, the analysts were biased or encouraged to be biased. They likely selected examples that closely matched and excluded examples of letters and words that did not. However, they did present a detailed analysis which, due to its sheer size, was impressive in the trial.

The defense did not have a gaggle of handwriting analysts to present to the jury and claimed that they did not have the budget to hire them. Some handwriting experts claimed they were discouraged from working for the defense, even threatened, so they chose not to do so.

There is much to consider in the ransom letters, and the handwriting is only a part, perhaps a minor role. We'll get back to this point soon.

To summarize what I tried to present in this section:

1. This evidence is very unusual. Usually, in a kidnapping, there is a ransom letter. "Give us a dollar or you'll never see your cat again. Go into the pet store on 43rd and Market Street and leave the dollar under the guppy tank. Do not involve the police. When we believe it is clear for us to get the ransom, we will return your tabby." In the Lindbergh case, there was an ongoing discussion between Jafsie and the kidnapper(s) via ads in the local Bronx newspapers from Jafsie, resulting in 15 handwritten letters from the kidnappers.
2. Many report that Hauptmann was beaten/abused during the time he was writing exemplars for the police.
3. I think it took some time to contemplate what was happening in the trial, and what conclusions were reached. In the books written about the case shortly after the trial, authors seem to conclude that Bruno was guilty. In books written decades later, authors realized that while the kidnappers identified themselves as a gang of five, there were no leads connected to anyone but Hauptmann, so the evidence was presented focusing on Hauptmann as the single kidnapper.
4. My goal in the sections that follow is not to compare Hauptmann's writing to that in the ransom letters. Instead, I want to compare the writing in the ransom letters because I do not believe, from the evidence, that one person wrote them all.

16C. Some Observations and Measurements

I was very fortunate in being allowed to make measurements on the actual ransom letters, and to photograph them all. They are presented here for you to study. The first ransom note ended with an unusual symbol which the kidnappers intended to put on all further correspondence, so the Lindberghs would know that the letters were from them. This was a smart thing to do. Hundreds of letters were received daily claiming to be from *the* kidnappers, from people trying to get the ransom money. I also provided at least one view of the envelopes that they came in when there were envelopes.

I made several measurements, each of which will tell a part of the story. I went to the New Jersey State Police Museum, where the ransom notes are kept. Each letter and envelope was in a separate folder, in a plastic sleeve. I wore cotton gloves but decided that I would not take them out of their protective covers – I could make measurements and photograph them through the plastic. I used a pencil to write down dimensions in my notebook just as a precaution – I wouldn't want to accidentally get ink on an historic document. I had a collection of wooden, metal, and plastic rulers, and when I compared them, they were not all the same! My set of plastic rulers were all the same, consistent, and accurate, and I decided to use those. I also felt it was important to use plastic rulers to handle these 80+-year-old letters, I didn't want to gouge one with a sharp metal ruler accidentally. I made all my measurements in millimeters (mm). If you are not familiar with what a millimeter or centimeter is, you can look them up in ALLISONweb. You will see that I took letter photos with a ruler nearby. Each photo will be slightly different, so you can *only use that one ruler to get information on dimensions of that one letter.*

Look through the pages in Chapter 16E and get a general idea of what they look like (Yes, now would be a good time,) then come back here.

(Watching the clock, pacing)

Welcome back. As you saw, there are images of the front (recto) and back (verso). I first want you to measure the width and height of each ransom letter. When I took photos (using the rulers in each image), I downloaded them to my computer and printed them. They appeared to be very similar in size to the originals, but they were *not* the same size, so I included with each page, each view, a ruler. Again, you can use ratios, as follows:

Each page has a ruler showing 15+ cm (150 mm). Measure in mm the distance on the page corresponding to those 150 mm.

Distance (figure)/150 mm = Ratio. You can use it to measure anything *on that page.*

There may be an easier way to do it. Here is a photo of a bookmark *with* a ruler in the same photo.

Figure 16C.1: I Choose a Bookmark And a Ruler

I'm going to use an index card and make two marks on it, which will represent the width of the bookmark in the figure. Then I'll use the ruler, which will be in the same photo, to determine, at whatever reduction or magnification we may have, the size of the bookmark.

Figure 16C.2: The Width of the Bookmark Transferred to an Index Card

I've made two marks such that the distance between them represents the width of the bookmark. Now I'll take that relative length and compare it to the ruler *in the same photo.*

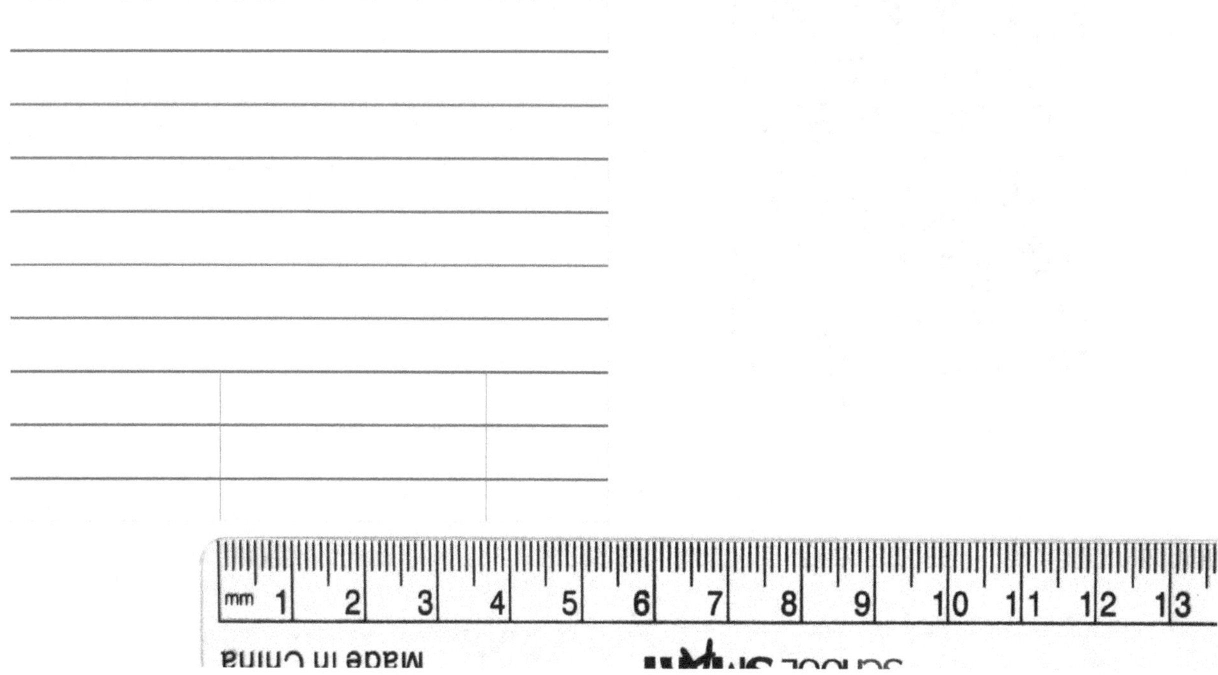

Figure 16C.3: Measuring that Distance with the Ruler in that Same Photo

From this, I lined up one line with the real "0" on the ruler, and then read off the number pointed to by the other line. It looks like the width of the bookmark falls between 36 and 37, so the best estimate I can make is 36.5 mm.

I want to make additional measurements on each of the ransom notes beyond the height and width of each letter. On the front page, if there is the singnature, I made the following two measurements, which I'd like you to confirm. I measured the distance from the bottom of the page to the imaginary line linking the three holes (actually to the middle of the center hole). The distance from the bottom of each letter to the center of the middle hole, we will call **a.** Then I measured the distance from the center of the hole (closest to the edge) to the edge of the ransom note. We will call that **b.** We will use them a little later.

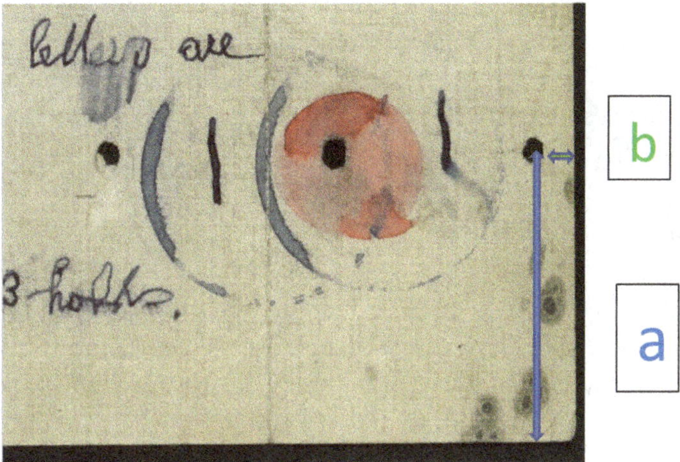

Figure 16C.4: The distances **a** and **b**.

I also made some measurements on the spacing of the holes, which I did *on the reverse side* of the ransom letters. Reading left to right on the reverse side of each letter, we will refer to the holes as hL, hC, and hR (for hole Left, hole Center and hole Right). First, to compute the hL-hC distance, I measured the distance from the outer edge of each, and the inner edge of each (x1o and x1i). I did the same for the pair hC-hR (x2o and x2i). Perhaps it will make more sense if you can see how these variables fit together.

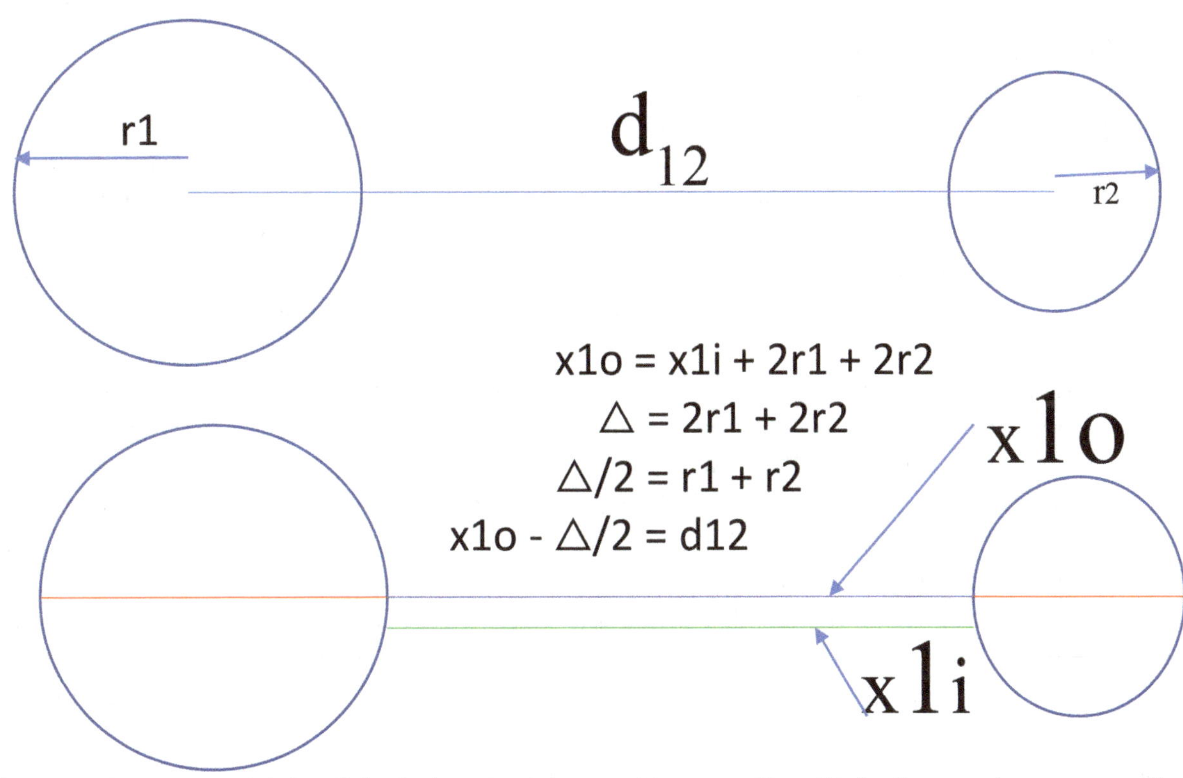

Figure 16C.5: A model for Calculating the Distance Between Two Hole Centers (not necessarily of the same sizes)

We want d12 and d23, the distances between pairs of holes, center to center, (1 to 2 and 2 to 3). We'll measure the distance from the outside edge of one hole to the outside edge of the other, x1o, and between the inside edges of both holes, x1i. The circle on the left has *diameter* d1, and the diameter for the one on the right is d2. The difference between the two lines, x1o-x1i is equal to d1 + d2 = delta. Delta/2 is equal to the radius of the first circle plus that of the second circle.

So, x1o – delta/2 = d12, our desired distance.

There are some dimensions that I want to discuss, and I have done that work for you. Your assignment is to check my work to be sure you know how to make the measurements, and to *read* each letter and, on the blank page(s) that follow each, write down what they say. I don't want your interpretation. If it says boad, write boad, not boat. Spend a little time with each word and write what you see. Try to make choices that make sense, assuming the writer either had a hard time with the English language or was trying his or her best to make it look that way. You have 15 letters to rewrite. They are messy, I know. For some words, you may have to work to decide what each letter is. As you work through them, you will hopefully find some helpful patterns – such as t's that are never crossed, and i's that are never dotted. Some individual letters are very distinctive and unusual, written the same way every time.

In this initial introduction to the letters, some parts may be too much of a mess to write anything down. I think someone worked hard to write in a way that suggested a German was writing English, poorly, or that the writer was trying to disguise his or her natural writing.

16D. Introduction to Handwriting Analysis

There are people you can hire to get someone's handwriting analyzed (graphology). They will go through the documents you provide and summarize their findings in a report. Perhaps the writer dots their i's with hearts. "The person is young and always very much in love." Some writers might not use punctuation. In that case, "they are a very anti-establishment spirit who tends to do what they want, not what they are told." They will tell you their innermost feelings if that's what you want. Hopefully you know that 1) this is not handwriting analysis, and 2) it's not real. It's certainly not an accepted science. Let's get that out of the way.

A typical handwriting analysis by a questioned document examiner, would involve having several examples of the person's real handwriting, and some questioned document, where the question is whether the person who wrote one sample also wrote the other. While there is some software that can be used for such a project, I believe most handwriting analysts prefer to do it manually. Preferably, the exemplars are recent, and nothing has changed in the person's life in the time that passed between the two samples. If the person is 80, we don't use a diary written at age 17 as a writing sample. In some cases, as people age, they get ailments such as Parkinson's disease, causing hand tremors that would undoubtedly change the appearance of their handwriting. In many cases, people try to disguise their handwriting, which takes time; so, when you ask for writing samples, push the person to write quickly, not giving them time to concentrate on a different writing style.

With the documents in hand, if everything is written on lined paper, that would be handled differently than unlined paper. In the latter, measuring variables such as the spacing between the lines could become useful. Spaces between words are studied. Then take a step back and look at the big picture between the two. Does the person underline often? Is their writing filled with exclamation points or quotation marks? Are there words or phrases that seem to appear often? Perhaps you will find some trend like these in their writing.

Let's start off with a simple example. A friend of mine had someone become very interested in him, possibly romantically. He was not interested in her, but she persisted until he eventually had to ask her to leave him alone; just go away. She did for a few months, but in February he received an unsigned valentine. He was concerned the woman was pursuing him again and asked me to do a handwriting analysis. The situation was not ideal. He had a handwritten letter from her, exhibit A, and there was the valentine, exhibit B, containing only a few words – not enough to do this correctly, but I wanted to share it to give you a sense of what goes into handwriting analysis.

We probably each have multiple handwriting (cursive) styles depending on whether what we are writing is formal or informal, whether it is just a personal note, like a shopping list, or something that will be read by others. Most people keep some stylistic aspects of the penmanship that they learned in grade school, but it's not a hard and fast rule.

OK, let's get to it. There was a Valentine, exhibit B, and an earlier letter, exhibit A. This was all the writing in Exhibit B.

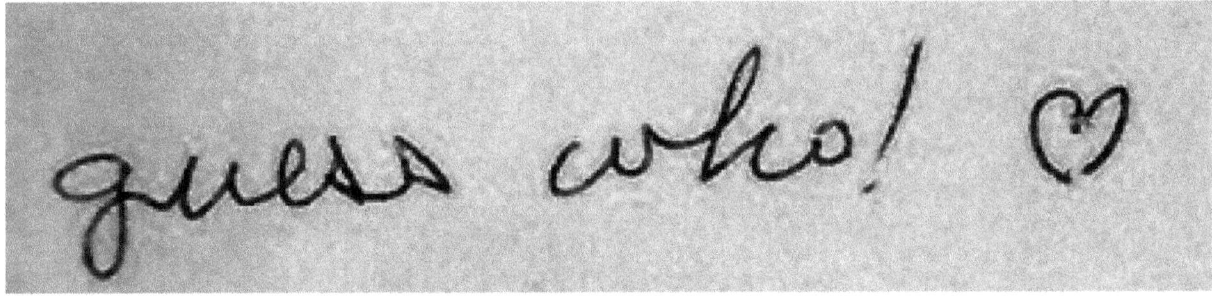

Figure 16.D.1: Exhibit B. Handwriting on the Valentine

There are only eight letters, one used twice, an exclamation point and a heart. This is obviously a very playful note. Exhibit A, which was signed, is different. Whoever wrote it was clearly in a different mood and appeared to have a lot to say since almost every inch of the paper is filled with their feelings. While it's not relevant, I did notice that there was frequent mention of friends/my friends –words used often.

The most important part of an examination is when the letters, or words, or letter combinations found in one set are compared with the other. Often this is physically done, where examples are cut out of exhibit A and placed on a page with samples from exhibit B, so we can see how similar the details are.

Here, because exhibit B is so small, we will do a letter-by-letter comparison. The first letter in exhibit B is a *g*. There are a few *g*'s in the example of the writing in exhibit A, *caring*, (line 8) and *gratitude* (line 12). Often, letters will be written differently depending on where they appear in a word. The *g* in *caring* (1. in Figure 16D.3) is a bit more elaborate than the simpler *g* in *gratitude*, and I'm going to focus on the *gratitude g* (2.) since it is at the beginning of a word, like *guess*. They both have the same general appearance. There is no line leading into the *g*, it has a healthy lower loop, and there is no pen lift between it and the next letter. So, with the limited number of exemplars, the *g*'s are *similar* in both documents.

There are several *u*'s. These include those in *sure* and *hurt* (line 2), *number* (line 4,) *gratitude* (line 12), *your* (line 14,) *judgmental* and *because* (line 16), *would* and *much* (line 17). In the first example, *sure* (4.), the *u* is in the interior of the word, but (as you can see in line 1) when a word begins with an *s*, it is often detached from the next letter, so a *u* after an *s* (4.) may have a slightly different appearance than the *u* in *hurt*. In some cases, words are compacted as a sentence reaches the end of the line, and writing styles may change a bit, but if you consider the *u* in *much* and *hurt* and *number* (5.) and *gratitude*, they all look very similar to the *u* in *guess*. The pen stroke moves smoothly into and out of the *u* connecting the adjacent letters and shows a writing style that is very simple and easy to read. They appear to match.

I'm <u>so</u> <u>sorry</u> you felt my behavior was "inappropriate."
I'm sure you realize how <u>deeply</u> that criticism hurt me.
I don't <u>ever</u> remember "looking up" your email or cell phone
number. Both of them are readily available on [redacted]
FB page. And, when one has Messenger on one's phone, all
one's FB friends can connect with you that way automatically.
I <u>never</u> intended to invade your privacy. If you check
my messages to you, every one of them was caring + supportive—
exactly what one would want in a friend. In fact, I sent
some of the same stickers to other friends, like [redacted]
[redacted]. They, like most of my other friends, reacted
with <u>smiles</u> + <u>gratitude</u>. <u>No</u> <u>one</u> <u>else</u> said I was being
inappropriate. I hope you can find
it in your heart to forgive me +
become more accepting, less critical +
less judgemental—like my other friends—because
it would make you a much happier person—and
more likeable.

With Love,

Figure 16D.2: Exhibit A

The next letter is an *e*, and there are many throughout exhibit A. The *e* is a simple loop connected to adjacent letters, just as the simple *e*'s found in words like *felt* (5.) (line 1), *realize* (6.) (line 2), *ever, remember, email, cell* (7.) (line 3), *number* (8), *them* and *ready* (line 4) with many other examples. The simple loop model for the cursive *e* is repeated throughout exhibit A and is the same form in Exhibit B. The letter often has a tilt to the right, by a few degrees.

The first word ends with an *ss*. The *ss* in the words *messenger* (line 5) and *messages* (10.) (line 8) are of a simple style but perhaps more distinctive than the double *s* in exhibit B, however, the placement changes. The *ss* is at the end of *guess*, while in the cases from the letter, the double *s*'s are always internal to the word. So, there are similar but multiple *s*'s in the writing style – such as the detached, almost printed *s* that starts words such as *sorry (9.)*, the internal double *s*'s such as in *messenger*, and terminal *s*'s such as in *was* (11.) (line 1), *has* (line 5), *was* (line 8) and *s*'s that start a word such as *smiles* (line 12). All the *s*'s are simple; in some cases, the swing back at the bottom of the *s* crosses back over the pen stroke that begins it. Sometimes it is obvious, and that stroke barely does so in *case* or *person*, (line 17). They are all very similar, and differences may be because there was a large space for only a few words in exhibit B. In such cases, a writing simplicity may be expected.

There are several *w*'s in exhibit A, but I'm going to focus on the *wh* combination, such as appears in *when* (12.) (line 5) and *what* (line 9). Both examples show a simple *w* with no lead in stroke, a curved line connecting it to the *h*, and very distinctive *h*'s which are found throughout exhibit A. The *h* starts with an upper loop, and the lower body moves away from the downward stroke, and peaks to the right - a distinctive *h*.

The last letter is a terminal *o*. In exhibit A there are many internal *o*'s and starting *o*'s such as *on* (line 4), *on* and *one*'s (line 5), *you* (line 6) etc. They usually have a small upper loop at the top of the o, while terminal o's such as in *to* (17.) (lines 7,8 and 10) are very clean and simple circles, with no stroke following the circle. The two exhibits match in this regard.

There is no exclamation point or heart in exhibit A, which is to be expected, because the two communications have very different tones/purposes.

Figure 16D.3: Comparing Exhibits A and B

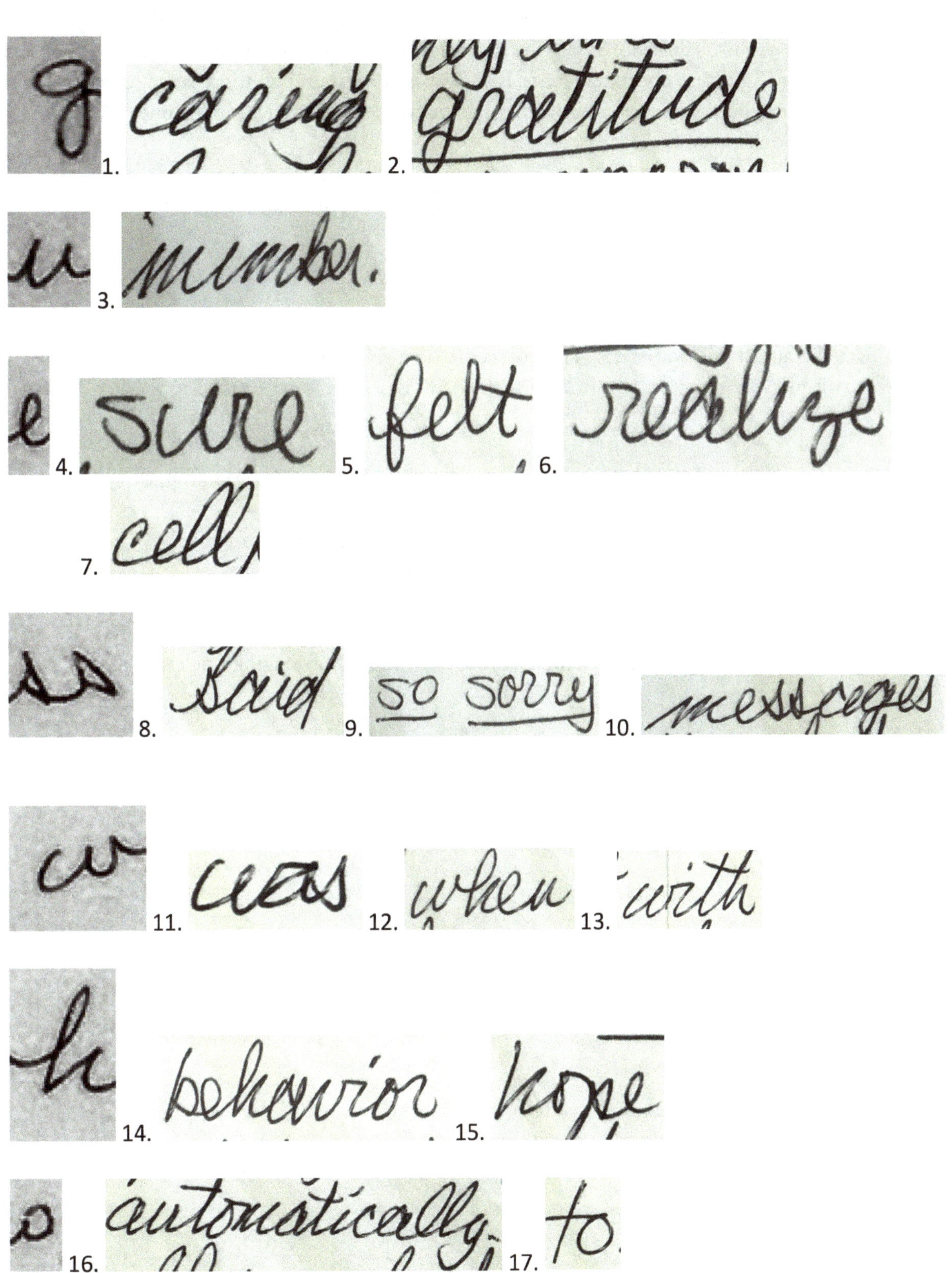

The words cut out from exhibit A, using a hobbyist's X-Acto knife, similar to a scalpel, are shown to the right of those of exhibit B. Samples 12.-15. show the similarity of the *h*'s. Words such as 10. show a double *s*, internal to the word. Examples 8 and 9 show *s*'s at the beginning of a word. Example 3 shows the simple *u*. That top loop on some of the *o*'s does not appear in 16. and 17., where the *o* is terminal in the word. 11.-13. show examples of the *w*. Often, every time a letter is used it is cut out and all those same letters are shown together. This is advantageous because you know that the analyst is not just picking the ones that match and ignoring the ones that don't.

This is, I hope, a good example for you to begin to think of ways to compare writing samples.

16E. THE Ransom Letters and some Measurements - Letter Dimensions

What follows are the actual ransom letters. The colors are off because I adjusted contrast on each to make them easier for you to read. See what you can do with them, based on what I asked for earlier. Determine for each:

- The width and height of each ransom letter, using the ruler shown in each figure
- The values for a and b, defined in Figure 16C.4
- The distances between the holes, using the model developed in Figure 16C.5
- Write what each letter says, following the instructions in Section 16C

FYI – The ransom letters were received over a short period of time. Occasionally two were received in one day. The first was received March 1 and the tenth was received April 1, averaging one every three days.

Ransom Letter #1 width:_157.5_ mm height: 177.5_mm a =___ mm b = ____ mm

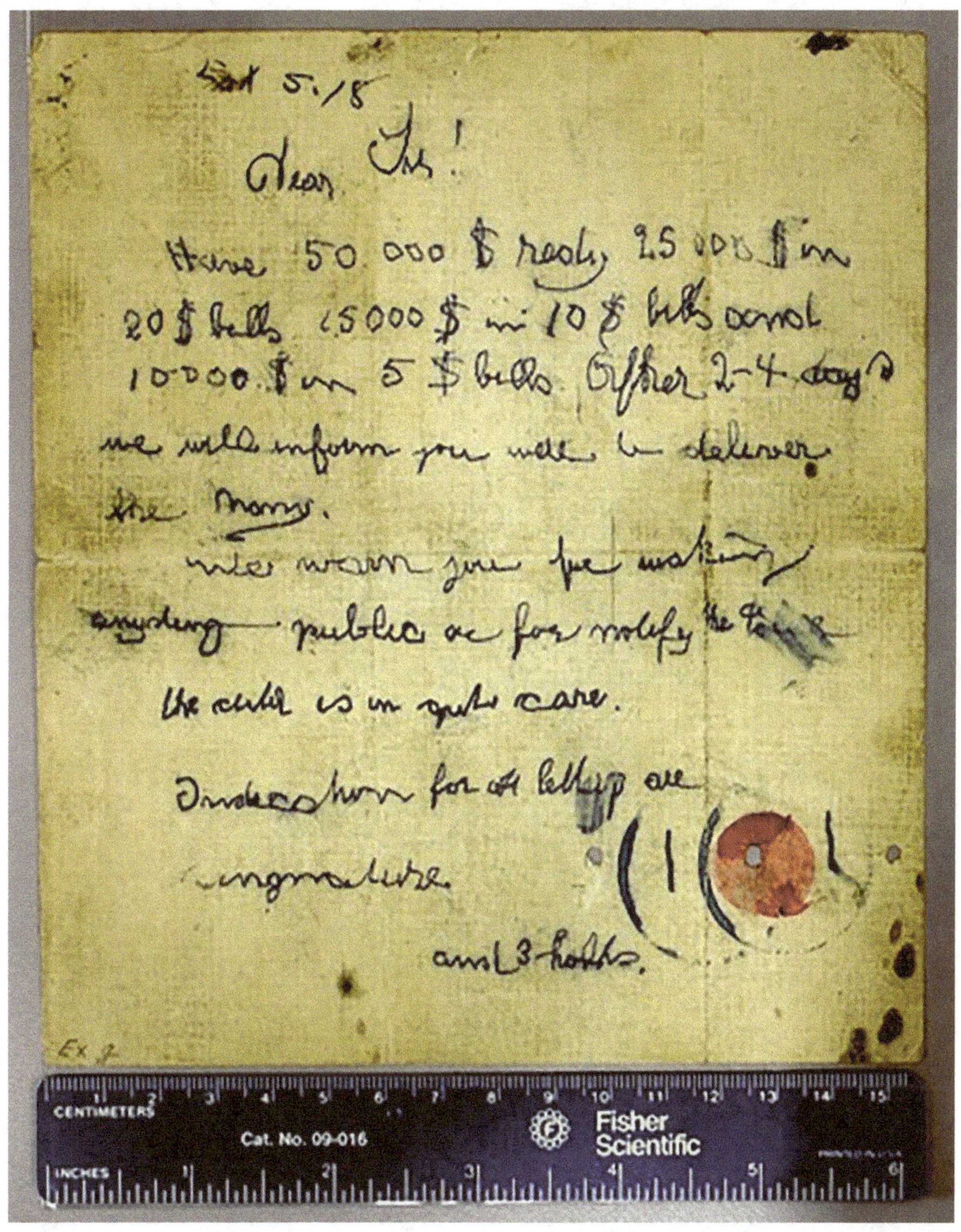

Sat 5.18

Dear Sir!

Have 50.000 $ redy 25 000 $ in 20 $ bills 15000 $ in 10 $ bills and 10000 $ in 5 $ bills After 2-4 days we will inform you were to deliver the mony.

We warn you for making anyding public or for notify the Police the child is in gute care.

Indication for all letters are singnature and 3 holes.

Ex 9

Letter #1 (verso). x1o = _____mm x1i = ____ mm x2o = ____mm x2i = ____mm

What the letter says:

Envelope for Ransom Letter #1

Ransom Letter #2 width:_157_mm height: _174_ mm a = ____ mm b = ____ mm

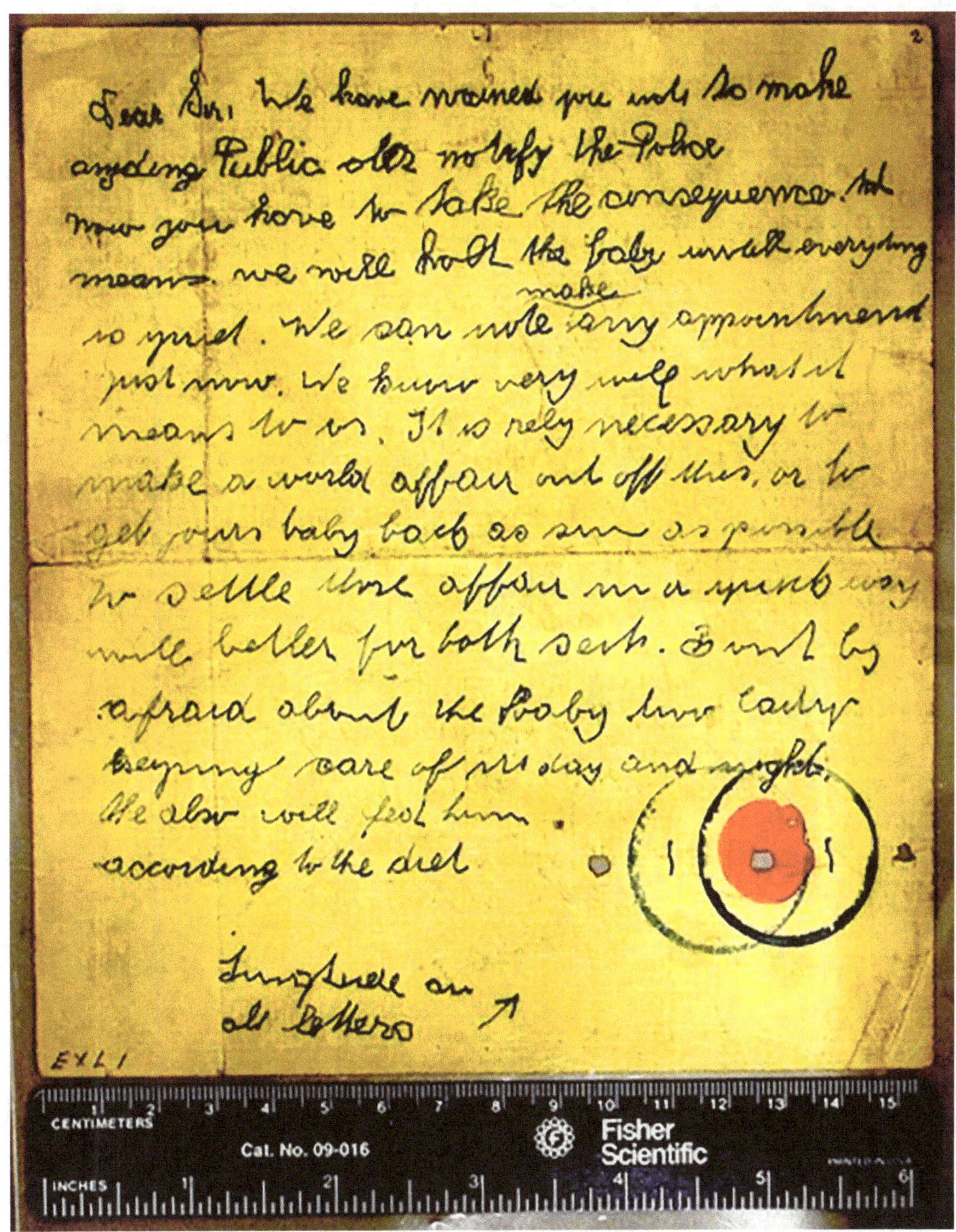

2

Dear Sir, We have warned you note to make
anyding Public also notify the Police
now you have to take the consequence. This
means we will hold the baby until everything
is quiet. We can note make any appointment
just now. We know very well what it
means to us. It is realy necessary to
make a world affair out off this, or to
get yours baby back as sun as possible
to settle those affair in a quick way
will better for both seits. Dont by
afraid about the baby two ladys
keeping care of its day and night.
She also will fed him
according to the diet

Singtuere on
all letters

EXL1

We are interested to send him back in
gut health. and ransom was made aus
for 50.000 $ but now we have to take
another person to it and probable have
to keep the baby for a longer time as we
expected. So the amount will be 70,000 $
20.000 in 50 $ bills 25.000 $ in 20 $ bills
15000 $ in 10 $ bills and 10.000 $ in 5 $ bills.
don't mark any bills. or take them
from one serial nomer. We will
inform you latter were to deliver the
mony. but we will not to so
until the Police is out of the case
and the Pappers are quiet.

Ex S 20

The Kidnaping was prepared
in yahrs. so we are prepared
for everyding

EX 41 (2dp)

CENTIMETERS 1 2 3 4 5 6 7 8 9 10 11 12 13 14 15
Cat. No. 09-016
Fisher Scientific
INCHES 1 2 3 4 5 6

Letter #2 (verso) x1o = ______mm x1i = _____ mm x2o = _____mm x2i = _____mm

What it says;

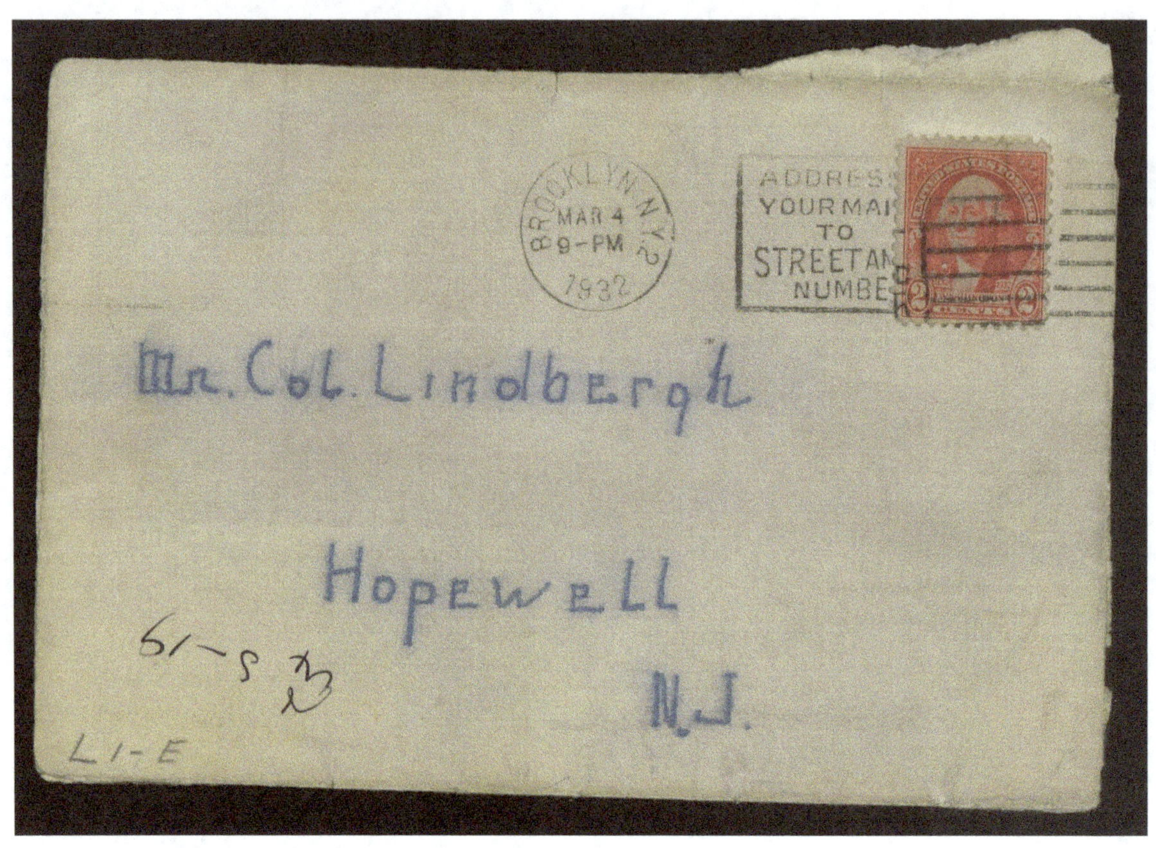

Envelope for Ransom Letter #2

Ransom Letter #3 width:__157__ mm height: _174__ mm a = ____ mm b = ____ mm

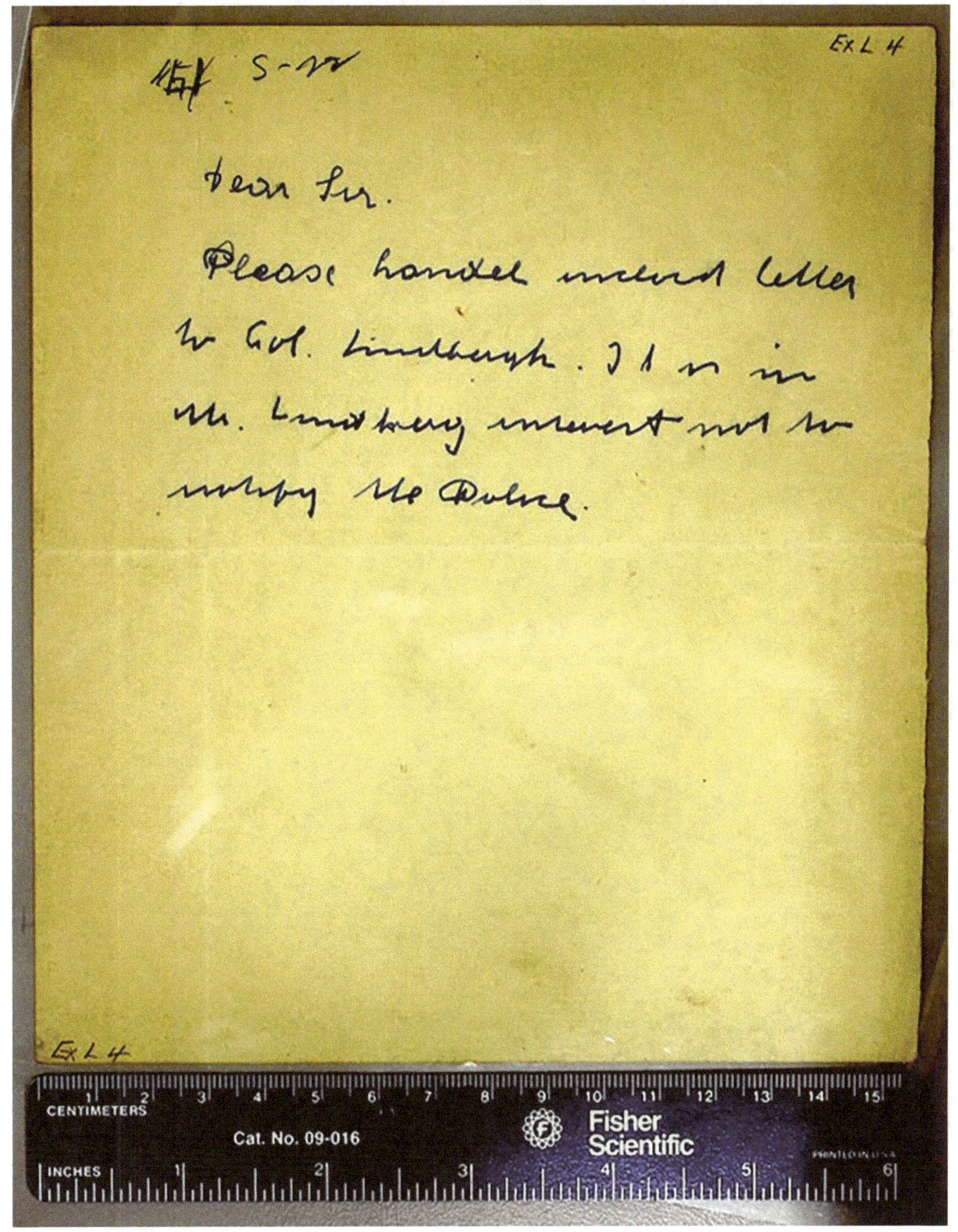

S-22

Ex L 4

Dear Sir.

Please handel inclosed letter to Col. Lindbergh. It is in Mr. Lindbergh interest not to notify the Police.

Ex L 4

Ransom Letter #3 (verso). x1o ______mm x1i = _____ mm x2o = _____mm x2i = _____mm

What it says:

Envelope for Ransom Letter #3

Ransom Letter #4 width:_157.5__ mm height: _178__ mm a = ____ mm b = ____ mm

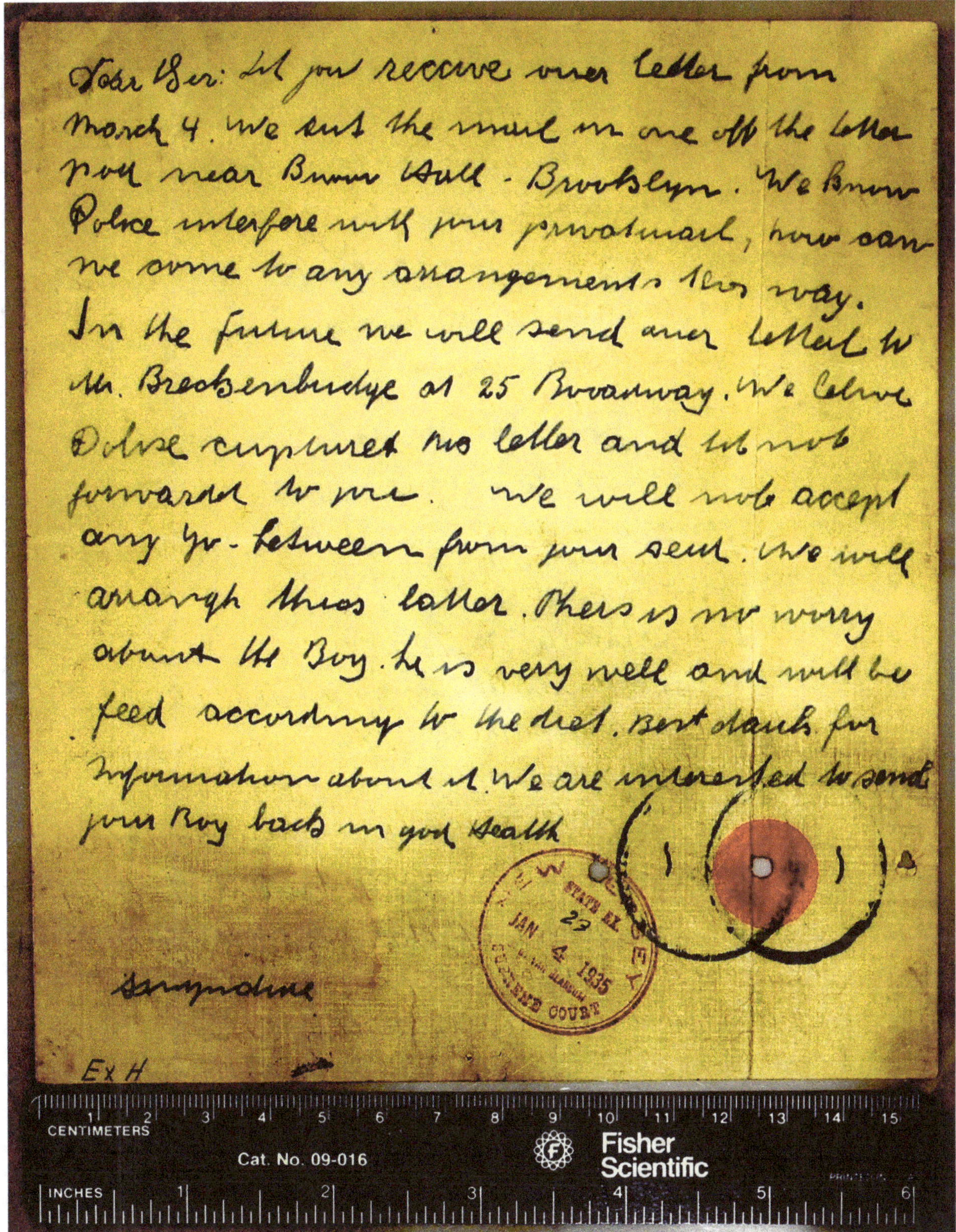

Dear Sir: Did you receive our letter from March 4. We sent the mail in one off the letter box near Burro Hall - Brooklyn. We know Police interfere with your private mail, how can we come to any arrangements this way. In the future we will send our letters to Mr. Breckenbridge at 25 Broadway. We believe Police captured our letter and let not forwarded to you. We will not accept any go-between from your sent. We will arrange theas latter. There is no worry about the Boy. He is very well and will be feed according to the diet. Best thanks for information about it. We are interested to send your Boy back in good health.

Singnature

Ex H

Is it nessisery to make a world affair out of
it, or to get your boy back as soon as possible:
Why did you ignore our letter which we
left in the room: the baby would be back
long ago. you would not get any result
from Police, because this kidnaping was
planed for a year allready. but we were afraid,
the boy would not be strong enough.
And ransom was made out for 50.000 $
but now we have to put another lady to it and
propperly have to hold the baby longer as we
expected so it will be 70 000 $.
20000 in 50 $ bills 25000 in 20 $ bills 15000
in 10 $ bills 10000 in 5 $ bills. we warn you again
not to mark any bills or take them from one serial
No. We will inform you latter how to deliver
the money, but not befor
the Police is out of this cace and the
pappers are quiet.
Please get a short notice about this letter in the
New-York American.

Ransom Letter #4 (verso) **x1o = _____mm x1i = ____ mm x2o = ____mm x2i = ____mm**

What it says:

Envelope for Ransom Letter #4

Ransom Letter #5 width:_135__ mm height: _165_ mm a = ___mm b = ____ mm

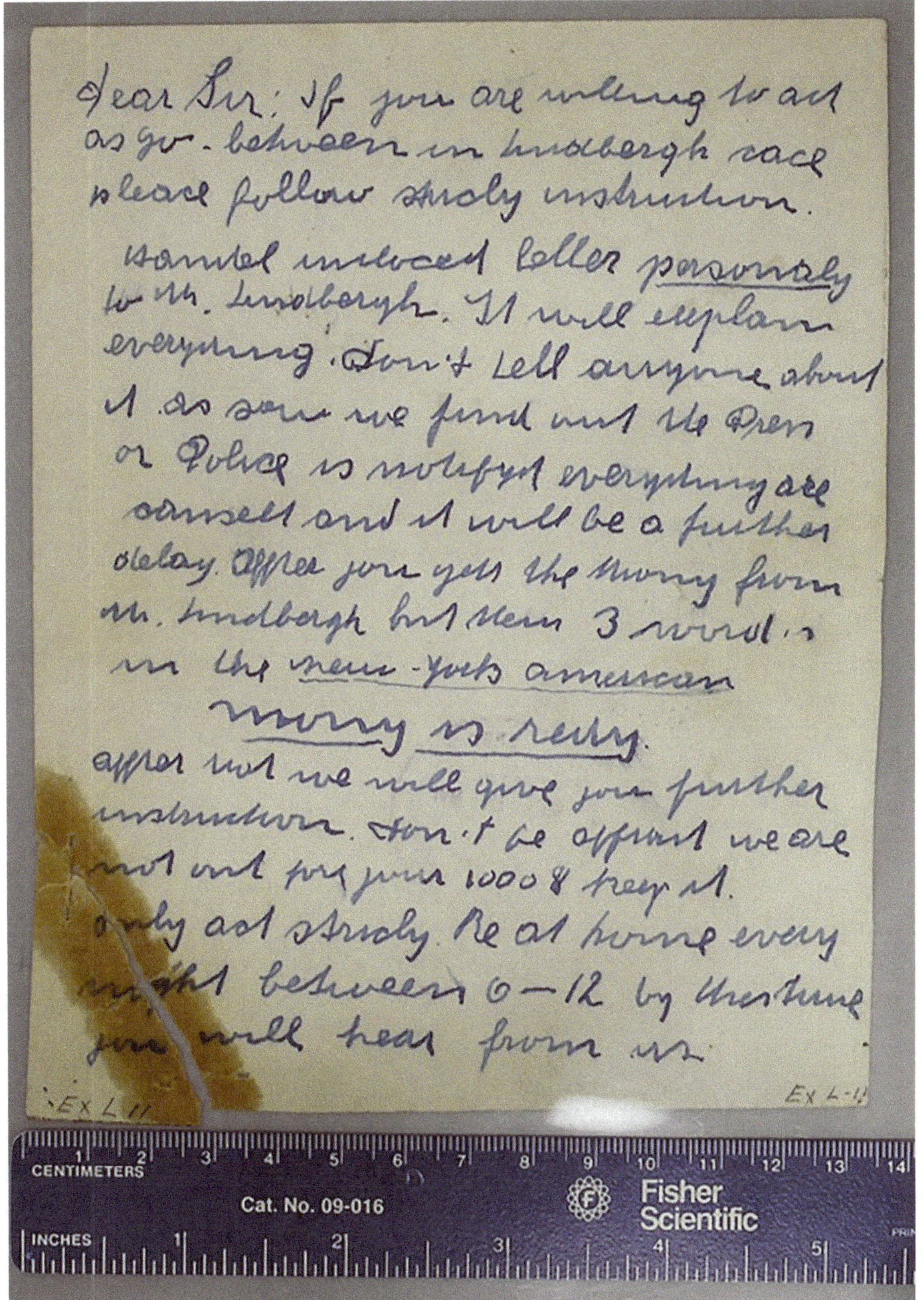

dear Sir: If you are willing to act as go-between in Lindbergh cace please follow stricly instruction.

Handel incloced letter personaly to Mr. Lindbergh. It will explain everyding. don't tell anyone about it. as soon we find out the Press or Police is notifyd everyding are cancell and it will be a further delay. Affter you gett the mony from Mr. Lindbergh put these 3 words in the New-York American

mony is redy.

Affter notit we will give you further instruction. don't be affrait we are not out for your 1000$ keep it. only act stricly. Be at home every night between 6–12 by this time you will hear from us.

Ex L 11 Ex L-11

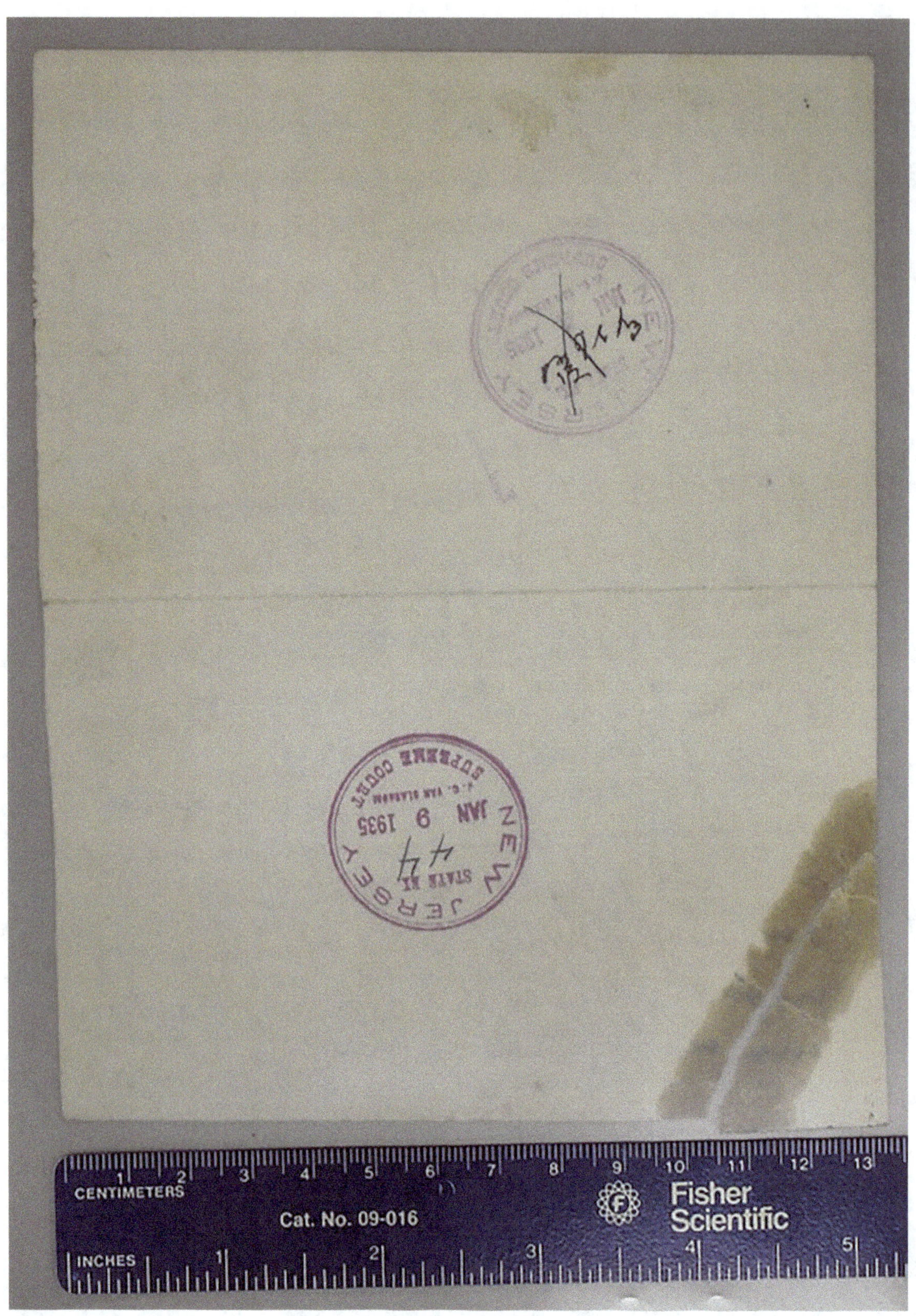

Ransom Letter #5 (verso)

What it Says:

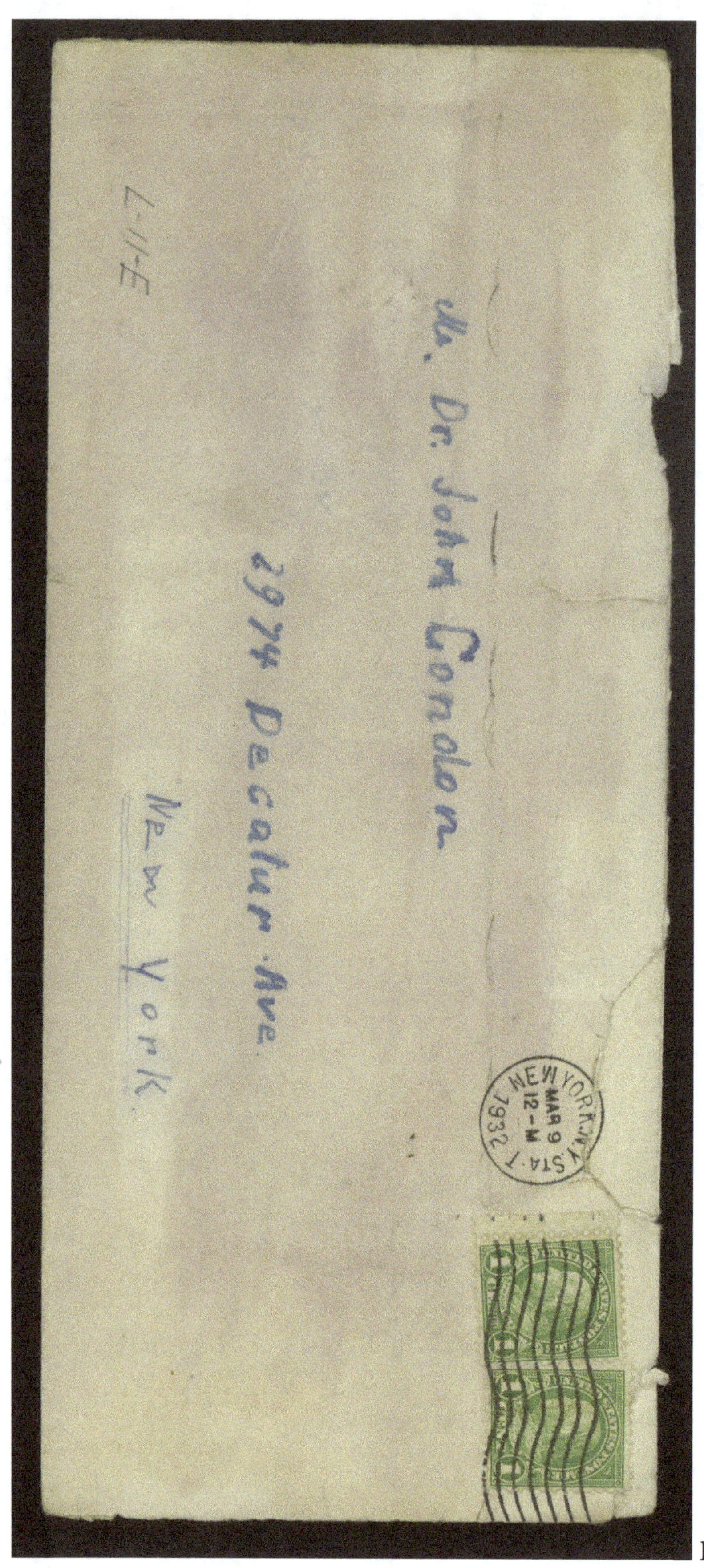
Mr. Dr. John Condon
2974 Decatur Ave
New York
NEW YORK, N.Y. STA. T
MAR 9
12-M
1932

Ransom Letter #5 Envelope

Ransom Letter #6 width:__157_ mm height:_177.5_ mm a = ____ mm b = ____ mm

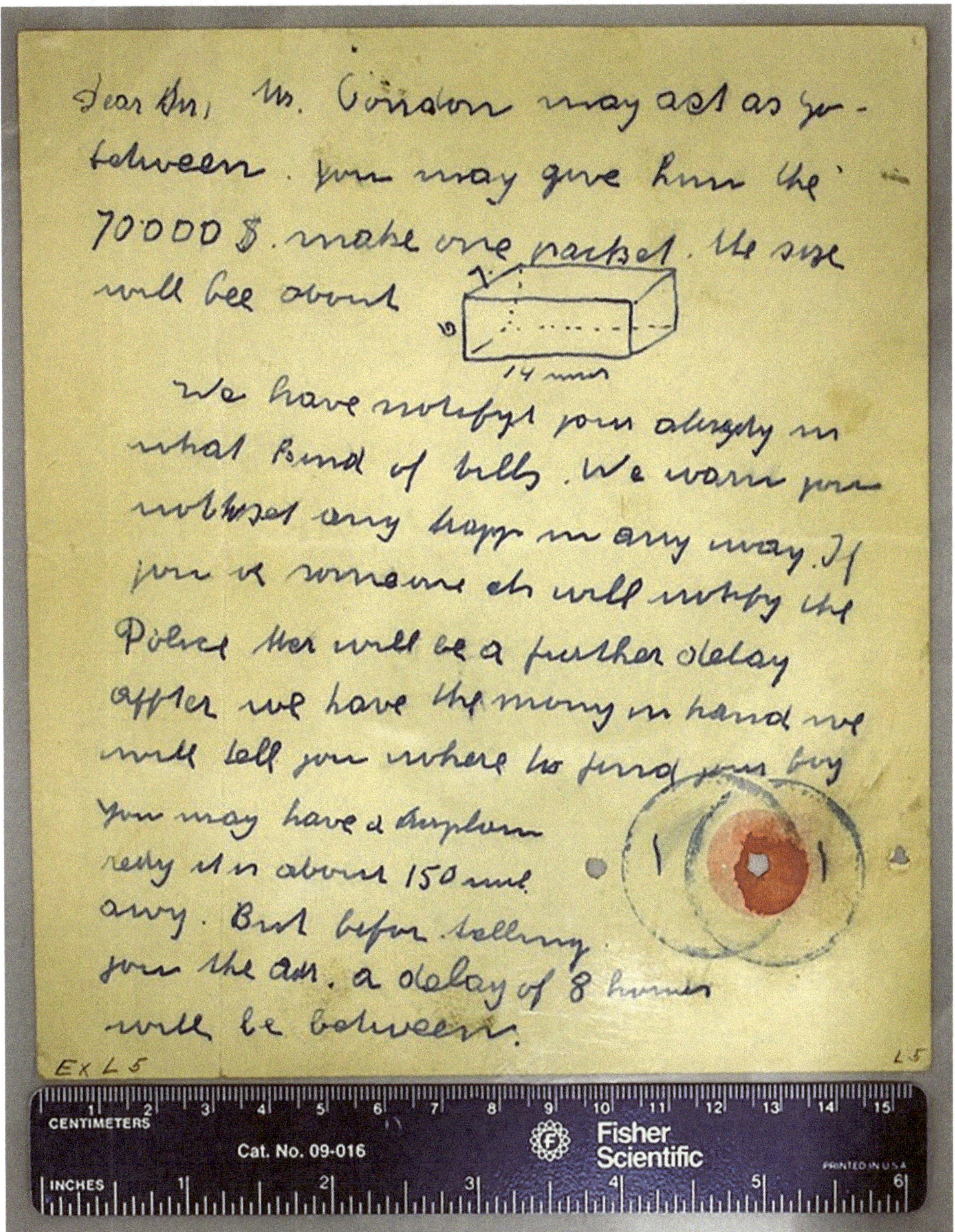

Dear Sir, Mr. Condon may act as go-between. You may give him the 70000 $. make one packet. the size will bee about

We have notify you already in what kind of bills. We warn you not to set any trapp in any way. If you or someone els will notify the Police ther will be a further delay affter we have the mony in hand we will tell you where to find your boy You may have a airplane redy it is about 150 mile awy. But befor telling you the adr. a delay of 8 houers will be between.

Ex L 5

L 5

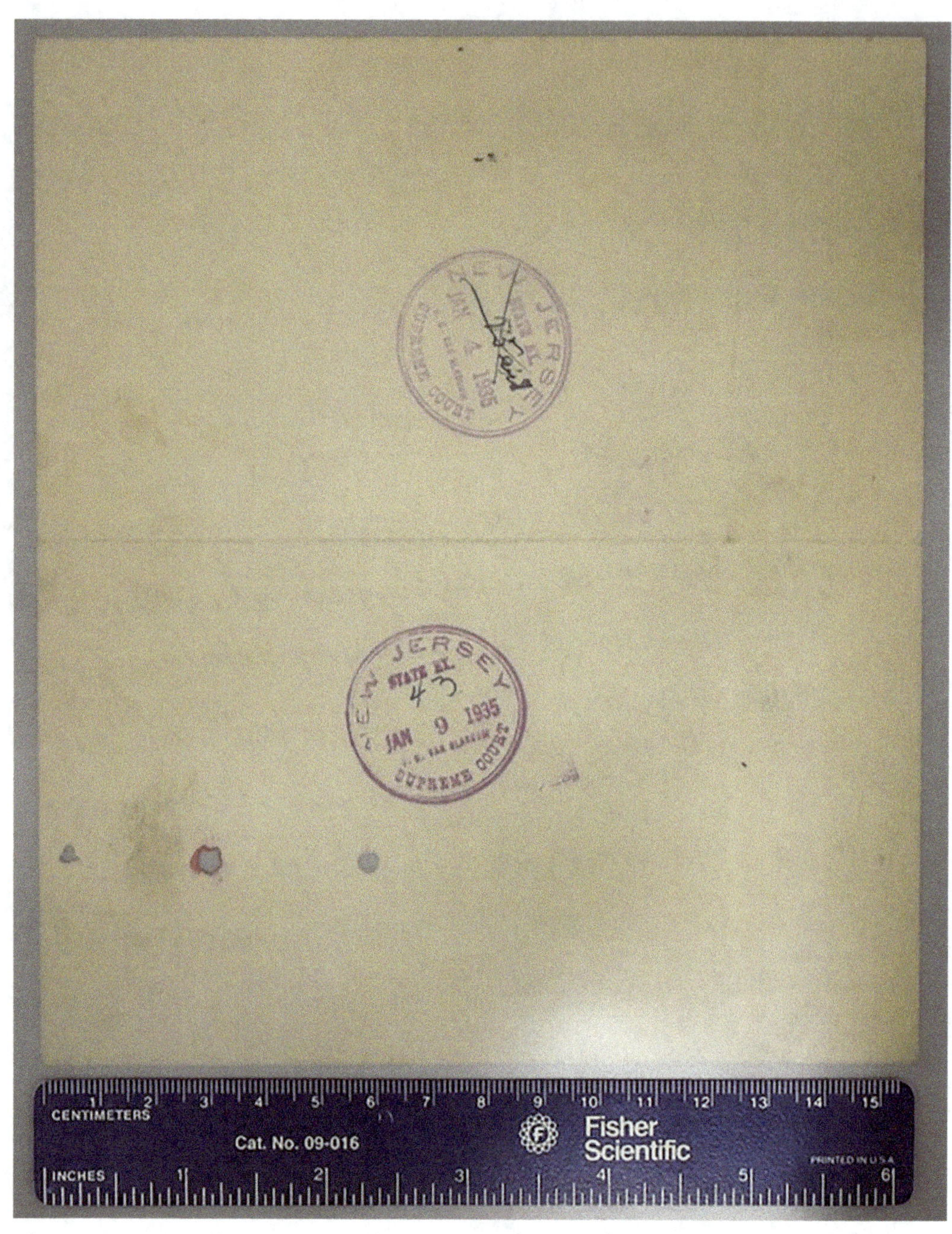

x1o = _____mm x1i = ____ mm x2o = ____mm x2i = _____mm Ransom Letter #6 (verso)

What it Says:

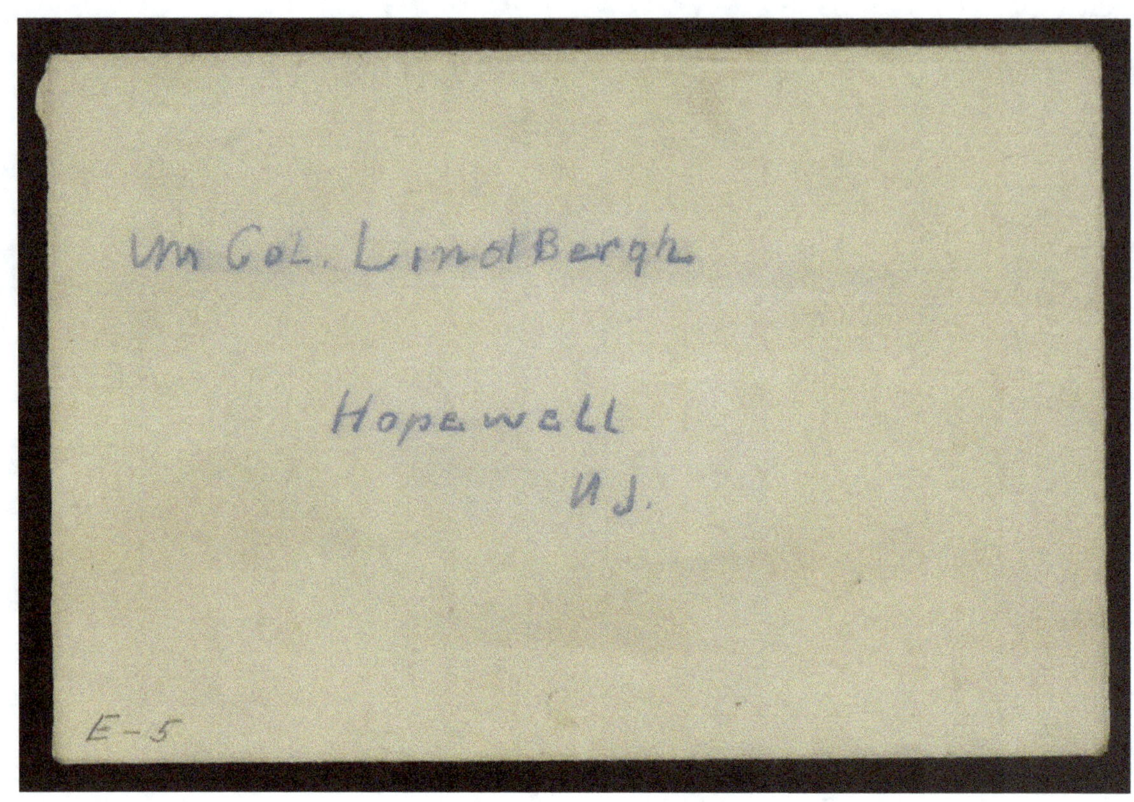

Envelope for Ransom Letter #6

Ransom Note #7 width:__157_ mm height: _177__ mm a = ____ mm b = ____ mm

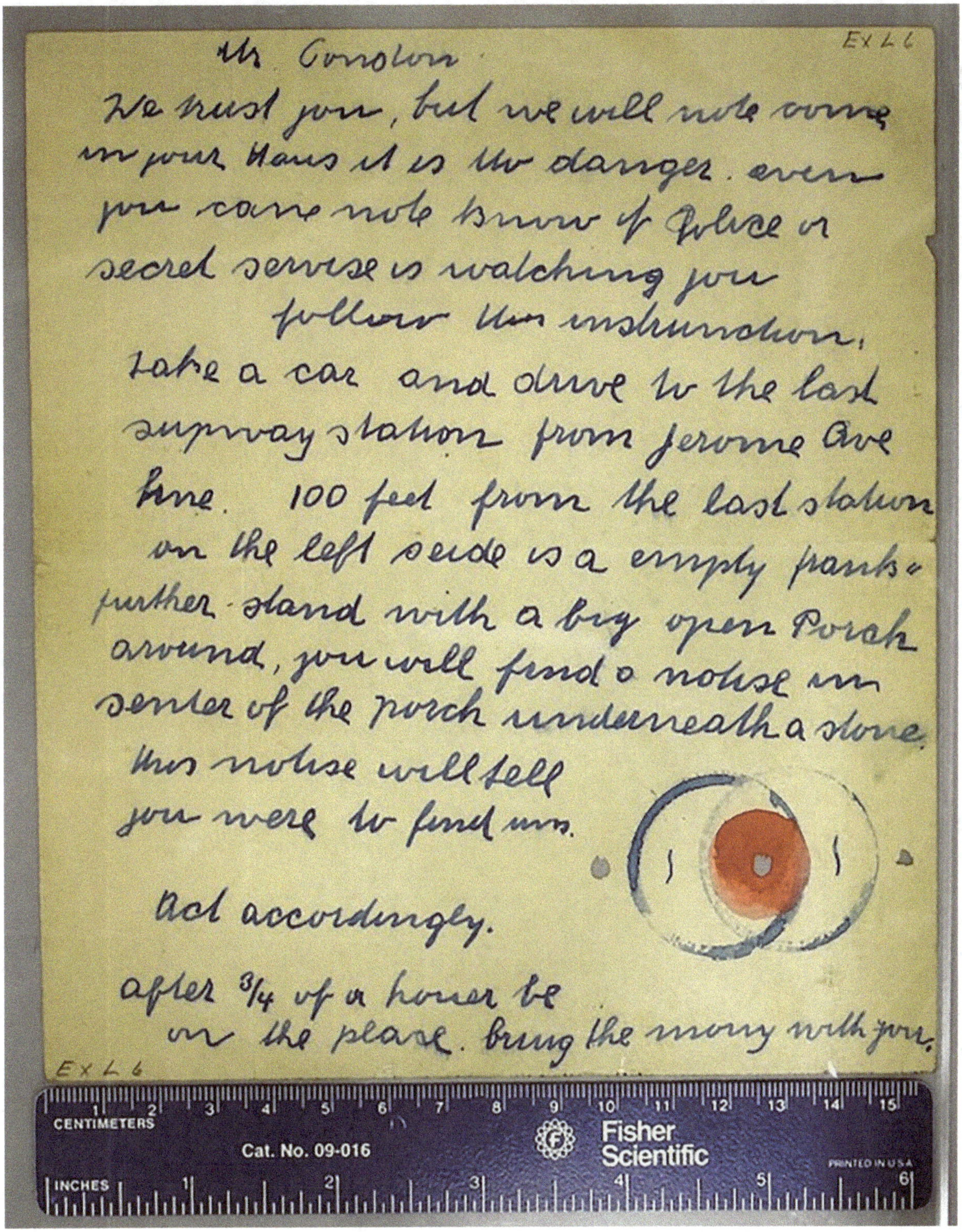

Ex L6

Mr. Condon.

We trust you, but we will note come
in your Haus it is to danger. even
you cane note know if Police or
secret servise is watching you
follow this instruction.
take a car and drive to the last
supway station from Jerome Ave
line. 100 feet from the last station
on the left seide is a empty frank-
further-stand with a big open Porch
around, you will find a notise in
senter of the porch underneath a stone.
this notise will tell
you were to find us.

Act accordingly.

after 3/4 of a houer be
on the place. bring the mony with you.

Ex L6

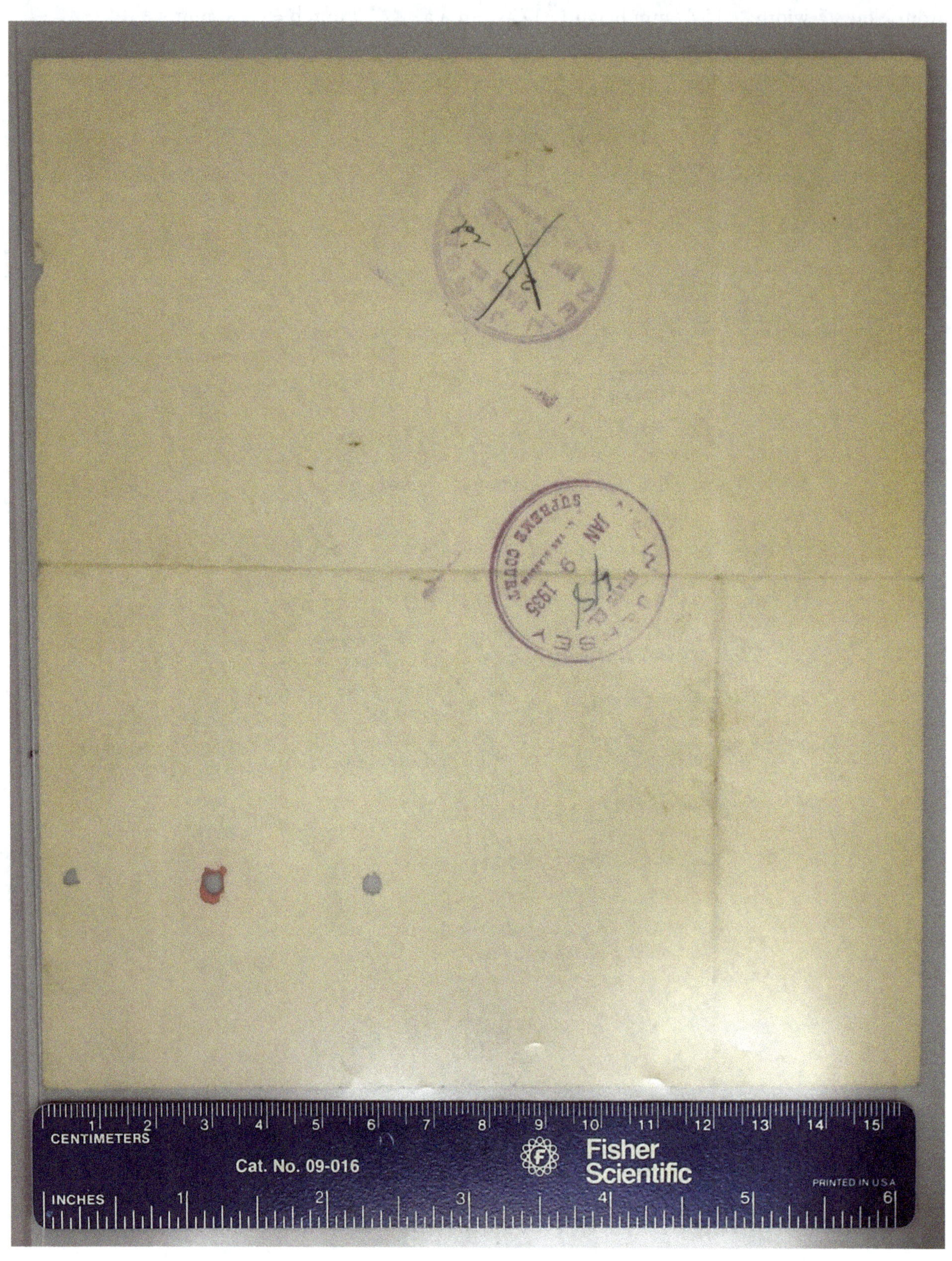

x1o = _____mm x1i = ____ mm x2o = ____mm x2i = ____mm Ransom Letter #7 (Verso)

What it says:

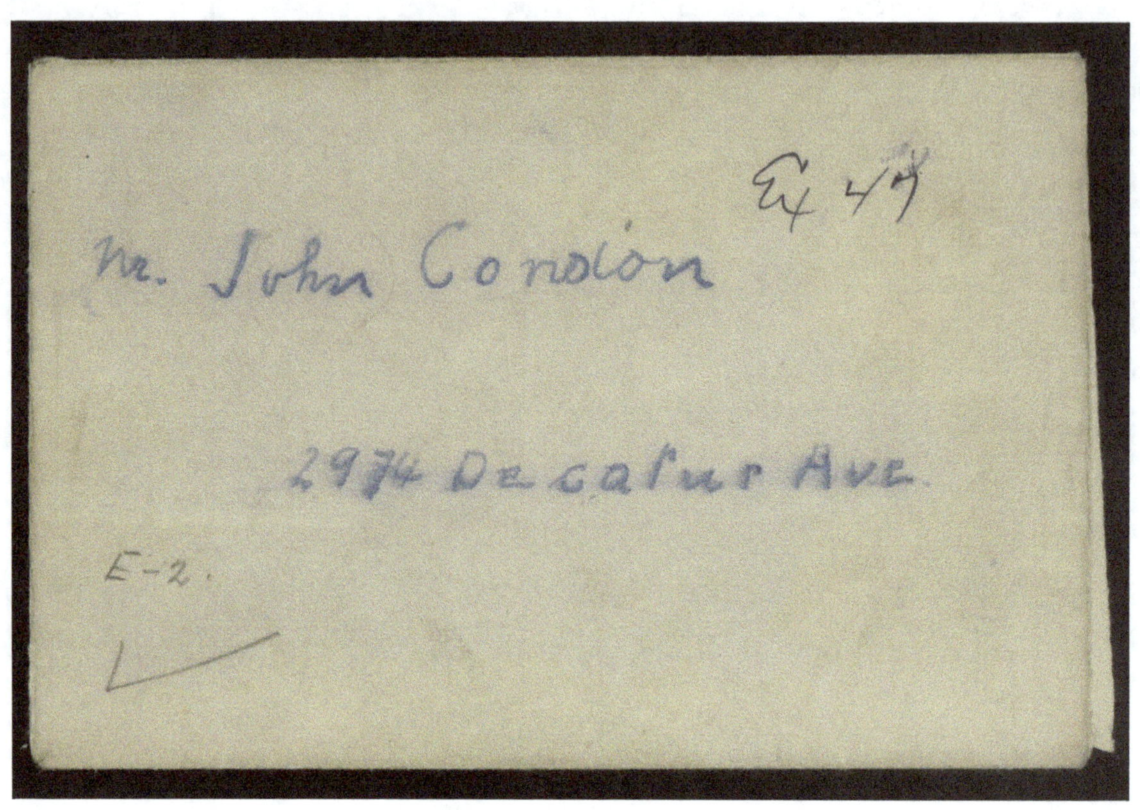

Envelope for Ransom Letter #7

Ransom Letter #8 width:_155.5_ mm height: _178.5_ mm a = ____ mm b = ____ mm

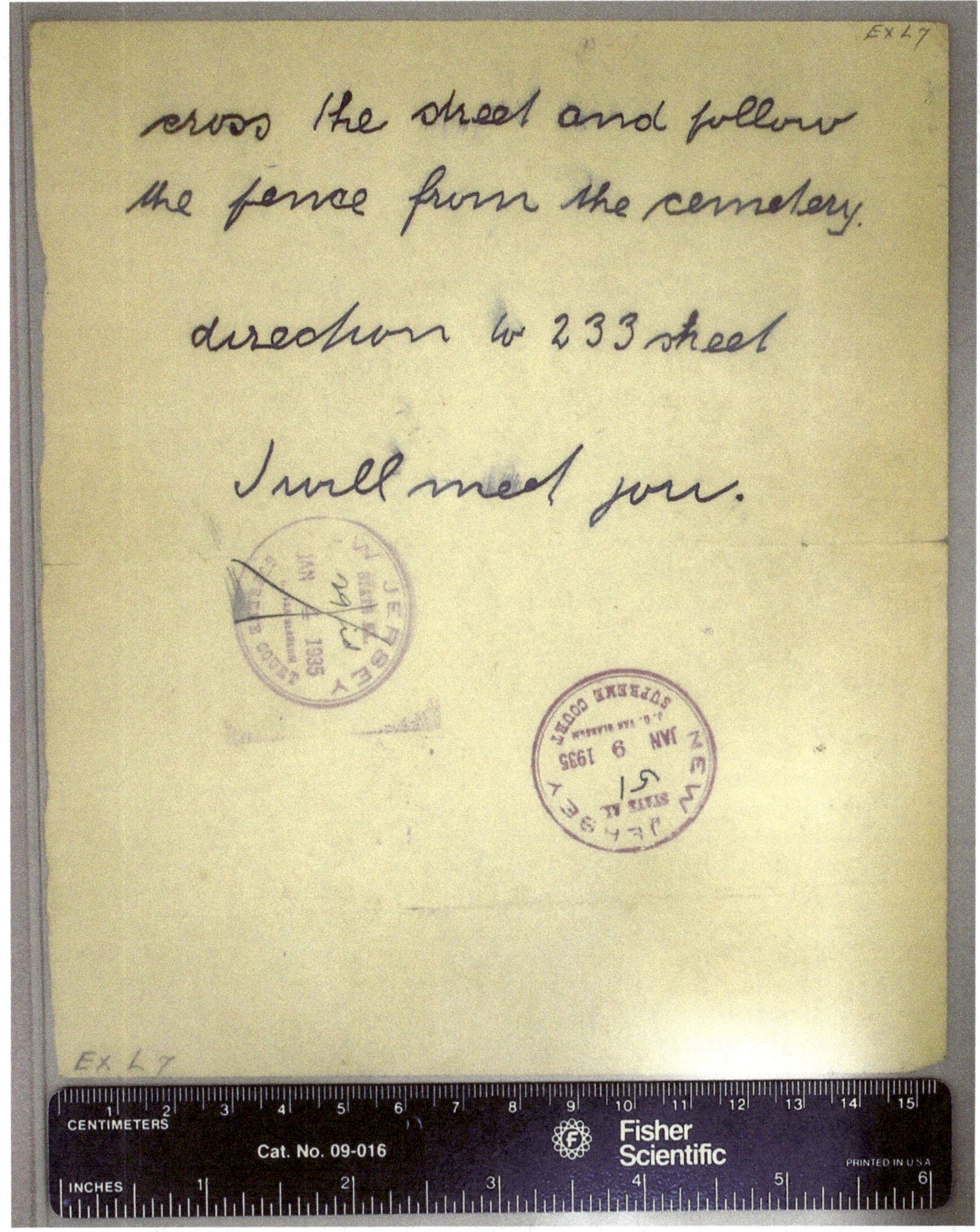

cross the street and follow
the fence from the cemetery.

direction to 233 street

I will meet you.

Ransom Letter #8 (verso)

What It Says:

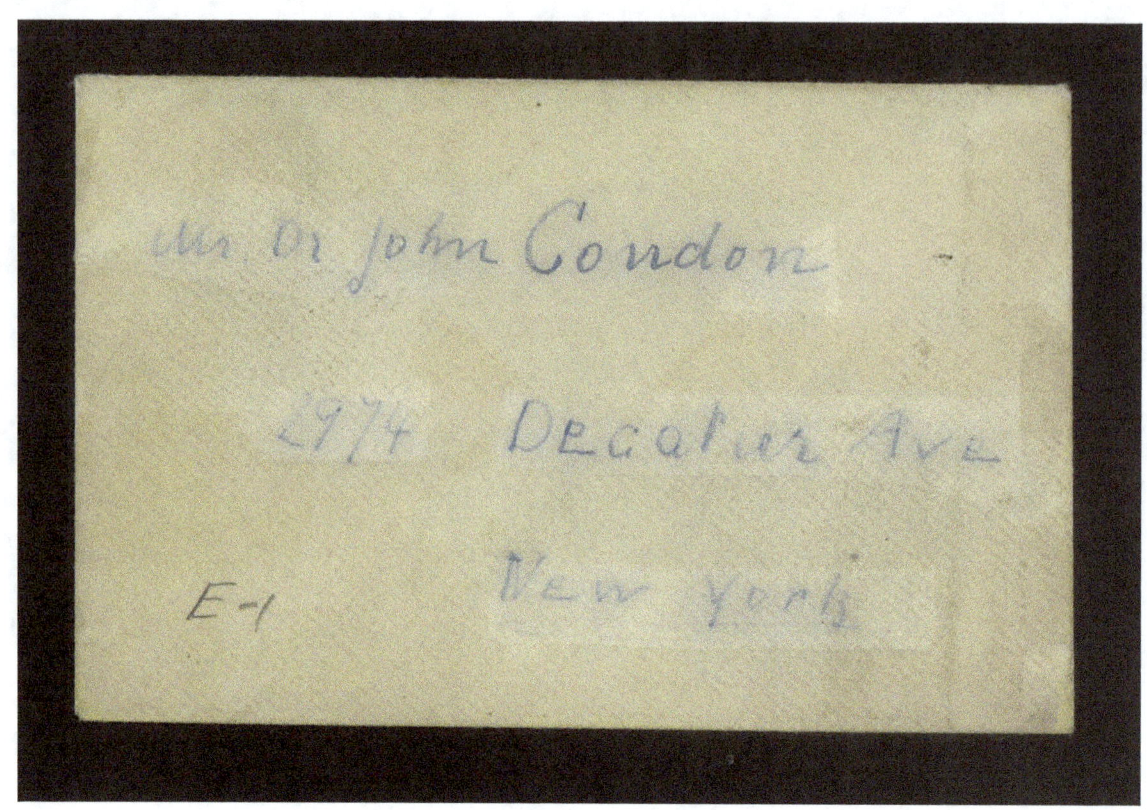

Envelope for Ransom Letter #8

Ransom Letter #9 width:_136.5_ mm height: _175_ mm a = ____ mm b = ____ mm

Dear Sir: Ouer man faile to collect the
mony. There are no more confidential
conference after the meeting from March
12. those arrangements to hazardous
for us. We will note allow ouer man
to confer in a way like befor.
circumstance will note allow us
to make a transfare like you wish.
It is impossibly for us. wy shuld we
move the baby and face danger. to
take another person to the place is
entirely out of question. It seems
you are afraid if we are the right
party and if the boy is allright. Well
you have ouer singnature. It is always
the same as the first one
specialy them 3 holes.

EX K

now we will send you the sleepingsuit
from the baby besides it means 3 $ extra
expenses because we have to pay
another one. Pleace tell Mrs. Lindbergh
note to worry the baby is well. we only
have to give him more food as the diet says.
You are willing to pay the 70000
note 50000 $ without seeing the baby first
or note. let us know about that in the
New York american. We can't do it other ways.
because we don't like to give up
ouer safty plase or to move the baby.
If you are willing to accept this deal
put these in the paper.
I accept mony is redy
ouer programm is:
after 8 houers we have the mony received
we will notify you where to find the
baby. If there is any trapp, you will be
responsible what
will follows.

Ex S-52

Ex K (2d p)

x1o = ______mm x1i = ____ mm x2o = ____mm x2i = ____mm Ransom Letter #9 verso

What it says:

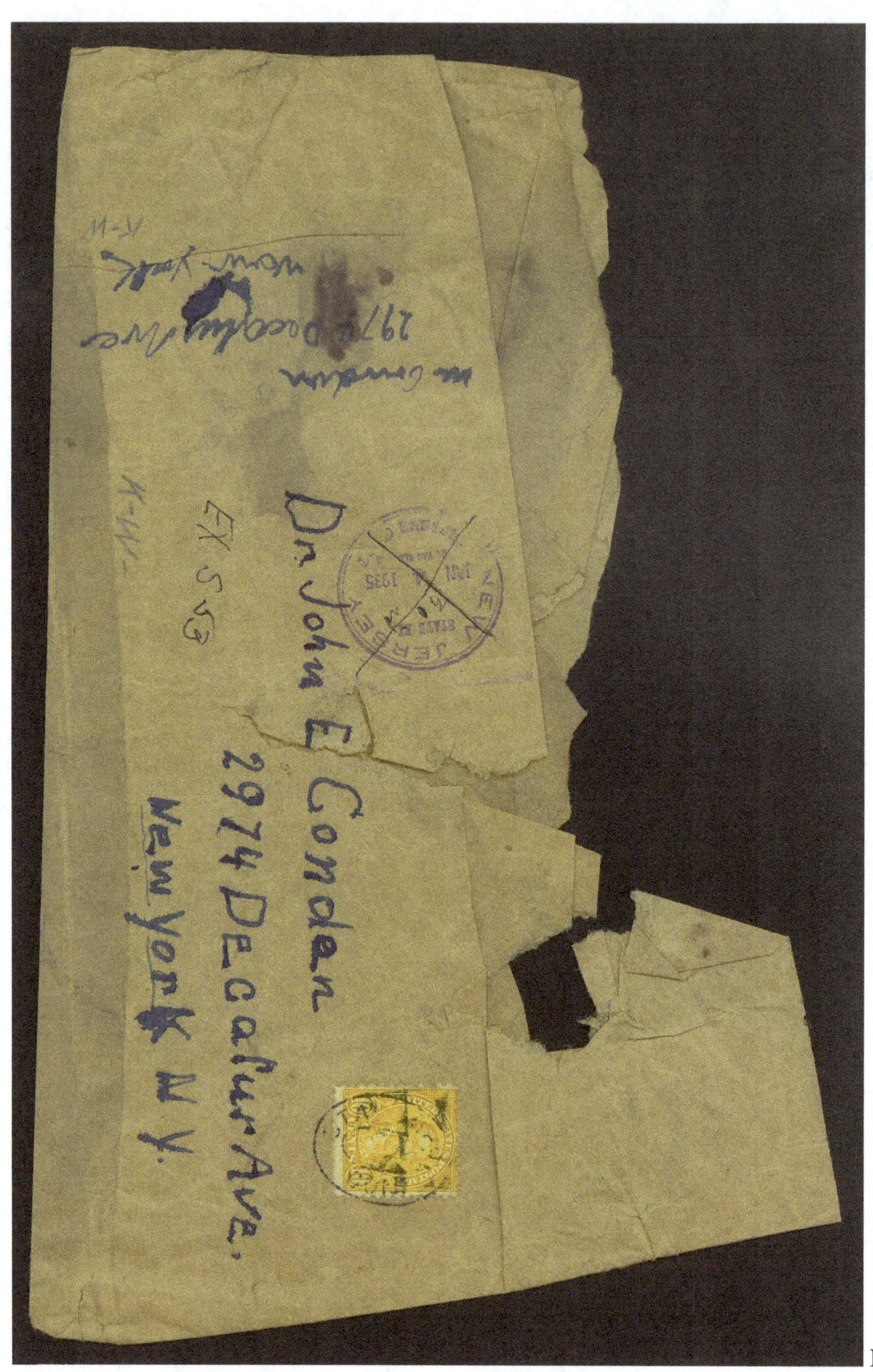
Dr John E Condon
2974 Decatur Ave.
New York N.Y.

Letter#9

Ransom Letter #10 width:__136_ mm height: _176.5_ mm a = ____ mm b = ____ mm

dear Sir: You and Mr Lindbergh know
our Program. If you don't accept
den we will wait until you
agree with our deal. we know
you have to come to us anyway
But why should'd Mrs. and Mr.
Lindbergh suffer longer as necessary
We will note communicate with
you or Mr Lindbergh until you write so
in the paper.
We will tell you again; this kidnaping case whas prepared for a
year already so the Police won't
have any looks to find us or the child
You only push everything farther out
til you send that
little package to
Mr Lindbergh: it contains
the sleepingsuit from the
the baby is well. Baby.

EX J

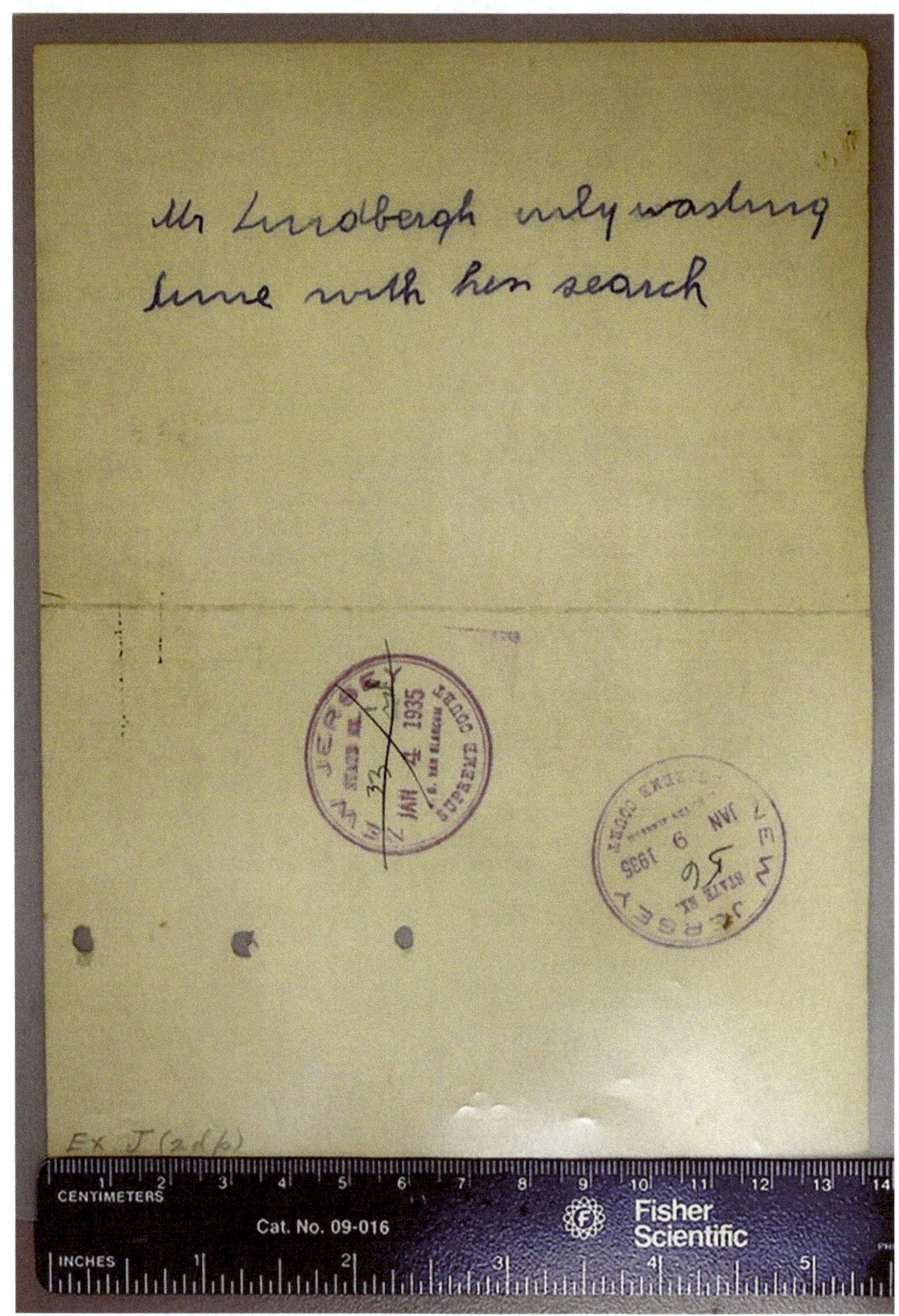

Mr Lindbergh only wasting
time with his search

Ex J (2d/c)

Ransom Letter #10 verso. x1o = _____mm x1i = ____ mm x2o = ____mm x2i = ____mm

What it says:

Envelope for ransom letter #10

Ransom Letter #11 width: 136.5 mm height: 179.5 mm a = ___ mm b = ___ mm

dear Sir: It is note necessary to furnish any code. you and Mr. Lindbergh know our Program very well. We will keep the child on our save plase until we have the money in hand, but if the deal is note closed until the 8 of April we will ask for 30000 more. - also note 70000 - 100000.

how can Mr. Lindbergh follow so many false clues he knows we are the right party our singnature is still the same as on the ransom note. But if Mr. Lindbergh likes to fool around for another month. - we can help it.

once he has to come to us anyway but if he keeps on waiting we will double our amount. there is absolute no fear about the child it is well.

Ex L2

CENTIMETERS Cat. No. 09-016 Fisher Scientific INCHES

x1o = _____mm x1i = ____ mm x2o = ____mm x2i = ____mm Ransom Letter #11

What it says:

Envelope for Ransom Letter #11

Ransom Letter #12 width:137 mm height: 178 mm a = ___ mm b = ____ mm

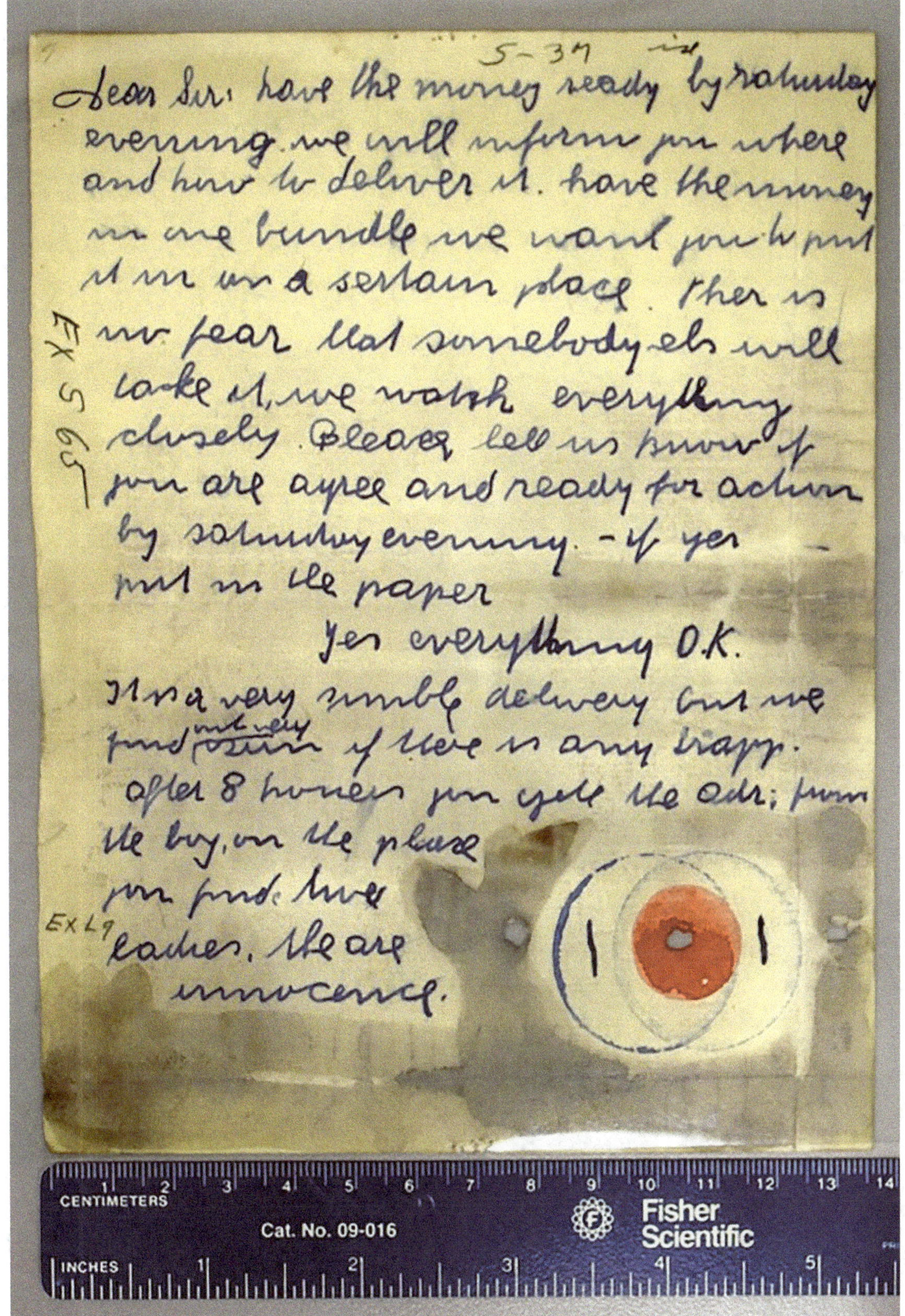

5-37

Dear Sir: have the money ready by saturday
evening. we will inform you where
and how to deliver it. have the money
in one bundle we want you to put
it in on a sertain place. ther is
no fear that somebody els will
take it, we watch everything
closely. Please let us know if
you are agree and ready for action
by saturday evening. - if yes
put in the paper
Yes everything O.K.
It is a very simple delivery but we
find out very soon if there is any trapp.
after 8 houers you gett the adr: from
the boy, on the place
you find two
ladies. the are
innocence.

EX 59

EX L9

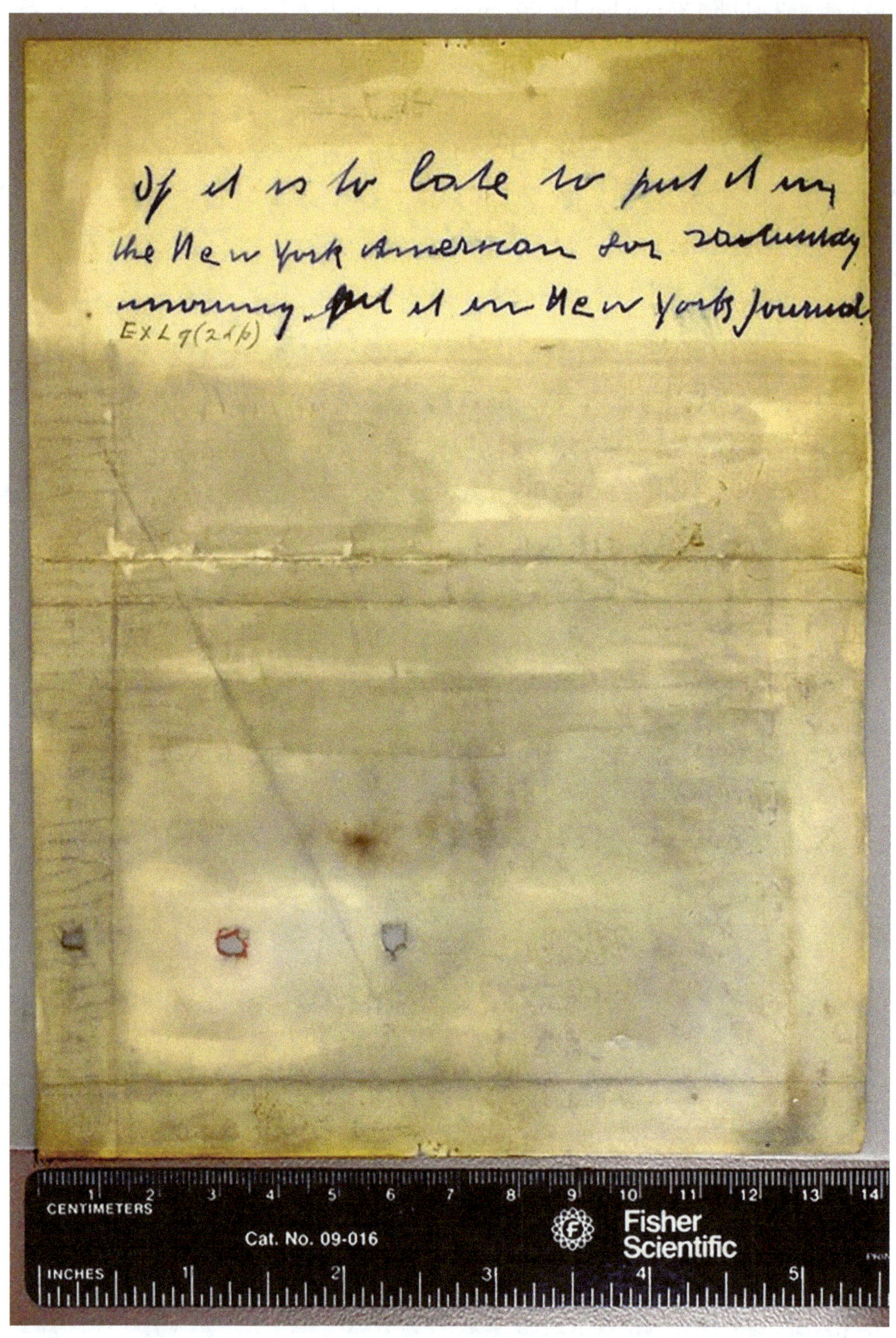

If it is to late to put it in
the New York American for saturday
morning. put it in New York Journal
EXL 9(2 of p)

x1o . __mm x1i = ___ mm x2o = ___ mm x2i = ___ mm Ransom Letter #12 (verso)

What it says:

Envelope for Ransom Letter #12

Ransom Letter #13 width: 137 mm height: 177. mm a = __ mm b = ___ mm

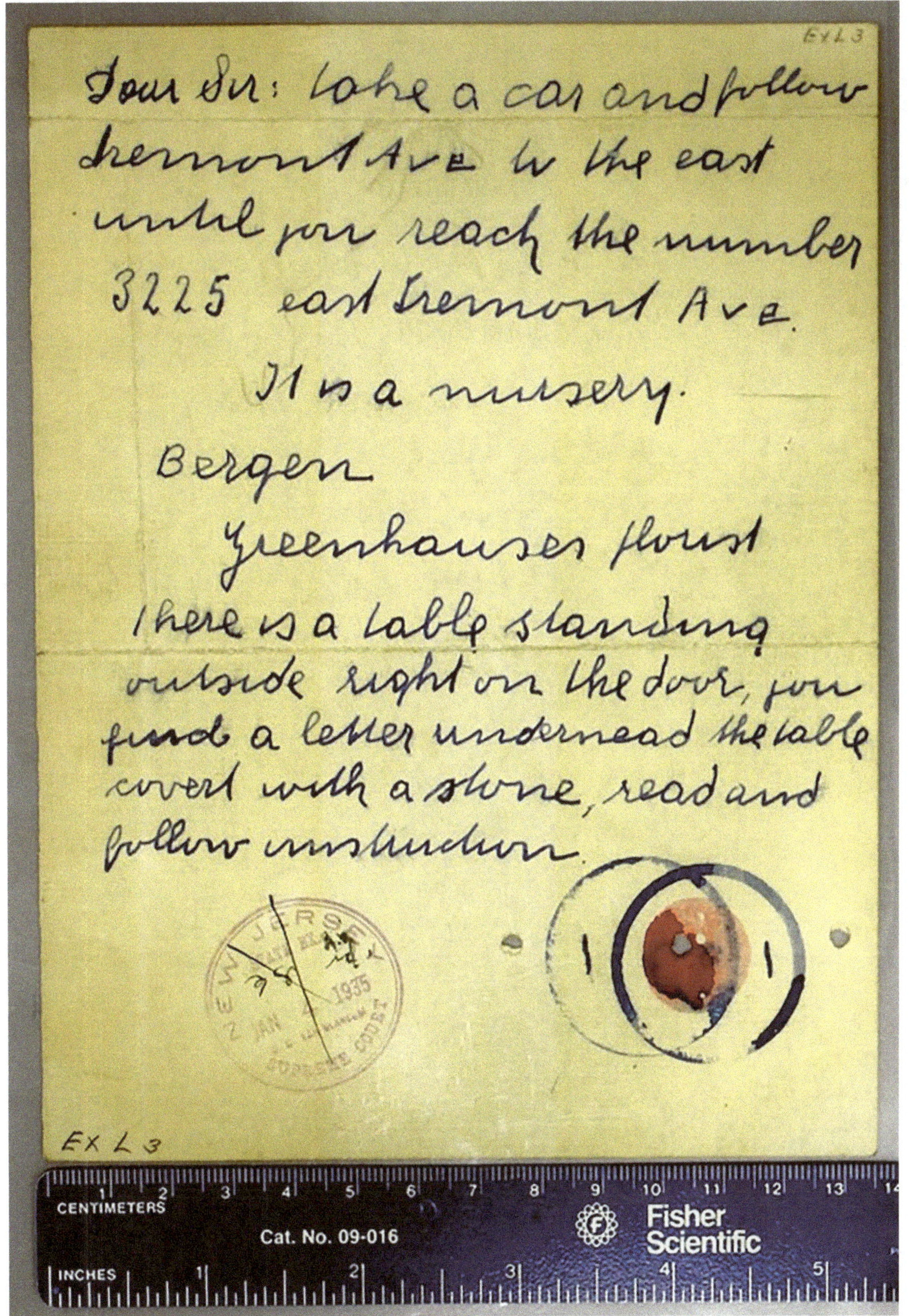

ExL3

Dear Sir: take a car and follow
tremont Ave to the east
until you reach the number
3225 east tremont Ave.

It is a nursery.

Bergen

greenhauses florist

there is a table standing
outside right on the door, you
find a letter underneat the table
covert with a stone, read and
follow instruction.

NEW JERSEY ... 1935 ... SUPREME COURT

EX L3

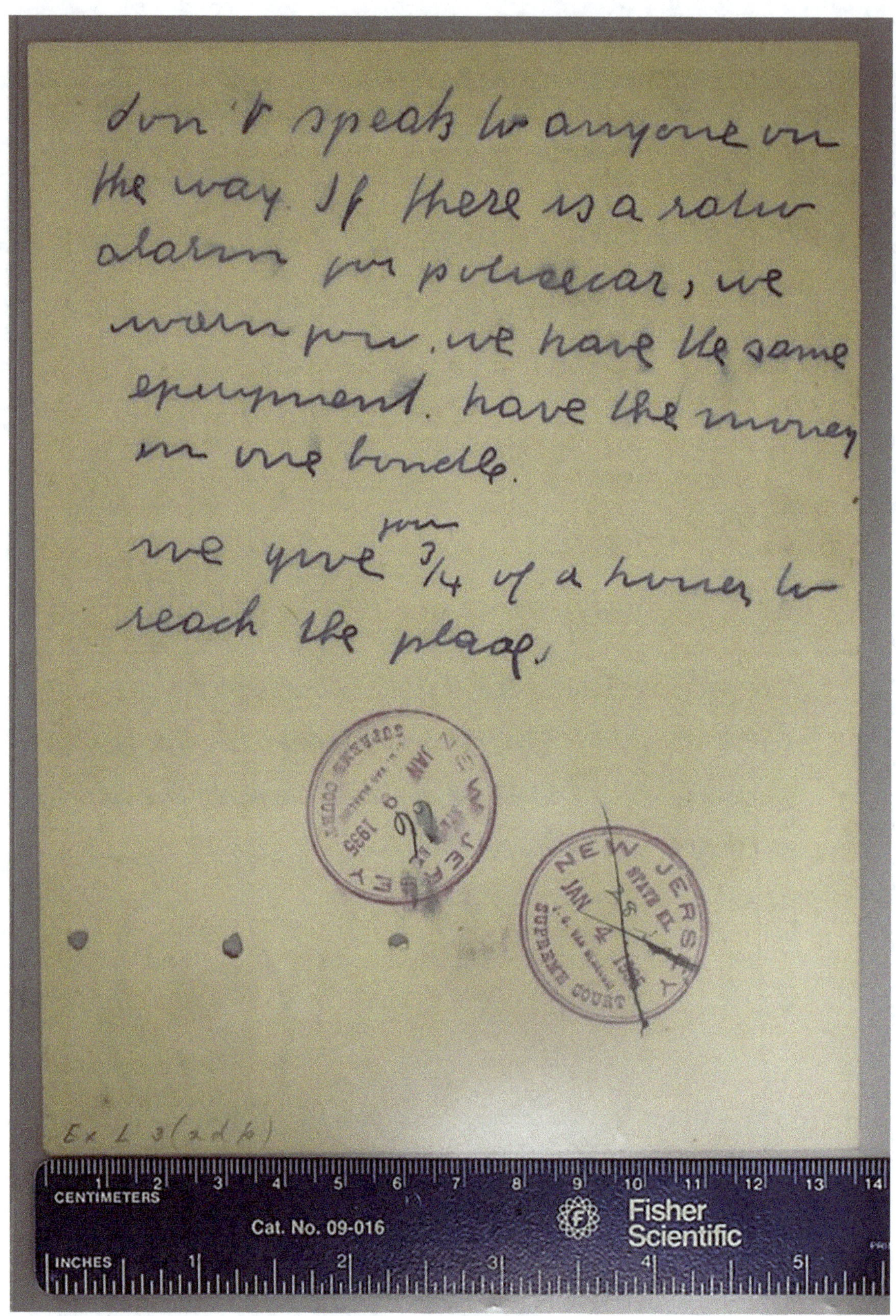

don't speak to anyone on
the way. If there is a ratio
alarm for policecar, we
warn you. we have the same
equipment. have the money
in one bundle.

we give you 3/4 of a houer to
reach the place.

x1o = ____ mm x1i = ___ mm x2o = ___ mm x2i = ___ mm Ransom Letter #13

What it says:

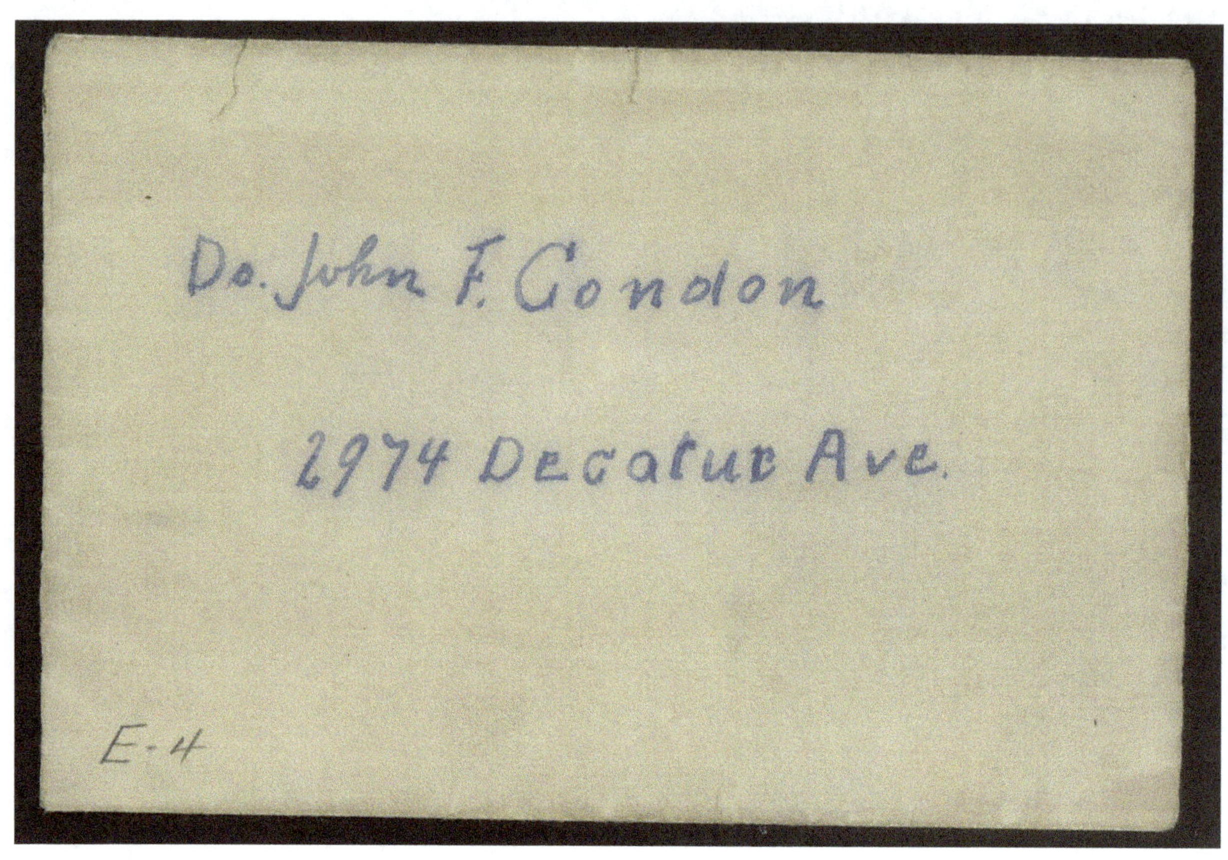

Do. John F. Condon

2974 Decatur Ave.

E-4

Envelope for Ransom Letter #13

Ransom Letter #14 width: 136 mm height: 178 mm a = ___ mm b = ___ mm

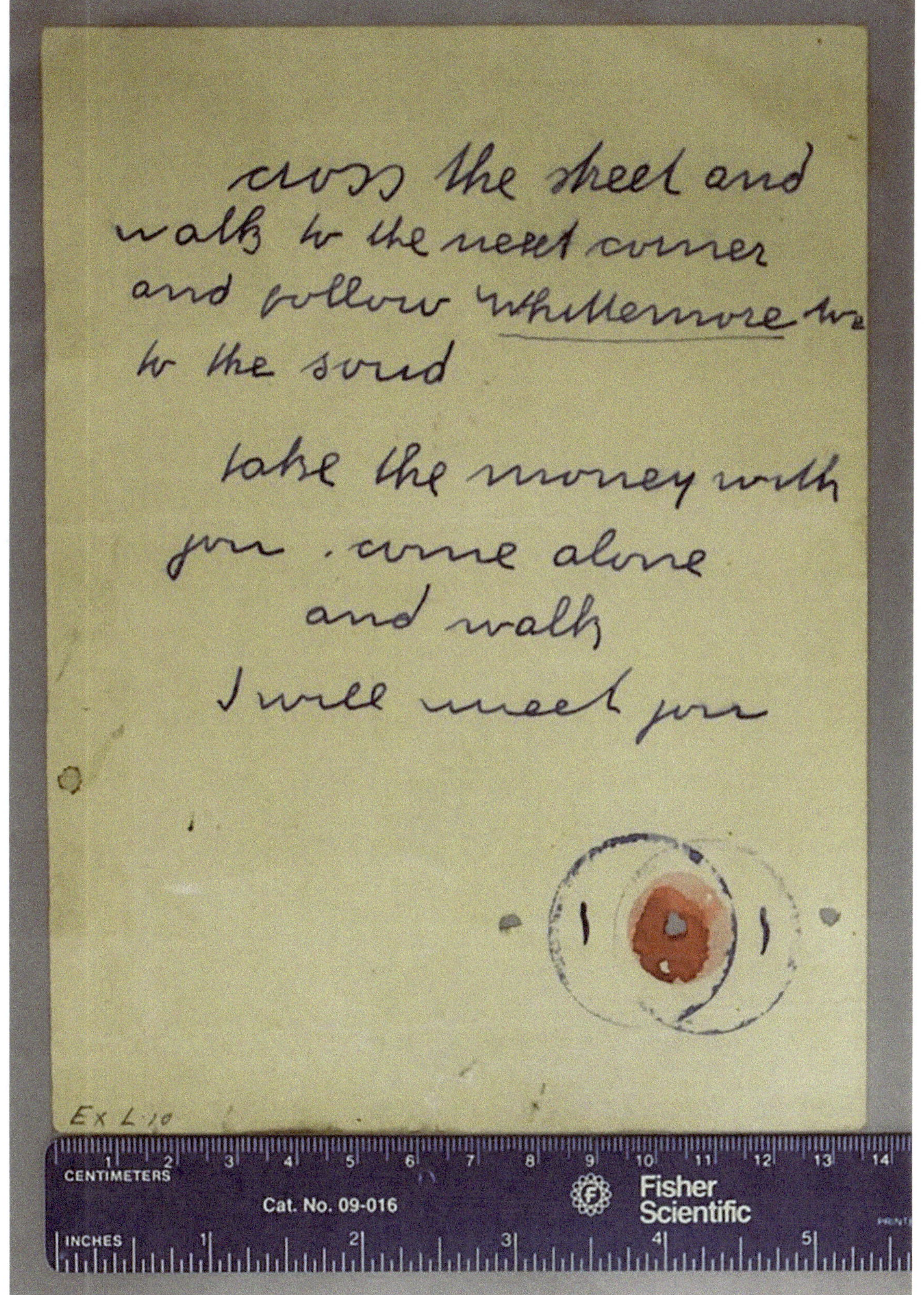

cross the sheet and
walk to the next corner
and follow Whittemore Av
to the soud

take the money with
you . come alone
and walk
I will meet you

Ex L-10

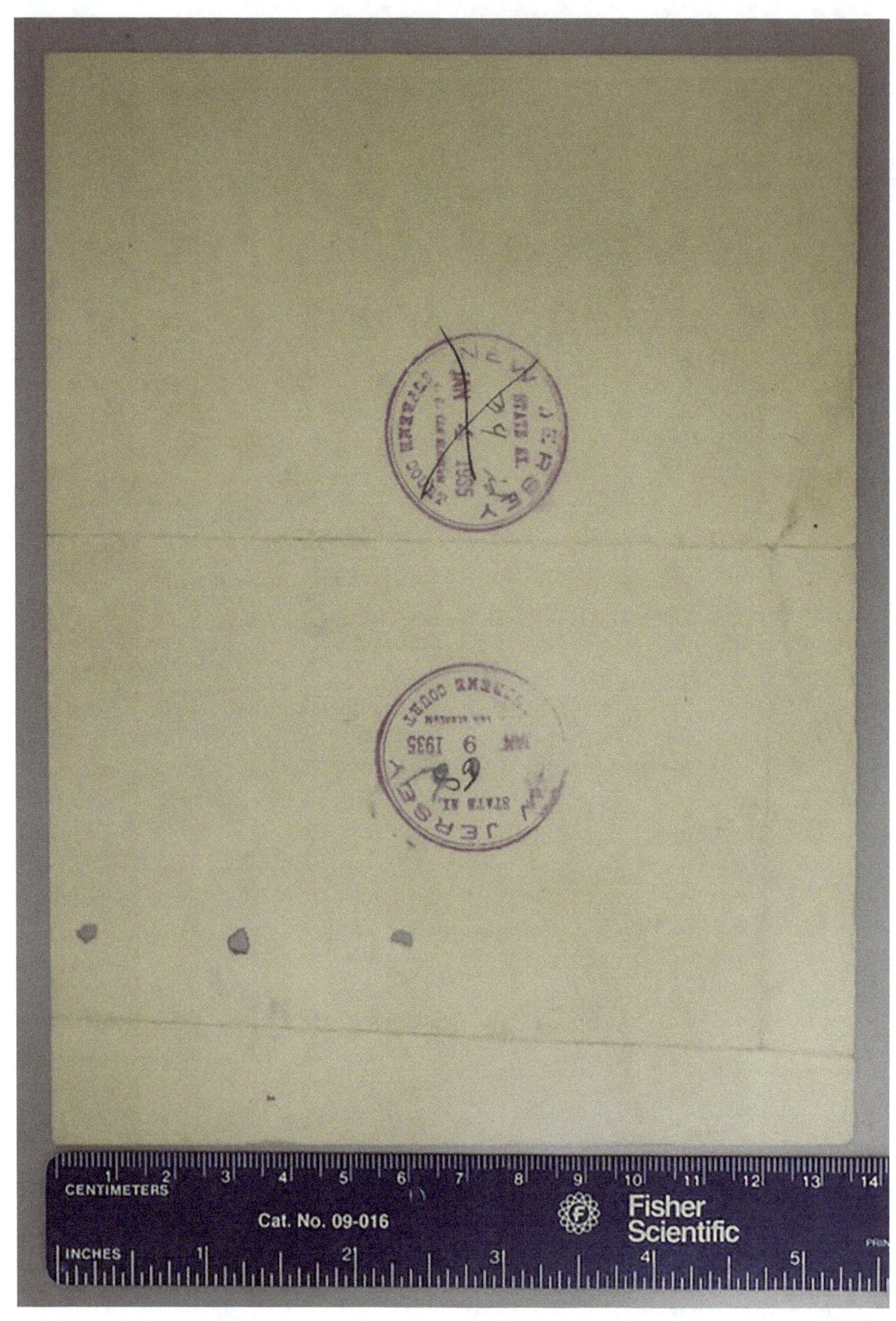

x1o = ___ mm x1i = ___ mm x2o =___ mm x2i = ___ mm. ransom letter #14 (verso)

What it says:

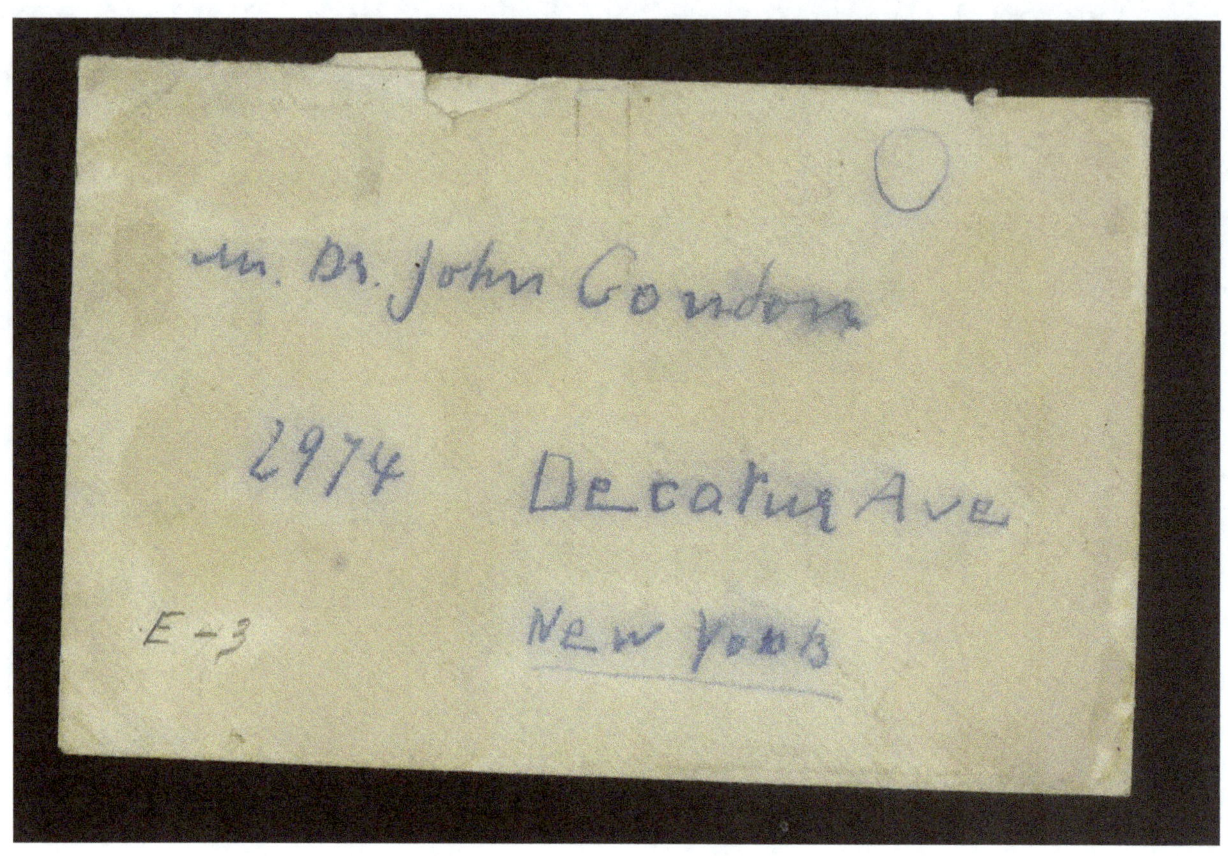

Envelope for Ransom Letter #14

Ransom letter #15 width: 158 mm height: 127 mm a = ___ mm b = ____ mm

No singnature; no holes

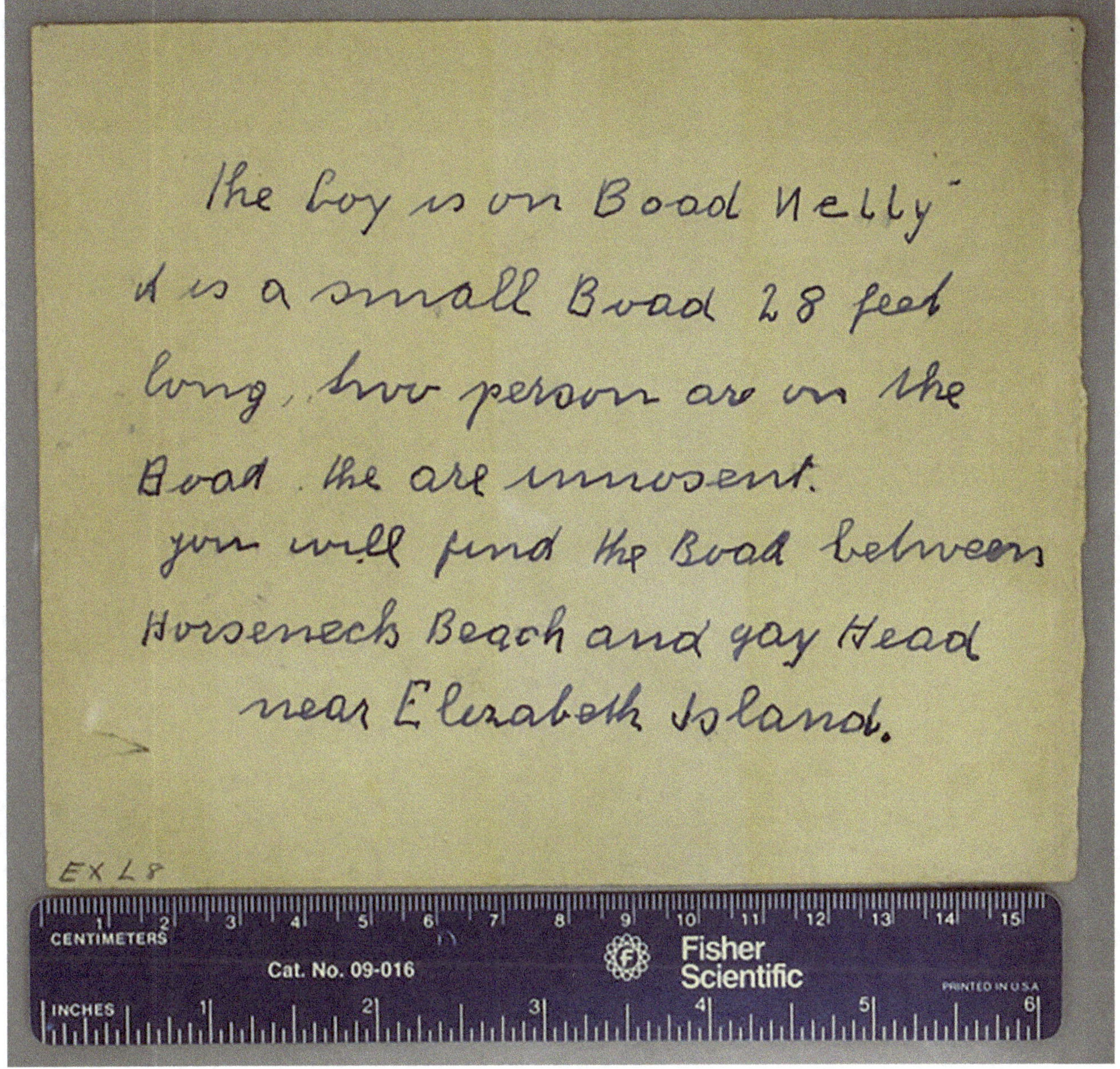
the boy is on Boad Nelly"
it is a small Boad 28 feet
long. two person are on the
Boad. the are innosent.
you will find the Boad between
Horseneck Beach and gay Head
near Elizabeth Island.

EX L8

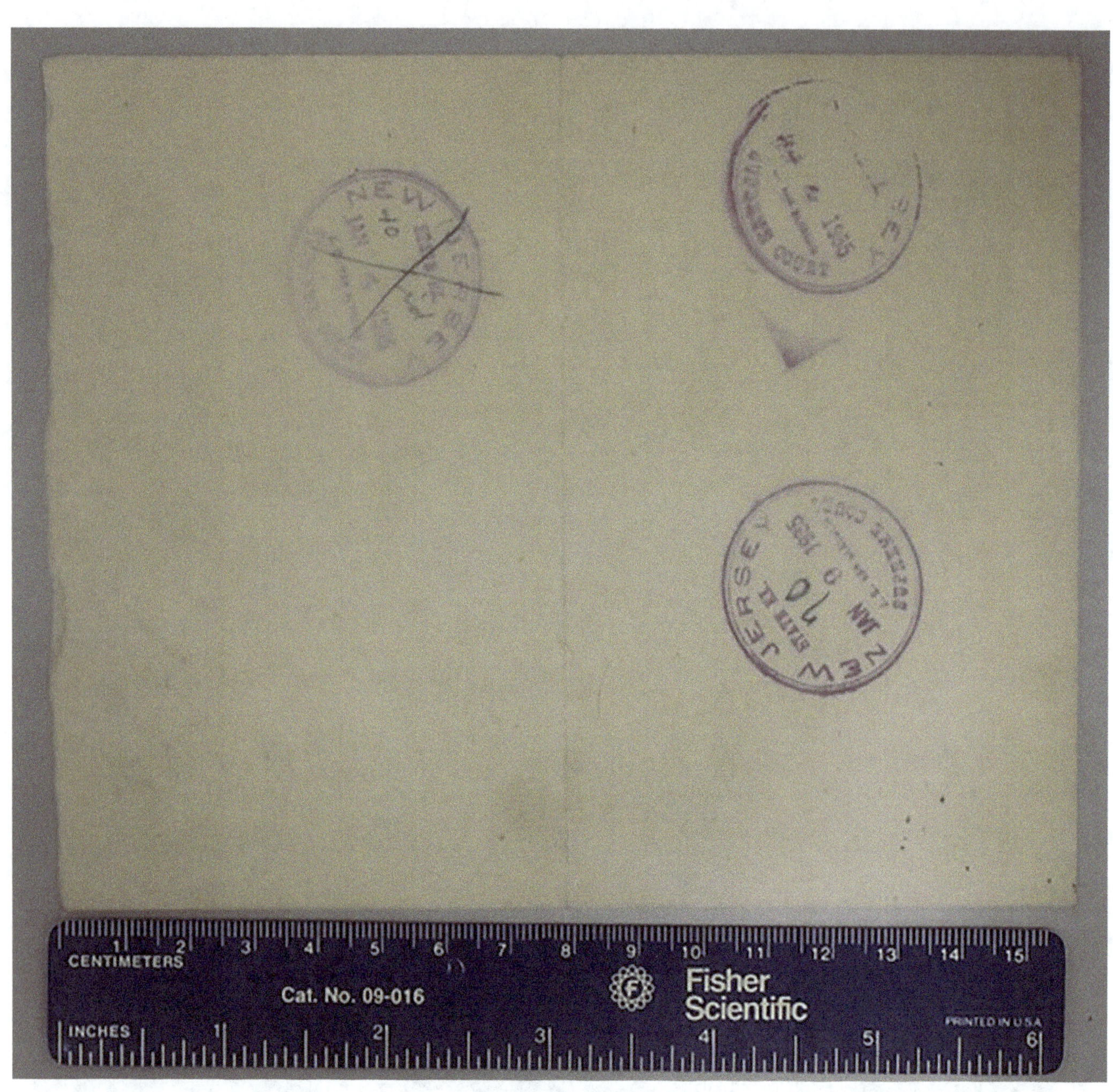

ransom letter #15 (verso)

What it says:

16F. Analysis of Measurements

16F1. The Paper they Wrote on

One of the first things that may catch your eye as you look over the actual ransom letters is that they are not on 8 ½ in. x 11 in. paper, the kind used in computer printers and copiers. But then, since it was nice stationery (two different kinds/styles), probably letter stationery, perhaps it came in various sizes. This was a time when people wrote letters to each other. The source of the paper might be a clue to who wrote them.

When I think about the writing of fifteen ransom letters, I don't imagine an organized mafia gang meeting in the back room of the Bada Bing Strip Club, each contributing to making sure there were spelling errors, errors in the creation of letters, etc. I imagine that it was a few (or less) people sitting around a kitchen table. When they needed an envelope, they would go to that "junk drawer" that everyone has in their dining room, with left-over Christmas cards and mismatched envelopes, perhaps some stationery, some pens, a few stamps, stuff that the family couldn't bear to throw away. Everybody had and probably still has one (or more) of these drawers. So, let us start with the paper itself. There are two kinds of paper in this set of 15 letters, and at least one page (or envelope) had a visible watermark on it, "Fifth Avenue," which was a brand of stationery that Woolworth's sold. That watermark was on the envelope of ransom letter #6.

I attempted to measure the size of each ransom letter. These are my results:

Table 16F1.1: Ransom Letter Sizes

Height x Width	Group
letter 1 176 x 157 mm	A
letter 2 176.5 x 157 mm	A
letter 3 178 x 156 mm	A
letter 4 178 x 157.5 mm	A
letter 5 167.5 x 135 mm	B
letter 6 178 x 158.5 mm	A
letter 7 177.5 x 157 mm	A
letter 8 179.5 x 157 mm	A
letter 9 178 x 137 mm	B
letter 10 179 x 135.5 mm	B
letter 11 179 x 136 mm	B
letter 12 179.5 x 136 mm	B
letter 13 177.5 x 135.5 mm	B
letter 14 180.5 x 135 mm	B
letter 15 159 x 125 mm	C

I measured directly with a ruler that gave me an answer in mm. If you'd prefer to know the values in inches, you can take my values in mm, then convert them to inches. I found for you a web calculator that converts into fractional inches, which most calculators won't do:

(https://www.rapidtables.com/convert/length/mm-to-inch.html).

That is, while a decimal equivalent in inches is correct, such as 4.25 inches, you may be more comfortable with that number reported as 4 ¼ inches.

I've made this set of measurements (and all others as well) multiple times. There are some values on each of the letters that are from a different set. I wanted to share those with you as well. It's a fact that, when you measure these letters trying to get millimeter precision, it's difficult and there is no single value. It depends in part on where you measure. The paper sizes can be irregular. Nonetheless, the trends are all consistent.

The values reported on the letters were also calculated using the rulers in the photos. The table (above) values were from the direct measurement (Table 16F1.1) and are hopefully more accurate. I believe the numbers I report here are within 1.5 mm of the real value because the width may depend on where on each letter it was measured. Also, the pen I used to determine ransom letter dimensions in Section 16E had a pen stroke width of almost 1 mm.

I'd like to show you how valuable *graphing* data can be. Keep in mind, for this I measured values in mm. It is difficult to measure in mm, because 1 mm is so small, and there is almost always a range of values because of a rough edge on the paper, so the width could be off by a mm. A few of the dimensions, such as for #5 and #15 suggests a different size paper. Ransom notes #5 and #15 are also similar because they do not have singnatures on them. Perhaps the writers didn't have what they needed with them to match the paper size and create a singnature. It's also useful to be sure that there are no incorrect numbers that stand out because of their magnitude. (For example, if all the values are around 7 inches and one measurement is less than an inch, or 100 inches, you might want to remeasure.) You can save time by making sure you have plausible numbers before you use them for anything. I did my best in this regard, making replicate measurements.

16F.2. Paper Size

I graphed all the letter dimensions, with height on the x (horizontal) axis and width on the y (vertical) axis. This is the result, using a simple X-Y graph.

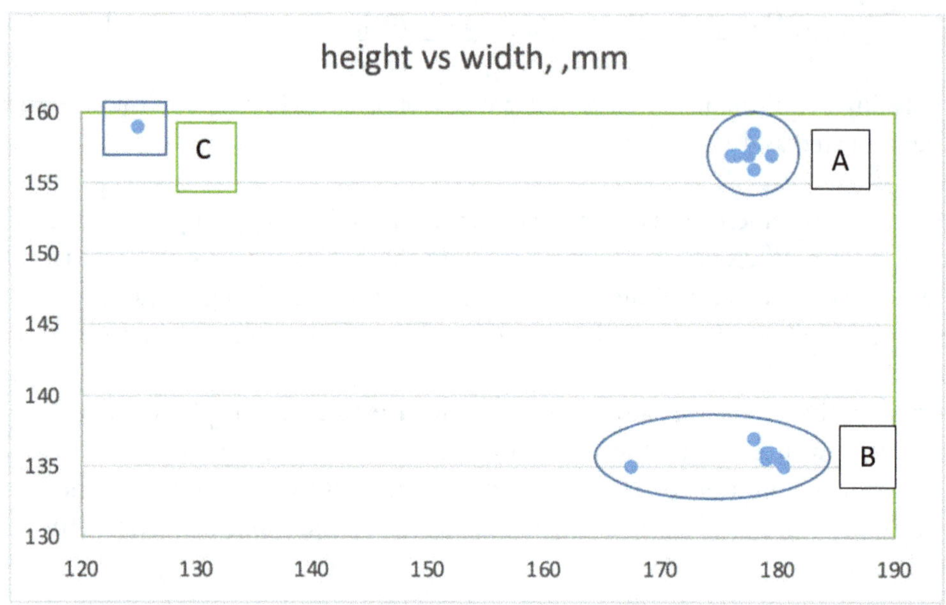

Figure 16F2.1: A Graph of Height vs. Width of each Ransom Letter.

Graphing the data is very useful. Here you can see that the points fall into three groups, (marked as A, B and C on Figure 16F2.1) indicating three different sized paper.

I report below, averages of the height and width for the three letter sizes, as well as converting some of them into inches.

Avg values.	height (mm)		width (mm)		values in inches
A avg	177.6.	x	157.1	=	6.99 in. x 6.18 in.
B avg	177.3	x	135.7	=	6.98 in x 5.41 in.
C avg	125.	x	159	=	4.92 in x 6.26 in

Q16F2.1: Is there a standard size of paper that is 7 inches by something larger than 6.18 inches, such that it could be cut once and give us a 6.99 x 6.18-inch page to write on?

A16F2.1: You should understand how the standard sizes of paper are created.

16F.3. Making Paper / Paper Dimensions

There are many standard sizes of paper that have specific uses, from business cards to posters. Paper is made/ cut today based on a variety of standards.

We'll start with dimensions of the A series paper sizes. The dimensions, as defined by the ISO 216 standard and are given in the table below the diagram in both millimeters and inches (cm measurements can be obtained by dividing mm values by 10). The A Series paper size chart, below, gives a visual representation of how the sizes relate to each other - for example, A5 is half of A4 size paper, and A2 (595 mm x 420 mm) is half of A1 (594 x 841 mm) size paper. Please see the ISO entry in ALLISONweb for additional details.

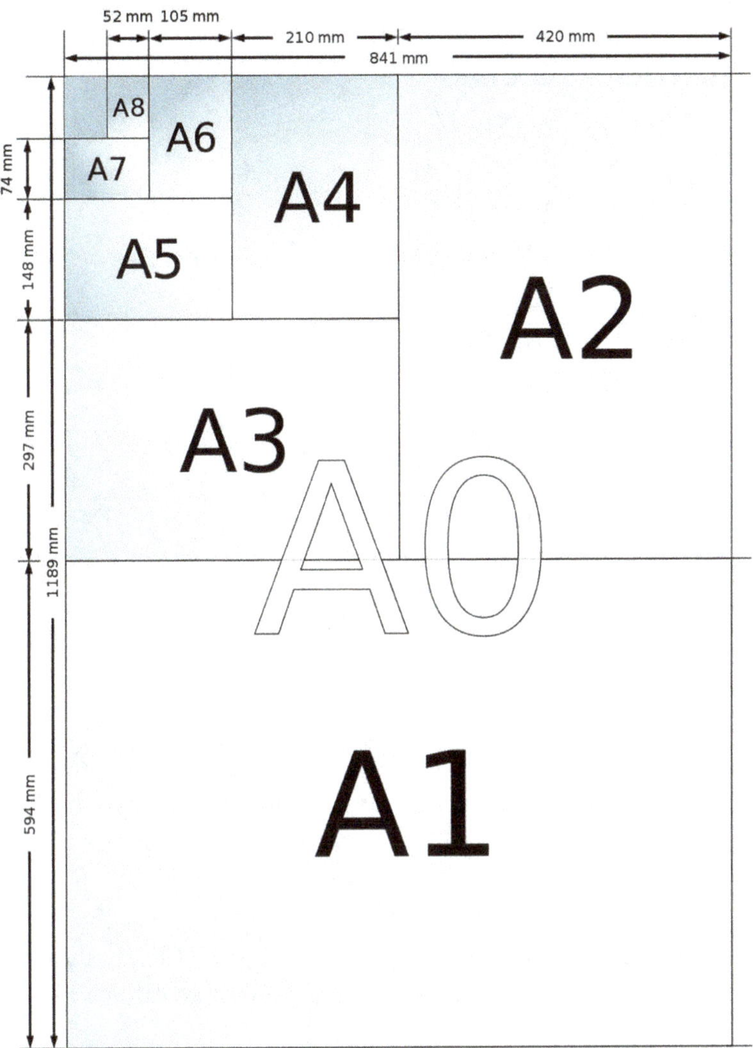

Figure 16F3.1: A Paper Sizes (www.papersizes.org/a-paper-sizes.htm)

All the A sizes have something in common, the length divided by the width is 1.4142, which is the square root of 2. That is, 1.4142 x 1.4142 = 2.

There is a less common series, the B series. The area of B series sheets is the average of successive A series sheets. So, B1 is between A0 and A1 in size, with an area of 0.707 m^2 (1 over the square root of two). As a result, B0 is 1 meter wide, and other sizes in the B series are a half, a quarter or further fractions of a meter wide. While less common in office use, B size paper is used for special applications. Posters use B-series paper or a close approximation.

The C series of standard paper sizes is commonly used for envelopes and is defined in ISO 269. The area of C series sheets is the average of the areas of the A and B series sizes of the same number. The area of a C3 sheet is the average of the areas of an A3 sheet and a B3 sheet. This means that C3 is slightly larger than A3, and slightly smaller than B3. Practically, this means that a letter written on A3 paper fits inside a C3 envelope, and C3 page fits inside a B3 envelope.

Table 16F.3.2: Paper Sizes (*in mm)*

Size	A series	B Series	C Series
0	841x1189	1000x1414	917x1297
1	594x841	707x1000	648x917
2	420x594	500x707	458x648
3	297x420	353x500	324x458
4	210x297	250x353	229x324
5	148x210	176x250	162x229
6	105x148	125x176	114x162
7	74x105	88x125	81x114
8	52x74	62x88	57x81
9	37x52	44x62	40x57
10	26x37	31x44	28x40

16F.4. Back to the Ransom Letter Sizes

A popular dimension for many of the ransom letters was 7 inches (along one side). It appears that there is no A size paper with that as one of the dimensions, or B or C. However, some are close. For example, 5B sheets of paper are 6.93 x 9.84 inches. This *could* have been the initial size of paper used for writing the ransom notes.

Back to our graph. The data points cluster into three sets, as Figure 16F2.1. shows. While it may look like all the points are not shown, this is because some points have the same value and are on top of each other.

Some have suggested that these were not the original paper sizes, but they were cut from larger pieces of paper. The letters are written on good paper. Perhaps each started out as a piece of letterhead, and the person's information was cut off the "top". If this were the case, the cut edge would always be the same edge, assuming the paper was only cut once. It had been suggested, by Albert Osborn (reported in the "FBI Files") that if you look very closely, with a microscope, the ransom letters 1 and 2 were at one time a single piece of paper, because the cut edges of each fit together exactly at a microscopic level. Osborn suggested that a piece of paper was first folded, then torn apart to yield the paper used for #1 and #2. If this were the case, we should be looking for a source of paper that is initially 12 3/8 inches wide by 7 inches high. That's an odd shape for a piece of paper.

16F.5. Time for another trick

If you look at the edges of the ransom letters, one edge on each is rough, the "cut edge". For these, there is only one "cut" edge, and it is always the left or right edge, never the top or bottom (as you hold it to read). You may be trying to see if there are any odd variations along an edge, perhaps over a six- or seven-inch edge. It is much easier to compare the edge to a smaller dimension – any variation will be easier to see.

Figure 16F5.1 is the relatively unusual ransom letter # 3. If you look at the edges, I'd guess that the right edge had been cut – cut or ripped or torn or somehow separated from a second piece of paper.

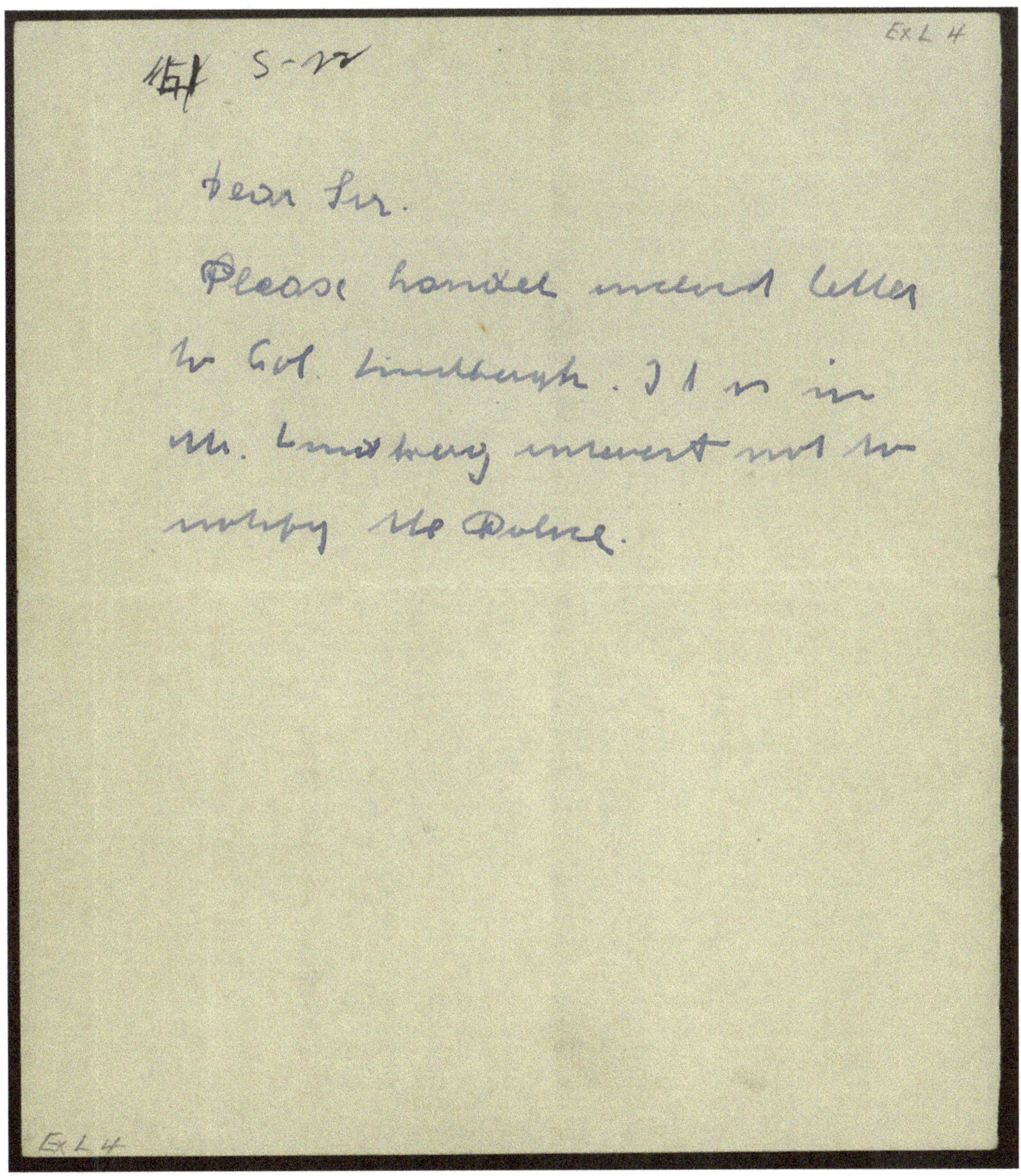

Ex L 4

Dear Sir.

Please handel inclosed letter to Col. Lindbergh. It is in Mr. Lindbergh interest not to notify the Police.

Ex L 4

Figure 16F.5.1. Ransom Letter #3

If you look down the edge, tilting the page, it is easier to see the wobble in the edge. Or, if you have a digital version of the image, you can compress it along that edge, making it much more obvious that this was a torn edge.

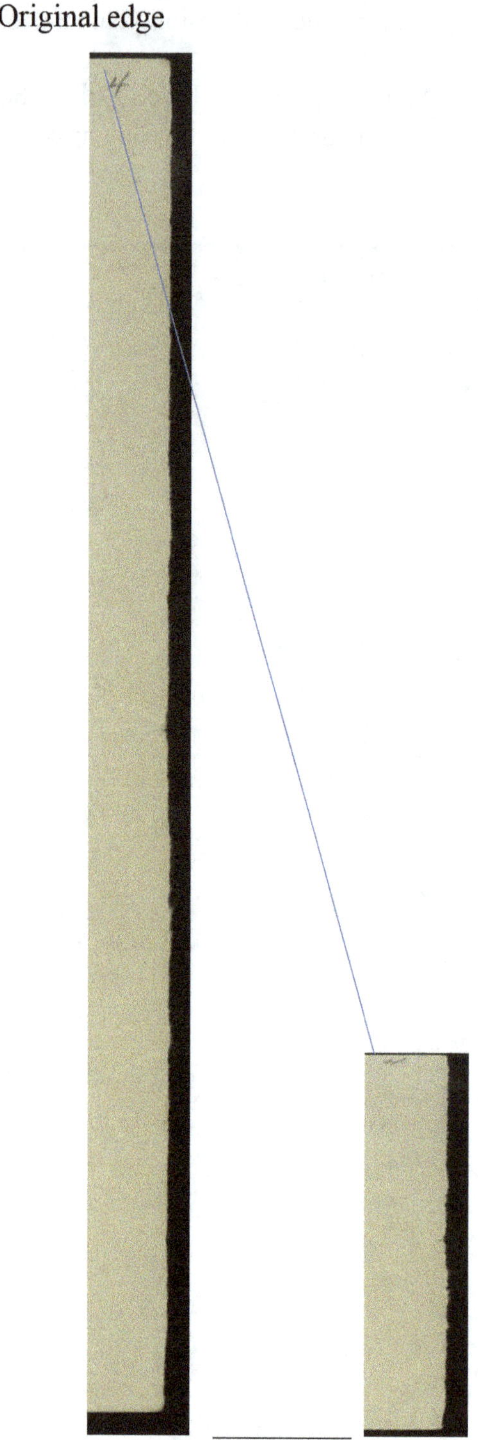

Figure 16F.5.2. The right edge was a torn edge.

Some of the ransom notes were cut on the left side, as you hold it to read, and some on the right side. I've sorted them by side-modified. The first thing to look for is which ones were cut or torn. Then I squeezed the images down to make alterations to the edges easier to see. Next, have any of them once been together as a single page? If so, the cuts should not be identical but be complimentary images of each other. I don't see any matches.

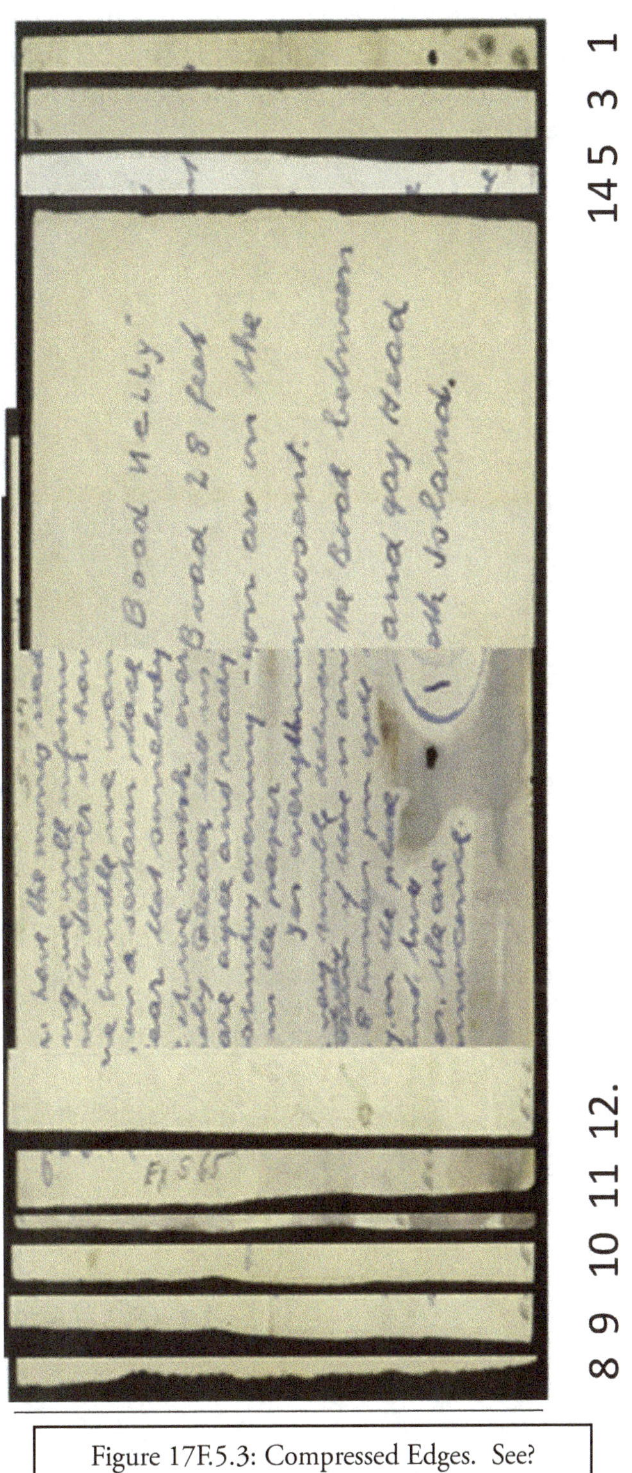

Figure 17F.5.3: Compressed Edges. See?

For the ones that we have, it appears that no two were together at one time, so perhaps they were cut off larger paper, but only by a single cut/tear. Some of them are very crudely cut, such as letter #9.

Q16F.5.1: Which choices that are presented above would not be a good choice to consider and why? That is, considering that some of the edges look cut and perhaps some ripped, which is most likely, or should we assume multiple mechanisms for cutting were used?
A16F.5.1: Figure it out! Take a piece of paper, preferably some good paper used for letter-writing, and divide the piece of paper into two pieces. Use a straight-edge and tear along it. Then cut with scissors. Cut along a straight edge with a razor blade or knife. Consider some likely possibilities and decide if the rough edges that we see correspond to any of your methods for dividing one piece of paper into two. Each method probably leaves a signature pattern. List them here.

Observations:

Torn paper:

Cut with Scissors:

Cut with Knife:

Cut with razor blade:

Other:

Again, a popular dimension for many of the ransom notes was 7 inches (along one side). It appears that there is no A size paper with that as one of the dimensions (or B or C). However, some are close. For example, 5B sheets of paper are 6.93 x 9.84 inches (we'll call it 7 x 10 in). This could have been the size paper used, with one cut, removing 4 inches off the side shown.

Figure 16F5.4: Making a 7 inch x 6 inch page

Searching using Google Images, I found a watercolor painting that was on a piece of watercolor paper that had one dimension of seven inches. I did a search of "watercolor 7 in x " in Google Images, and found that 7 inches was a common dimension on many small watercolors such as:

a. *Window Box on Royal Street*, Watercolor on paper
   Joan Dagradi, 7 in x 5 in
b. *Foothills Farm,* Watercolor on paper
   Mary Ann Valvoda, 7 in x 9 ¾ in.
c. *Cow Boy*, Watercolor, (Whidbey Art Gallery, Langley, WA)
   Judi Nyerges 7 in x 10 in.

These led to my finding that even though "regular" paper is not routinely made/sold with this unusual dimension, some watercolor paper is. Here are a few examples, of paper with one edge being seven inches, that I found.

1. Bee Paper Company
   Aquabee Landscape Sketch
   Esquisse – 50 sheet pad, Natural White Sheet, "Dual Sized"
   7" x 15" (17.78 x 38.10 cm)
   This is interesting. When I said that Ransom notes #1 and #2 were initially together, and that would mean the original page was 12 3/8 by 7 inches, I considered that this commercially available paper, made for artists, could have been converted into two letters. This Bee paper is 7 inches by more than 6 inches, so the original could have been 7" x 15", large enough to make two letters, but not like this:

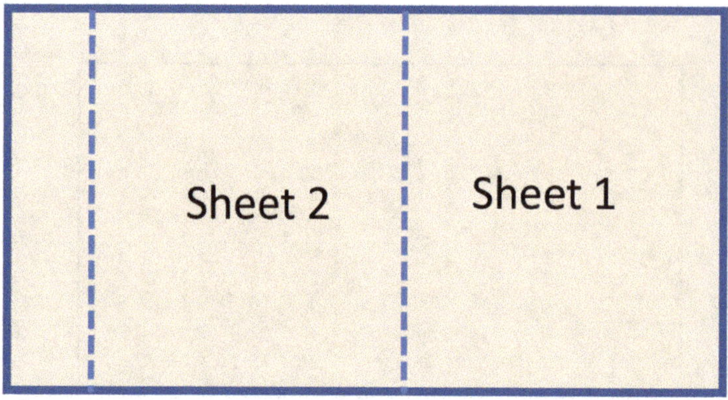

Figure 16F5.5: Wrong way to cut out two ransom letters

Sheet 1 is fine, but Sheet 2 has two cut edges, which we've not seen in the set. However, if I cut a piece out of the middle, roughly 3 inches wide, I'd have two 7 in x 6 in sheets, each having only one cut edge.

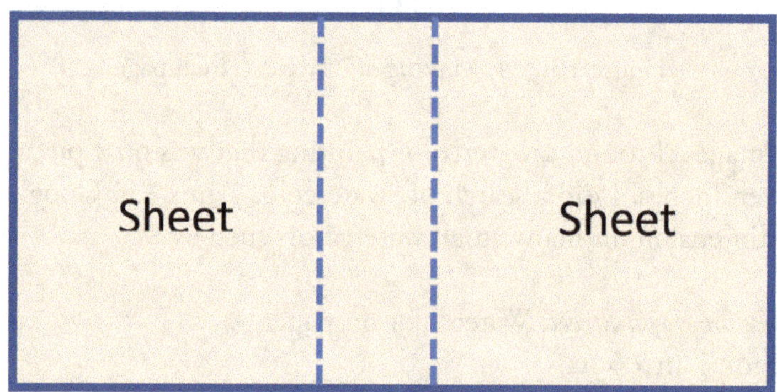

Figure 16F5.6: Correct way to get 2 Ransom Letters From one page.

2. Handcrafted Genuine Leather Antique Traveler Journal with Parchment Paper (5" x 7") Lewis and Clark Series by Viatori.

I find this interesting – considering the possibility that the paper was originally pages in a book or journal that had to be cut out. There is a problem with the size of the pages here since most of the letters were more than five inches wide. Still, I like the idea.

3. V&A (Victoria and Albert Museum, London) – B5 Notebooks – ruled or blank; 80 pages each, 7 x 10" (176 x 250 mm) One could cut one page and make one ransom note, retaining the 7-inch dimension.

4. Pentalic Acid-free paper Sketch book; wire-bound; heavyweight, 80 sheets 70 lb. paper, 7 inches x 7 inches. Most of the ransom letters could have been made from a sketchbook like this because the width was almost always less than 7 inches.

5. Pentalithic Field Book; wire-bound, watercolor; 7 in x 10 in. 24 sheets, 140 lb. paper. Another possible choice.

6. ARCHES, Watercolor Paper book, Cold Pressed 140 lb. 15 sheets, 10 x 7 in (260 x 180 mm) 100% cotton

There are at least two types of paper that were used in the ransom letters, both linen-type paper. Perhaps someone was purposely mixing up the paper type to further confuse Police.

The paper I found here was interesting but watercolor paper tends to be heavier than writing paper- clearly different.

16F.6. Other Possible Leads

I tried to find as many products as I could from Woolworth's 5 and 10 Cent Store – they were everywhere in the 1930s. Woolworth's sold small books on interesting current topics – sometimes educational, sometimes how-to books. I don't know if they had blank pages in them, but it appears that the pages are the same size as some of the ransom notes. If there was a blank page in the back, they may have cut the blank page out and used it.

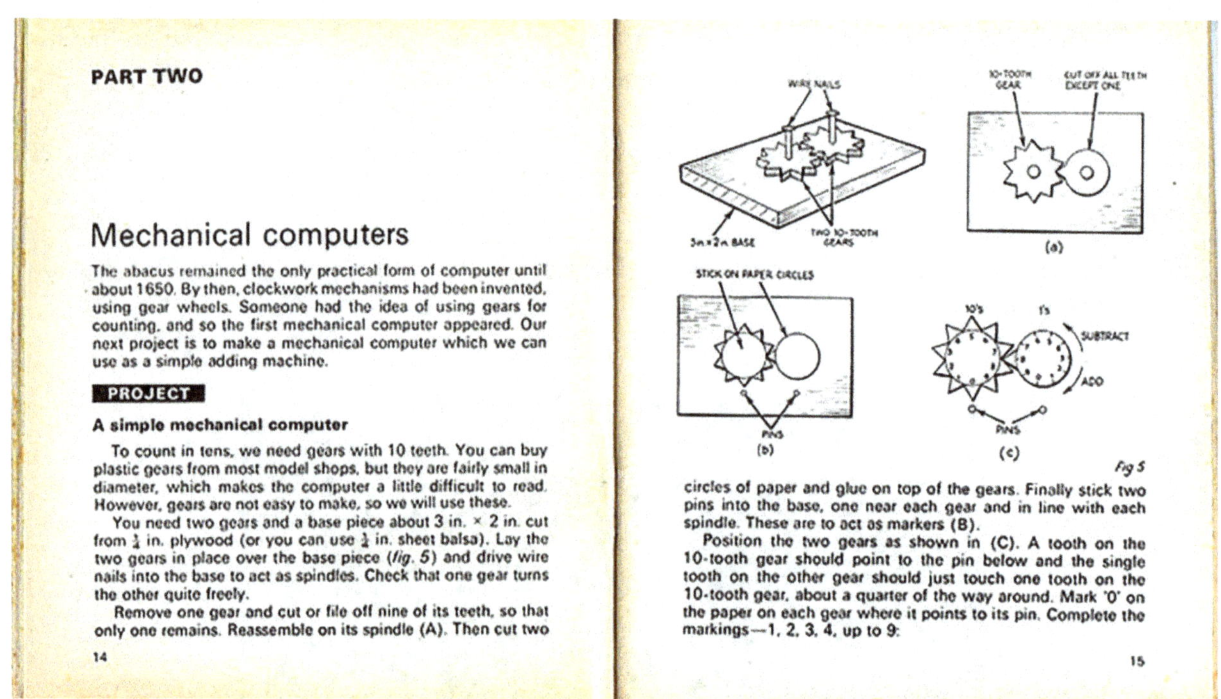

PART TWO

Mechanical computers

The abacus remained the only practical form of computer until about 1650. By then, clockwork mechanisms had been invented, using gear wheels. Someone had the idea of using gears for counting, and so the first mechanical computer appeared. Our next project is to make a mechanical computer which we can use as a simple adding machine.

PROJECT

A simple mechanical computer

To count in tens, we need gears with 10 teeth. You can buy plastic gears from most model shops, but they are fairly small in diameter, which makes the computer a little difficult to read. However, gears are not easy to make, so we will use these.

You need two gears and a base piece about 3 in. × 2 in. cut from ¼ in. plywood (or you can use ¼ in. sheet balsa). Lay the two gears in place over the base piece (*fig. 5*) and drive wire nails into the base to act as spindles. Check that one gear turns the other quite freely.

Remove one gear and cut or file off nine of its teeth, so that only one remains. Reassemble on its spindle (A). Then cut two

14

circles of paper and glue on top of the gears. Finally stick two pins into the base, one near each gear and in line with each spindle. These are to act as markers (B).

Position the two gears as shown in (C). A tooth on the 10-tooth gear should point to the pin below and the single tooth on the other gear should just touch one tooth on the 10-tooth gear, about a quarter of the way around. Mark '0' on the paper on each gear where it points to its pin. Complete the markings—1, 2, 3, 4, up to 9:

15

Figure 16F.6.1: Inside a typical Woolworth book

Shown above are two pages from one of Woolworth's books on computers. A ransom letter was placed over a page, and it just fits. I don't know if there were any blank pages that could have been used from the back of the book.

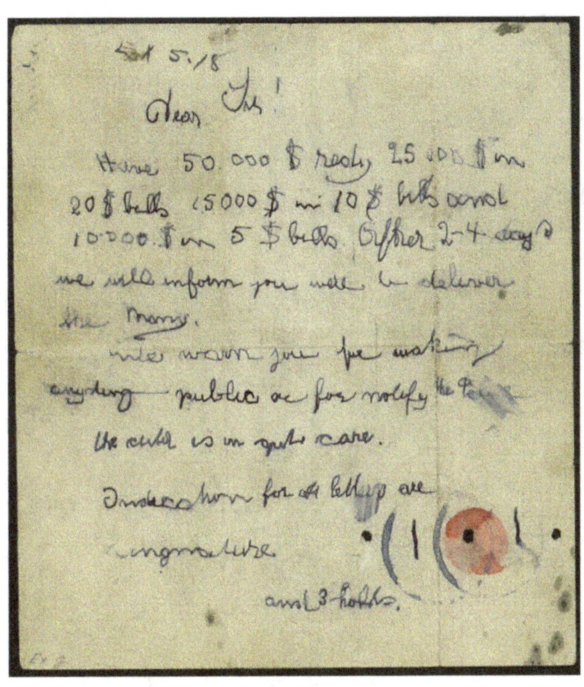

5/18

Dear Sir!

Have 50.000 $ redy 25 000 $ in 20 $ bills 15000 $ in 10 $ bills and 10.000 $ in 5 $ bills. After 2–4 days we will inform you were to deliver the mony.

We warn you for making anyding public or for notify the Po[illegible]

the child is in gute care.

Indication for all letters are singnature and 3 holes.

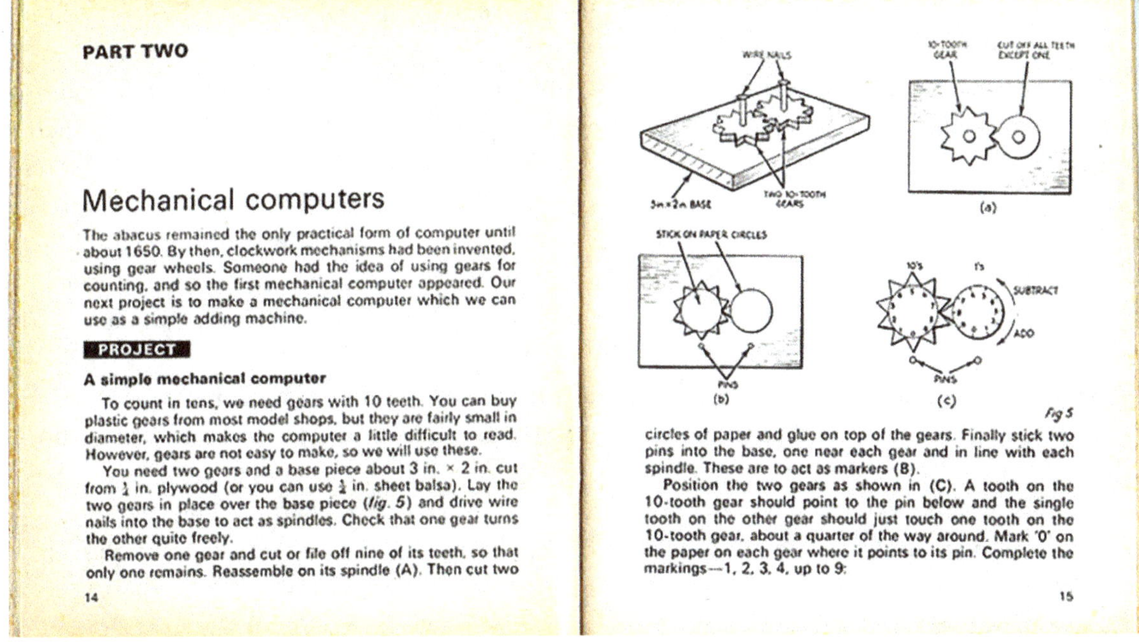

PART TWO

Mechanical computers

The abacus remained the only practical form of computer until about 1650. By then, clockwork mechanisms had been invented, using gear wheels. Someone had the idea of using gears for counting, and so the first mechanical computer appeared. Our next project is to make a mechanical computer which we can use as a simple adding machine.

PROJECT

A simple mechanical computer

To count in tens, we need gears with 10 teeth. You can buy plastic gears from most model shops, but they are fairly small in diameter, which makes the computer a little difficult to read. However, gears are not easy to make, so we will use these.

You need two gears and a base piece about 3 in. × 2 in. cut from ¼ in. plywood (or you can use ¼ in. sheet balsa). Lay the two gears in place over the base piece (*fig. 5*) and drive wire nails into the base to act as spindles. Check that one gear turns the other quite freely.

Remove one gear and cut or file off nine of its teeth, so that only one remains. Reassemble on its spindle (A). Then cut two

14

circles of paper and glue on top of the gears. Finally stick two pins into the base, one near each gear and in line with each spindle. These are to act as markers (B).

Position the two gears as shown in (C). A tooth on the 10-tooth gear should point to the pin below and the single tooth on the other gear should just touch one tooth on the 10-tooth gear, about a quarter of the way around. Mark '0' on the paper on each gear where it points to its pin. Complete the markings—1, 2, 3, 4, up to 9:

15

Figure 16F.6.2 A Ransom Letter Matches a Book Page

Suppose the ransom letters were cut out of a book, like a journal, where the pages were initially bound. If you look carefully at the ransom letters, some show a larger border on the torn side, with the author not being able to get as close to the inside edge that was perhaps intact when the note was written, and then cut out.

Here are two examples where the writing goes out close to one edge, but is not as close to the other, possibly suggesting that the pages were initially bound in a journal or book. The writing goes out to the right edge but not to the left side of the page. (Or, perhaps they were left-handed?)

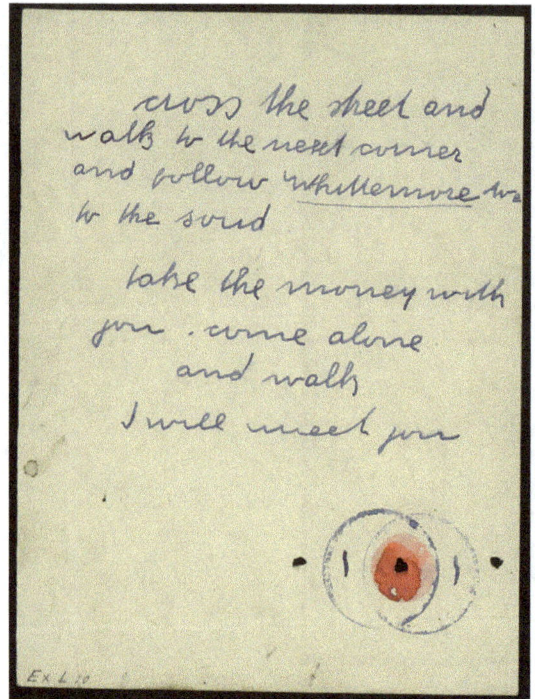

cross the street and
walk to the next corner
and follow Whittemore Av
to the soud

take the money with
you. come alone
and walk
I will meet you

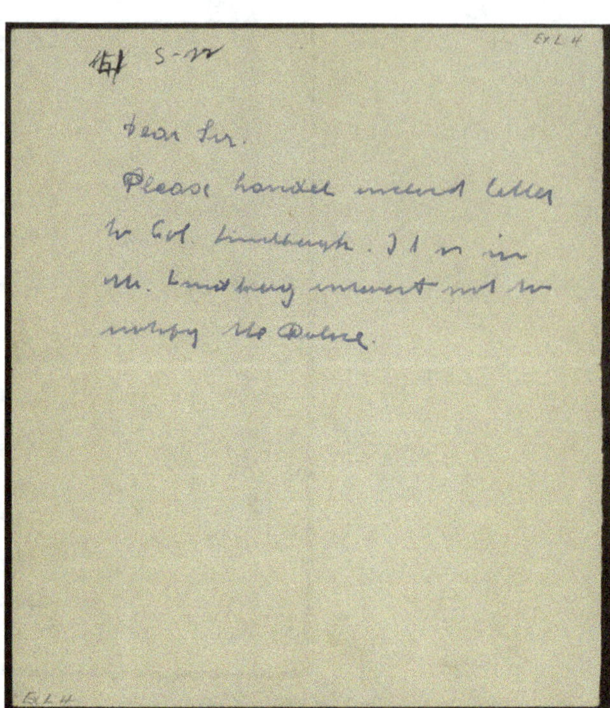

Dear Sir.

Please handel incl. letter
to Col. Lindbergh. It is in
Mr. Lindbergh interest not to
notify the Police.

Figure 16F.6.3: Why is the text shifted to the right?

So, for 14 out of the 15 ransom letters, I believe they could be explained as pages initially in a bound journal (not ruled) in which the pages were 7 in. high and more than 6.3 in wide, but not an artist's sketchbook or watercolor paper.

One final point: Not only did Albert Osborn observe that the first two ransom letters were written on one sheet of paper that had been torn in half, he also reported that both letters had been inserted into envelopes with the same Fifth Avenue watermark. I could only find one envelope with the Fifth Avenue watermark.

I should say a few things about watermarks. I had the opportunity to read several correspondences regarding watermarks on the ransom letters. Apparently the first two ransom letters had watermarks. One had a *KR* on it and the other, *ONE*. Put together, the watermark was *KRETONE*. The General Manager of the Hopper Paper Co. in Illinois reported that it was their paper/their watermark on the letters. They would sell it to the Sangamon Co., also in Illinois, "who are converters". They converted the paper into envelopes and writing paper for the S.S. Kresge Company (main office – Detroit). Kresge had a warehouse in Brooklyn, from where they would distribute to stores in their district.

"The sheet of paper is 5 3/8 inches wide and 7 inches long. It is apparently one half of an ordinary folded sheet of writing paper which had been torn into two pieces," one letter said. [I think that measurement is just a little bit off.] The problem is that the original sheet would have been 10 ¾ inches wide and 7 inches long. I had, earlier, suggested that the original sheet would have been at least 12 3/8 in x 7 in.

The paper type is called ivory.

In all of my searching for the right paper, this may be it, if all of the correspondences regarding watermarks, in the State Police Museum files, are authentic. The only concern is that these correspondences indicate that they made paper that could be torn in half to get the desired size. If that is true, wouldn't they have found all the letters of the *KRETONE* watermark, rather than just the *KR* and the *ONE?*

I returned to the State Police Museum to find the two letters that had the KR and ONE watermarks. What I (we) found was one. It was ransom letter #13. If you hold it to read it, the rough edge is on your left. In the lower left corner is a KR and the upper left corner is ONE.

16G. Reading the Ransom Letters

As I indicated earlier, my goal here is to compare the ransom letters to see if they were written by the same person, *not* to determine if Hauptmann wrote the ransom letters.

Let's look through them together. Go back and reread each one, make a note of anything unusual (That should be easy), then come back to this chapter.

Ransom Letter #1 The Nursery Letter. Anne and Betty had the time and certainly the motivation to find a ransom letter in the nursery after they found the baby missing, but it was Charles who found it when he returned to the room – some say in the crib, most say on the windowsill where the damaged shutter was.

The *D* of Dear and *S* of Sir are very odd letter shapes that are not commonly used in any language I could find. The exclamation point that follows the first two words is a German touch, as is the trend of putting the *$* dollar sign after the numerical amount. In line 2 there is the author's widely used *d*, written as a circle followed by a vertical line, *o*|. Keep track of this in subsequent letters.

Redy and *mony* are incorrectly spelled. "*The child is in gut care*" is a classic example of spelling errors made by these kidnappers.

Since this is the first letter, it is the one in which they introduce the singnature, two open circles, one closed, two wavy lines, and three holes, always in the front right corner of each letter.

It is difficult at times to count errors in the letters because the penmanship is so poor. *After* looks like it's been through a train wreck, and the *s* added to *2-4 day* is very far away.

Let's think about a characteristic of these letters – undotted *i*'s and uncrossed *t*'s. I see the words *Sir, in, in, in, bills, bills, will, inform, with*(?), *anyding, public, notify, child, is, in, singnature* – all words with *i*'s, none of them dotted. Now look at the *t*'s in *to, notify, the, the, gut, letters, singnature* – I don't think any of the *t*'s are crossed except the strange *t* in *gut* which may be a crossed *t*. While this is subjective, it appears that there are 48 words, seven (about 15%) of which are misspelled, and eight are illegible. Also, there are seven dollar signs, and each of them is unique.

Before we go further, get a blank piece of paper. I want you to fill the page with writing. Tell me about *your* interest or disinterest in the Lindbergh kidnapping trial. Write at least six sentences. Don't take your time; write fast. I want you to do something special. Don't dot any of your *i*'s or cross any of your *t*'s. If you accidentally dot or cross, don't worry about it, just keep writing.

Ready? Go.

Now I want you to go through what you wrote. How many words did you write? How many *i*'s were present? How many were dotted? How many *t*'s were present? How many of them were crossed?

Number of words:
Number of i's:
Number of t's:
Number of dotted i's:
Number of crossed t's:
Fraction of t's crossed:
Fraction of i's dotted:

I've had students do this in class. Some had an awful time following the directions – they are just too used to adding dots and crosses. For others, it is easy to keep their concentration for one page. How did you do? This may help us to understand if the quirky letters were just the way the author wrote, or if they had a list of items they incorporated into every letter, such as uncrossed *t*'s.

Ransom Letter #2. The letter tells the Lindberghs again not to notify the police (too late), but since they did, we must wait until everything calms down. They also acknowledge that the Lindberghs had published in the paper the feeding instructions from Little Charlie's doctor, and they agreed to follow the diet. It seems like a very reasonable letter, urging the Lindberghs to get this over with and get their baby back. They also justify why the ransom had to be raised to $70,000. This letter is very different, covering both sides of the page, totaling 219 words. Of them, roughly 16 are misspelled (about 7%). They still begin with an unusual *D* in *Dear.* I'm not sure why they didn't want any bills from one serial number (or what that even means). I don't think they understood how serial numbers are assigned to currency. Also, it appears that the first several lines are a mess but the writing evens out after that. As you read each letter, underline words that you think are misspelled.

Ransom Letters #3 and #4: These were both sent in the same envelope, addressed to Col. Breckenridge, Lindbergh's friend, and lawyer. The kidnappers were worried that the Police were reading all of Lindbergh's mail, so they sent these ransom letters to Lindbergh through Breckenridge. Here it seems much more natural not to cross any of the *t*'s, although at the end of the second line, the *i* in *in* seems to be dotted. Still, an unusual version of a *D* in *Dear Sir* is used. The *!* following the salutation is gone. The capital *P* is certainly unique, in the last word, Police. Apparently, the *P* was drawn over in *Please* to resemble a more typical capital *P*. In the accompanying letter #4 to Lindbergh (still *Dear Sir* – must be a form letter!), there is a very unusual *k* used in line 3 (*Brooklyn*) and someone is still modifying the *P* of *Police* (line 3, and 8). *Police* is spelled correctly in line 4 but incorrectly in line 8. It seems that we have come a long way from Ransom Letter #1 – *Dear Sir* is now just part of the first line, but that may be because this is a long letter. In the next to last line of the front page of Letter #4, the word *send* is written with a normal *d*, not the *o|* version we had been seeing in earlier letters. In the third line from the bottom, there appears to be the word *best.* I believe it is usually easy to see when someone touched up a word or letter, because extra ink is there, and the letter is darker. Fountain pens usually don't randomly release different amounts of ink. If there is a common feature of fountain pen writing, it's that the writing gets lighter as the ink reservoir empties. So, in *Best,* it seems someone went over the *t* to make sure it was crossed! Perhaps one person was writing, and one was looking for places to touch up. As in other letters, capital letters seem to show up unexpectedly, such as the capitalized *Boy,* twice on the front page. (Again, it's a German thing.) Strange *k*'s continue to appear in words such as *back.* It almost seems as if they forgot to disguise their writing and had to get back to it at the end – "*the mony, but not before the Police is out of the cace and the papers are quiet.*" The wide, uncrossed *t* is used several times in that sentence, although several versions of that letter appear. But, of course, the big surprise is in their discussion of how they want the ransom, now $70,000. This is worth reviewing.

Ransom Letter #1- Ransom Demand
25000$ in 20$ bills
15000$ in 10$ bills
10000$ in 5$ bills
Total: 50.000$

Ransom Letter #2 - Ransom Demand
20.000 in 50$ bills
25.000$ in 20$ bills
15000$ in 10$ bills
10.000$ in 5$ bills
TOTAL: 70,000$

Ransom Letter #4 Ransom Demand (again!)
20000 in 50$ bills
25000 in 25$ bills
15000 in 10$ bills
10000 in 5$ bills
TOTAL: 70.000$

Why would they request the $70K twice? In Ransom Letter #2 they seemed to be following European standards by using a period/decimal point when writing numbers, but they forget about that by Letter #4. And of course, there is the major "error," if not done on purpose, to look like they weren't from the U.S.: the request for part of the ransom in 25$ bills! I'd like to get a few of those as well!

Ransom Letter #5. We're still using the second model of having *Dear Sir* just being part of the first line. It appears that, long ago, the corner of the letter became detached, and a person thoughtlessly taped it back on. The tape did not last, but the adhesive remained on the page. (Mark says there was also a time when the pieces were stapled together!). This appears to be the first letter addressed to Dr. Condon. They seem to be underlining words -- for emphasis, I suppose. There were no underlined words in the first ransom letter. Letter #5 is to Condon, who has offered $1000 of his own money to add to the ransom. Their response was "keep it." The writer has been consistent in words he/she misspells such as *anyding, mony,* and *redy.* They do make a mistake asking Condon to be home every night between 0-12 because they wanted to call him. Most interpret that as 10-12 P.M. There is no signature on this letter; I suppose Condon didn't need it.

Ransom Letter #6. They finally approve Condon as a go-between, and Condon immediately goes to the Lindbergh house for approval. Here the ransom letter author(s) draws and defines the dimensions of the "packet" size for holding the 70000$, 6 x 7 x 14 inches. Why do they care what the size of the package is? And why did "package" eventually lead to the use of a box? The envelope is incompletely addressed and has no postage on it. Very different from previous letters.

(If you haven't figured it out yet, stamps such as those on the back(verso) of letter #6 and an occasional handwritten date or note, are evidence stamps. For example, the envelope for letter #6 has an E-5 written in pencil in the corner, some sort of police code – not on the envelope originally from the kidnappers. The date is when the document was submitted/accepted into evidence for the trial.)

Ransom Letters #7 and #8. Another ransom letter to Dr. Condon. It instructs him where to go to find the next letter. This is the beginning of the actual payoff of the ransom and return of Little Charlie! ("Bring the mony with you."). The author's spelling may be improving. As is often the case, they spell harder words correctly and the easier words incorrectly. Condon followed the instructions to the next ransom letter - #8. It is short, with no singnature. The misspelled street in *233 Sheet* may look like it's been fixed to have the *h* look more like a (crossed) *t* and an *r*. Not much to discuss here, but it is one of the ransom letters with a very rough left edge, so there's no doubt that the stationery they were using is not of a standard size. There are seventeen words in letter #8, and all of them are spelled correctly. Unfortunately, while the ransom was discussed this very night, and Dr. Condon got to meet "Cemetery John" for the first time, no ransom was paid; no baby returned.

Ransom Letter #9. While the letter is long (about 250 words), there are about 22 words misspelled (about 9%). The letter refers to their first meeting of Condon and John and indicates that it will never happen again. For some reason, they assume that the Lindberghs are unsure if they are dealing with the right group, the one with the baby, so they offer to send Little Charlie's sleeping suit as proof. They are curious about what the Lindberghs are prepared to pay. They promise to give them the location of Little Charlie within eight hours after the ransom is paid. (They sound like a very reasonable band of kidnappers.). When this letter was sent, the baby's sleeper, or at least another Dr. Denton's, was also sent to the Lindberghs.

Ransom Letter #10. Again, it appears that while there are still misspellings, some of the unique features found in earlier letters, such as the o| for d, have disappeared. They are getting impatient, saying the Lindberghs are just wasting time. The back of letter #10 could be a good example of having a large space between the writing and the paper's edge on the left side of the back side, however this seems to contradict the proposal that the sheet was cut out of a journal.

Ransom Letter #11. This is another letter that has been tested using silver nitrate in an attempt to find fingerprints. A few fingerprints have appeared, although occasionally, the process is very slow, so the fingerprints may have developed long after the silver nitrate was applied.

Ransom Letter #12. It looks like *Dear Sir:* (with a colon, on the first line) has replaced the *Dear Sir!* that had its own line in the first ransom letter. It may be useful to point out a very silly error that is probably not in anyone's vocabulary. When the word New is used. the *N* is occasionally backwards and perhaps they have someone in charge of writing it incorrectly again when it was accidentally written correctly.

Ransom Letter #13. Another letter to Dr. Condon, their go-between. This one leads him to a florist, and to a table under which another letter directs him to the second cemetery, where Condon and Cemetery John will have their second and last visit. It is one of the few times that *police* is not capitalized, and again, letter #13 looks so much different than letter #1. Are we sure they were all written by the same person? Really? The found letter, #14, instructs Condon where to bring the money (a second cemetery) and to come alone.

Ransom Letter #15. The last of the set, it has no singnature. This is the famous *the boy is on the Boad Nelly* letter. Some "facts" should be simple and clear. Even you can read Ransom Letter #15 and know what it says. However, one source (Brant J. & Renaud E. 1932) reported that Little Charlie was being held on the 28 foot-yacht, Sally. (For the record, 28 feet is small for a sailboat, hardly a yacht.) *Boad* must mean boat because it is 28 feet long and two people are on the boat taking care of Little Charlie. But again, *boad* is not German for *boat*. Every *Boad* is spelled with a normal *d*, no *o*|'s anymore. Based on this letter, the search began for a boat named Nelly. Condon and Lindbergh borrowed a plane and searched the waters near Elizabeth Island and Gay Head (look it up), but no such boat was found, none was on record. Some handwriting experts believe the letter's author had a hard time writing this letter; he kept writing his own address. If you blow up the letter, it looks like he originally wrote "road" not "boat." Also, Gay Head may have initially been Gun Hill, the neighborhood where Jafsie and John met (Gardner, L, C. 2012). $50,000 had been paid for the ransom, and this was the last communication. The kidnappers had vanished with the money, and there was no real information provided on the location of Little Charlie. Keep in mind that this was only half of the conversation between Dr. Condon (on behalf of the Lindberghs) and the kidnappers. The kidnappers wrote letters, and Condon replied in the newspapers. If you would like more information on the other half of the conversation (Condon's newspaper posts) you can find them in the sources listed below.

Q: So, what do you think? Were the letters all written by the same person?

Q: Is the author of the letters German or Scandinavian, or American?

Many have attempted to "translate" the ransom letters (now including you). One place where you can find them (They count 13 letters) is

http.lindberghkidnappinghoax.com/ransom.html.

You might also look at:

Charles Lindbergh, American Aviator (http:www. Charleslindbergh.com/kidnap/index.asp)
(Linden, D.O. Famous Trials)
And
Falzini M.W. Archival Ramblings 9 Sept. 2008

I didn't want to share these with you until you attempted to interpret the letters yourself. These web sites may clear up some of the words on these pages that are impossible to read.

16H. Letters, Envelopes and Folding

Many have suggested that one person wrote all the ransom letters. They had no choice when they only had one suspect. Perhaps they never considered the envelopes. Whoever addressed the envelopes usually printed in a block style and had very different handwriting compared to whoever wrote the letters.

One aspect that I find interesting is that the ransom letters have fold lines, so we should be able to virtually fold the letters and put them into the envelopes as the author of the letters did.

The stationery is an unusual shape, and the letters were folded in unique ways to put them into envelopes. Consider ransom letter #4. If one enhances the letter a little one can see the fold lines. If you fold along those lines and compare that folded shape with the dimensions of the envelope, it's often an unusual fit, with the folded ransom note sometimes being much smaller than the envelope – odd mismatches.

Most of the envelopes are stamped and postmarked – none are postmarked in New Jersey, all in New York.

Q16H.1: Consider the envelope for ransom letter #12. Is it real or something possibly added to the evidence later?

A16H.1: I don't have photos of the envelopes with rulers in the same photo. How can we estimate the dimensions of the envelope? The envelope holds a red (crimson rose) 2 cent Washington stamp. These were used in 1932. The postmark is Fordham Station April something, 1932. Could this be real, or is it just planted evidence? It seems legitimate. The Washington Bicentennial series of stamps first went on sale January 1, 1932.

(Side Note: The Fordham Station is adjacent to the Rose Hill Campus of Fordham University. Fordham U. began as St. John's College, until 1907. It has three campuses. Rose Hill, the original Fordham campus is in the Bronx, located at the intersection of Fordham Road and East 190th Street. John Condon was both a student and an instructor at Fordham University).

Q16H2: There were many similar Washington stamps made in the first part of the century. How do you identify a stamp to make sure you know the date it was printed?

A16H2: There are things to look for. Was it part of a sheet or a coil? The key is the perforations. Perforations are rows of holes punched between stamps to make them easier to separate. For example, from 1919 to 1921, there were 1 cent Washington stamps made. Some were perforated 11 x 10, others 10 x 11, others 10 x 10, others 11 x 11. These are each considered to be unique stamps within the series. You should understand what perforations are and how to measure them. If the stamp was originally part of a coil, it would only have perforations on the sides. Stamps made in sheets have perforations on all four sides. You can get a perforation gauge like the one shown below, from Mystic Stamp Co. for only a few dollars.

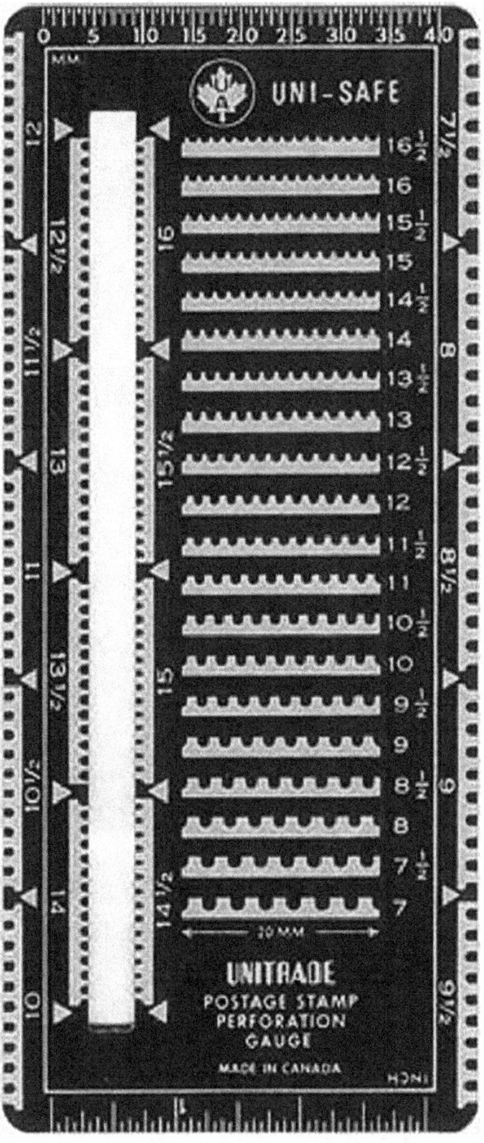

Figure 16H.1. Perforation Gauge

Concerning the use of stamps, in 1885 the rate for a 1-ounce letter was two cents. In 1917, that went up to 3 cents, per ounce, and back down to 2 cents by 1919. The rate returned to 3 cents in 1932, where it stayed until 1958. Probably people were used to buying 2 cent stamps for letters, although when the increase to 3 cents was announced, some went out and bought 1 cent stamps since they had 2 cents stamps already in their possession. This may explain why some letters have two 1 cent stamps on them rather than a 2-cent stamp. In the present, as of January 2019, postage required for a one-ounce letter is 55 cents.

When trying to identify a particular stamp, how do you do it? What do you look for? If you are interested, there are catalogs on the internet and free catalogs that you can request. One of the larger stamp companies in the US is the Mystic Stamp Company (America's Leading Stamp Dealer). You can request a free copy of their current US Stamp Catalog at:

https://www.mysticstamp.com/Advertisement-Response/FREE-US-Postage-Stamp- Catalog/SC2S/

If you're going to take advantage of a free stamp catalog, make sure they're in color and make sure they use a standard designation system (usually the Scott Catalog number). There are often dozens of great books on stamp collecting in your library.

Figure 16H.2. The envelope for letter #12

The 2-cent red Washington on the envelope for ransom letter #12 is perf. 11 x 10.5, meaning there are 11 perforations every 2 cm horizontally and 10.5 perforations for every 2 cm vertically. I counted the perforations, and estimated the size of the stamp to be 20.9 mm x 24.8 mm, and used that to estimate the size of the envelope as 139 x 87 mm.

I folded ransom letter #12 in half. Several fold lines are visible on letter #12. I had measured the ransom letter #12 to be 179.5 mm x 136 mm. If I fold it in half, the dimensions should be 89.8 mm x 136 mm. It will not fit in the envelope with only one fold. In the long dimension, the envelope is 139 mm, and the letter is 136 mm, which is fine, but the 89.8 mm high folded letter will not fit into an envelope that is only 87 mm high.

Rule for future investigators: Take the time to do it again and do it better this time. Let's talk about stamps some more. The 1932 Washington 2 cent stamp was part of a set of stamps with the theme of our first President. They were all the same size. I found an authentic ½ cent brown Washington from that set, which I measured to be 26 mm x 21 mm, very close to the value I estimated for the stamp, 24.8 mm x 20.9 mm. So, using the stamp to estimate the size of the envelope worked well, and I'm going to continue to work with the estimated dimensions of the envelope for letter #12 to be 139 x 87 mm.

Back to the ransom letter #12. The letter is 179.5 x 136 mm, so if I fold it in half, I get a folded letter that is 179.5/2 x 136 mm = 89.75 x 136 mm. However, there was no fold at the halfway mark of the height. I see two fold lines in the middle of the page. I see up to six possible fold lines.

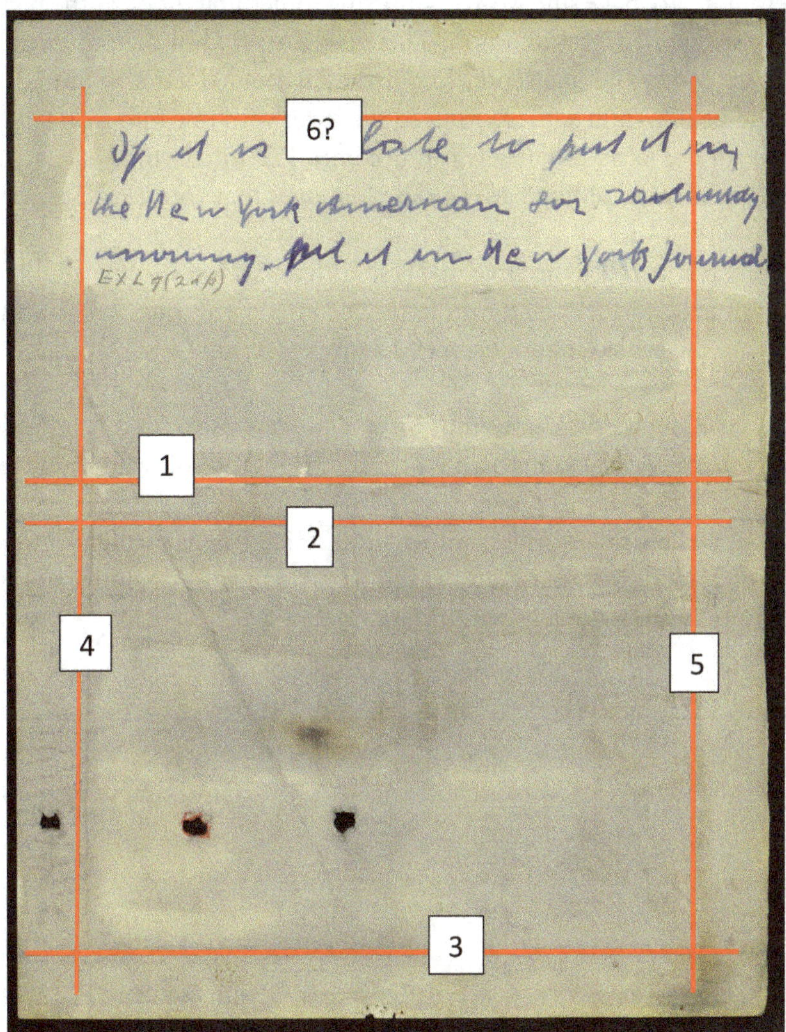

If it is late to put it in the New York American for Saturday morning. put it in New York Journal

Figure 16H.3: Letter #12 and its fold lines

Let's consider folding the letter again, this time using the fold lines instead of assuming anything.

Letter# 12 and its envelope were messy ones because they put a solution of silver nitrate on it in places, not on the ink, to find fingerprints. So, the dark area at the top of the back of the ransom letter is just darkened silver nitrate. I can't be sure if there is a fold line up there too or not.

One fold, we decided, does not make a small enough letter for this envelope. I'll keep folding. If I fold both sides in along the fold lines, the width becomes 111 mm. If I fold the top down the height is 81mm, and if I fold the top and bottom in, then the folded letter becomes 74 mm wide. So, if the letter is folded five times along folds that can be seen, it will fit in the envelope.

I did these by cutting out letter #12 verso and physically folding it, then measuring dimensions using the ruler that was on that same page. It seems like a crazy way to fold a letter, but if you fold along 1,2,3,4 and 5, it will fit into the envelope. Certainly not traditional. I remember when I was in school, we learned how to fold letters.

I'm going to check a few more, to make sure we're not missing something. Look at the pictures for ransom letter #2 and its envelope. The letter is 157 x 176.5 mm. There is a clear fold in the center, and one up the left side as you read the front of letter #2. The one center fold makes my folded letter 88 mm high x 157 mm wide. I calculated the envelope to be 92.7 mm x 141.5 mm, so the letter with one fold won't fit. If I then fold it along the fold on the right side of the page, the new width becomes 128 mm, which is less than 141.5 mm, so the letter now fits, with a very different folding pattern. The fold lines that you see are the ones that were used.

I'm going to do one more, just because the envelope is so different. Consider ransom letter #3. The one horizontal fold does fold it in half, so 156 x 178 mm letter becomes a 156 mm x 89 mm folded letter. If I fold it on the left side fold line, the folded letter becomes 129 mm x 89 mm.

The envelope has two 1 cent green Franklin stamps on it. They are also 26 x 21 mm. Using the stamp as my ruler, I calculated that the envelope is 94 mm high x 219 mm wide. So, I only need one fold, and the letter fits.

So why is there a fold on the left side of the front of letter #3? I was particularly interested in this because some stationery is sold prefolded, with matching envelopes. There is a possibility that the prefold could fall within the page after it was cut to size, as shown in Figure 16H.4.

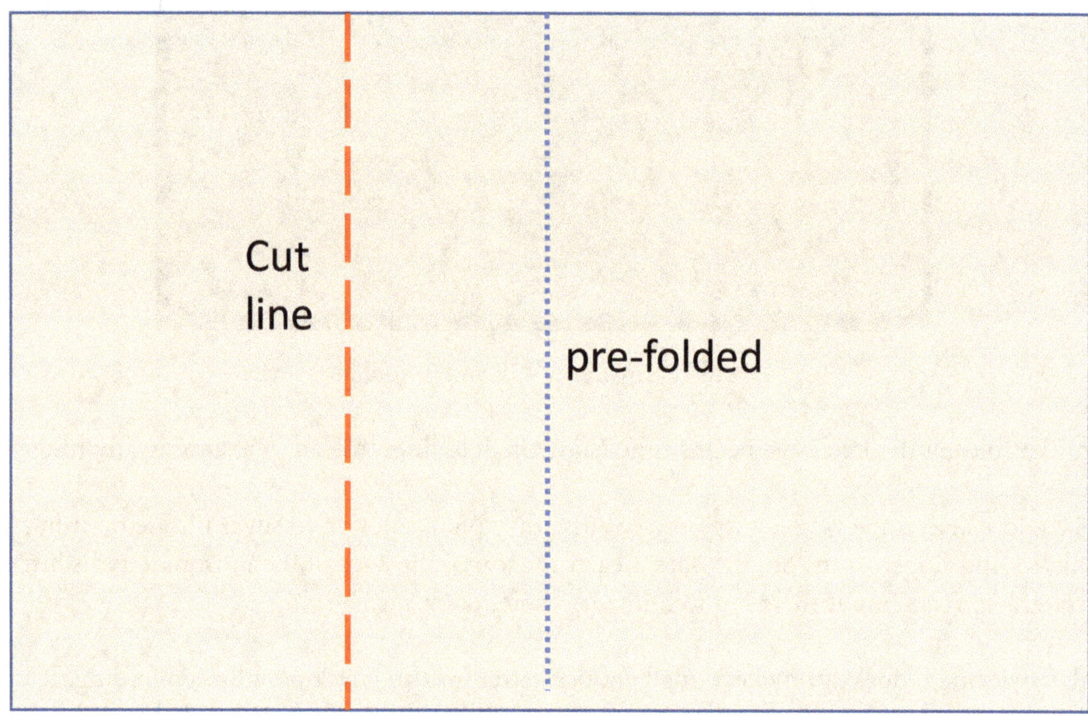

Figure 16H.4: Cutting Pre-Folded Stationery

This would be very interesting, suggesting that some of the fold lines were not ones made to put the letter into the envelope.

Q: What is the flaw in this argument?

A: Look again at Ransom Letter #3. If the prefolded page was cut as shown, the cut edge would be close to the fold, but the cut edge is on the other side, so this could not be the case.

161. The Language Used, and Lawrence Welk

Let's consider some of the ransom letters, focusing on the language used. We can't know if the author's first language is English, German, or Scandinavian. Ransom Letter #1 starts with Dear Sir! That's not the punctuation taught in American schools, but it is used in Germany. The ThoughtCo web site,
https://www.thoughtco.com/how-to-write-a-letter-in-german-1445260
states

> "The more modern way is to end the greeting is a comma, however, you may come across the old-fashioned pre-computer/e-mail way of putting an exclamation point at the end of the greeting: *Liebe Maria!*"
> (where Liebe is the German equivalent of "Dear," used for females).

So, someone knew something about how Germans construct correspondence. If someone was trying to hide his or her writing style, that person did a pretty good job here.

It is noteworthy that money is designated with the dollar sign following the amount, such as 50.000 $. If you look up "Currency Symbol" in Wikipedia, it states that, for many currencies in the English-speaking world and Latin America, the currency symbol comes before the amount (e.g., $50.00). The Cape Verdean Escudo places the symbol in place of the decimal point, (e.g., 20$00), and in many parts of Europe, including Germany, the symbol is placed after the amount (e.g. 20.50$). There are many misspelled words such as *mony*, and the child is in *gut care*. In the first ransom letter the writer(s) refer to their strange symbol as their *singnature*, and this spelling is consistently used.

The second ransom note starts by: *We have warned you not to make anyding public or notify the police*, with random use of capital letters.

> Mark Falzini comments
>
> Random, or the capitalization of a noun (German grammar rule)
>
> Author comments
>
> You can learn French, German, Italian and other languages at the ThoughtCo. (thoughtco.com). One of the topics covered is capitalization. One simple rule: all German nouns are capitalized. We need to appreciate the recent German history of this rule.
>
> There was a formal change in German rules of spelling in 1901. In 1924, the Swiss BVR was created with the goal of eliminating most capitalization in German. In the 1930s many supported this. In 1996, in Vienna, representatives from all the German-speaking countries signed an agreement to adopt new spelling reforms, including the capitalization-of-nouns rule. Again, current rules differ from when the ransom letters were written.

The letter looks so much more like a real letter. I would just assume they were written by different people, although again no *t*'s are crossed or *i*'s dotted. The baby is in *gut* health. And we will *note* do so … In some cases, simple words are misspelled, while more complicated words are spelled correctly. Does it seem to you as if a German in the U.S. is using his best version of English but often letting German words sneak in? Let's set the record straight. *Anyding* is not German for *anything* (although Haring claims it is in "The Hand of Hauptmann", concluding that the ransom letters' author was German.) *Gut* is German for *good. Note* is not German for *not*, however it is the German word for *grade. Boad* does not mean *anything* in German.

Perhaps the author(s) was/were trying to <u>sound</u> like a German American. Perhaps trying so hard to mask his or her real handwriting, living close to a German community and hearing German speech, the author was trying to make the letter read like broken English, belonging to a German. Let's assume that Germans (or at least one German), as they learn the English language, mispronounce words like anything, as anyding. My question is: *If you mispronounce words, is that how you write them too?*

I'm going to propose that the answer to that is <u>no</u>, and the reason is Lawrence Welk.

Lawrence Welk was an American bandleader who hosted *The Lawrence Welk Show* on television from 1951 to 1982. Welk was born in Strasburg, North Dakota – specifically in the German-speaking part of the town. He spoke with an accent, known for his "Wunnerful, wunnerful" and "Thanka you thanka you, ladies anda gentlemen." So, we have a German American who incorrectly pronounces words. Is there any connection between how he pronounced words and how he wrote them? Did he not *know* how to spell wonderful because he couldn't pronounce it correctly?

Let's find out! Here is a letter written by Lawrence Welk.

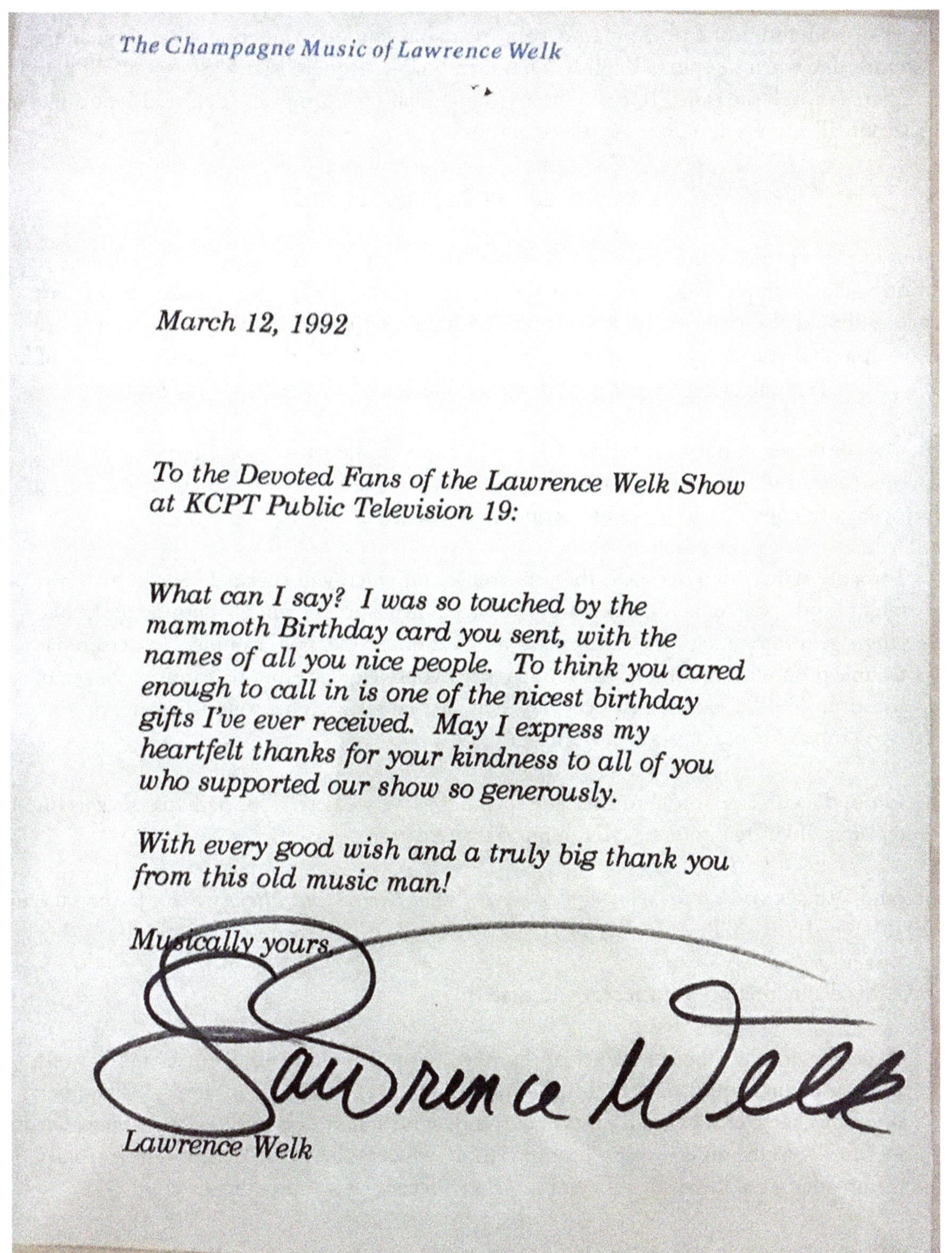
The Champagne Music of Lawrence Welk

March 12, 1992

To the Devoted Fans of the Lawrence Welk Show
at KCPT Public Television 19:

What can I say? I was so touched by the mammoth Birthday card you sent, with the names of all you nice people. To think you cared enough to call in is one of the nicest birthday gifts I've ever received. May I express my heartfelt thanks for your kindness to all of you who supported our show so generously.

With every good wish and a truly big thank you from this old music man!

Musically yours,

Lawrence Welk

Lawrence Welk

Figure 16I.1: A letter from Lawrence Welk.

I see no indication that the typed letter 16I.1 was typed by his secretary. I also found a handwritten postcard from Mr. Welk. The postcard has no German words in it, and there are no words spelled as they may have been incorrectly spoken.

So, possibly the poor English used in the ransom letters is nothing other than a handwriting style created by a kidnapper to frame someone of German descent. Perhaps you are wondering what someone of German descent sounds like when he speaks English. That's reasonable. If there is any interest at all, help is on the internet. There is a web site called IDEA – International Dialects of English Archive. If you'd like to hear a German accent, all you need to do is ask. Check it out at

www.dialectsarchive.com/germanyt-5.

In addition to the recorded voice, there is *Scholarly Commentary* that evaluates how the dialect changes the spoken words – for example, *d* changes to *t* at the end of a word, so a speaker's spoken *bird* is *birt*. (What a great find!). I should also point out that story writers often wrestle with how to handle characters' accents. Some may use a phonetic representation when spelling out a word, but this is not an indication of how people would write. "A phonetic representation creates the illusion of an accent, for the readers."

I need to say a little more, not to trivialize this topic. Suppose the writer was German who spoke English with a German accent. According to an article, *Why do people have an accent?* By Betty Birmer. (https://www.linguisticsociety.org/content/why-do-some-people-have-accent):

> "Broadly stated, your accent is the way you sound when you speak. There are two different kinds of accents. One is a 'foreign' accent'; this occurs when a person speaks one language using some of the rules or sounds of another one. For example, if a person has trouble pronouncing some of the sounds of a second language they're learning, they may substitute similar sounds that occur in their first language. This sounds wrong, or 'foreign', to native speakers of the language."

The question is, does an accent lead to alternate spellings as we see here? This perhaps takes us into the area of sociolinguistics. If you're interested, you might start here:

Gatlin, B. and Wanaek, J. *Relations Among Children's Use of Dialect and Literacy Skills* J. Speech Lang Hear Res 58(4) 2015 pp1306-1328.

They make this distinction between accent and dialect:

> "Accents typically differ in quality of the voice, pronunciation and distinction of vowels and consonants, stress, and prosody. Although grammar, semantics, vocabulary, and other language characteristics often vary concurrently with accent, the word «accent» may refer specifically to the differences in pronunciation, whereas the word "dialect" encompasses the broader set of linguistic differences. Often "accent" is a subset of «dialect»."

Much of their interests are if/how an accent affects reading and more importantly comprehension in a second language, but spelling is a part of literacy. In their mathematical analysis of data, they conclude:

> "The random effects weighted effect size for the spelling and writing component was significant and negative, but small in magnitude"

suggesting that an accent has only a small influence on spelling.

Letter #4 indicates that the kidnappers think the police read Lindbergh's mail, and they don't want the police involved in any way (too late), so they decided to send future letters to Col. Breckenridge, Lindbergh's lawyer and friend. How do they know who Lindbergh's friends are, and their addresses? As mentioned previously, Anne Lindbergh was so concerned about Little Charlie because he had some minor physical problems, and the doctor had him on a specific diet. Anne published the diet in the newspaper asking the kidnappers to please follow it, and they indicate that they would.

Notice how the body of the letter starts on the same line as Dear Sir in Letter #4 – very different from Letter #1.

In **Letter #5**, the kidnappers adopt Jafsie as someone to maintain communications, and they start working on a system where he communicates through small posts in the local Bronx papers, posting short messages such as "money is ready" (or *redy*, according to the ransom letter.)

In **Letter #8**, again there are no dotted *i*'s or crossed *t*'s, but not a singnature either. Was this rushed, not planned out in advance? Look at the right side of the page – it is a very ragged edge. This was either cut or torn from a larger piece of paper, and many of the letters are similar in this regard.

Ransom Letter #9: *We will note allow ouer man to confer in a way lieke befor.* This is typical of some of the spelling errors in earlier letters, but all the ransom letters do not look the same. Compared to letter #1, letter #9 is much neater. Note that the singnature overlaps the writing here, showing that the singnature was made on the page before the letter was written.

Letter #10: Again, the writing overlaps with parts of the singnature.

Letter #11: Concerning the child, I believe the last sentence indicates that *it is well* – very unusual to not refer to the child as a boy or girl. (Lindbergh was known to sometimes refer to his son as *it*.) This letter is very messy compared to the previous ones because a police expert in fingerprinting again tried to find intact fingerprints on the letter, using an aqueous solution of silver nitrate. Silver interacts with the chemical components in the fingerprint, and they turn black/grey. The investigator "painted" a silver nitrate solution over part of the letter, which did turn darker. Still, there are no fingerprints with sufficient detail to be useful for comparisons with prints of suspects.

Letter #13: By now, you should have noticed that the paper has changed. We can't know if the author of the letters tried to be consistent in his/her inconsistencies or not. They report an address as 3225 East Tremont Ave, written in a combination of script and printing. The abbreviation *Ave.* in particular, is unique, printed as three separated letters.

Letter #14: Perhaps a hastily written note, perhaps not by the usual writer; the Dear Sir is missing, and there are few words per line. It almost looks like poetry!

Letter #15: A very jagged left edge and no signature; what is going on? Readers assume Boad Nellie refers to a 28-foot long boat. The kidnappers seem very comfortable in telling the Lindberghs what to do. *There are two people on the boad. They are innocent.* Oh, ok, so we shouldn't try to get any answers out of them or include them in the "gang" responsible for the kidnapping. We should just smile at them and take the child? I don't think the police would feel comfortable with just a "tip of the hat" to gang members based on this letter.

The police had a man in jail, and they wanted this to be the end of it – they had no leads on other members of the gang. It is better to blame it all on one person, including the handwriting, and several testified at the trial that the handwriting in the letters matched that squeezed out of Hauptmann. However, the envelopes are a different matter. In some cases, we only have one side of the envelope to see. Starting with the second ransom letter envelope, the writing is very blocky, printed, upper case *E*'s are used as lower case, and since they are now printing, or someone else is printing, new styles appear, such as writing a lower-case *d* as an *ol.* Do you see that in Letter #1? Look for the word *deliver*. Not there. Ransom letter #2 – *diet*. No. Ransom letter #13 – *door*, still a typical *d*. Was a second writer in charge of the envelopes?

Even the placement of the address is inconsistent, as seen by envelope #6. Some envelopes list the city; others do not.

One handwriting analyst thought all ten singnatures were made at the same time ("practically duplicates of each other"). Perhaps he had poor vision.

In closing, I just must point out …

There is a website belonging to Tess Milom, called "The Morbid Linguist/The Open Journal of a Consulting Forensic Linguist" (http://morbidlinguist.blogspot.com/2019/07/native-language-analysis-for-german.html). She uses "native language analysis". In this blog she evaluates the Lindbergh ransom letters in a post entitled *Native Language Analysis for German Transference Features in the Lindbergh Kidnapping Notes* (Sept.23, 2019). Her results were inconclusive. She discusses the method used and sources of data on language structures in a June 10, 2019 post, *Crossed in Translation*. It's beyond the scope of this book, but very interesting work.

16J. The Handwriting.

As you look through the ransom letters, keep in mind the conclusion of all the handwriting analysts who testified that they were all written by the same person.

16J.1. What Does the Handwriting tell You?

Many had stated that not only was Hauptmann abused when the police hastily collected handwriting samples from him, but there is an old video on YouTube:

https://www.youtube.com/watch?v=cW_WpKoqxts

which, at about 5:20, discusses how the ransom letters were modified, so the handwriting looks more like *his* handwriting. Specifically, they rounded off letters such as a's in the ransom letters so they would look more like Hauptmann's normal handwriting. It does seem like many individual characters have darker parts to them as if someone had written over them to reshape them. There are also numerous examples where letters such as an ending *e* in a word were added, or a characteristic flair at the end of a word added. Let me show you a few.

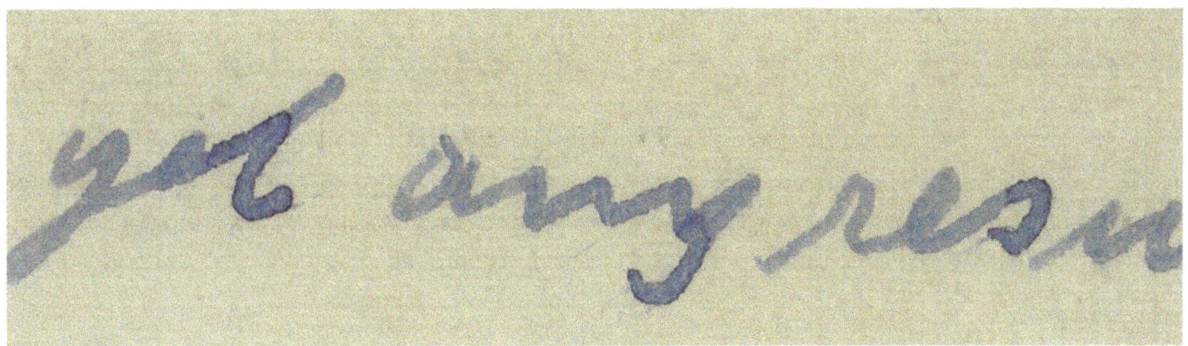

Here it appears that a tail was added to *any* and the *s* was written over, perhaps to get a better-shaped character for comparison with Hauptmann's penmanship.

Here, *e*'s were possibly added or modified in both Police and becauce.

Extra ink on more *e*'s.

Reshaping an *a*; rewriting a *b* in *big*.

There's lots of extra ink in this one sentence – *e*'s at the ends of words, reshaping the *a* in because, uncrossed *t*'s, undotted *i*'s, and some evidence of the way a *d* was written, as an *o* followed by a separate vertical line, that sometimes doesn't even touch the *o* portion, so their *d* becomes *o*|.

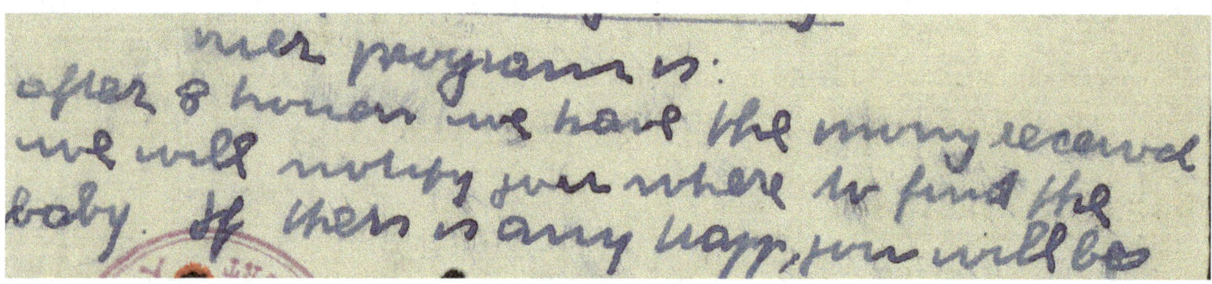

There's a sea of *e*'s in the above example. It's amazing how many e̲'s have extra ink – having been modified or perhaps even added using a different pen. I don't think it's just how "that pen" wrote. Pens usually are not sensitive enough to know when they have come to the last letter in a word.

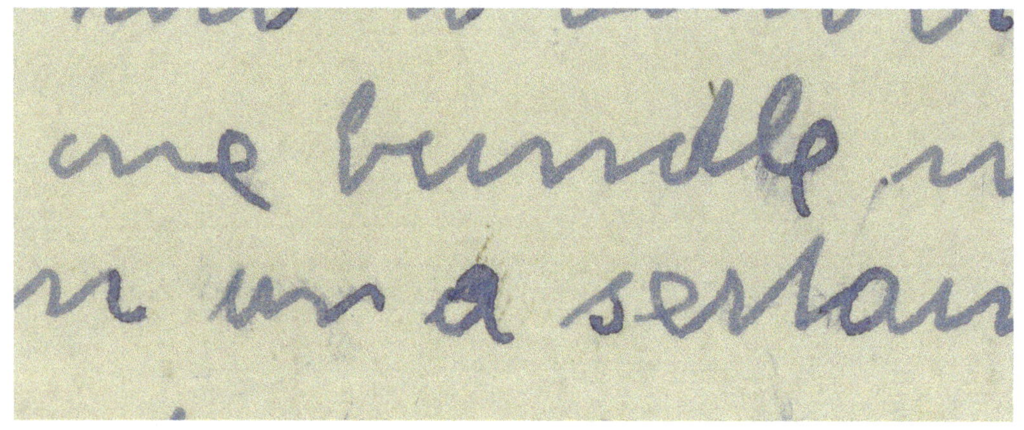

More *e*'s added or modified. A fairly clearly modified *a*. Again, they are reshaping *a*'s.

16J.2. The Penmanship

Cursive ("writing" not printing) is obviously not the same all over the world. In many countries, schools teach "penmanship," often in a national way. Students are shown how to write individual letters correctly and go through writing drills for an academic year or more (but if you attempt to write with your left hand, I hear the nun may smack you with a ruler). In some schools, the alphabet may be permanently painted across the top of the blackboard, showing the order in which each pen stroke is made and how. The students, then, all work from this same set. If the school had enough money to spend, it might have used workbooks that drill the students on all writing the same way. We have done this in the US, and style books from the past can be found on the web. For example, below is the writing style called the ZanerBloser style from a 1938 US Copybook. The same was used in the 1931 Copybook.

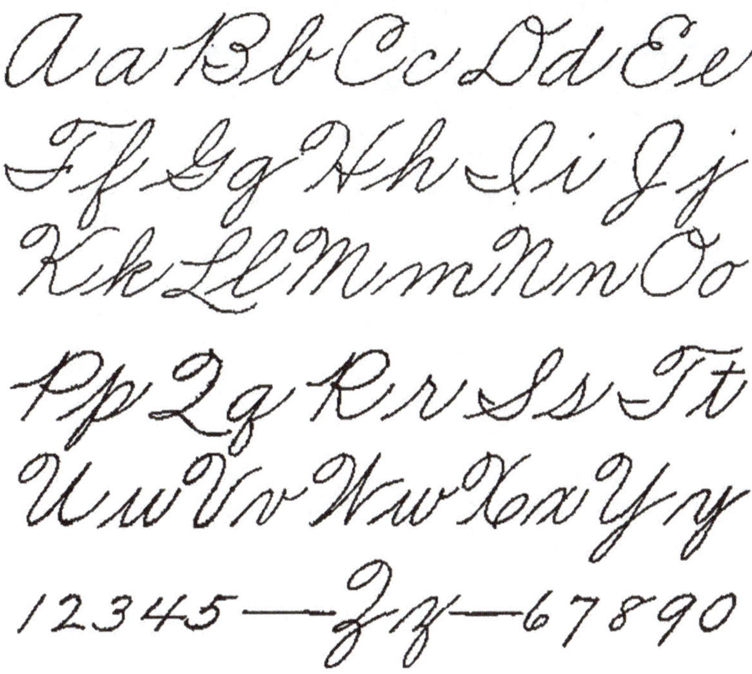

Some writing experts claim that they can determine where you come from, specifically where you were trained to write in cursive, from the shapes of letters. While our writing ultimately (d)evolves into its own unique style, still there are characteristics of the style we initially learned that will always be retained in *our* writing and in that of fellow students who learned the same style.

The ransom letters, while at times so messy as to border on unreadable, have some unique styles when it comes to certain characters. Could these be the key to whether the writer is German or not?

I decided to go on a quest, looking at script writing styles from earlier in the 20th century, from the US, Germany, and some European countries. I picked some targets to try to find. The first was the fascinating *Dear Sir* in Ransom Letter #1. It is often different in subsequent letters, always interesting.

From Ransom Letter #1

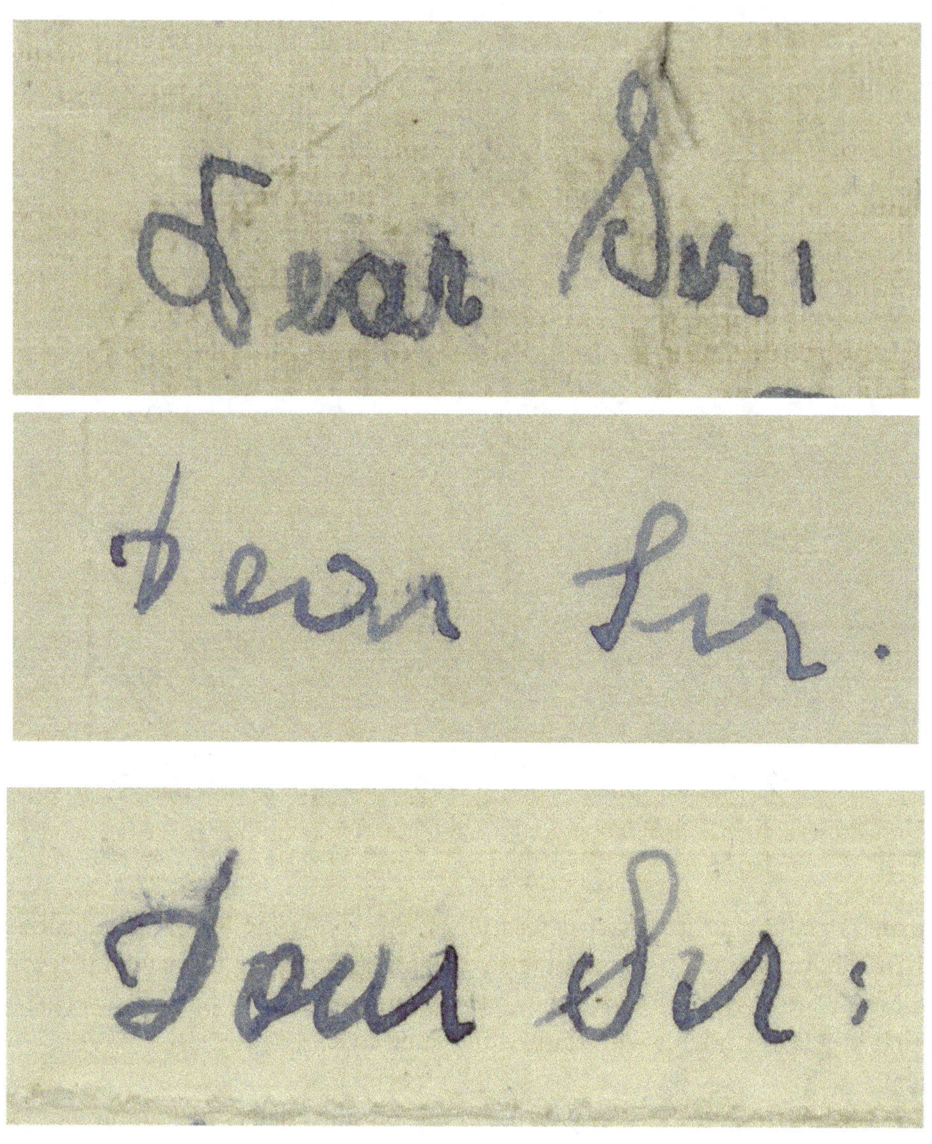

Do you think these Dear Sir's, from multiple ransom letters, were written by the same person?

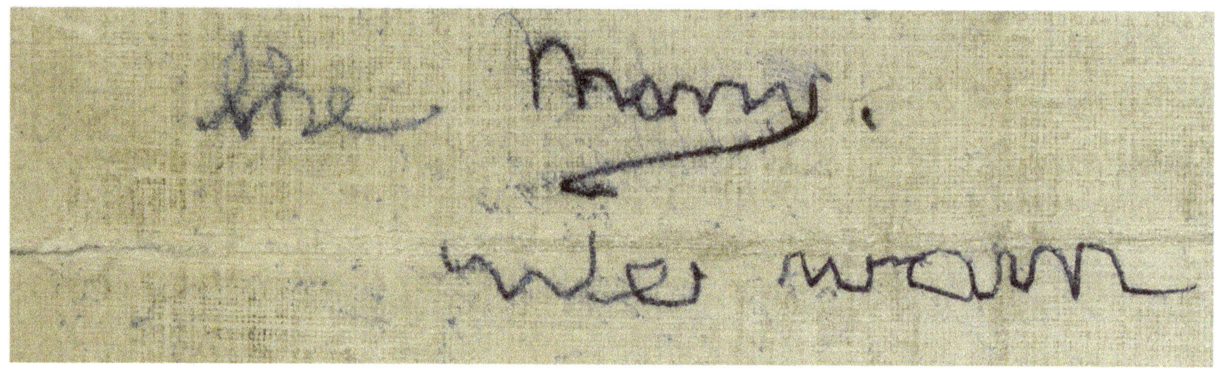

In the above, *we warn* shows a substantial variation just in the *w*'s. And the *a* of *warn* certainly does not match most of the others. I think it's clear that the *We warn* was written using the left hand of a right-hander (or the reverse).

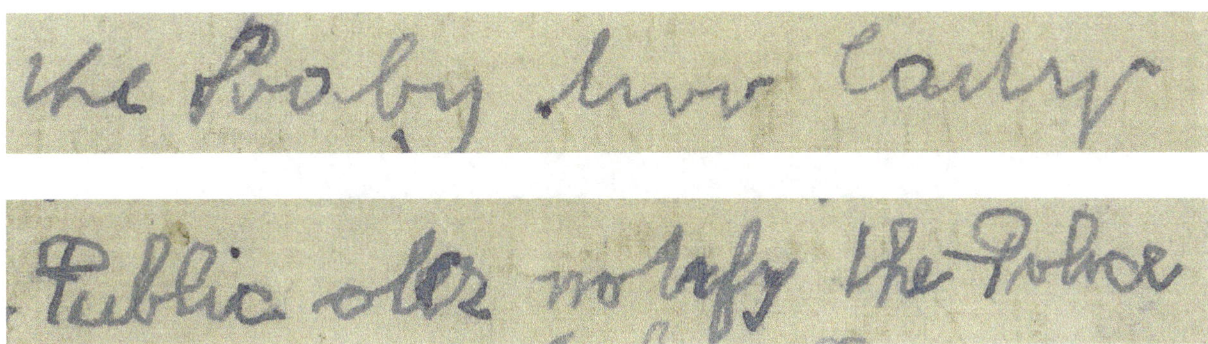

In the two partial lines show above, the *b* of baby is demolished as a letter, but they still managed to put a nice top on the *a* of *early* and *baby*. The word *older* has substantially extra ink on it.

I like these examples (above) because they apparently forgot that one of the other writers was not crossing *t*'s, so they crossed the uncrossed *t*'s when they found them, sometimes making the *t*'s that end words look like a star.

Above we see more touched-ups, and the open *o,* but other times they fixed both. Above, we see the lower-case *d,* again made up of two discrete parts, with the two pieces separated. The capital *B* also looks modified here (below), as do all the letters except for the *o.*

The possibility has been pointed out that the authors initially, not thinking, started to write out their own address so this word was supposed to be Road, before they converted the *R* into a *B.*

Three examples from envelopes follow:

The Mr., the *r*'s of Mr. and Doctor, as well as the *J* change in these three examples, while the *ol* form of *d* remains the same. I think the order of titles is appropriate. I was introduced in Germany as Herr Professor Doctor Allison – the order that is always followed there. I am a man first, then a college teacher, and finally, my degree of doctor.

The increasing mixture of capital and lower case *B*s and *E*s is shown above. They do know how to write but are trying to create a cryptic style. Perhaps the envelope writer never got the email.

The most popular handwriting style in Germany at the time is shown here:

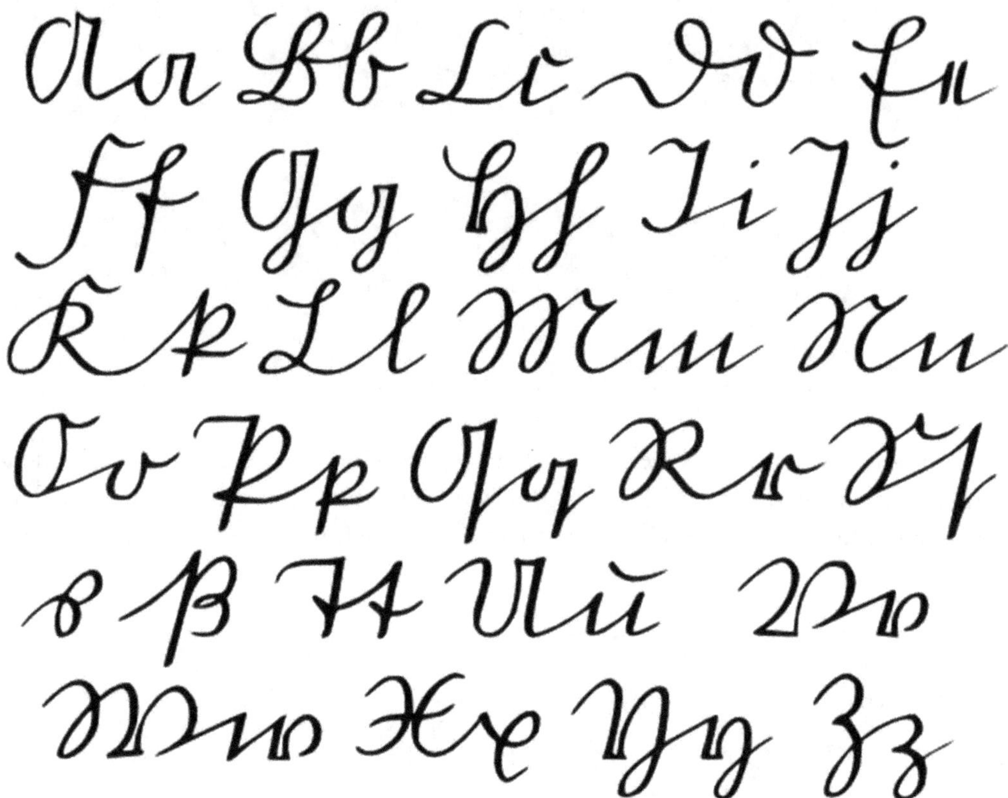

or this older Popular German script:

Aa Bb Cc Dd Ee Ff Gg Hh Ii

Jj Kk Ll Mm Nn Oo Pp Qq Rr

Ss Tt Uu Vv Ww Xx Yy Zz

ä ö ü final s ch ck ß tz mm nn

The *d*'s and the *s*'s are very different from ours, and your own personal writing style would take you from our traditional letters to ones closer to those shown in the letters, perhaps. I've stared at the letters; I've stared at the envelopes and looked at the comparisons with Bruno Hauptmann's writing and the ransom notes, and I just cannot conclude that there was a single writer.

The older style shown above is the Sutterline style, another popular style of script that was taught in Germany 1865-1916, which would probably be about when Hauptmann was learning how to write in the lower grades of school.

Hauptmann was born in 1899.

I've looked at many other writing styles for various time periods, and I don't really see the style in which these *D*'s and *S*'s are written as we've seen in the first few ransom letters! I can only conclude that both Hauptmann and the letter writers were working hard to cover up their real handwriting, creating all sorts of plausible characters and trying to use them consistently.

The first letter is almost unique in that, while the pen strokes are shaky and awkwardly written, the pen used for the first letter seems to have a finer point than that used for the other ransom letters.

Was there a single writer? I personally believe multiple writers are likely, if there was only one writer. it doesn't appear that it was Hauptmann.

Random fun fact: There are apps, of course, for your phone, that can help you learn how to write in cursive. Even for a child, they can show a letter on the screen, show how it was written, and then if it's a touchscreen, allow the child to write the letter on the screen correctly. There were a few apps of this type for my iPhone, and they taught how to write in several different languages. For at least two of the apps, which I purchased, one of the languages was German. When I installed them, neither had a working German component as advertised. (Gut ding I'm note paranoid.)

ransom letters — Hauptmann handwriting

Shown above are side-by-side comparisons used at the trial to prove Bruno wrote the ransom letters. I find it hard to believe these were shown to a judge and jury. I'm not sure what the first two words are. The second two appear to be *next* and *Bronx*, with similar *x*'s. However, the *n*'s in each word are different. If the third line, *is* and *yes* are presumably meant to show the *s*'s are the same, and if these were the closest they could find, it's certainly not a useful comparison. If the last two words are meant to show the similarity of *a*'s, the *a* in *part* has been modified. Also, the *t* in *part* is crossed while the *t* in the above *the*, typical of the ransom letters, is not. I believe that all the visual aids concerning writing that were used in the case were prepared as part of the case against Hauptmann. A few were borrowed by the defense and used to prove he was <u>not</u> the author. This would have been a good collection of comparisons to do so.

A copy of a handwritten letter from Bruno Hauptmann to the Governor, asking for help, is available on the internet. This was written while he was in jail, waiting to be executed. You will be surprised at the good handwriting; the letter contains few spelling errors, and all his *t*'s were crossed, and *i*'s were dotted. It looked nothing like any of the ransom letters. It can be found at this very useful website:

http://jimfisher.edinboro.edu/lindbergh/writing.html

There are also requested writings that Hauptmann made the night he was arrested that were used as exemplars of his writing style on this web site.

There also exists a very long, 5000-word letter that Hauptmann wrote to his mother in Germany, explaining his innocence, which she never received. It was kept by the warden of The Trenton State Prison. He didn't want it to create additional controversy if it was released to the public. It's easy to find if you'd like to look.

16K. Image J and Some Image J Images

One of the tools that I have in my laboratory is the software called Image J. The software is free, and it can run on your computer.

Since we are not in 1932, we have many computer tools that we can use to help analyze evidence. One that I often use is this freeware for analyzing photos and stacks of photos. It has been developed over the years by both the National Institutes of Health (NIH) and by users.

Image J is a powerful program for manipulating images. It's like iPhoto or the program you got with your digital camera to improve digital photos after you've taken them. However, often, you don't know precisely what you are doing. You click on a button or move a slider to enhance contrast. You don't know what you've done, but the picture looks better. In Image J you can see exactly what you do and can see how a fundamental change alters the result. Plus, it does things with digital images (pictures) that you can't imagine, like split a color image into its component images, or do image math (divide an image by another image).

IMAGE J is easy to find on the web to download, and there are many tutorials as well, so if you want a powerful image analysis tool that can do very useful manipulations, download a free copy of Image J.

Providing a full tutorial here for the program is beyond the scope of the book, so let me introduce you to a few of the realities of digital photography.

The figure below shows a black and white photograph of some boats "on the hard."

Figure 16K.1. A digital photo called "Boats"

When this file is opened in Image J, it informs you that the picture is 397x453 pixels, 8 bit, 176K.

Since the image is digital, it is made up of an array of points called pixels. There is a table that describes it in the computer (phone), that lists each position (x,y) and the intensity of the pixel at that position. The upper left side corner is x,y = (0,0). x gets larger as you move to the right; y gets larger as you move down. So, a picture is a set of all possible coordinates with intensity information for each. It says there are 397 x 453 pixels or points that make up the image. The total number of pixels is then 397 x 453 = 179,841 total pixels. So, the image size is 179 thousand points, or, in math shorthand, 179K (K = kilo = 1000). There are digital cameras now that can shoot images that have megapixels in them, that's a thousand times more points. As the number of pixels increases, resolution usually goes up.

There is also information in the black and white file on your computer that tells you, for each location, what should you put there? A white dot? A black dot? Something in between? For each location (x,y) there is an intensity number associated with it between 0 and 255 (this means there are 256 greyscale tones that could be used at each point in a black and white image.) This is the definition of the "8 bit" part of the label. For this system, the blackest black corresponds to an intensity number of zero, and a value of 255 corresponds to the whitest white. All other values fall between black and white – 256 total shades of gray. We rarely think about it, but since we have a table with three columns of numbers, we need to know what shade of gray corresponds to what intensity number. This is called a lookup table (LUT), where numbers are converted to grays. This is purely an artificial thing. There are many lookup tables that we can select in addition to a collection of grays. There are lookup tables that tell you what COLOR to put at a location if there is a certain intensity value there.

Also, useful to understand is the concept of a histogram. The program looks through every pixel and adds up the number that had an Intensity value of zero, then 1, up to 255. Then it makes a graph that shows you how the points are distributed. Below is a typical histogram.

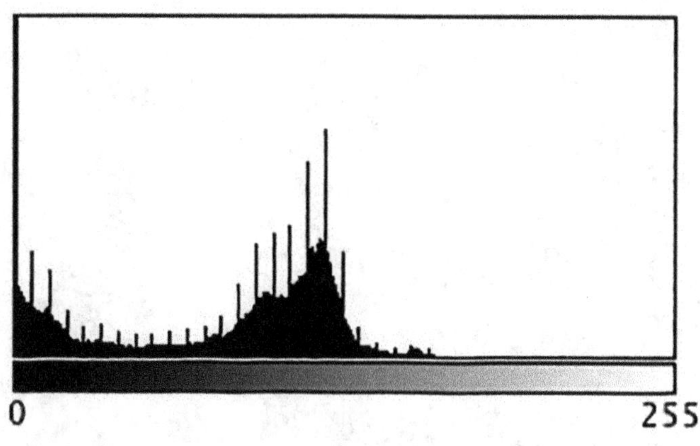

Figure 16K.2. A Histogram, and below it, a LUT

The graph shows that the number of pixels with each intensity value on the graph; below the data is the lookup table that was being used. 0 = black, 255 = white. What one usually prefers is an image with a histogram that covers the entire possible range. It looks like in the range of 175-255, where you will see the brightest of whites, there are no pixels that have those intensity values, although there are lots of pixels that have intensity values of zero. So, we're not using the entire range of greys. If we redefine the pixel value, we can convert the values to span from 0 to 255, that's the brightest, best photo you can get. If we have a range of 256 values, why not use them all? We can convert to a new look-up-table (LUT) that will do that.

Figure 16K.3. The same photo using the full range of possible intensity values

The photo looks much better when we use all the pixel greyscale values, especially the whiter ones. Our eyes are not necessarily built to distinguish similar shades of grey, but no worries, there are many creative LUTS out there. We can count out numbers from 0-255 and assign a different color to each number. I'm going to replot this using a LUT called *sixteen colors*.

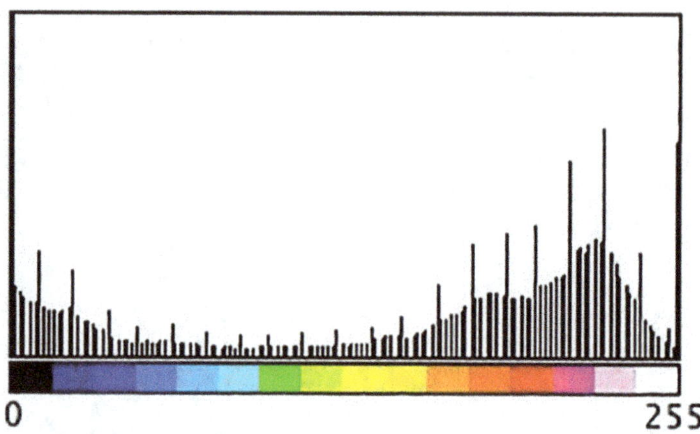

Count: 179841　Min: 0
Mean: 147.291　Max: 255
StdDev: 87.726　Mode: 0 (13043)

Figure 16K.4. An expanded range of intensity values with the *sixteen colors* LUT, also shown

This LUT associates different colors with the pixel intensity values, where now 0 is black, and 255 is white, but in this case, there are colors in between.

Figure 16K. 5. Same photo, different LUT

If we apply this color LUT to our boat photo, this is what it looks like. You never know when a very different LUT can help you see things you didn't before. The name on the boat on the right stands out with this LUT, but not so much with the greyscale LUT.

If you can at least understand pixels, histograms, and LUTS, that's a good start for searching for hidden treasures in a photograph – especially if it is of a document of interest.

One fascinating aspect of Image J is that when you start to use it, perhaps there are 50 possible things you can do. People have developed extra tools that you can add to your Image J to make it much more useful to you. These are called plug-ins, and they give additional power to the program. You might be able to find a set of plug-ins just for analyzing documents. It would have options in it like comparing the shapes of letters. If you were studying dinosaur bones, comparing letters would be of no use. Perhaps you'd like to be able to measure the length and thickness of a bone from a photo. There may be collections of plug-ins just for dinosaur doctors and other sets of plug-ins for document examiners, which turn your basic Image J platform into something that does just what you want to do. Plug-ins are free, and people who use Image J often find a way to create a new plug-in and share it with the rest of us.

Go to https://imagej.net/Introduction to learn more about Image J.

I want to show you a few aspects of the ransom letters that I found and encourage you to see what you can discover. I was interested in the concept of letters in words being modified, with what appears to be a slightly darker ink (or more ink), to add a character or to make a's look more rounded like Hauptmann's writing. It is simple to change the contrast of a document to more clearly pick out letters that are a little darker from those that are a bit lighter, but giving the image higher contrast, making the light points much lighter and the dark points much darker. This is what a typical ransom letter looks like when this is done.

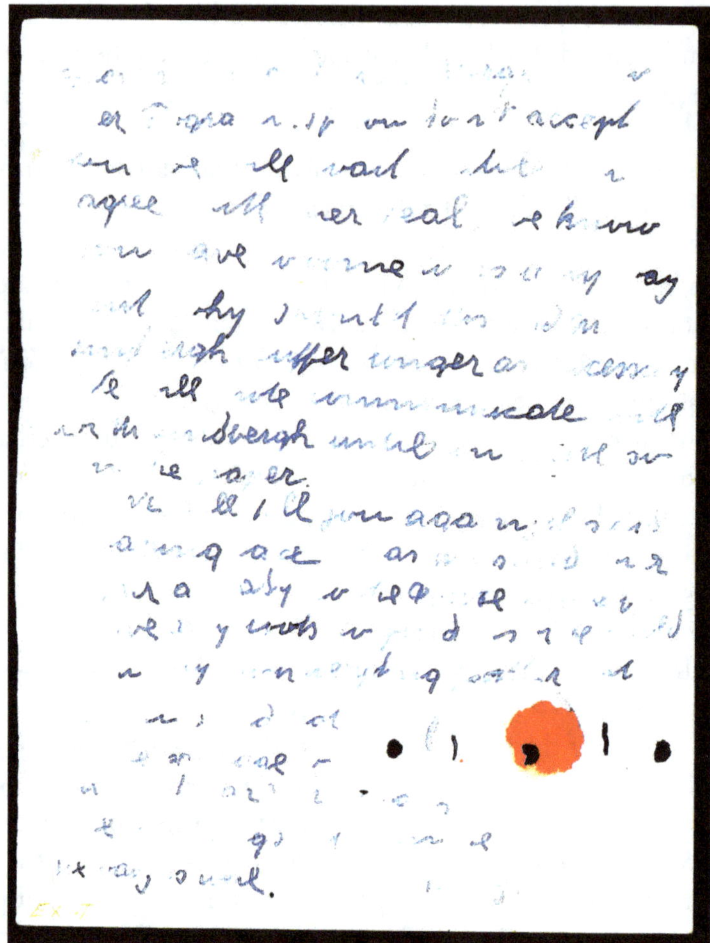

Figure 16K.6. A ransom letter, enhanced

This is not what you see if you do the same with a regular handwritten letter. If I were a conspiracy theorist, I'd suggest that if the darker letters are all put together, there is a secret message there waiting to be read, but that is not the case.

By working with contrast and saturation and selecting a variety of LUTs, I started looking where there was nothing. "Nothing" tended to be on the back sides of the letters where often there is no writing. Through many trials and errors, I found a combination of operations that took me to this view of the back of a ransom letter.

Figure 16K.7. Enhanced back of a ransom letter

I found writing on it! You can also see the fold lines much clearer and a smudged but real fingerprint on the center bottom of the page. However, the excitement lies in finding writing. Was this the impression of writing on another page that was not a ransom letter? What additional can it tell us? I analyzed several ransom notes and found 'invisible' writing on all of them. As I began to unravel these mysterious messages, I first saw that the words and letters to the words were all written backwards - very strange. I then reversed the writing on the other side of the page and realized that this is what I was discovering – the writing from the other side of the pages. It was exciting for a moment, and this is the nature of scientific research. Sometimes we rediscover what we already should know.

Fortunately, it gets better. There is an operation in Image J that lets you separate intensity values so you can see, for example, where a boundary may be between all points with intensity values less than 140 and all numbers more than 142. There may be some pixels with values just a little higher or lower than all the others, and we can find them, perhaps to help find where the letters were folded.

Other than finding fold lines, one would expect paper to be fairly homogeneous in terms of the intensity values for all the points that are not part of the writing or singnature, but there are some unusual patterns here (shown below). There is a stripe of pixels of different intensity values on at least two of the ransom letters. Shown below is what I found for letters #10 and #13.

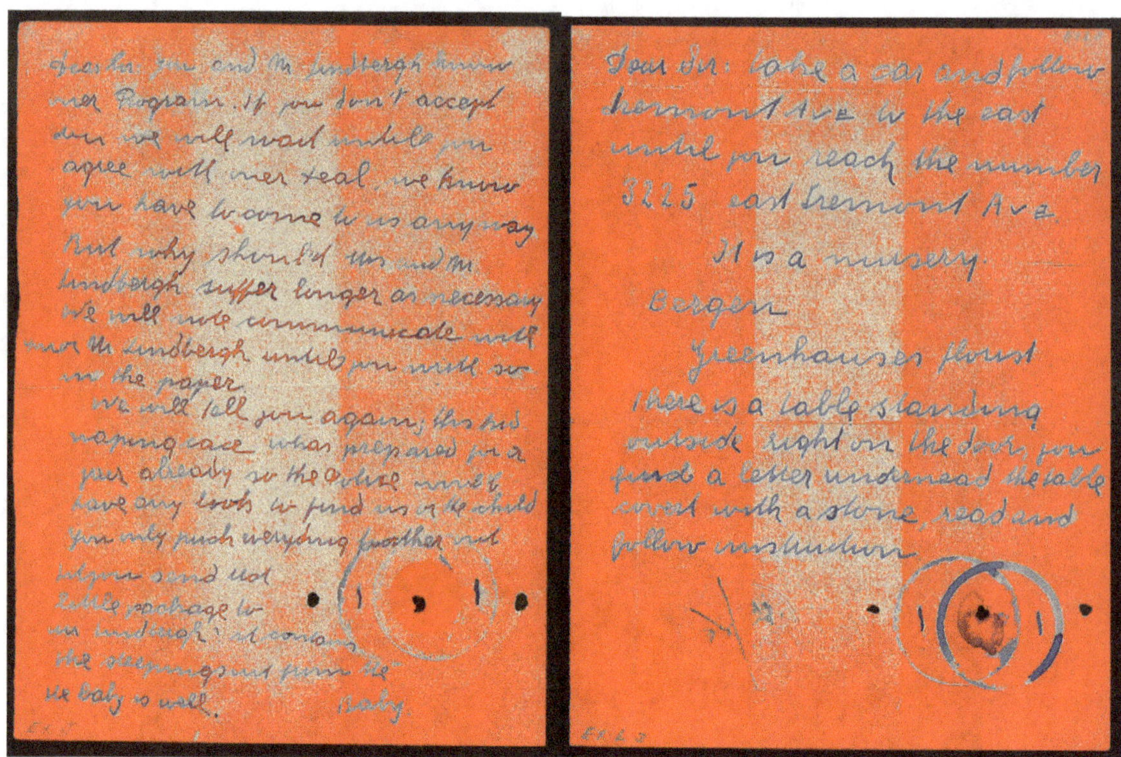

Dear Sir: you and Mr Lindbergh know our Program. If you don't accept den we will wait until you agree with our deal. we know you have to come to us anyway But why should Mrs and Mr Lindbergh suffer longer as necessary We will not communicate with you or Mr Lindbergh until you write so in the paper.
We will tell you again; this kidnapping case whas prepared for a year already so the Police won't have any look to find us or the child You only puch everything farther out did you send that little package to Mr Lindbergh? it contains the sleepingsuit from the baby. the baby is well. Baby

Dear Sir: take a car and follow Tremont Ave to the east until you reach the number 3225 east Tremont Ave. It is a nursery. Bergen Greenhauses florist there is a table standing outside right on the door, you find a letter underneath the table covert with a stone, read and follow instruction.

Figure 16K.8: Finding stripes on Letters #10 (left) and #13 (right)

They are in the same place on each page. What does it remind you of?

It could be an imprint of a bookmark. I thought of small blank books that I often buy to write in, that are loosely held closed by a paper band around a few books, such as that shown below.

Figure 16K.9. Paper Band holding a journal together

The size of this paper strip is very similar to the stripe found on the two ransom letters.

Shown below is an 8-pack stationery set (envelopes and writing paper wrapped in a brown paper band) as an example of how paper bands are used.

(I liked the bookmark idea, but think about putting one in a book – usually not in the middle of a page.)

Figure 16K.10. Stationery held together with a paper band

Perhaps it was just a physically compressed part of a few pages made from a bookmark. I still believe that there are several aspects of the ransom letters, from the single cut/ripped edge to the appearance of a band, that would be consistent with the paper coming from what at one time was a blank, bound journal.

I used ratios for the Image J-enhanced pages where I found the stripes and determined that the white stripe on letter #10 is 1 17/32 inches wide, and on letter #13 it is 1 13/32 in. wide. I had a set of three small notebooks that were bound in a paper strip, which was 1 3/8 in. wide – unusually close to being 1 12/32 in wide:

Figure 16K.11. Paper band around small blank booklets

although in some stationery sets, they use a ribbon a fraction of an inch wide to hold the envelopes or notes together.

I want to share with you one other thing I found using Image J. With a good, scanned image, you always have the option of blowing it up, almost like having a microscope at your disposal.

I was looking at the cut edges, hoping to find out how they were cut. Wouldn't you measure the distance, make some marks, draw a line, and then cut along the line? You don't see any evidence of such lines … or do you?

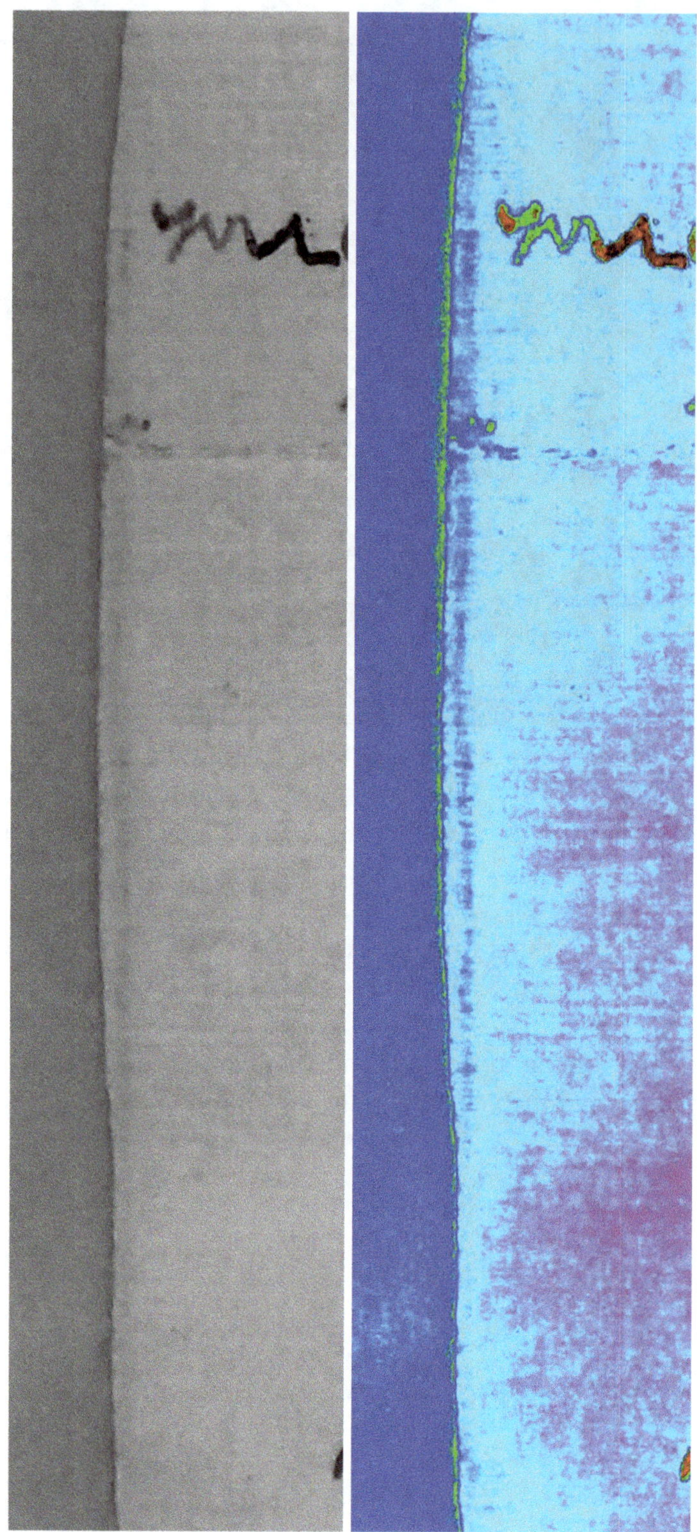

Figure 16K.12. A portion of a cut edge - Left, black and white LUT; Right, using a color LUT

On one ransom letter I see a faint, straight line that must have been used to make the cut. If I choose a color LUT, it is easier to see. This observation suggests that the pages were more likely cut then torn.

CHAPTER 17
THE SINGNATURE – INTRODUCTION

Let me start by saying, again – What a mess! What is this thing? A message or more distraction? You can't know until you start looking into signs and seals. And before we do that, we should define it in as much detail as we can.

Qualitatively, the singnature has three equally spaced holes, two blue open circles, one red filled circle, and two wavy lines. It always is on the front side of a ransom letter, not at the end if the message carries over to the backside. It appears to fall in the same place, reproducibly, on each letter that carries one.

Gardner (Gardner, L.C. 2012) made an insightful comment. He wrote that the kidnappers created an ideal singnature. It is impossible to copy, even if you had the original in front of you!

As you learn more about it, you will appreciate how insightful Gardner's comment is.

Most who have something to say about the singnature suggest that the red circle was made using the cork from a red fountain pen ink bottle, and the circles were made with the bottom of an ink bottle, that had been "dipped in blue fountain pen ink." I think we can consider these but should, at the very least, confirm. If this were the actual seal of some organization, one would expect it to look better. The red circle in the middle is usually blotchy and incomplete, as are the blue circles. The blue circles seem randomly placed, and whatever they chose as an applicator for the blue circles should have been replaced with something that could do a better job. When I look at the singnatures, I imagine that someone set a shot glass down on one of the ransom letters and left a circular stain of who knows what, and that gave them the idea.

Some of the holes look somewhat round; some are almost triangular. If you look at the backside of the holes, many have paper that was once the hole, and has been punched out but not completely punched off the page; a fragment remains, hanging. Who knows how they looked just after they were made? We can only know about their appearance more than 80 years later.

If I mention the phrase "hanging chad", you might be old enough to know its significance. If not, there is a short explanation in ALLISONweb for you.

17A. What Is It? What Does It Mean?

Before we get into too many singnature details, I'm sure you want to know what it means.

I did buy a copy of Koch's *The Book of Signs* (493 primitive and medieval symbols) (R. Koch 1930/1955), and there is nothing in there that looks like the singnature. I purchased *Masonic and Occult Symbols Illustrated (728 Illustrations)* (C. Burns, 1998). Once I was in that section of Amazon Books, there were many choices. I also purchased Cooper's *An Illustrated Encyclopedia of Traditional Symbols* (210 Illustrations) (J.C. Cooper, 1978) and E. Lehner's *Symbols Signs & Signets* (1350 Illustrations) (E. Lehner, 1950). I could find nothing in these sources that resembles the singnature.

Perhaps I should conclude that it is as it appears, a mess of ink that indicates the letter came from THE kidnappers, so it serves its purpose. Perhaps in this way, it is like the ladder – designed only to give the police something to do, where all theories are irrelevant.

Over the years, many have "reported" what the symbol is, and of course, those explanations have been repeated by others. But no one seems to back up their facts by showing us the symbol they cite. When you investigate them further, you find that none of them match.

But today we have the internet. We have tools such as Google Images. I spent many days there and did see several symbols that have *something* in common with the kidnappers' singnature. I also investigated all the proposed symbols. I'll share what I can here:

Figure 17A.1. unidentified location

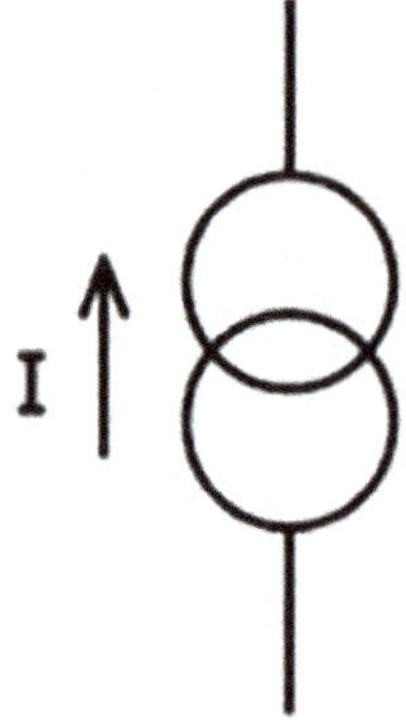

Figure 17A.2. A symbol used in electronic circuit diagrams

Figure 17A.3. Supposedly a Scientologist's secret bunker

Figure 17A.4. A crop circle

Figure 17A.5. Vatican City in Rome (left)

The symbol at the right (above) is the symbol of the Catholic Church. It evolved from the Greek spelling of Jesus Christ, IESOUS XPISTOS. Sometimes they use an overlapping I and X called the iota-chi, or an overlapping X and P as shown above, called the chi-rho.

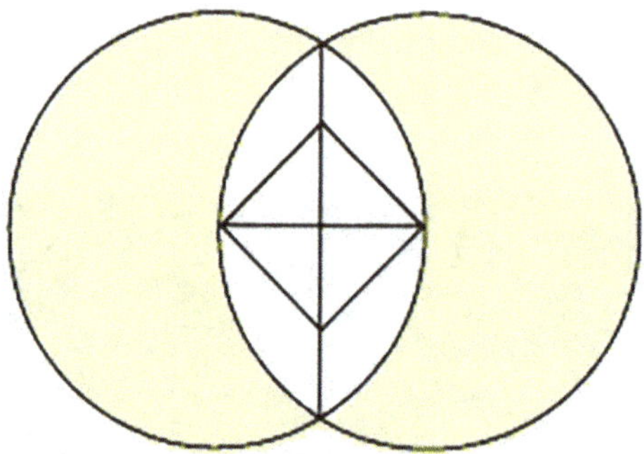

Figure 17A.6. Vesica Piscis, a pattern "through which all geometric shapes are born."

If you're curious, there is an interesting article entitled *The Ripper* [yes, Jack], *Jesus Christ and the Lindbergh Tragedy* (Westcott, T. 2004) that discusses it.

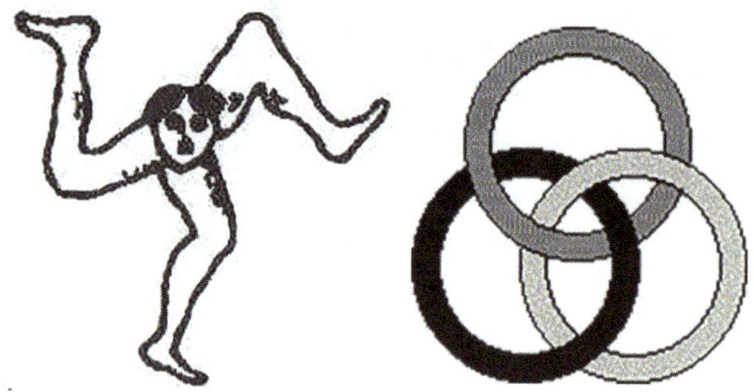

Figure 17A.7. The Trigamba

A popular explanation was that the singnature was a symbol of an Italian or Sicilian gang, called the Trigamba. (See the ALLISONweb for more information on the Trigamba.) Two versions are shown in Figure 17A.7.

Figure 17A.8. The Krupp Arms, A German Military Trademark, and Ballentine Beer's three-ring sign

There was a U.S. beer, Ballentine Beer, that used the three-ring sign.

Figure 17A.9. Aleister Crowley's Solar Phallus from *The Equinox*. Crowley was an occultist and founder of the religion *Thelema*

You can learn more about him through Ozzy Osbourne's song, *Mr. Crowley (Blizzard of Ozz,* 1980).

Figure 17A.10. A City Monument

Olympic Symbol

Kool Cigarettes

Figure 17A.11. Errata, all equally unlikely

> Mark Falzini comments
>
> You left out the Chalice Well in Glastonbury, England.
>
> Author comments
>
> You are right! Let me take care of that.

The Chalice Well is found in Glastonbury, England. Pottery shards dating back to the Paleolithic Age found near the well suggest that it has been in use for two thousand years or more. The cover of the well is shown in Figure 17A.13. It feeds into the pool shown in Figure 17A.14.

Figure 17A.13. Cover of the Chalice well

Figure 17A.14. The pool fed by the well

While it does not match the singnature, I chose to include the three-ring sign of Ballentine beer. Just as their add suggests it was created by accident; I have a feeling it was perhaps (as I've said before) a wet shot glass put down on a ransom letter being constructed that eventually lead to the singnature. I tried to find out what the singnature meant, and so far, I can only conclude that it has no meaning.

There are some very dramatic interpretations of the symbol where one blue circle is supposed to represent Lindbergh and the other circle Hauptmann, with the red circle representing Little Charlie between them. The small wavy lines represent water, over which the pilots fly, to represent the fact that Hauptmann also had a great interest in flying, and in the end the child was supposedly kept in a boat, so we need water in the image. Very creative! But probably no.

I have one final lead. The FBI of course had a file on the Lindbergh case, certainly not accessible to the public at the time (Fensch, 2001, p. 398). Four special agents prepared a summary report on the file's contents for the period March 1, 1932, through February 1934; it was the basis for a report made by Special Agent T.H. Sisk on February 16, 1934. The file contained a letter received by the New York Division in September 1933 from John J. Pawelczyk. He wrote to point out that he copyrighted a radio puzzle in September 1931 and copyrighted a symbol very similar to the singnature. His handwriting was compared to the ransom letters - not a match. His symbol was of the same general design, using overlapping circles to represent radio dials. This could be the basis for the singnature design. The puzzle was released before the kidnapping. However, if it had any popularity, it would have been recognized at the time. I could find no record of Pawelczyk's symbol.

Conclusion: The singnature is too sloppy to be relevant, but the search for its meaning obviously keeps many occupied. Until someone can show me that it is legitimate, I'll assume it has no meaning and functions to indicate that certain letters are from the kidnapper(s), as they explained.

17B. The Holes, Part One

Assignment: Make some holes in paper using a punch, a nail, a screw, a pencil point, a pen point, etc. Be creative. First, think about the variables in poking a hole in paper. There is a tool. Perhaps a nail. You can also get very different results if you punch through a single sheet or a few at the same time, and whether you have a sponge under the paper, a small stack of paper towels or napkins, or perhaps a hard surface. Look at the holes in the signatures of the ransom letters (front and back) and see if any of the real holes match any of the ones you made.

Q17B.1: Do you think you found how the holes were made, and could your observations be relevant?

A17B.1: First list the variables that you investigated. (Variables: tool used, number of sheets punched at one time, soft or hard support under the pages, etc.). Don't be lazy; investigate all the variables you can think of. Then complete the table.

	Tool Used & Other Variables	Hole Appearance
1.		
2.		
3.		
4.		
5.		
6.		
7.		
8.		
9.		
10.		

17C. How to Assemble a Singnature

Q17C.1: Was there a specific order in which the components of a ransom note were made? We should briefly consider the order if any because we can.

A17C.1: Consider the singnature of Letter #7. Shown below are the front and the back sides.

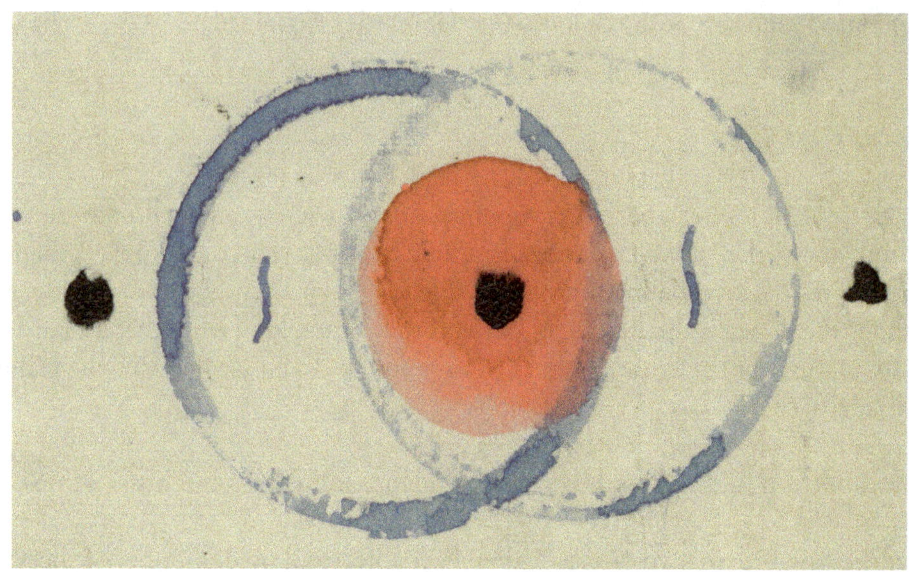

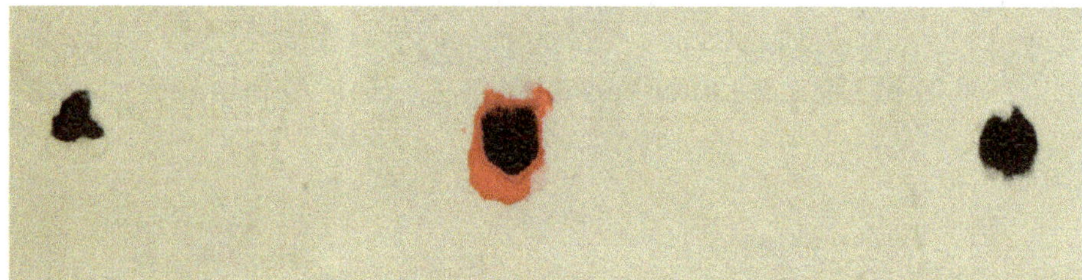

Figure 17C.1. The singnature, front and back, from Letter #7

This is not the only letter where the red from the center circle bleeds through the center hole, suggesting that the holes (at least the middle hole) are(is) made first.

Look at the blue circles of the singnature, and the relative position of the writing on the page; there are multiple instances where the writing runs over the top of one of the blue circles (ransom letters 2, 4 and 6, for example). This would be consistent with the singnature being created after the holes, and before the text for that specific ransom letter. In some cases, the blue circles are completely separated from the red circle; in other cases, one is on top of the other, so it appears that the red circle was put on the paper first, with the larger blue circles following (more on the blue circles shortly). The order appears to be: holes, red circle, blue circles, probably wavy lines, and last, the message.

Q17C.2: Do you think the singnature is of any importance at all? What does it signify? Is it just like the ladder – something made to take time and attention away from important aspects of the case?

A17C.2:

Mark Falzini comments

The ladder isn't an important aspect of the case?

Author comments

Numerous sources suggest that the ladder was not used in the kidnapping. There were apparently holes in the ground that show the ladder was put up to the Nursery window. If all three sections were used, it would have rested against the broken shutter, and entry into the window would have been impossible. If only two sections were used it would have been too short. The holes in the ground suggest the ladder was set up just outside the first floor office window where Lindbergh was sitting at the time of the kidnapping, with no curtains on the window. The "True Story of the Lindbergh Kidnapping" reports that the ladder indentations in the soft soggy ground were too shallow for the ladder to have actually been used.

17D. Creating the Blue Circles

Continuing on the question of "How was it made?", let's move to the larger blue, open circles, of the signature. Go back to the ransom notes and look at them. They are all very messy for something so important, and let me say for the tenth time, it is unclear why the kidnappers would have accepted something of such inferior quality if it had a real meaning to them.

17D.1 Circle Size and Pattern

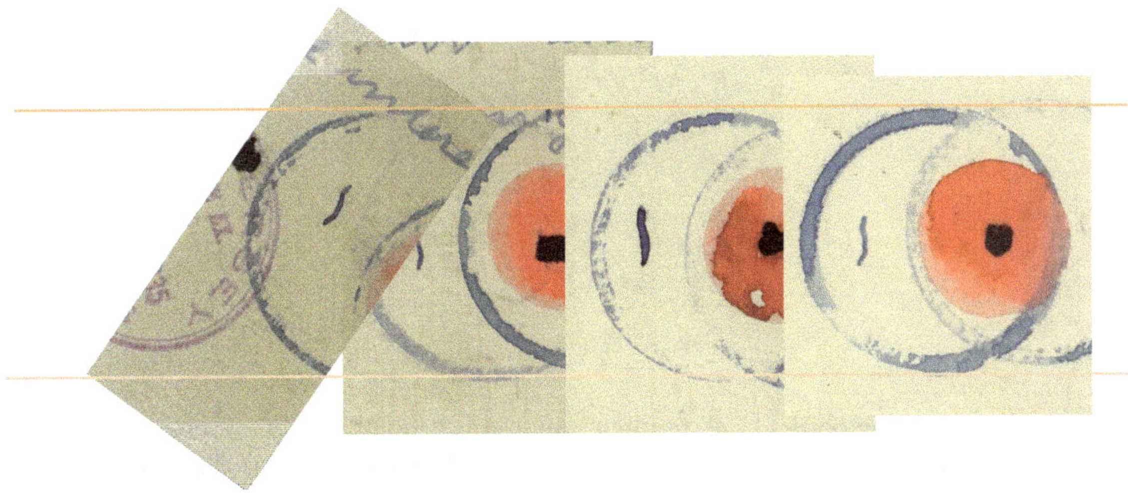

Figure 17D.1.1. Some partial blue circles

Blue circles on multiple letters all appear to have the same diameter, suggesting that the same tool was used for each one. They are 32 mm in diameter (outer diameter, o.d.), depending on the thickness of the line (roughly 2 mm), are often incomplete circles, fade to nothing for some, and are dark and thick for others. Again, in the lab, we experimented with several possible "stamps," possible blue liquids that may have been readily available and considered prior suggestions.

The pattern seen shows that, if a bottle was used, the bottle bottom had a continuous set of small dimples around the outer edge. Not all bottles are made with such a pattern. Adding that to the edge of a bottle's base is called stippling.

Figure 17D.1.2. Completing a blue circle from fragments

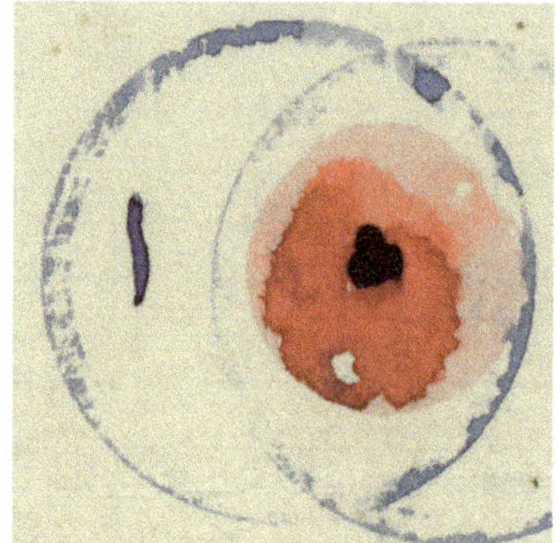

Figure 17D.1.3. A Complete Blue Circle

There are several reasons why bottles have stippling. Often this is found on beer bottles or bottles used for medicine. Stippling patterns are just on the outside base edge where contact occurs. If it is something like a beer bottle, it may contain stippling around the outer base edge because cold bottles in a humid environment sweat and the sweat tends to run down to the base, making the bottles unstable, easy to slide or slip over;

stippling is added to the base to make it more stable. Many base perimeter-type stipplings looks like small crescents ((((((((. Sometimes seen on modern wine bottles it looks more like ()()()()()()()(). Stippling on a bottle may also be added because the bottles are moved on a conveyor belt when filled, and stability at that point is required.

Many things may be found on bottle bottoms such as makers' marks, and various marks caused by the method of bottle construction; pontil marks, ejection marks, seams, or specific information requested by the bottle user.

It has been suggested that the bottom of a round ink bottle was somehow exposed to writing ink, then used as a stamp for the singnature's blue circles.

17D.2. Bottle Bottoms, Sizes, and Patterns

Figure 17D.2.1. shows the measurement of the diameter of a typical (old) ink bottle. The digital caliper reports 2.19 inches, which is roughly 2 3/16 inches (55.6 mm).

Figure 17D.2.1. Measuring The bottom of an ink bottle from the early 1900s

Many ink bottles have been cast (Molten glass is poured into a metal form to create the bottle shape), and the bottom of ink bottles often have raised letters indicating the name of the company or "This Container Made in the USA," so if raised portions of the bottom of a bottle were used to deposit a small amount of blue liquid, we would see company names or product names; we do not.

Figure 17D.2.2. An inverted ink bottle

The bottom rim of this ink bottle (above) has a diameter of ~ 45 mm. The blue circle has a diameter of 32 mm. To create a smaller size blue circle, a smaller glass bottle could have been used, but likely not an ink bottle.

About the only thing we can conclude is that they probably used some kind of glass bottle bottom, which inefficiently picked up some blue liquid to stamp with. Sometimes the stamp is sufficient to yield some structural details of the stamp, and sometimes it's just not available.

17D.3. Stipple Measurements on Ransom Letters

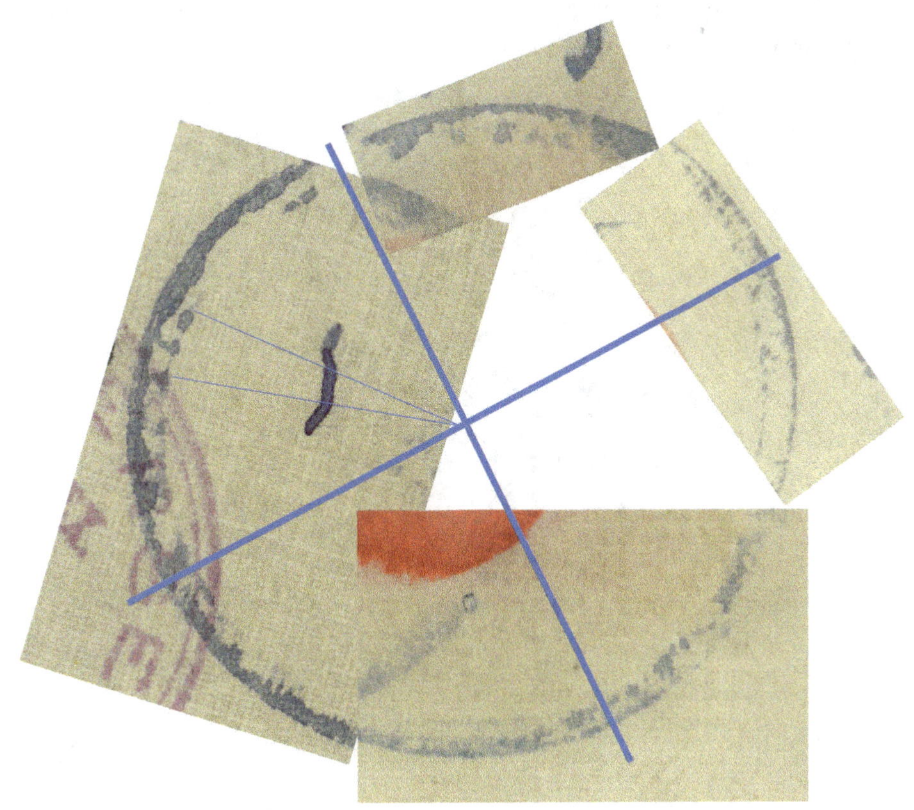

Figure 17D.3.1. Counting Stipples on the bottle used to make a blue circle

I did my best to find the approximate center, as shown above. I considered three well-defined stipples. They corresponded to an angle from the center of 12 degrees. So approximately every six degrees is another stipple. Six degrees, including the starting stipple contains 1+ 6/6 = 2 stipples, 12 degrees contains 1 + 12/6 = 3 stipples, so 360 degrees would contain [1 + 360/6] = 61 stipples around the full circumference of the bottle edge. One can see more than three stipples in a row. I marked the first three and three more and measured the angle. The measurement depends on how accurately I can locate the center of the circle from a partial arc. For six stipples, I determined the angle containing them to be 34 degrees. This would correspond to 54 stipples for the entire circumference, less than the 61 approximated using only three stipples to estimate the corresponding angle.

One can certainly understand why the circles are often incomplete, sometimes detailed enough to see the spacing between the stipples; on other occasions the partial circle is thick and full. Glass is not a good medium for absorbing ink. To study this, I would select an ink and soak a paper towel in it, push the bottom of a bottle into the wet paper towel, then "print" with it. It depends on whether the stippling is helping in picking up ink, which it does not do uniformly; the glass does not have sufficient affinity for the ink, and so the print depends on the amount of ink available and the surface of the glass. Shown in the next section (18D.4) are some examples made in my laboratory using a 32mm OD bottle and inks on paper. Clearly the bottle is variable in its ability to pick up inks and the result also depends on what the liquid is.

17D.4. Bottle Candidates – Sizes and Patterns

Here are some typical glass bottles that have a special textured edge on the bottom or some other writing that would appear if the glassware were used as a "stamp".

Figure 17D.4.1. The bottom of a bottle with stippling and other marks

For the figure shown above, which has a very dense set of stipples, I divided the circle into quarters, and a 90-degree portion of that circle contained roughly 25, so there would be approximately 100 stipples for the entire 360 degrees. The stipples here are too close to each other, so one would need to find a candidate with a larger space between stipples to make the blue singnature circle.

Figure 17D.4.2. Stippling on the bottom of a liquor bottle (flask shaped)

My "typical" ink bottles had bottom diameters of 1.904 and 2.198 inches (48.36 and 55.83 mm), much bigger than the singnature circles. In my Chemistry Department stockroom, there were many bottles to look through. Some were bottles that may have been purchased a while ago and were never used because an experiment changed. I first looked for bottles with stippling on the bottom, then looked for bottles with diameters close in size to the circle. Kimble, one of the largest makers of glass products for scientific work, makes an amber dropper bottle, a small 30 mL (1 fluid oz.) capacity bottle that has an OD of 32 mm. It comes with a screw cap, bulb and glass dropper. They also made amber Boston round bottles, and clear Boston round bottles with a 30 mL (1 mL = 1 milli-Liter) capacity and 32 mm OD bottle. (Boston is a reference to the shape – simple round bottles)

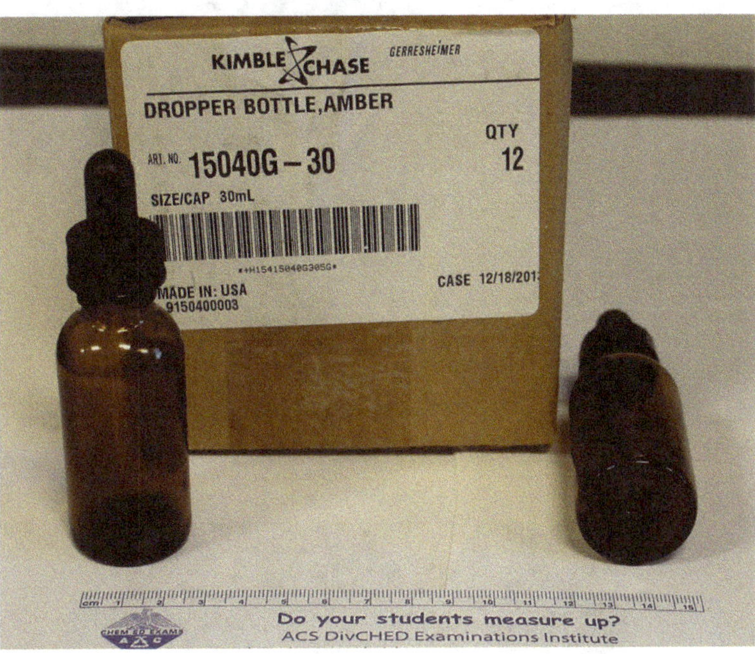

Figure 17D.4.3. 30 mL Boston dropper bottle

Figure 17D.4.4. Small bottles with stippling

Figure 17D.4.4 shows similar size bottles that have stippling and/or other printing on the bottoms. For example, the clear bottle on the left side has a double set of stipples. I divided the bottom into four (90 degree) quarters; each had 15 stipples, for a total of approximately 60 stipples around the circumference.

Here is the bottom of another small bottle with stippling, again with a double row of points.

Figure 17D.4.5. Stippling

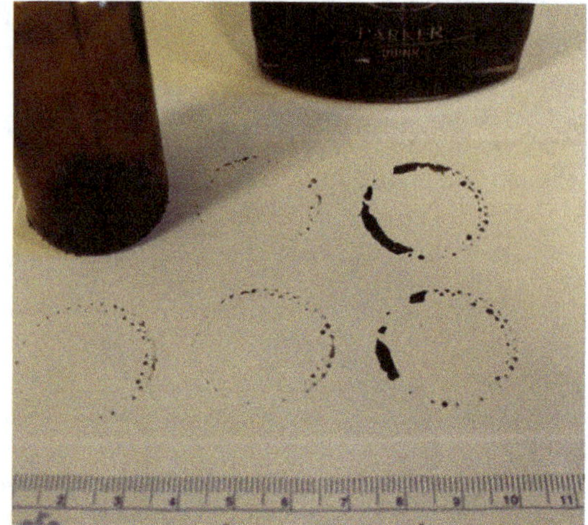

Figure 17D.4.6. "Printing" with a bottle bottom

Figure 17D.4.6 shows several stamps made using two fountain pen inks, where the bottom of a #12 bottle was dabbed onto a paper towel soaked in the ink. The stamps all look different. In the top figure, there are stipples on two circles of very similar radii, each with 17 corresponding to 180 degrees, so 34 for 360 degrees, the complete bottle circumference. Such small bottles are commonly used in research labs. If a bottle like this were found in the home, it would most likely be from a pharmacy – a small bottle of ear drops, for example.

17D.5. Not Bottles

There are many items, not just bottles, that have a similar diameter and features around the edge. Consider, for example – wristwatch cases. Many can be found in the 24-56 mm diameter range and could have around the edge *scallops*, a repeating *pattern* of some kind, or even *diamonds* around the edge. The ransom letter singnature appears to have about six within a 34-degree angle for a total of 54-61. One watch that I picked had about 65 "features" around the face.

Figure 17D.5.1. There are roughly 65 features around this watch casing

Figure 17D.5.2. I estimate there are 46 diamonds around the face of this watch

So, there are many possible items – bottles, watches, anything round with a repetitive pattern on it, that could be a candidate for making the blue circles. Whatever it is has a poor attraction for ink or an aqueous solution (such as glass or polished metal), so it only picks up a small and variable amount of ink. There are small bottles that are 32 mm wide and have stippling around the edge. Ink bottles are larger than the blue singnature circles in general, so it is doubtful that one was used to make the blue circles.

A curiosity: Below is ransom letter #4, unusual because there is an evidence stamp on the front. It is also possibly unusual because, if you look closely at that stamp and one blue circle, it seems like the blue circle ink is on top of the stamp. Does it look like that to you, and if so, why could it be important?

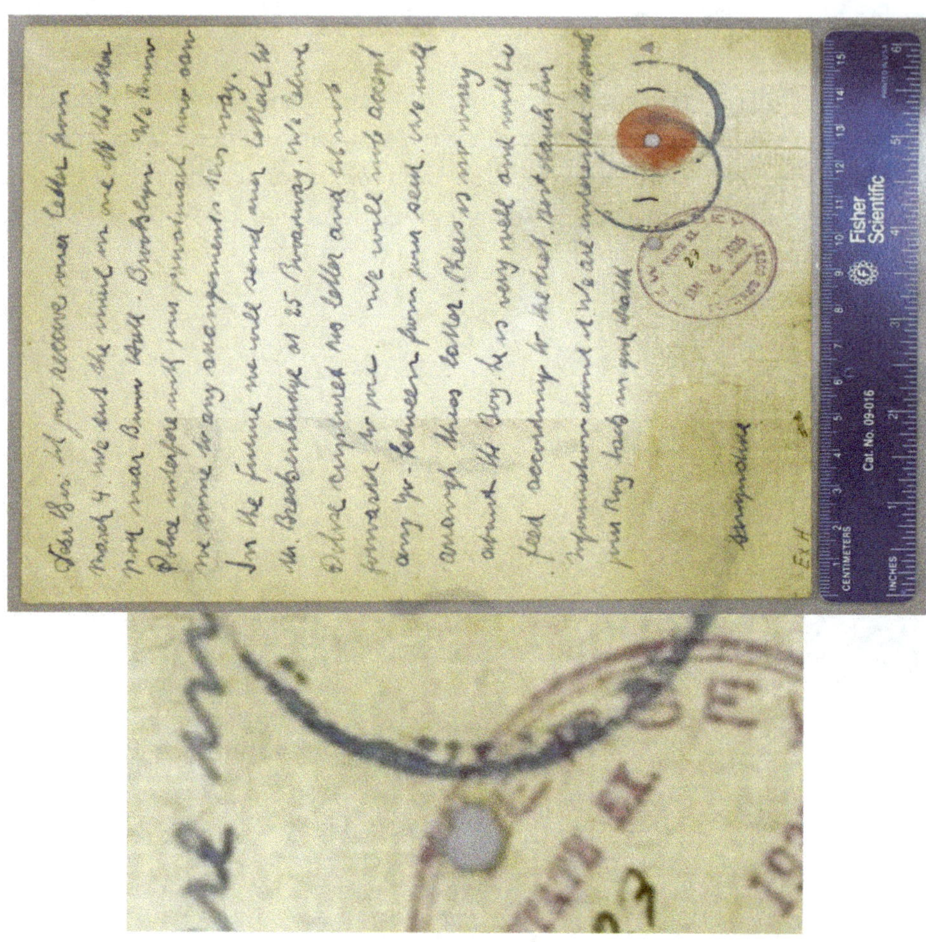

17E. The Red Circle

17E.1. How was it Made?

It was suggested that a cork from an ink bottle was used. Since it appears that the holes were made before the red circle, at least the author(s) could roughly center it on the center hole. I have spent some time traveling around the Northeast U.S. (New England, a great place for antique shopping) and I now have a small collection of ink bottles (without their corks).

17E2. Cork?

The corks are not what one might think of; most corks are tapered. The corks used in ink bottles, like wine bottle corks, are usually cylindrical, but may be different than a wine bottle cork because those used in ink bottles would often be beveled at the end. Many of the ink bottle corks would have a plastic top glued on to make it easier to pull the cork out. Often the corks for ink bottles looked like that shown in Figure 17E2.2.

Figure 17E2.1. Two old ink bottles – side and bottom views

Figure 17E2.2. Cork for an ink bottle – small, rounded/beveled bottom

We will talk about the dyes/colors later. First let's consider the shapes. The red circle appears to have a diameter of 11/16" (17.5 mm), 0.68 inches. (Note: 12/16" is ¾"). Below are some ink bottles. This was a time when manufacturers were switching from corked bottles to wider mouth bottles with thin metal screw tops.

Figure 17E2.3. Waterman's Ink Bottle – note short cork

Wine bottle corks are a little too large to fit an ink bottle. There is a #9 Superior Grade Straight Cork used in wine bottles. These corks are 15/16 inches in diameter and 1 1/2 inches long and are slightly chamfered on both ends for easier insertion. (The sharp edge around the cork is rounded off). These corks will give a good tight fit with a standard fifth size wine bottle that uses a finished cork or has a 3/4-inch opening. While these may be found in a wine bottle, some aspects of the size and details are to assist in using them with a corker, a mechanism that forces corks into a smaller opening on the bottles. There is also a smaller #7 straight cork (13/16" diameter), and a larger #10 straight cork (1 in. diameter), both of which are too large to have been used to make the red imprint.

My Chemistry Department stockroom has a large collection of cork stoppers of different sizes, and the one which can be used as a stamp to make the same size circle as the red circle is a number 8 cork stopper. They are 27 mm long, 17.5 mm diameter at one end and 22 mm (0.68 inches) diameter at the other end. These are perfect for making the red circle, but since they are tapered, they would not be used in an ink bottle.

(Cork stoppers such as this can be purchased from a number of laboratory supplies distributors, such as widgetco (www.widgetco.com/8-cork-stoppers-cork-plugs) - $0.31 each in lots of > 100, $0.11 each in lots > 1000.)

17E.3. Finding THAT Cork

I believe that a size 8 cork stopper could have been used as a "stamp" to make the red circles – by dipping the small end in a red liquid and then pressing it against the paper. It is a very imprecise process, and whether there is good coverage or not depends on the paper, the ink, and the tool used, and *how* the tool was used (single touch, touch and press, touch and twist, etc.)

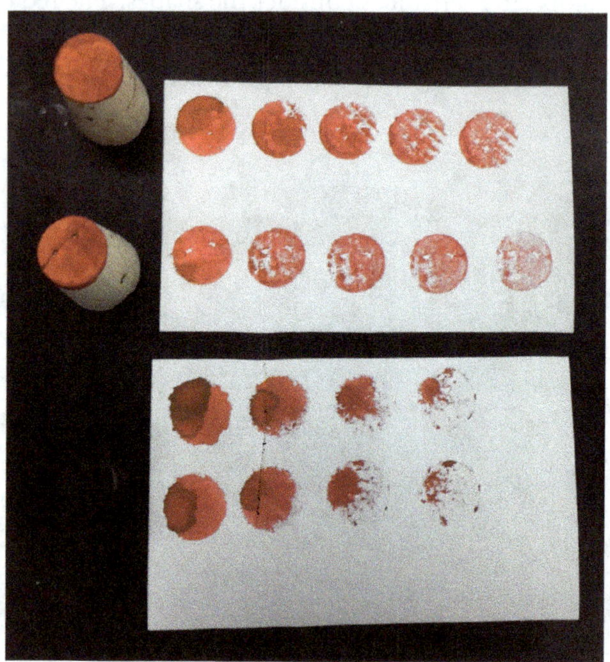

Figure 17E.3.1. Using corks (top) and a rubber stopper (below) as stamps

Figure 17E.3.1 shows the results of an experiment that we performed many different times with many different red liquids, papers, and possible "stamps." In some cases, red liquids would be picked up by the "stamp," to make multiple impressions. The top card was an experiment using a size 8 cork stopper (small end) and below, a similar size rubber stopper. The two materials adsorb and release the red liquid ink very differently. We observed something interesting. While the small end of a cork stopper may have a variety of physical features, only some of those are shown in its "stamp". However, we would often see one or two small round spots in the stamp where no red would be deposited. This was only observed with cork stoppers.

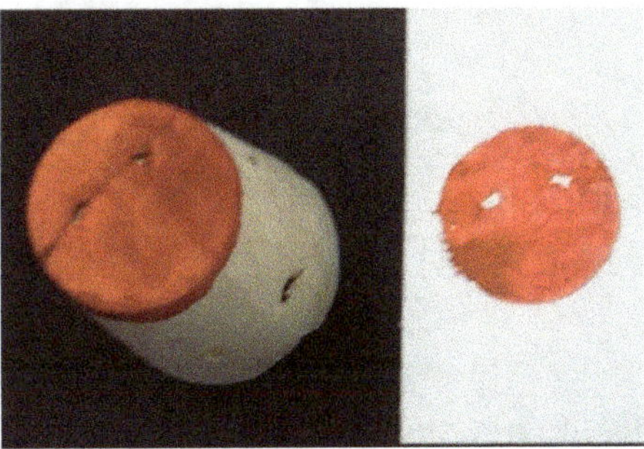

Figure 17E.3.2. Stamping with a cork can leave a signature with small "voids"

Similar small holes in the printed red circle were also seen in the ransom letters.

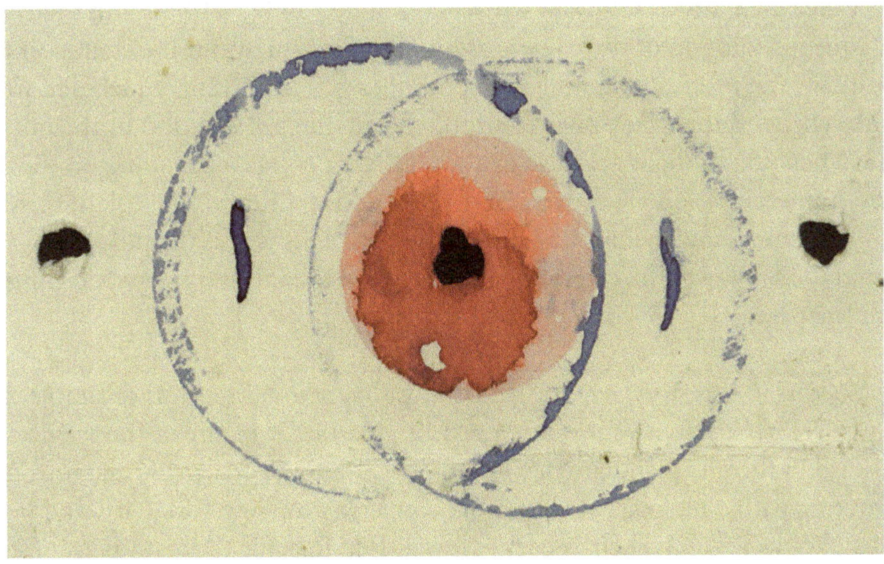

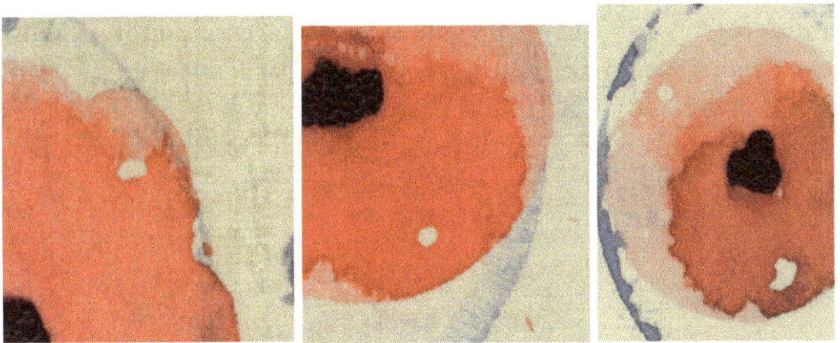

Figure 17E.3.3. Some of the signatures showing voids in the red circle

These small circular voids seem to correlate strongly with the use of a cork stopper, so we will assume it was a cork, but not a cork from an ink bottle or a wine bottle. Instead, it was a cork from an academic lab, possibly a pharmacy, or a laboratory supply house. Perhaps someone had them "around the lab/around the house" for some reason, although that reason has not made itself apparent to date.

17E.4. Stamping with a cork

If a cork was used, dipped into a red liquid, there are other variables to consider. For different red liquids, using a cork to stamp, does it make blotchy red circles or are they homogeneous, and does the color match that of the red circle?

We show results here for a few kinds of red colorants. One type may be found in the bathroom or kitchen and happens to be a red liquid. The second type is a commercial red ink, usually sold for use with fountain pens. Some companies make fountain pen inks that use the same formulation that was used at the turn of the century. In some cases, I started with a bottle of a red dye (a powder) and usually added a small amount to water to make a solution. If I start with red dye 40 (s) [the (s) stands for solid] and add it to water, the solution I make is called an *aq*ueous solution, written as red dye 40 (aq). It's easy to pretend an ink containing a dye and an aqueous solution of the dye are essentially the same from the standpoint of the color, but that's not necessarily so. Pen inks contain multiple components. The solvent, which doesn't have to be water, is referred to as the vehicle. Buffers may be present to regulate the pH (acidity) of the ink, so it doesn't start to dissolve the metal pen point. Some dyes also exhibit different colors, depending on the pH of the vehicle. Compounds called humectants control the rate of drying. Resins, often viscous plant or synthetic materials, may be present to determine how the ink flows from the pen. This is also the purpose of lubricants in inks. Surfactants are often used to lower the surface tension between the ink and the paper, controlling how much the ink spreads on the page.

We do have a few doctors in this story, who might be most likely to have access to simple tools of a scientific trade available – one is Dr. Condon, who is not an M.D. or a Ph.D. in any of the sciences. Perhaps the one remaining scientist is Lindbergh's grandfather, who was a well-known dentist. At the time of the kidnapping, Lindbergh was working with a biologist at Columbia University in New York City, and perhaps, also NYU, and would have had access to items such as corks as well. Red inks for fountain pens often contain the dye eosin. Blue inks often contain a triarylmethane dye. While most inks use dyes as colorants, which adhere to, and essentially "stain" the paper, there is another colorant option – pigments. Pigments are very fine colored particles that do not dissolve in water and are present in ink as a suspension. Pigments are similarly used in paints. The two interact with paper in different ways. Pigment particles lodge between the fibers that make up the paper, and since they are not soluble in solvents, they cannot be washed out of the paper as dyes can. Dyes essentially stain the paper fibers, and can often be washed off with the appropriate solvent.

17E.5. Testing Red Liquids

Let me show you some cork stamping results.

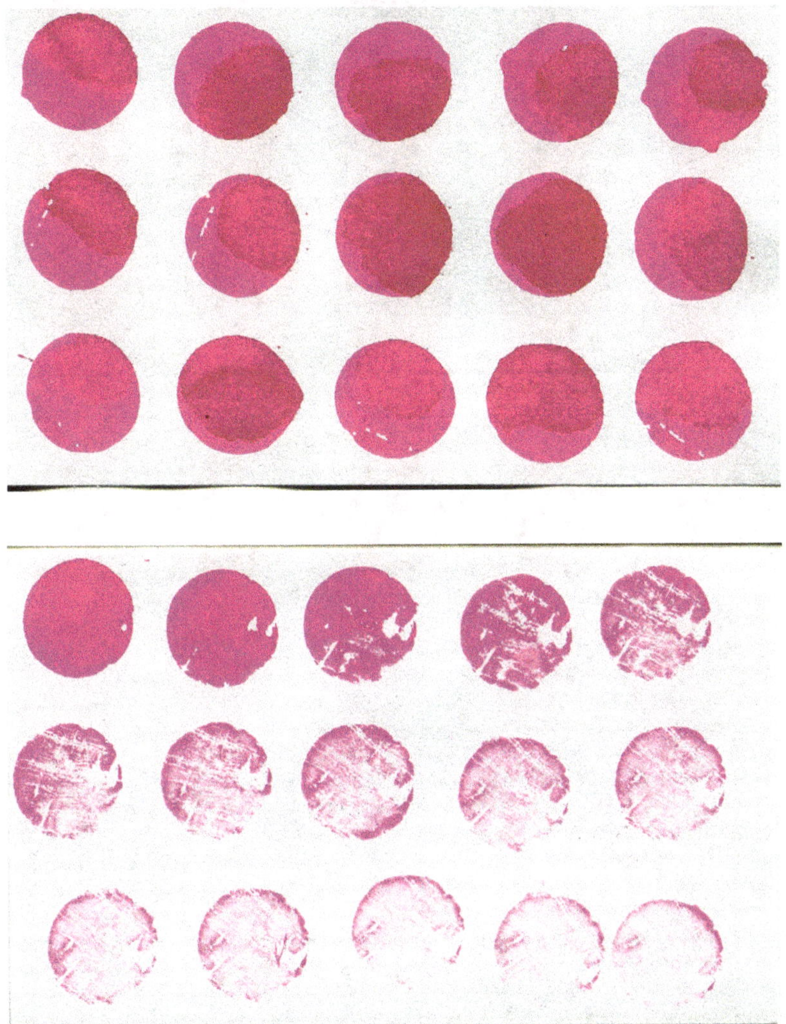

Figure 17E.5.1. Bordeaux Inkz

The top card shows multiple stampings, with a freshly loaded cork each time. The second card shows one dip into the ink, with successive stamps to see how quickly the cork face becomes depleted of ink.

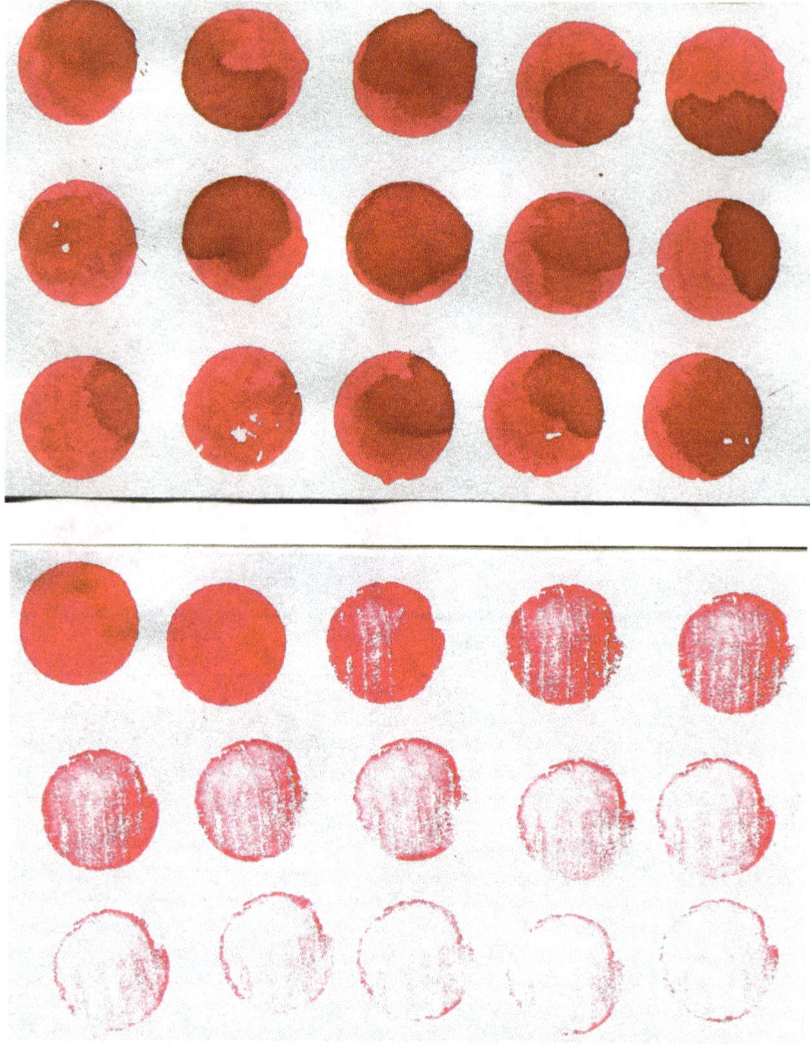

Figure 17E.5.2. The liquid is Levenger Ink; the color is cardinal red

Coverage is *fairly* complete in Figure 17E5.2, which would be expected because that is what inks do on paper.

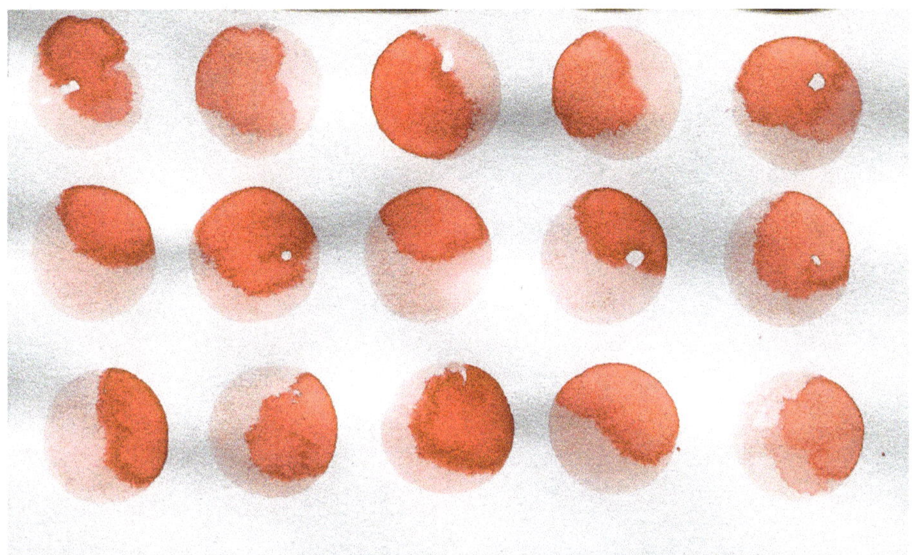

Figure 17E5.3. The Dye is Direct Red 23; Aqueous Solution

The print is blotchy, and the color is similar to that in the ransom letters.

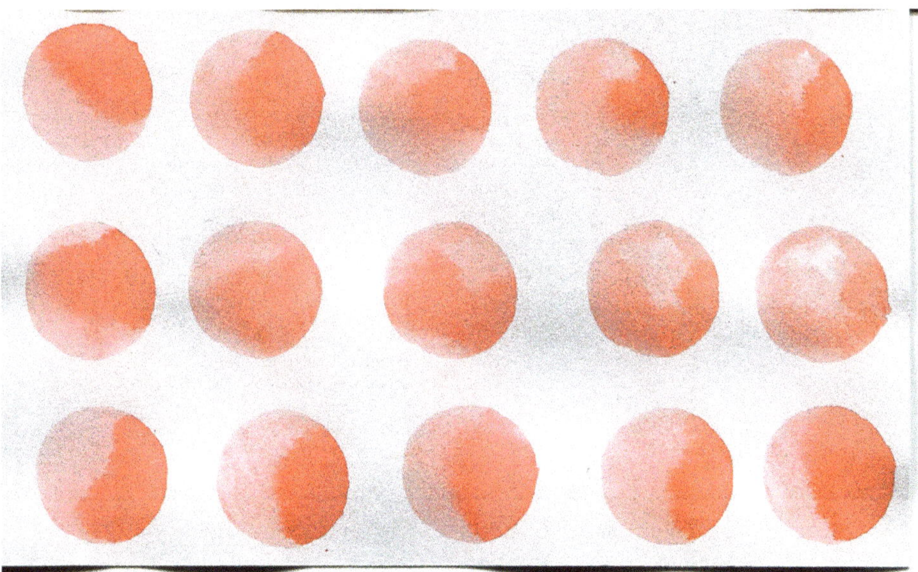

Figure 17E.5.4 Congo Red, aqueous solution

The coverage is poor and and the intensity is less than on the ransom letters.

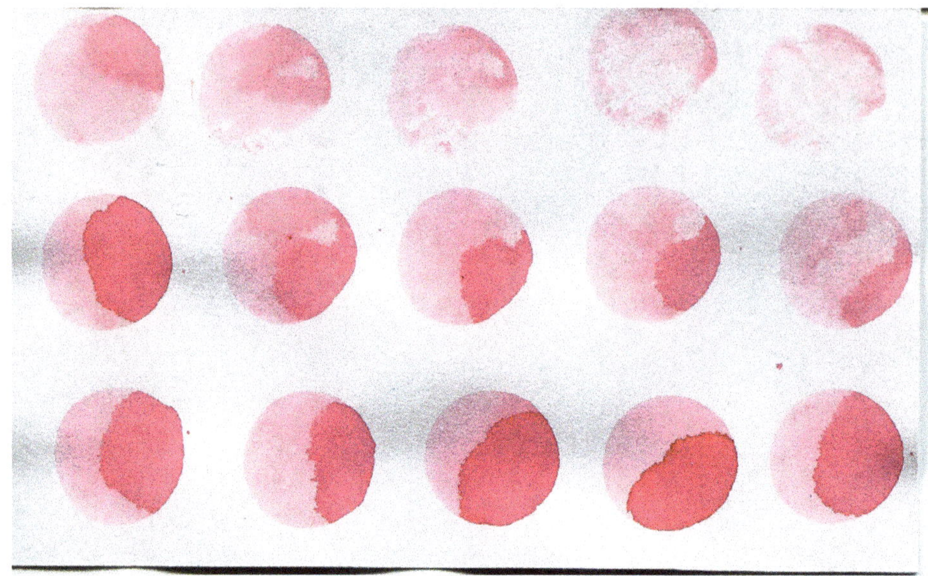

Figure 17E.5.5. Direct Red 81 aqueous solution

Figure 17E.5.6. Eosin Y – Aqueous Solution

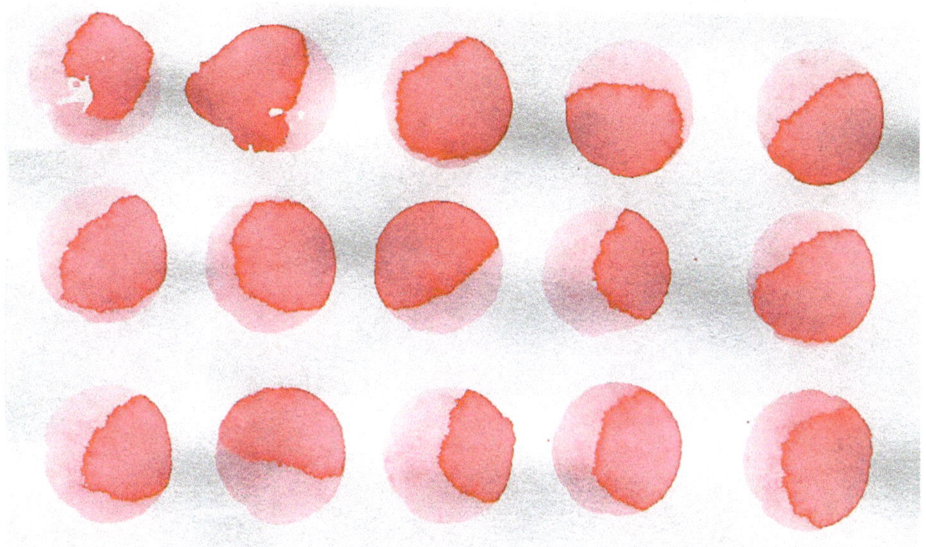

Figure 17E.5.7. New Cocchine (a dye used in inks) – aqueous solution

Figure 17E.5.8. New Fuscin (a dye used in inks) – aqueous solution

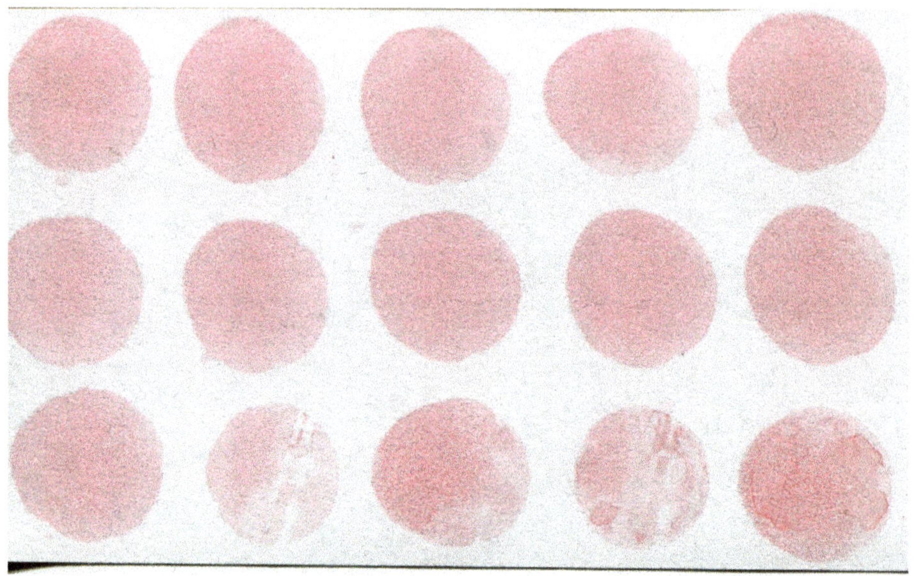

Figure 17E5.9. Oil Red O (a dye) – in ethyl acetate

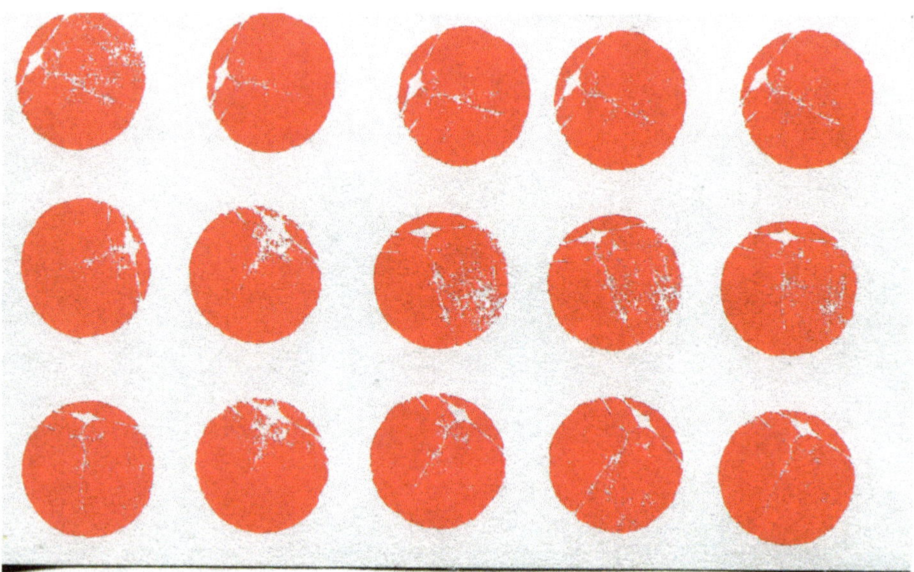

Figure 17E.5.10. Red ink from a red felt stamp pad

Stamp pads provide even coverage.

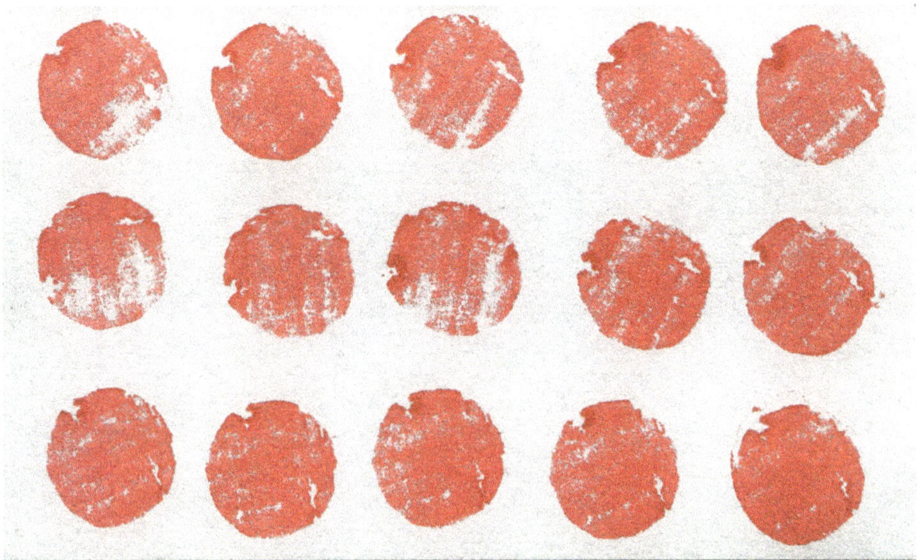

Figure 17E.5.11. Red ink from a gel stamp pad

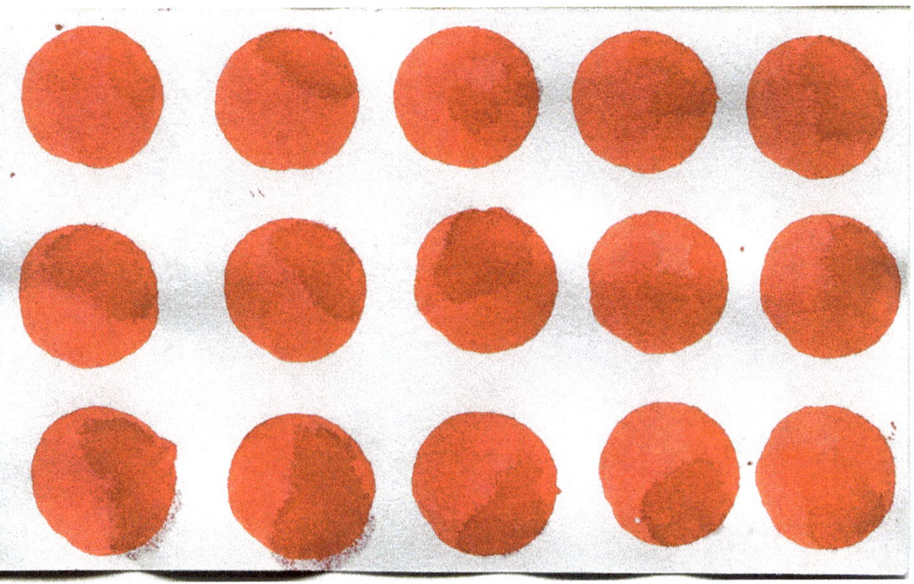

17E.5.12. Red food dye – contains red dye #3/also known as red dye #40

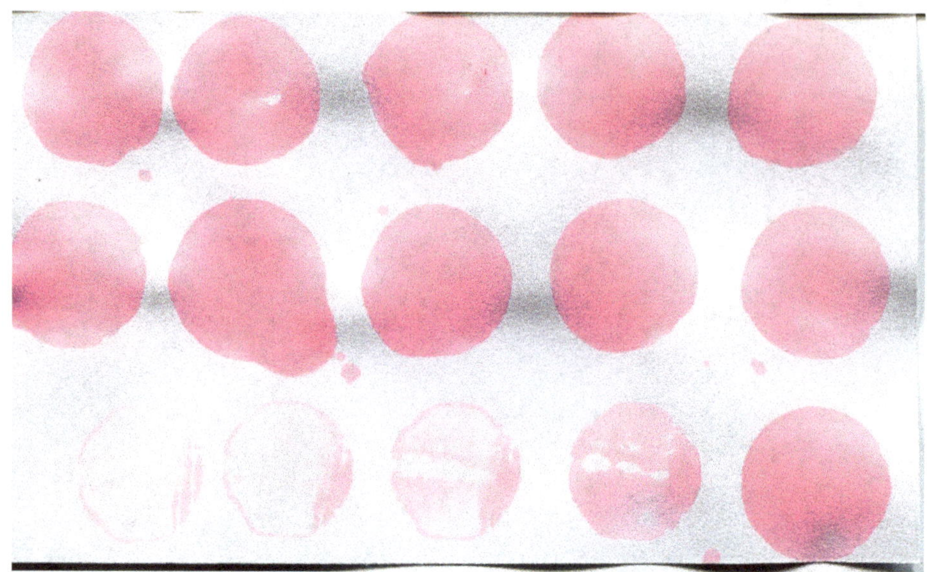

Figure 17E.5.13. Merthiolate tincture – right out of the medicine cabinet bottle

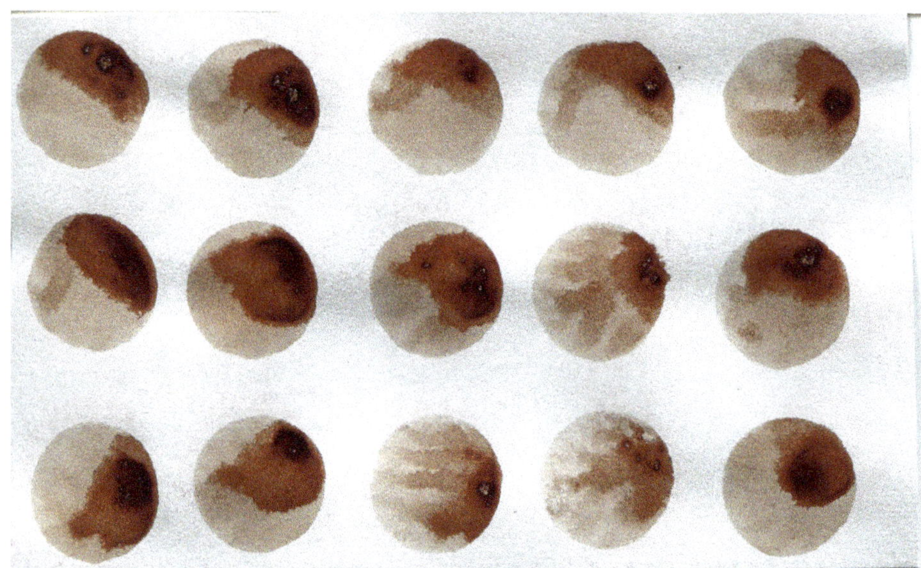

Figure 17E.5.14. Pig's blood

Figure 17E.5.15. Noodler's ink (Nikita)

You can rule out some candidates based on color. Sometimes the color is just not right, or the intensity of the color is off. You may find a good color match using ink catalogs. Do you see a match between the red center circle of the singnature, and any colors shown here?

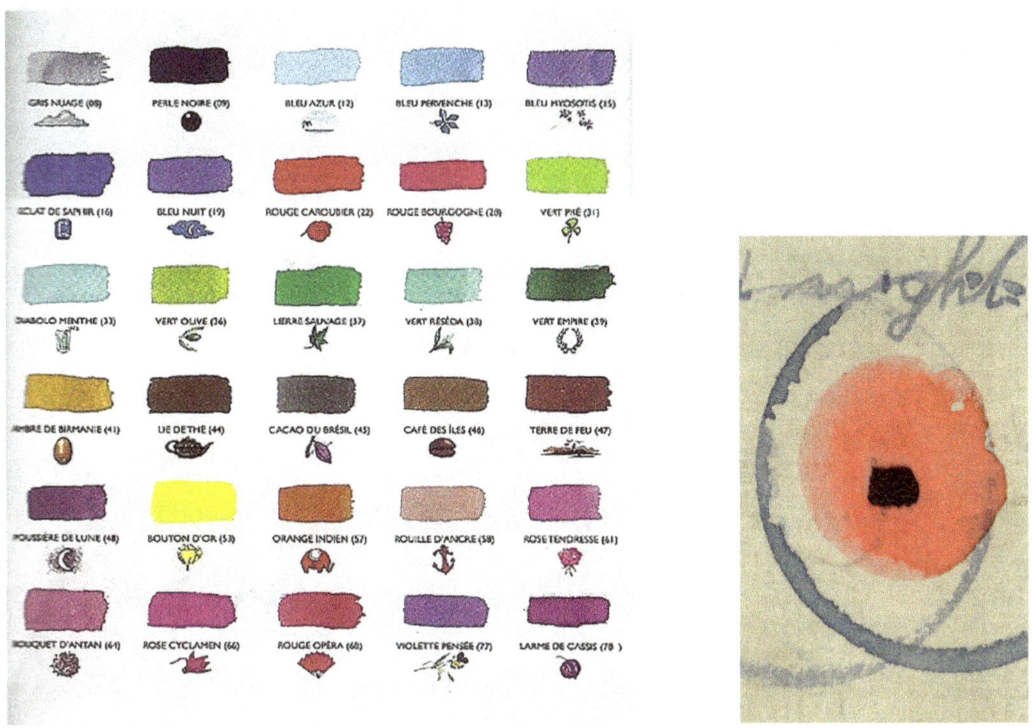

Figure 17E.5.16. J. Herbin fountain pen inks

Figure 17E.5.17. Pelikan Edelstein Premium Inks

Figure 17E.5.18. Diamine Fountain Pen Inks

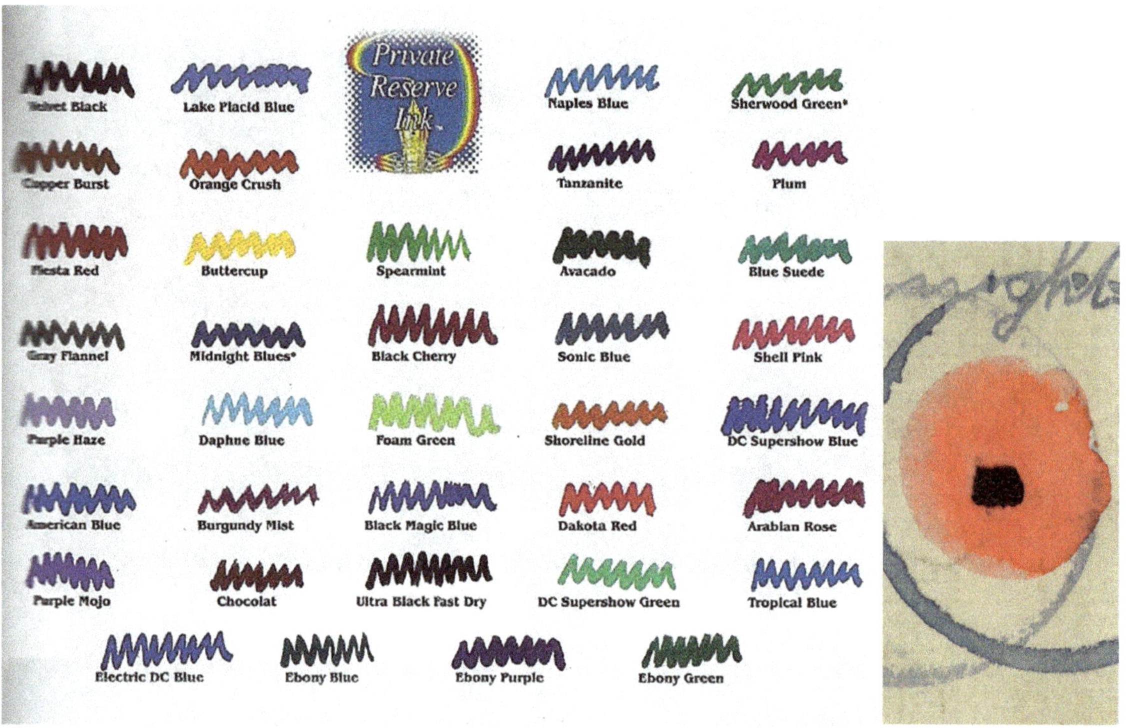

Figure 17E.5.19. Private Reserve Ink

Figure 17E.5.20. Noodler's Ink

These samples are from the *Goldspot Fine Writing and Luxury Gifts Catalog*. They carry the following warning: "Please use the sample charts … as a reference to select your color ink. Note that due to computer imaging and the difficulty in matching true color in natural versus artificial light, the ink colors are not exact depictions of the real ink. These swatches are meant to be used as a guide to help show a general idea of the color differences." I think the most substantial difference between the singnature red and the red inks is the intensity of the color. It can look like a washed-out red ink. Perhaps it wasn't an ink at all.

There is no shortage of candidate red liquids. Consider "powdered gelatin deserts", which you probably know as Jell-O. Jell-O has been around for a long time – trademarked in 1897. It contains gelatin, sweeteners, artificial flavors, and artificial colors. (Jell-O shots were invented later). In 1923, the Jell-O Co. introduced D-Zerta, a low-calorie version of Jell-O. Royal Gelatin came out in 1925 and was one of the many gelatin competitors by 1930.

We tested them. I had a box of Jell-O (strawberry) and Royal Gelatin (Cherry) that were probably 30+ years old (both had Red Dye 40 in them) and a much older box (family collection) of D-Zerta (raspberry) that only confessed to having artificial color in it. FD&C (Federal Food, Drug and Cosmetics Act) Red 40 was also in my assorted food color and egg dyes from McCormick.

The colors were often surprising. For example, pig's blood, which was red when we used it, became brown when applied to paper. Cranberry juice turned grey on paper. The gelatin deserts were not sufficiently intense in color; neither was cherry juice (which, surprisingly, didn't rely on its natural color but had the dye Red 40 added).

Merthiolate was pinkish, as was Erythrosine (aq). Methyl red turned brown.

We tested some makeups and red lipsticks. Since lipstick is wax based, if you put a little on a cork and stamp it on paper, you can easily identify it by the waxy feel and uniform coverage.

In conclusion, it appears that real inks do what they should, they make a homogeneous filled circle while aqueous solutions of red dyes always look much more like the singnature red circles.

Q17E.5.1: In terms of the color, is one closer to the real red circle on the ransom notes?

A17E.5.1: Perhaps the red food dye most closely resembles the color. That could look good because it was used directly from the (small) bottle. To correctly use food colors, here are the directions:

Mix ½ cup of boiling water, 1 tsp vinegar, and 10-20 drops of food color in a cup, depending on what is being colored (such as if we were dying Easter eggs.). If we wanted to make a red cake, we would probably add 50 drops of their red food dye concentrate into the cake mix.

No, we're not done yet. We have other tools at our disposal. Perhaps the red food dye most closely resembles the color so far, but we don't have to just look at the color and find similar materials, we can measure the color, which we will do in the next chapters.

A final few questions for you now:

Q: 17E.5.2: What was unique about Dr. Condon's correspondences?

A: 17E.5.2: He wrote in purple ink, which he formulated himself.

Q 17E.5.3: How does one make purple?

A 17E.5.3: One way is to mix something red with something blue.

You should try to make some solid red circles, like I just showed you. You can find a cork somewhere; its size is unimportant for testing. Find some red liquids. Do the results differ if you stamp on an index card vs. good quality stationery? Try it!

17F. Color Analysis- Ultraviolet/Visible Spectroscopy

17F.1. Color

Q. 17F.1.1: What is color? How would *you* define it?
A. 17F.1.1: When our eyes are exposed to certain kinds of light, characterized by a specific wavelength or frequency, our brain creates what we call a color for the image in our head. Almost all our minds do the same thing. Orange is orange for all of us, not plaid for some of us and apple green to others.

17F.2. Light

Q#17F.2.1: What is light?
A#17F.2.1: The sun is our primary source of light. It makes a wide range of electromagnetic radiation. The energy of a particular light particle depends on the wavelength. It sometimes can be a particle, called a photon, and other times it is more like a wave of energy that propagates through space – like a sine wave that alternates from a maximum positive value to a maximum negative value, passing through zero each time it repeats itself. Electromagnetic radiation means that it has an electrical component that oscillates, and a magnetic component, oscillating at the same frequency. These two fields are at right angles to each other. The electromagnetic wave moves at the speed of light, and one can think about the frequency of the oscillations or the distance it travels corresponding to one complete oscillation (such as peak-to-peak or trough-to-trough) as its *wavelength*.

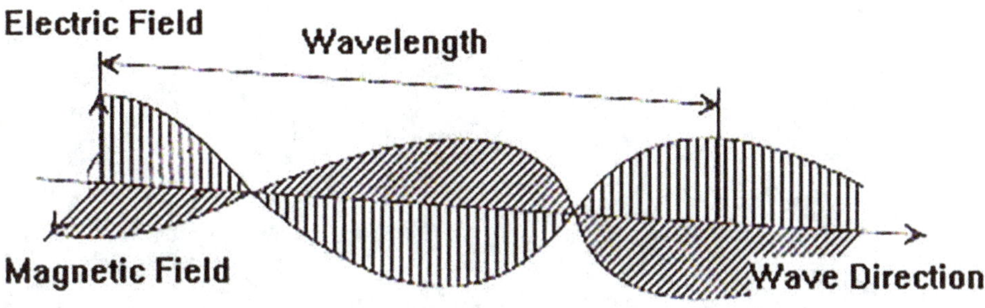

Figure 17F.2.1. An electromagnetic wave propagating through space

Figure 17F.2.2 shows that the sun generates all the different kinds of electromagnetic radiation from gamma rays and ultraviolet light (which we can't see), infrared through radio waves (which we also can't see). There is just a very small portion of all possible wavelengths that our eyes respond to – in the range from about 350 nm (blue/purple) up to almost 800 nm (red). The nm stands for nanometers. That's all our eyes can see. If we could see gamma rays, infrared light, radio waves, etc. we could never see where we are going!

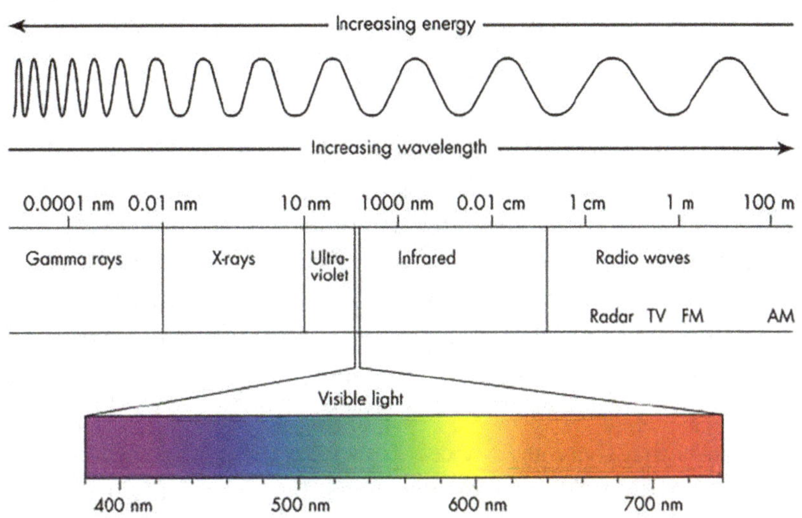

Figure #17F.2.2. The electromagnetic spectrum and what we call light

Much of what we know about light we can attribute to the work of Sir Isaac Newton. He was the first to take light from the sun, coming into his dark laboratory through a small hole in his curtain, and put, in the path of this beam of white light, a glass prism as shown in Figure 17F.2.3. What he saw, using the prism in the orientation shown, was that the light separated into its component colors (just like the colors of a rainbow). The light that was bent the least was the red component, and the light that was bent the most was violet. He even showed that if you separated white light into its component colors, you could combine them all with a second prism and you'd get white light back. There is not a discrete band of "red" then one of "orange." It is a continuously varying distribution that changes from red to reddish orange to orangish red to orange, etc.

Figure 17F.2.3. Newton making history

Q17F.2.1: Why is a banana yellow?
A17F.2.1: There are molecules in the banana skin that interact with the white light from the sun, but not in the way you may think. White light has all the colors in it. The banana absorbs all those colors except for yellow, which it reflects, so your eyes only see those yellow photons.

We have rods and cones in our eyes. At very low light levels, only the rods respond, and they only deliver black and white information to your brain. So, when it is very dark, and you can barely see things, your vision is black and white. In addition to rods, there are cones in our eyes – three types. They contain different pigments, so they respond to different colors. They respond to red, green, or blue light. Many colors are made up of contributions due to these three primary colors, so when the cones transfer information from your eyes to your brain, it is the combination of responses of the three different types of cones that your brain processes and decides on what color it will display on your mind's screen.

The important point so far is that there are devices like a glass prism that can be used to separate the components of light in space ('spatially'). We have other devices that can do this, and a popular choice today is a grating, which is a surface scored with lines very close together. A prism is a transmissive device, meaning the light passes through it. A grating can be a reflective device, meaning light shining on it is reflected at different angles depending on the wavelengths of its components. There are also transmission gratings, which also has parallel lines etched on the surface, very close together. Can you think of anything that has lines on it very close together on a reflective surface? A CD or DVD does, and when light bounces off one, you often see what seems like a rainbow. The light is being separated in space.

17F.3. How Do We Analyze Light?

A device that separates light spatially based on the component wavelengths is called a monochromator. The one we used is a very small, portable unit that connects to a computer. The instrument is sold by Ocean Optics (Largo, FL).

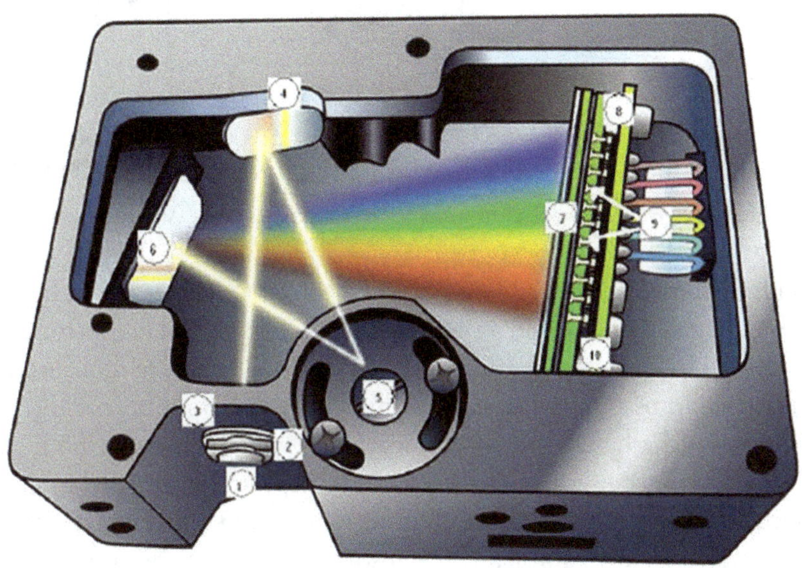

Figure 17F.3.1. Ocean Optics spectrometer

The light that we want to analyze is introduced to the instrument via a fiber optic flexible tubing, connected to the input, labeled as 1. The light enters the compartment, bounces off a mirror, and reflects onto a reflection grating. Light comes off the grating at different angles depending on the wavelength(s). As the light separates in space, it bounces off another mirror, and then the separated light impinges on a light detector. It is like a detector in a digital camera, which has a two-dimensional array of light detectors that we will call pixels, but here, we only have an array of pixels that is one pixel wide and 512 pixels long. Since the grating doesn't move, the light is always separated the same way, so pixel #1 (at one end of the detector) detects photons of a wavelength of 1000 nm. The next one detects photons at a wavelength of 999, then 998, etc. At the other end, pixels are detecting 250 nm photons. The component light waves are separated in space, and a detector of the light is a spatial array. The computer assists in reading every pixel, understanding what wavelength each is detecting, and recording the intensity of the light at that wavelength. When a monochromator has a light detector attached to it like this one does, it is called a spectrometer.

The components that I used to analyze the colors of various inks on paper are shown here.

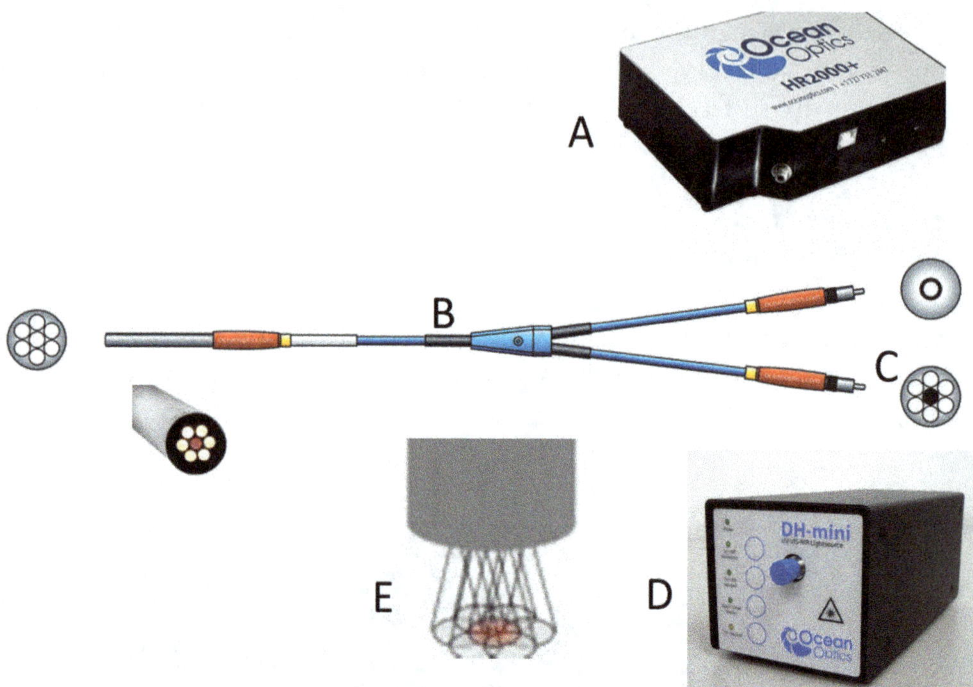

Figure 17F.3.2. Components used to do reflectance UV-Vis spectroscopy.

I start with a light source, shown in Figure 17F3.2, as D, which puts out white light. I have a fiber optic probe, B, that I can use to measure colors on a surface. It has six optical fibers surrounding one central fiber. The six fibers are connected to the white light source. If I put the end close to a surface, the pattern shown in E results. The surface is illuminated with white light. Light that bounces off the surface is collected by the center fiber which carries the light to the spectrometer, A, which analyzes the intensity of light at each wavelength in the 250-1000 nm range and creates a UV-Vis spectrum, usually an absorption spectrum. It analyzes a white surface first to document the colors in the white light, and then collects data when the white light is illuminating a pen stroke, for example, which absorbs some colors but not others. (F.Y.I., A black surface absorbs all colors, and reflects none. A white surface absorbs no colors and reflects whatever light shines on it.) A second spectrum is collected. When the two are compared, the computer generates an absorption spectrum telling us how much of the light was absorbed at each wavelength.

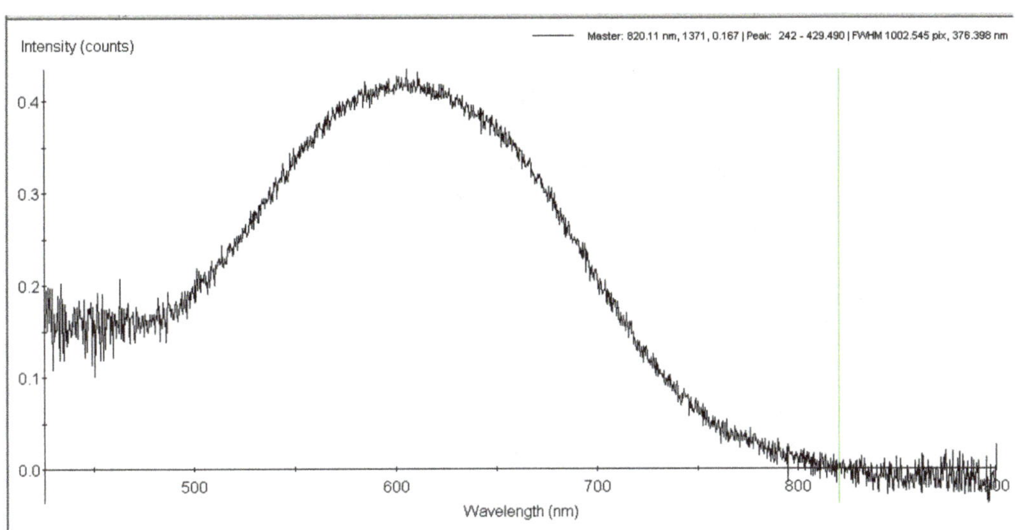

Figure 17F.3.3. An Absorption spectrum of the blue (writing) ink on ransom letter #2.

Here is an absorption spectrum obtained for ink on paper. It tells you how efficient the ink is at absorbing light over the range of wavelengths (colors) shown. You can see that no light is absorbed above 800 nm and only a fraction of the blue light in the 250-500 nm light is absorbed. The highest absorbance occurs at around 580 nm, referred to as λ(max).

So, we can direct the probe to different places on the letters and obtain absorbance spectra (technically reflectance spectra) of whatever color is under the probe, illuminating the sample with a light source and analyzing the reflected light with a spectrometer.

The spectrum shown in Figure 17F.3.3 is of the blue ink used to write ransom letter #2. The next figure shows the spectrum of the blue ink used to make the blue circles in the signature, from Ransom Letter #13. The question is, do the spectra tell us that the two inks are the same, or was some other blue substance used when making the singnature?

17F.4. Describing Spectra – Blue Inks

Usually not much is done with UV-Vis spectra except for visual comparison and quantitative analysis (often done at a single wavelength λ (lambda)). There is no reason why we couldn't make the comparison process more quantitative. (Warning: Analytical chemists will scowl at you if you ever make the following mistake. A single graph such as that shown in Figure 17F.3.3 is a *spectrum*. That is the singular form of the word. If you have two of them, you don't have two spectrums, you have two *spectra*. The word spectra is the plural form of the word spectrum. While we're at it, most people who make measurements may refer to their data and may write that their "data is shown in a Table." No, no! The word data is the plural form of datum, so their data *are* shown in a Table.)

The spectrum is a constant for a specific material, but the intensity of the spectrum (the y axis) depends not only on the compound, but the amount present, so don't make decisions by looking at the y axis values. It is the shape of the curve that is important. So how could we define the shape?

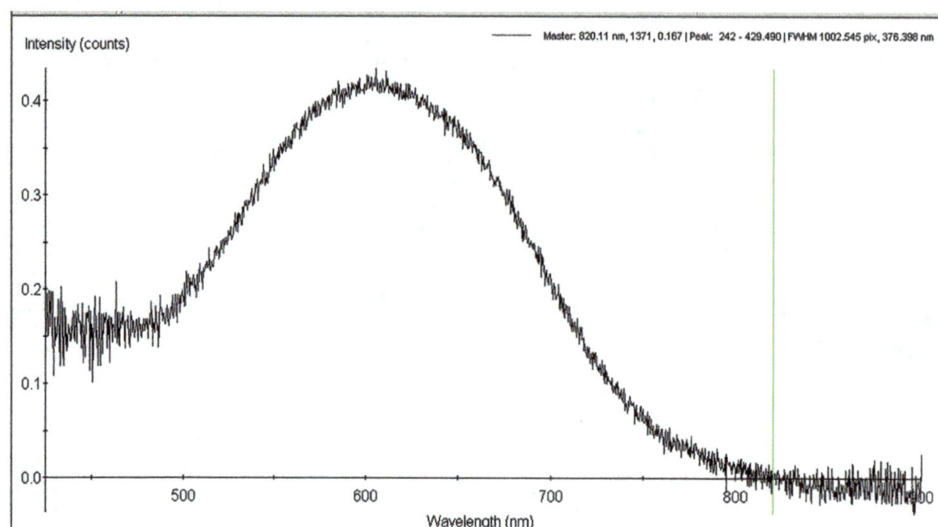

Figure 17F.4.1: Absorption spectrum of the blue ink used to make the blue circles of the singnature, Ransom Letter #13.

We can do some measurements and compare them to others, taking advantage of the fact that the spectrum shape for a particular compound would be constant. We could make some observations on Fig. 17F.4.1 such as the absorbance is flat up to about 500 nm where it starts to rise (reading left to right). The maximum value appears to be at about 580 nm, λ (max). The absorbance then starts to fall and goes to essentially zero by 800 nm.

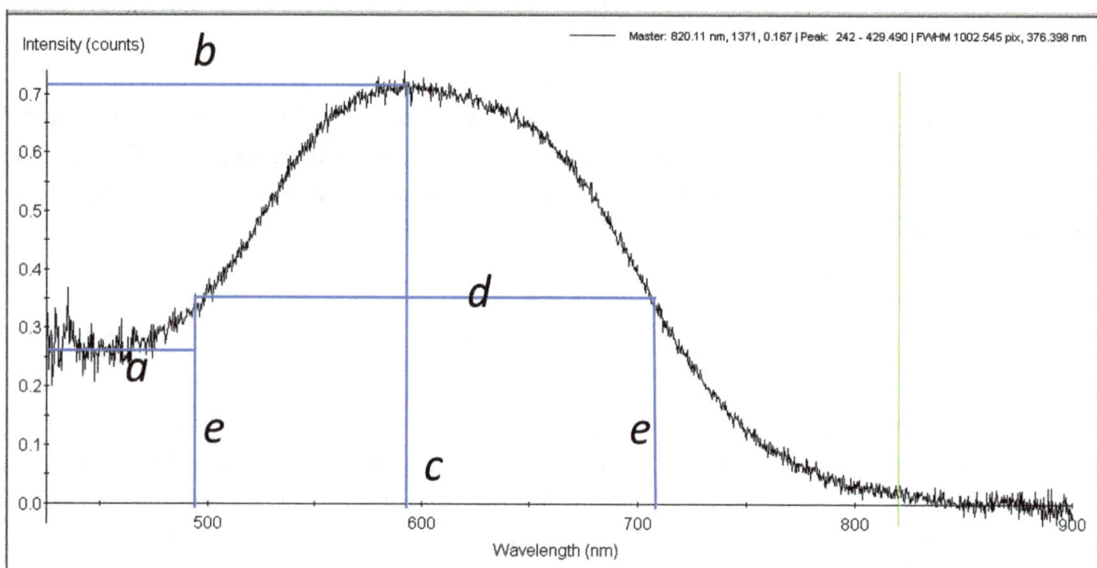

Figure 17F.4.2: Variables we could calculate for an absorption spectrum to make comparisons more quantitative.

I'm suggesting in Figure 17F.4.2 that there are some numbers we could determine to characterize a spectrum, that we could then compare with the same quantities for another spectrum, to determine how "similar" the two are. If I draw line *b* to the point that appears to be the highest point in the curve, then drop a vertical line *c* down to the x-axis, we can determine the wavelength corresponding to the maximum intensity, λ (max).

For Figure 17F.4.2, the top of the curve is *b* = 0.72, and the level of the flat portion below 500 nm, *a,* is at 0.26, so that ratio should always be constant. *a*/*b* = 0.26/0.72 x 100 = 36%. The flat portion is 36% as intense as the curve's peak. This should always be true no matter what the exact values happen to be. From the top of the curve, I dropped a line down to the wavelength axis. It intersects just below 600 nm. With a ruler, I measured the distance from 500 to 600 nm on that axis to understand, for my particular magnified view of Figure 17F.4.2, a certain distance along that axis corresponds to a certain wavelength range. I then used it to calculate in nm the distance from 500 nm to the intersection point, which was 95 nm, so the maximum is at a wavelength of 595 nm. The vertical line *c* is 0.72 intensity units high – that is the height of the curve. Half-height is then 0.36. A common spectral feature calculated is "width-at-half-height". So, at half-height (0.36 on the vertical scale), I drew line *d* from one side of the curve to the other, the width at 0.36. The length of the line *d,* in units of wavelength (nm) is 215 nm. So, these are some values that we could calculate if we had spectra that looked similar, and we wanted to compare them.

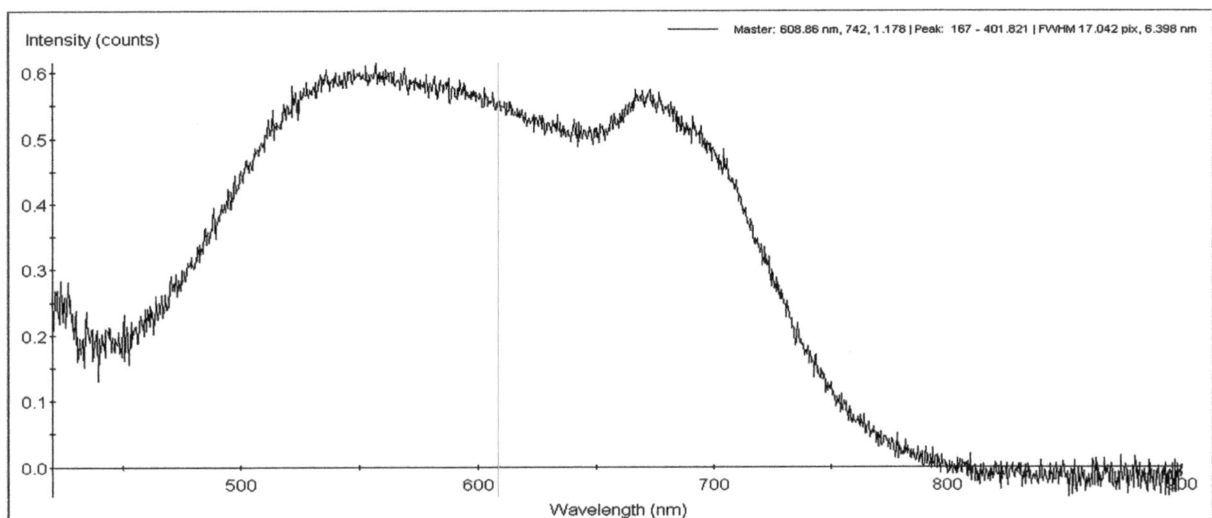

Figure 17F.4.3: Spectrum of blue ballpoint pen ink.

Figure 17F.4.3 (above) is of another blue ink, that of a blue ballpoint pen ink. This spectrum falls into a different category since it has two maxima. One could determine each one as part of numerically defining the spectrum.

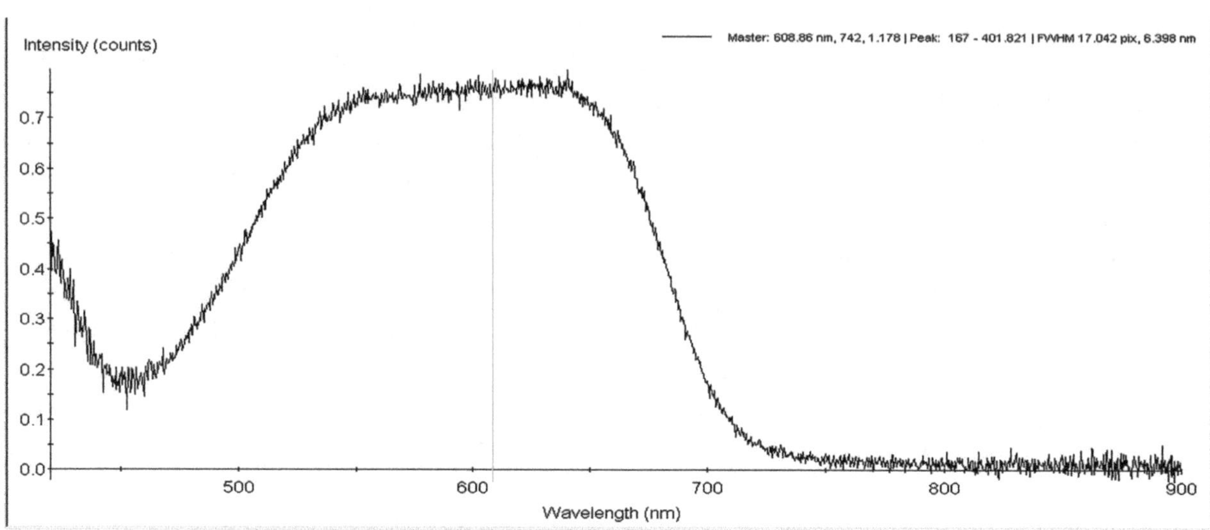

Figure 17F.4.4: Spectrum of blue ink from a felt-tip pen.

The spectrum above, Figure 17F.4.4 is of another blue ink, the ink from a felt tip pen. It is sufficiently different from the earlier spectra to indicate that it doesn't match with anything else shown so far. It is a broad curve, essentially flat-topped, and drops very quickly between 650 nm and 700 nm.

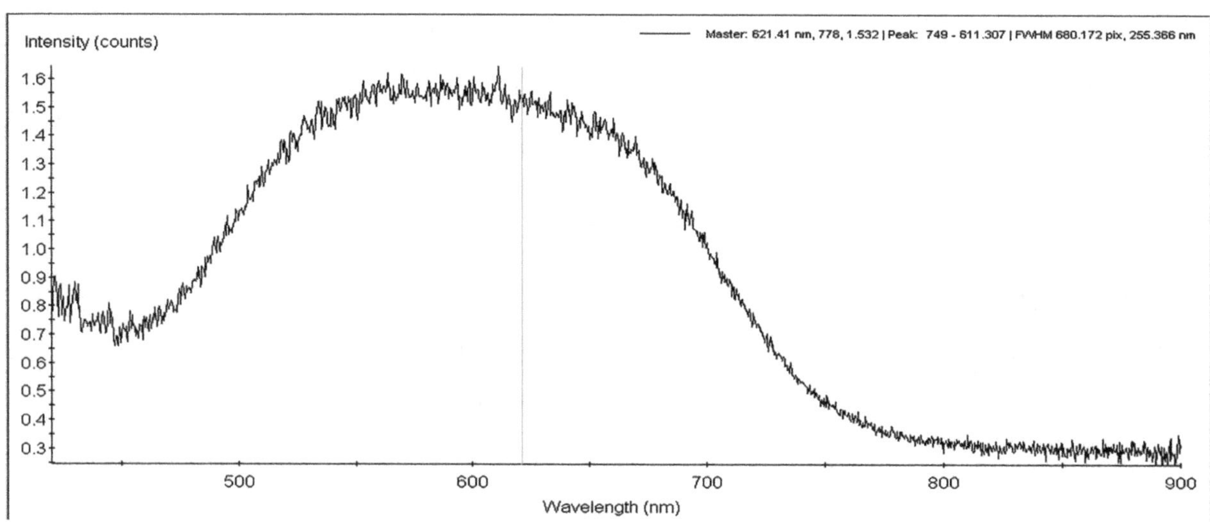

Figure 17F.4.5: Waterman blue fountain pen ink.

This is an ink that has been around for a long time, likely with very few changes. Does it match Figure 18F.4.1 (signature blue circle ink)?

The width at half height for the blue letter handwriting is 196 nm, for the circle is 215 nm and is 225 nm for the Waterman Fountain Pen Ink. The flat-top in the Waterman Ink spectrum makes it distinctly different than the other two.

I'm not going to present an exhaustive set of spectra here, but of the experiments we've done, the blue circle ink does appear to be most like the ink used in writing the letter (Figure 17F.3.3).

17F.5: The Red Spot.

Since we're discussing UV-visible spectra, let's move to the red spot in the singnature.

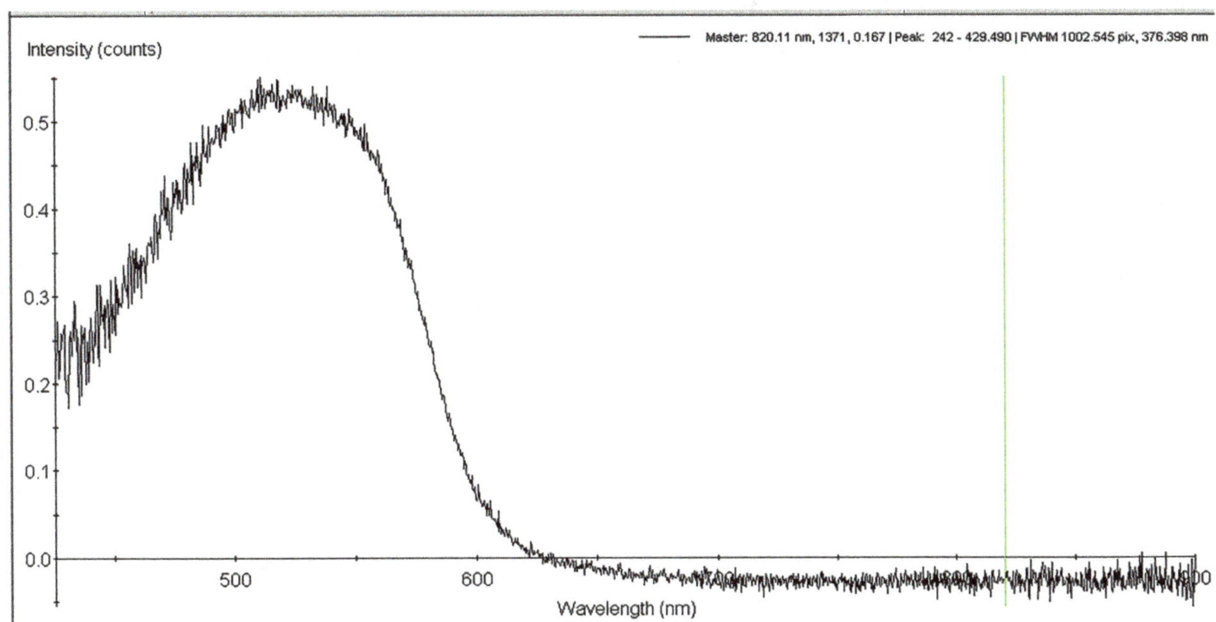

Figure 17F.5.1: Spectrum of the red spot ink, ransom letter #2

The spectrum peaks at a lower wavelength value and drops to almost zero by 600 nm, so the ink does not absorb above ~625 nm, allowing all the red light to be reflected, thus the ink is red.

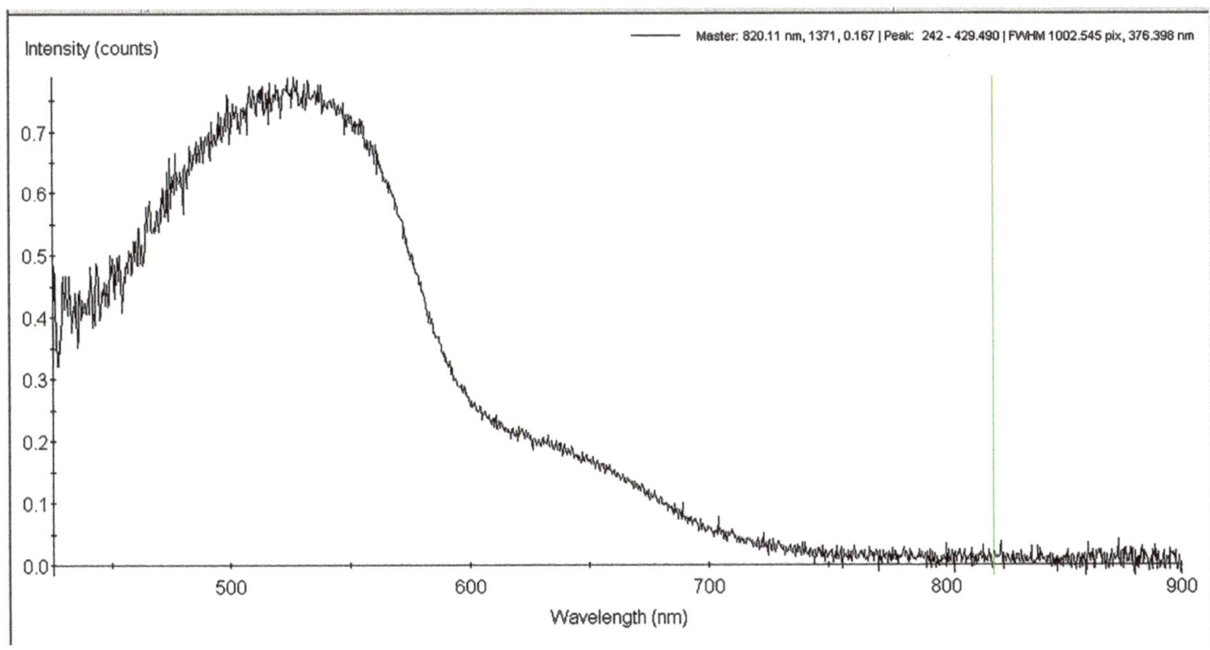

Figure 17F.5.2: Spectrum of red ink from letter #13.

The spectrum shown above, of the red spot ink from letter #13, looks nothing much like the previous spectrum, from the red spot of letter #2. Figure 17F.5.2 shows what looks like a spectrum similar to that shown for the spot of letter #2 if you look at the left side of the spectrum, with a second, smaller "hump" between 600-750 nm. I'm proposing that the part of the red circle of letter #13 chosen was contaminated with some blue ink, which is responsible for the hump on the right side. If you go back and look at letter #13, the blue circle on the right side of the singnature goes through the red circle, contaminating it with blue ink.

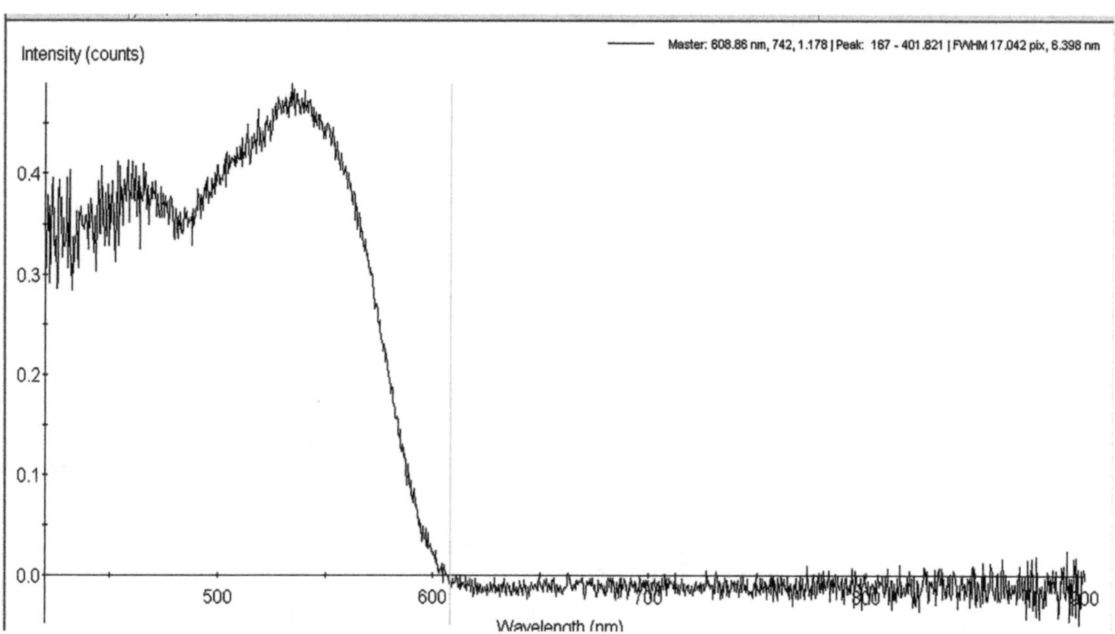

Figure 17F.5.3: Spectrum of a red ballpoint pen ink (usually rhodamine B or rhodamine 6G).

We would probably handle Figure 17F.5.3 as a spectrum with two maxima (note: maxima is the pleural form of maximum).

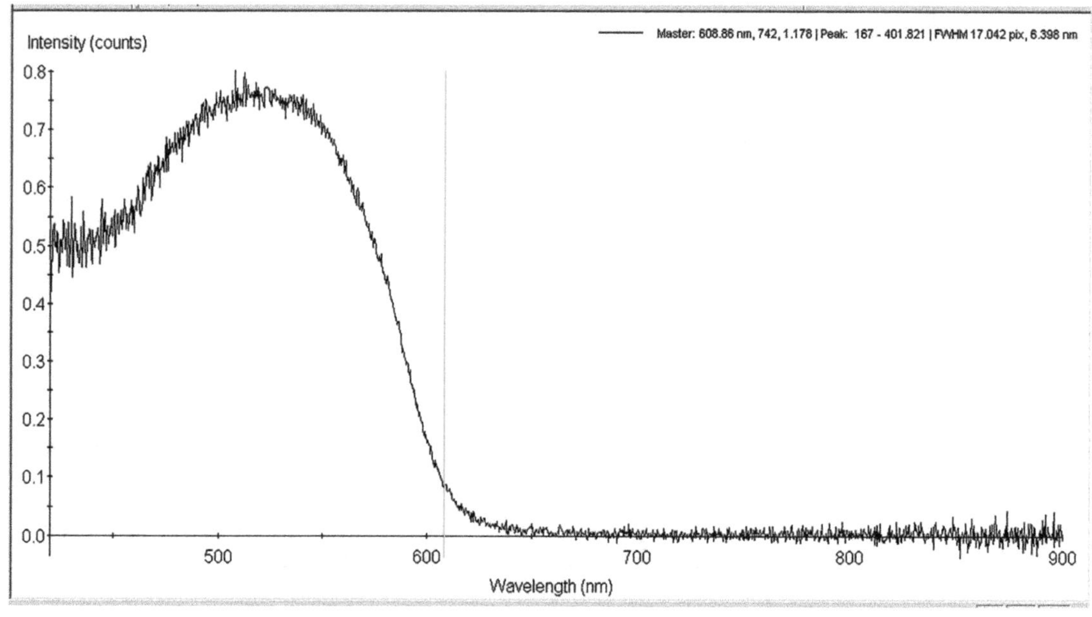

Figure 17F.5.4: Spectrum of a red felt tip pen ink.

Apart from the slightly different region below 400 nm, the spectrum is like Figure 17F.5.1 (red spot from letter #2).

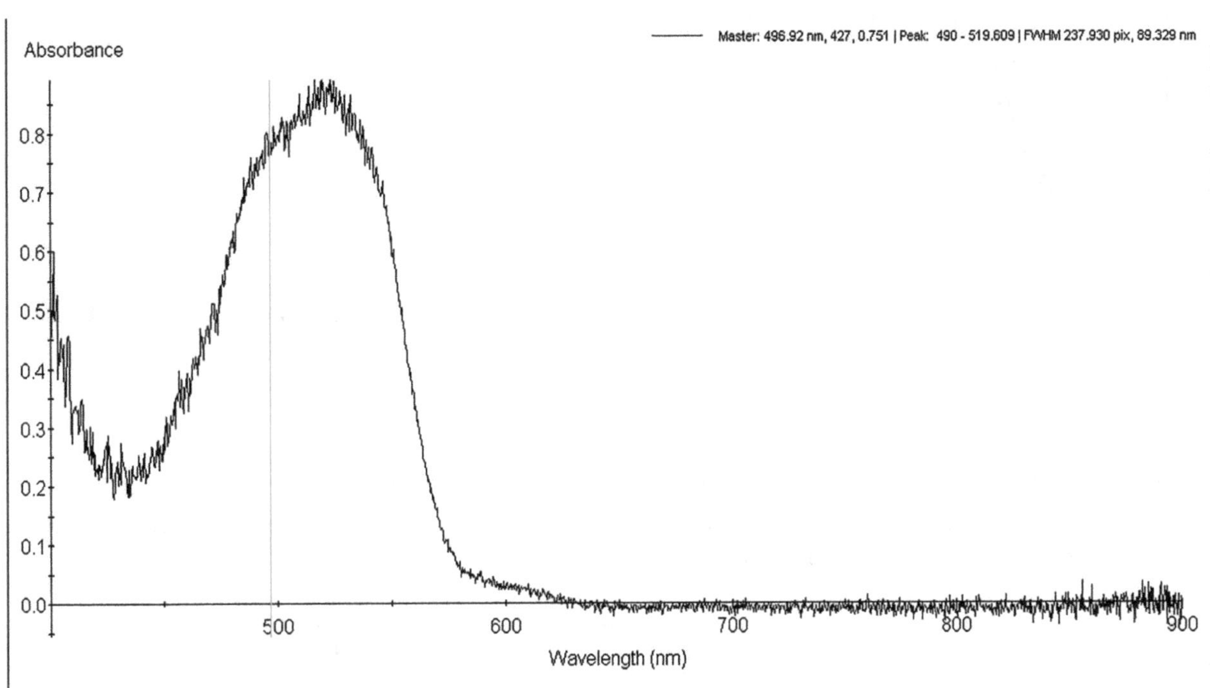

Figure 17F.5.5: Spectrum of eosin (aq), which was reportedly used in making the singnature.

I can see no similarity between Fig. 17F.5.5 and any other spectrum.

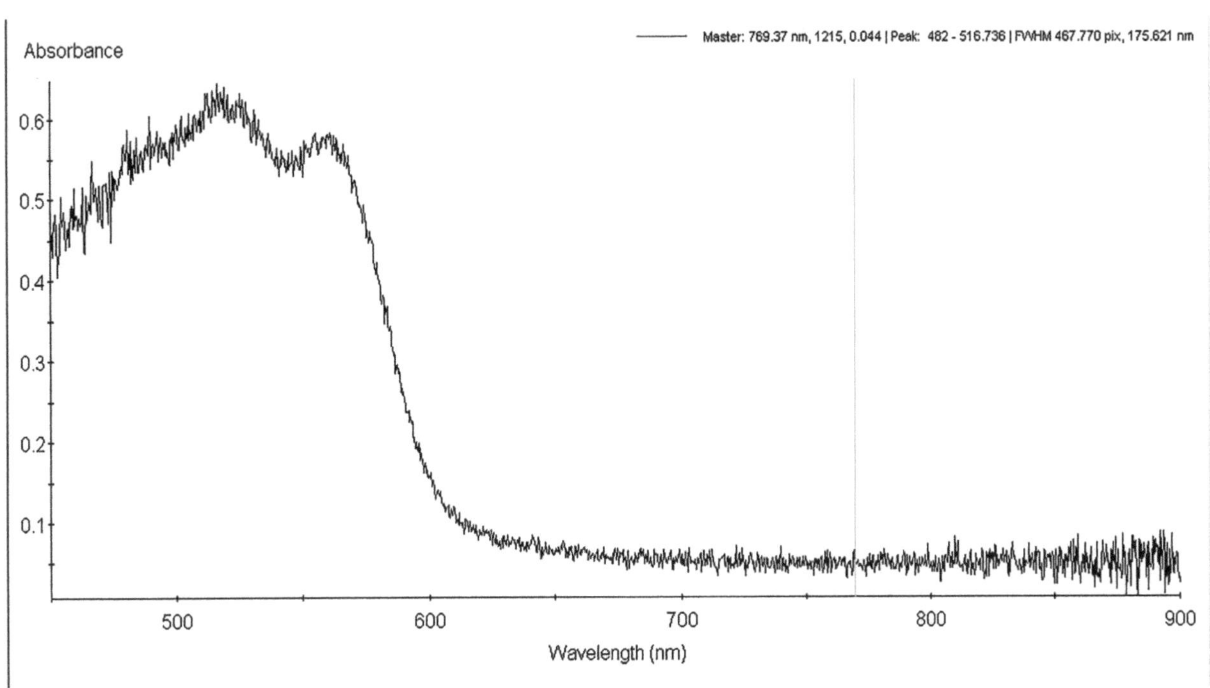

Figure 17F.5.6: Spectrum of carmine, also known as carminic acid.

Carmine shows a double-λ (max) spectrum. Carmine has been used to dye fabrics but not so much in pens.

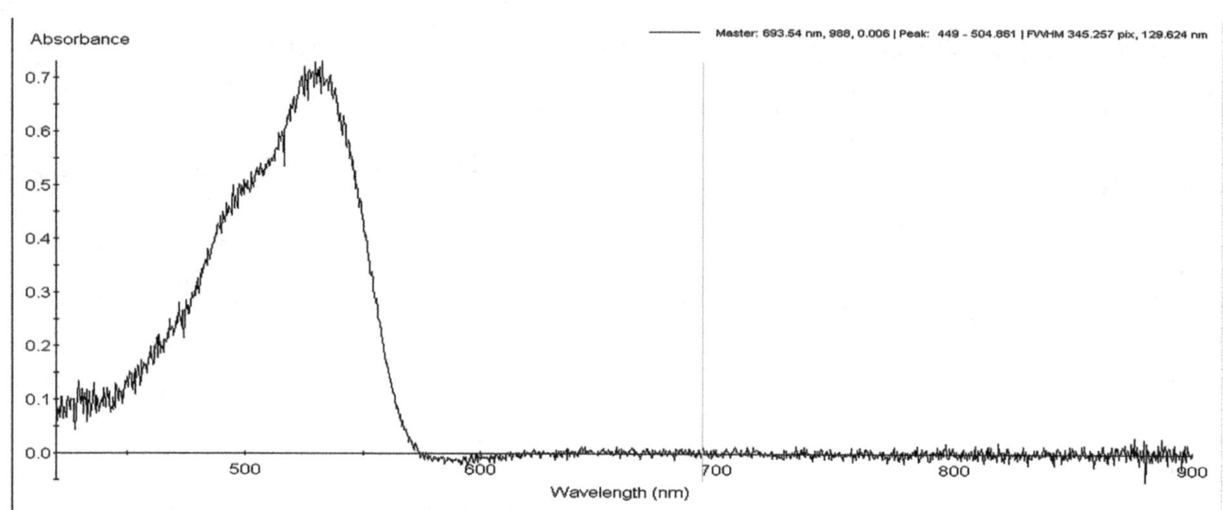

Figure 17F.5.7: The spectrum of merthiolate.

Tincture of Merthiolate is a red liquid, alcohol-based, that could be found in the medicine cabinets at the time (still available in small bottles on Amazon.com). Interestingly, the small bottle is 31 mm wide, although the spectrum doesn't match that of the red signature spot.

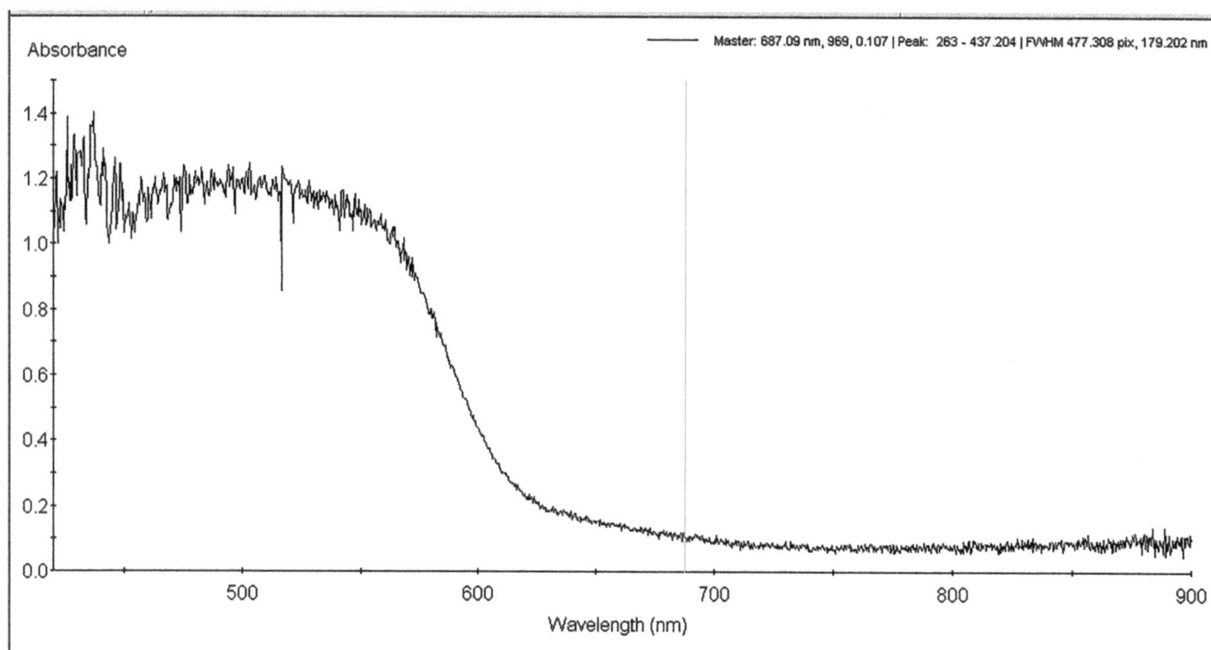

Figure 17F.5.8: The spectrum of Shaefer red fountain pen ink. Not a match.

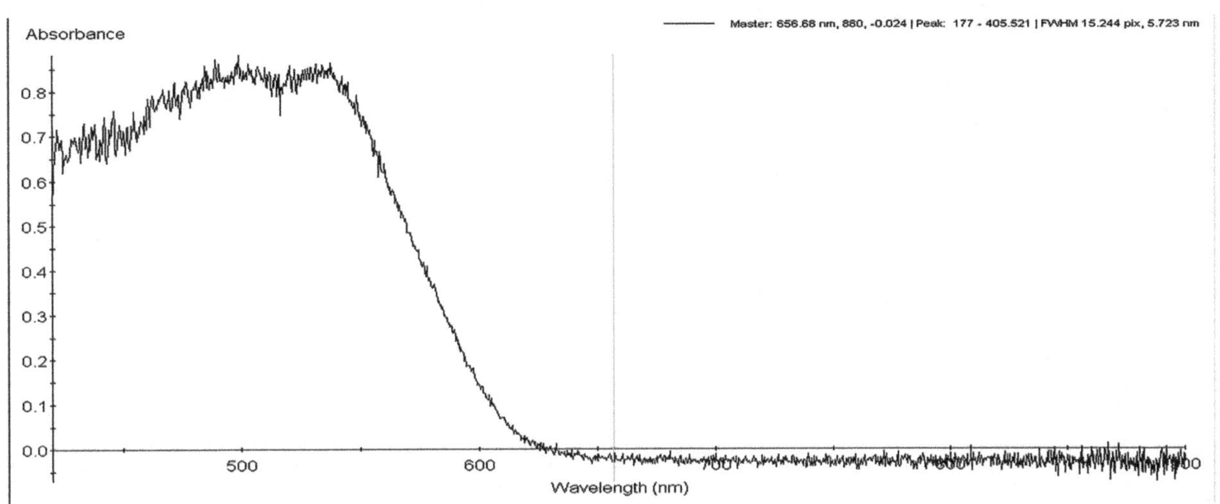

Figure 17F.5.9: Spectrum of red food coloring. Again, not a match.

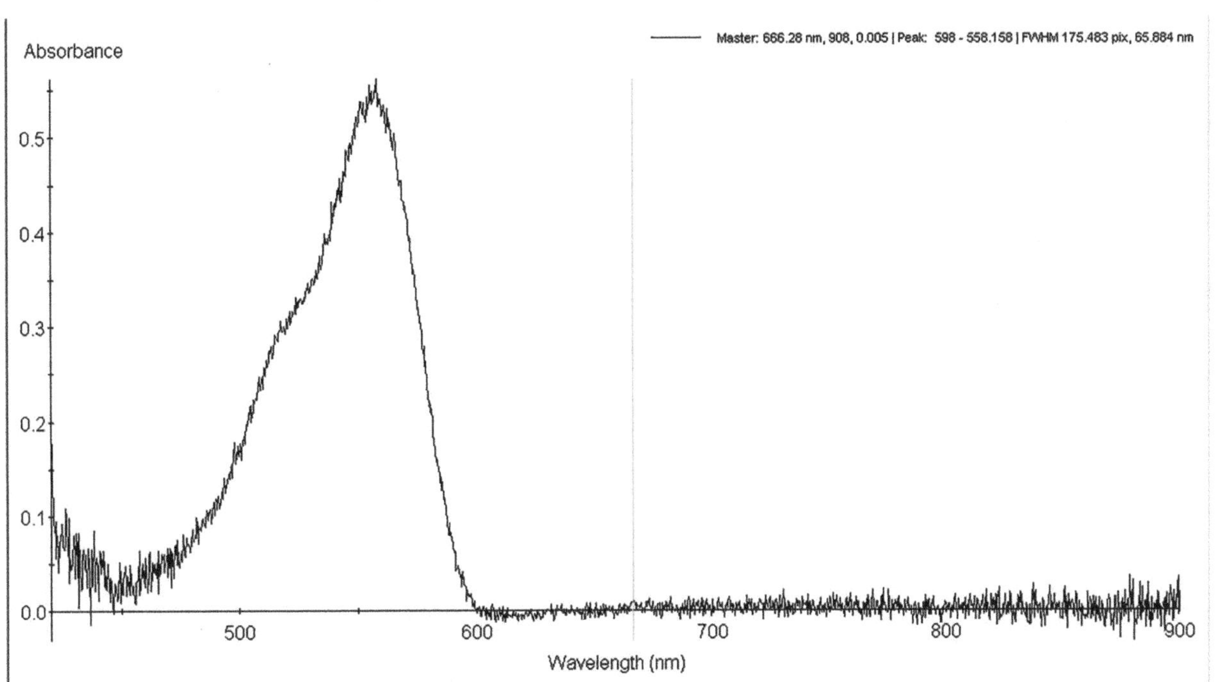

Figure 17F.5.10: Spectrum of Rhodamine B, a common dye for red pen inks, usually ballpoint pen inks.

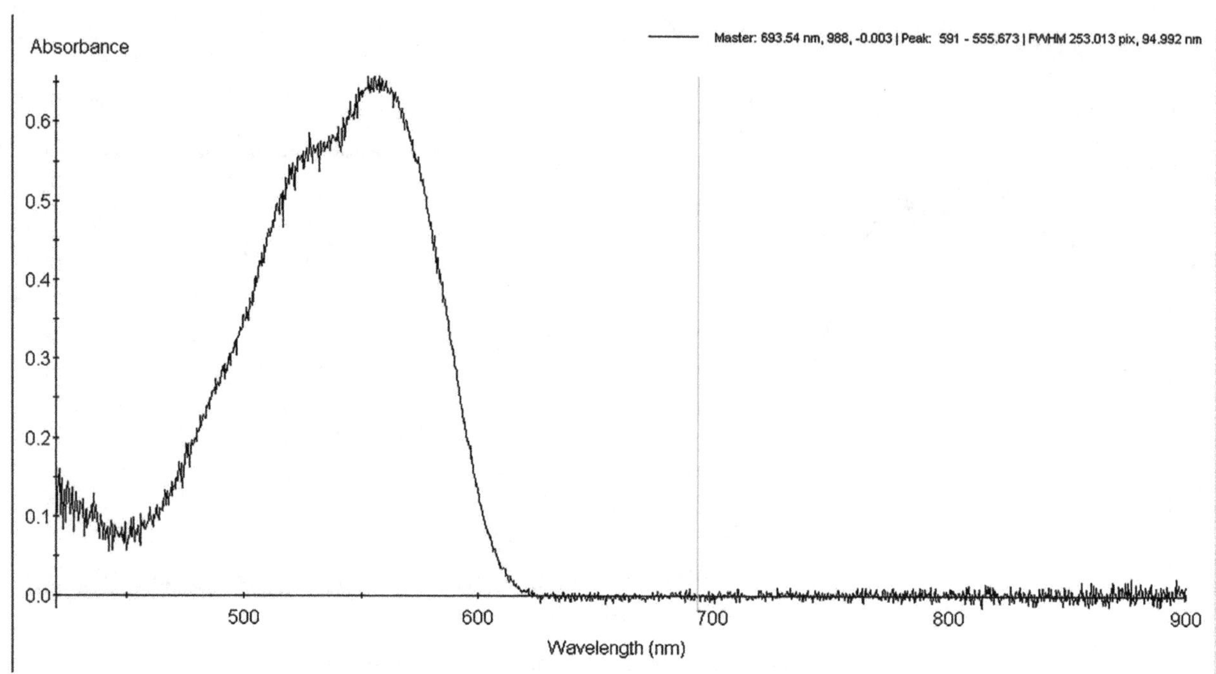

Figure 17F5.11: Spectrum of Bordeaux Red Fountain Pen ink.

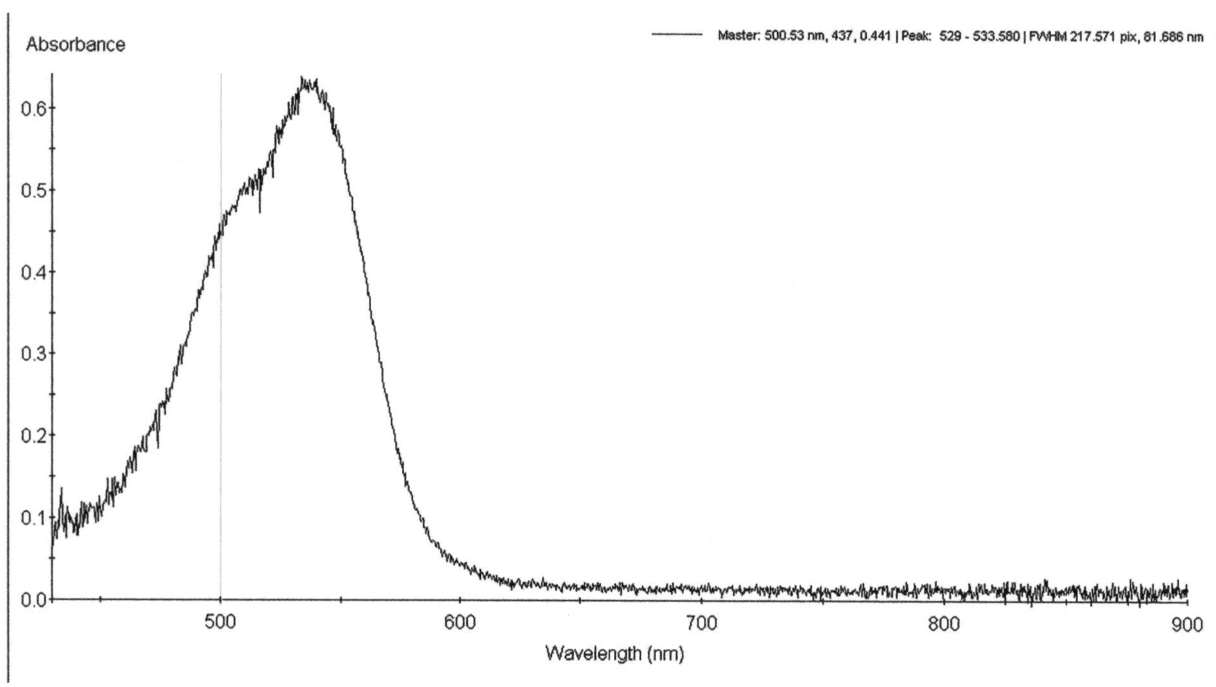

Figure 17F5.12: Spectrum of Rhodamine 6G.

The spectra of Rhodamine 6G and Rhodamine B are similar, as are their structures.

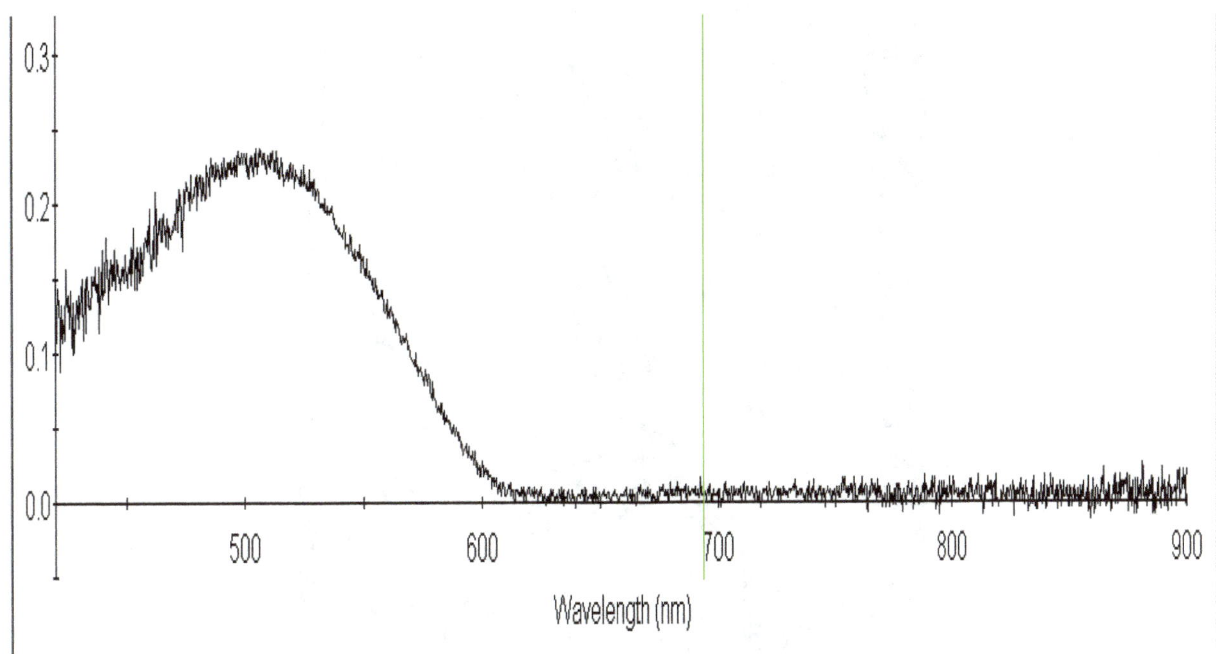

Figure 17F.5.13: The Spectrum of Direct Red 23

The spectra in Figures 17F.3.3 and 17F.4.1 do have the most in common, although there are other variables to consider.

17G. The Holes in the Singnature and the Story of the Table.

17G.1: There was a Table.

There is, in the Lindbergh kidnapping story, a famous table. Bear with me; its importance will soon be revealed. When its secret was discovered, The Table was taken to the police, but no police records remain. There were only a few newspaper articles, none of them very accurate, from 1948 … oh, and there was that one other article that appeared in the *New York Times* in 2004.

Figure 17G.1.1: The Table, minus it's top

The photo above is a State Police photo, so they had it in their possession at one time, except possibly for the top. The table is now gone, except for the top piece of wood shown, which is called the brace. The brace is not the tabletop; that had been removed, and its location is not known.

It appears to me that this table might have been sold as a kit. There are four legs attached to the main body, the pedestal. Sometimes such tables have ornately carved pedestals containing something like a carved pineapple, although this is relatively simple, more shaped like an acorn. It appears that there is a nut at the bottom of the pedestal. It looks like there *may* be a threaded rod that goes the length of it to hold it together. You can see the other end of the threaded rod coming out the top (or perhaps a section of threaded rod comes out of each end of the pedestal). Figure 17G.1.2 shows the brace; also, a State Police photo from 1948.

Figure 17G.1.2: The brace from the table.

The photo seems to have been taken from above while the brace was still attached to the pedestal. The center threaded rod can be seen in the middle, and there are holes for four screws, to hold the brace to the pedestal around the center rod. The center threaded rod casts two shadows; it appears that two light sources were used to illuminate the brace while photographing it.

There are three holes on each side of the brace. The wood on the sides where the holes are is lighter than the rest of the brace. This is because the holes had screws that secured two pieces of wood to the two edges. Since those parts of the brace was not exposed to air, they did not darken due to oxidation, explaining the two light "stripes" down the two sides. Perhaps two pieces of wood were screwed to the ends of the brace to lift the top higher above the brace, to accommodate a drawer. This is a common table construction. There is also lighter wood encircling the center threaded rod, suggesting that there was probably at least a washer and a nut on top, and the washer limited exposure of the wood to air, and oxidation.

During my Christmas trip through New England looking for ink bottles, I stayed in some old inns that had period furniture. Here is a photo of a Duncan Phyfe-style table, called a drum table because it doesn't just have a flat top attached to the brace, but a shallow "drum". It was at the Griswold Inn in Essex, CT. The space between the brace and top has room for a drawer in this case.

Figure 17G.1.3: A Duncan Phyfe-style drum table.

[Duncan Phyfe made furniture in America from the 1800s through the 1840s. He was known for his high-quality woods (mahogany, black walnut, cherry, and other hardwoods), and unique carvings on furniture parts.]

17G.2: The Table was Called a Mersman Table.

The table has always been called the Mersman Table because that's how it was reportedly identified by the owner of the furniture store where it was purchased. Mersman furniture was made in Ohio. It looks like a rather inexpensive piece of furniture. The State Police Museum has a copy of the Mersman catalog from 1932. The pieces in this very nice catalog are very nice, well made, of fine woods.

Figure 17G.2.1: The 1932 Mersman catalog

Perhaps they also made a line of inexpensive tables. The add below suggests this, although it is an advertisement from 1950.

OHIO ADVERTISEMENT SEPT 1950
FAMOUS MERSMAN QUALITY TABLES
19.95
Graceful 18th century style group ::: use one or all pieces. All have 5-ply Mahogany veneer tops and shelves; beautiful finishes and fine details.

Figure 17G.2.2: A Mersman Table Newspaper Advertisement, 1950

I'm not sure that the manufacturer is important at all, but it may be. Others have tracked down Mersman table ads and report that the table looks similar to their products but not identical.

17G.3: The Table was news because it contained a confession.

Figure 17G1.1 shows most of the table. The top had been removed by the owner for repairs. When the brace was exposed, he saw writing on it. It was discovered in 1948, but we don't know when the confession, written on the brace in pencil, was made. It could have been made when the table was being made, or the day before it was reported, for all we know. When the writing on the brace was discovered, it was reported to the police (it was surprising that it was ever found – when is the last time you took your sofa apart and looked at the wood for messages?).

Here is one of the few newspaper articles on The Table, from 1948.

LINDBERGH CASE

Nashuan Finds Confession Note at Bottom of Table

Former Nashuan, Elmer Bollard, now living in South Plainfield, NJ, revived the internationally-known Lindbergh kidnaping when he discovered a "confession note" found on the bottom of a table he purchased in Plainfield eight years ago.

BOILARD who was a machinist with the Flather Machine shop here 20 years ago, discovered the note while he was repairing a table, an imitation Duncan Phyfe. It was written in German and in indelible pencil. on a foot-square block of wood reinforcing the joint of the pedestal and the top of the table.

The gist of the unsigned note was this: The writer was one of a gang of kidnapers who hatched the kidnap plot in Hamburg, Germany. Bruno Hauptmann was innocent of the crime. The ransom note was buried in Summit, NJ.

BOILARD took the block of wood to a friend who translated it after which Boilard went to South Plainfield police. They in turn, called in State Police Capt Arthur Keaton, chief inspector of the state police and a veteran of the Hauptmann case who was assigned to the problem.

The table was purchased in 1940 in the Watchung Furniture house, Plainfield, but Albert Weisman, president of the furniture store could throw no light on the case. He said neither Borough nor state police had questioned him so far.

ACCORDING to store records, the table was sold to the former Nashuan between eight and nine years ago and it was new at the time. There were no German-speaking employes then, Mr Weisman said. Manufacturer of the table was an out of state concern, Mersman Table Co of Salina, Ohio.

Hauptmann was executed in Trenton, NJ, April 3, 1936 after being convicted of kidnaping and killing Charles A. Lindbergh's son.

NASHUA TELEGRAPH
NOV 24, 1948

Figure 17G.3.1: A Newspaper Article from 1948

It appeared in the Nashua Telegraph on Nov. 24, 1948. Apparently, those who reside on the planet Nashua like to refer to themselves as Nashuans. It tells the story of Elmer Bollard, a resident of South Plainfield, NJ, who bought the table at the Wachung Furniture House in Plainfield in 1940. While he was a Plainfield resident, he had lived in Nashua before that, so is identified by the Nashua Telegraph as a Nashuan. The table was of interest because Elmer found, written on the brace, a confession concerning the Lindbergh kidnapping. Keep in mind, this was discovered in 1948 (the kidnapping was in 1932).

On this brace was writing – handwritten in pencil. It was in German. Typical of anything written related to the case, there were misspellings that would not have been expected for a German author, although the first part of the message is probably understandable only to a German. The message started with part of an old German song about a prostitute and then claimed Hauptmann was innocent, that there was a "gang" who pulled off the kidnapping, still free, and the author was one of them. It claimed that most of the ransom money was buried in Summit, NJ.

Since we have official State Police photos, we know that they had the table at one time but now all they have is the brace. When the confession was found it was labeled as a hoax.

I won't keep you in suspense any longer. Here is what was written on the brace:

(http: www.lindberghkidnappinghoax.com/brace)

In Hamburg da bin ich gewesen in Samet und in Seide gekleidet
Meinen Namen den darf ich nicht nennen
Denn (this is taken from an old German sailor's song)

(In Hamburg I wore velvet and silk,
I am not allowed to tell you my name
Because)

Ich war einer der Kidnapper des Lindberg babys
und nicht Bruno Richard Hauptmann

(I was one of the kidnappers of the Lindbergh baby
and not Bruno Richard Hauptmann)

Der Rest des Lösesgeldes liegt in Summit New Jersey begraben.

(The rest of the ransom money lies buried in Summit New Jersey.)

N.S.D.A.P.
(These were the initials of what at the time was the German Nazi Party)

Q17G.3.1: Who would even think to write a "confession" on a piece of wood that was an interior part of a table, where probably no one would ever look? What would be their reason for doing such a thing?

A17G.3.1: (Your answer here. Good luck.). ____
____
____

The brace writing is hard to read. I have made a few attempts, using Image J, to enhance the writing on the brace; they are shown here.

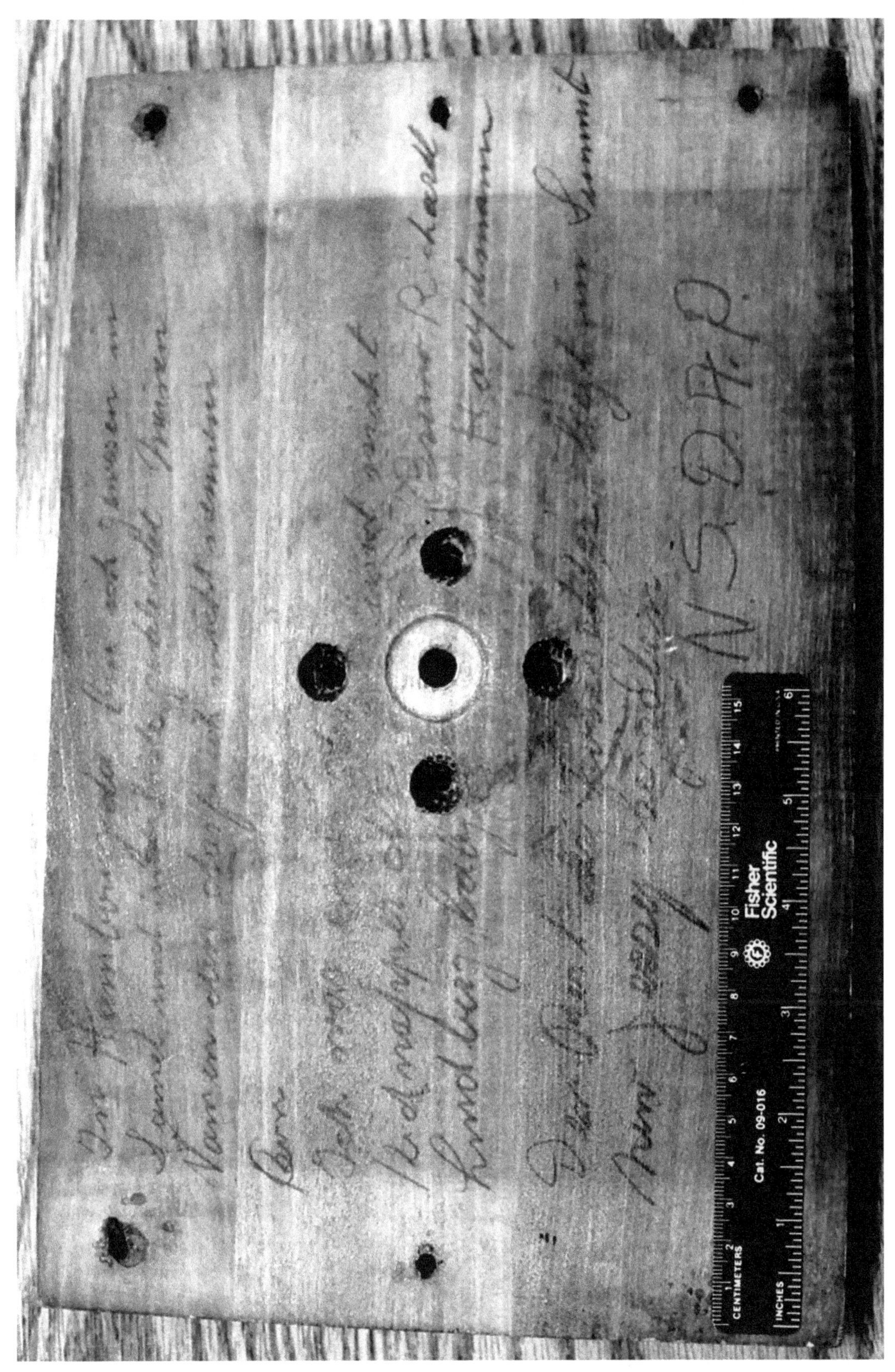
Fisher Scientific
Cat. No. 09-016
CENTIMETERS
INCHES

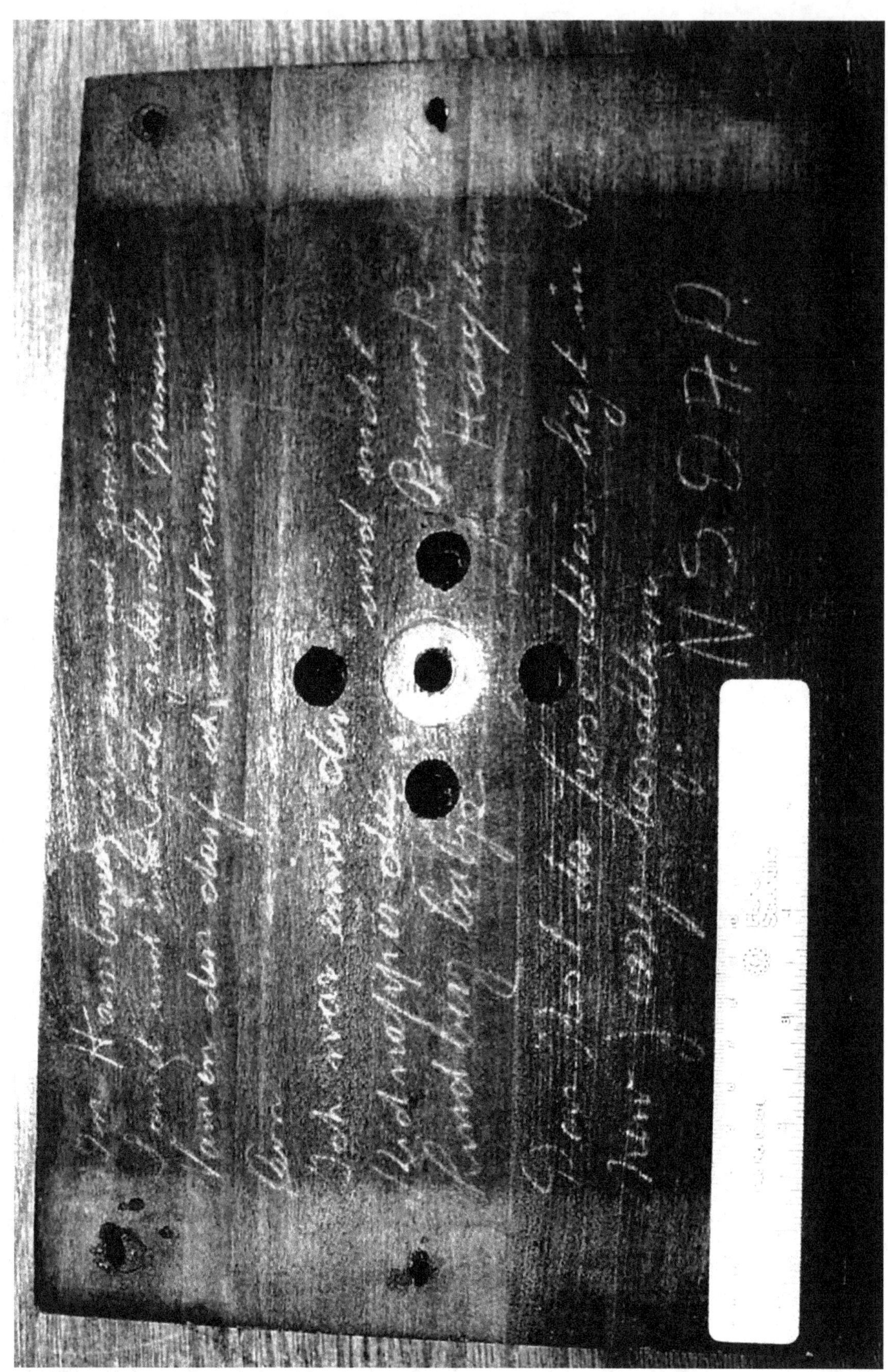
N.S.D.A.P.

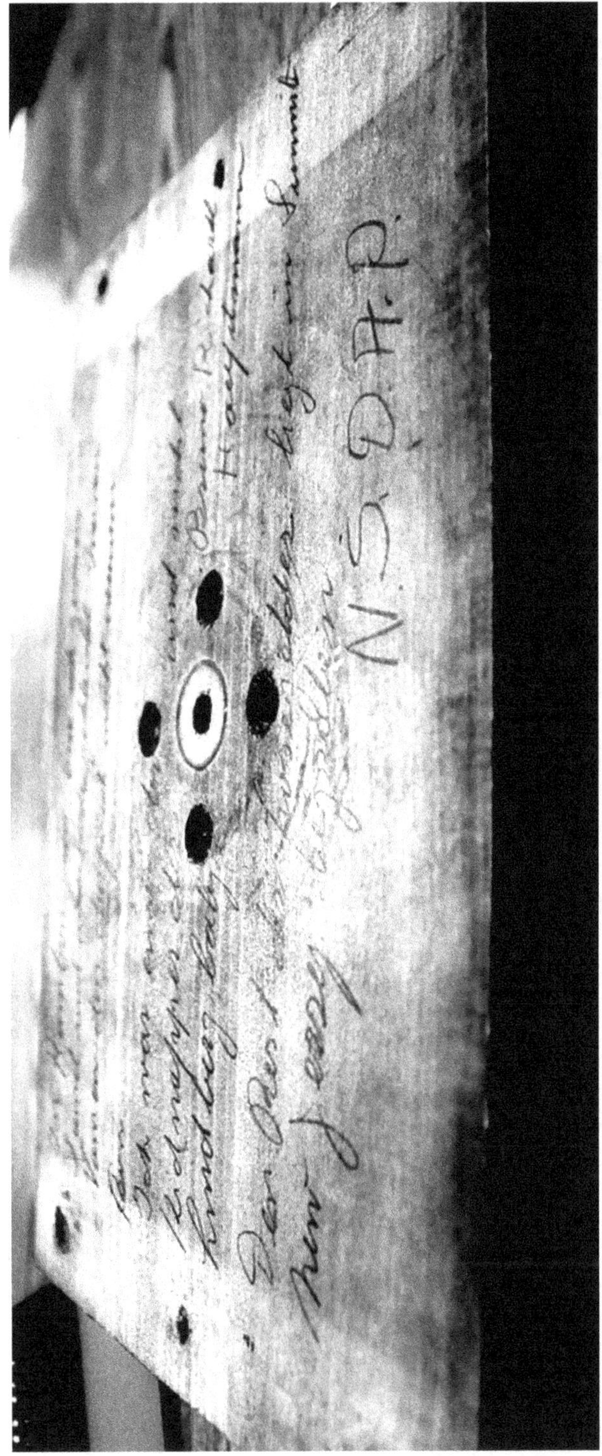

Figures 17G.3.2-4: Enhancing the writing of the brace using Image J.

The writing on the brace is entirely different from that in the ransom letters. I see dotted *i*'s, crossed *t*'s. There is no comparison of this "typical" writing to the substandard writing on the letters.

17G.4: The Table is now gone, except for the Brace.

The table is no longer in the possession of the State Police; perhaps once it was called a hoax, they threw it away or returned it to the owner. But Mark Falzini found a piece of wood, when unpacking a box related to the Lindbergh case, and realized it was THE BRACE from THE TABLE with THE CONFESSION on it. It was "retrieved from an old crate stored in a warehouse at New Jersey State Police Headquarters". "Rummaging through the contents of this long-ignored create, which included shoes and collectibles from the 1935 Lindbergh Trial", Falzini found the brace.

Mark knows what every good forensic scientist and every good scientist in general knows – at some point, you need to take a step back and take a fresh look at what you have. So, Mark looked. In particular, he looked past the confession, at the board of holes.

17G.5: The Brace and Mark Falzini.

Soon after, his findings appeared in the *New York Times*, in the *Jerseyana* section, June 22, 2003. You can find it the story at:

> www.Lindberghkidnappinghoax.com/brace.html.

The *Times* article by Becky Batcha is entitled *This Case Never Closes/Crime Buffs Abuzz as Key Piece of Evidence Resurfaces in Kidnapping of Lindbergh Baby.* Mark noticed that the spacing of the holes looked like the spacing of the holes in the signatures of the ransom letters. *The Ti*mes story reports "a series of holes in the board lines up with the original Lindbergh ransom letters. The coincidence suggests that the board is the template that was used to puncture the three-hole pattern that the police in the Lindbergh investigation came to recognize as the kidnappers' signature.

Many of the most active hobbyists, writers and researchers traveled to Ewing, NJ to see for themselves that the letter holes lined up with those in the brace. There was excitement related to the topic again. Several experts were quoted in the *Times* article indicating that this *was* the template used to make the ransom letters.

I feel I should comment on Mark Falzini and how he has given his career to helping others with aspects of the Lindbergh case. I appreciate Mark as a Lindbergh colleague in part because of how he once described himself:

> "I'm exposed to so much information, I'm baffled. And if I pick one thing I believe, then when someone else comes [and] I go to help them with their theory, I'm going to be blocked. By taking their theory for the day, I'm better able to help them, but also, in a selfish way, I get to help myself and learn more."

Q17G.5.1: Suppose you were Mark's assistant. What would you have suggested to be done next?
A17G.5.1:

17G.6: The Holes and Mark Falzini.

Get out your rulers and calculators. There are measurements that I have not seen made yet. This should be interesting.

Figure 17G6.1: The Brace Today

The brace is a woodblock that is 322 mm long, 208 mm wide, and 25 mm high. It has a hole in the center for the threaded rod that was probably topped off with a washer and nut. There are four holes around the center hole for screws to fasten the brace to the pedestal. The light-colored stripes on each edge of the top of the brace are 38 and 37 mm wide, and the three holes in each light stripe were separated by 78-82 mm.

Below are two more recent images that I made with rulers in the photos.

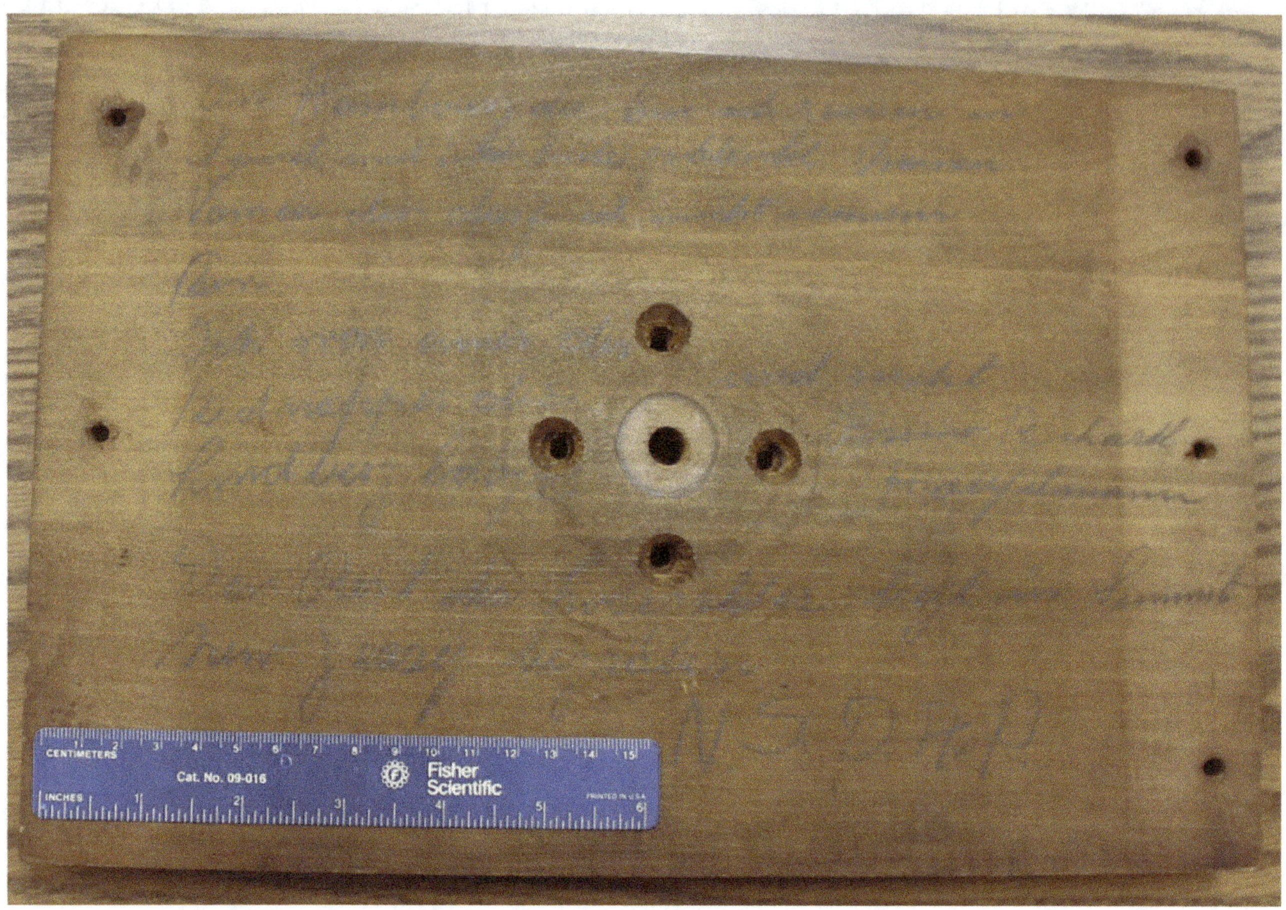

Figure 17G.6.2: Top of the Brace with a Ruler

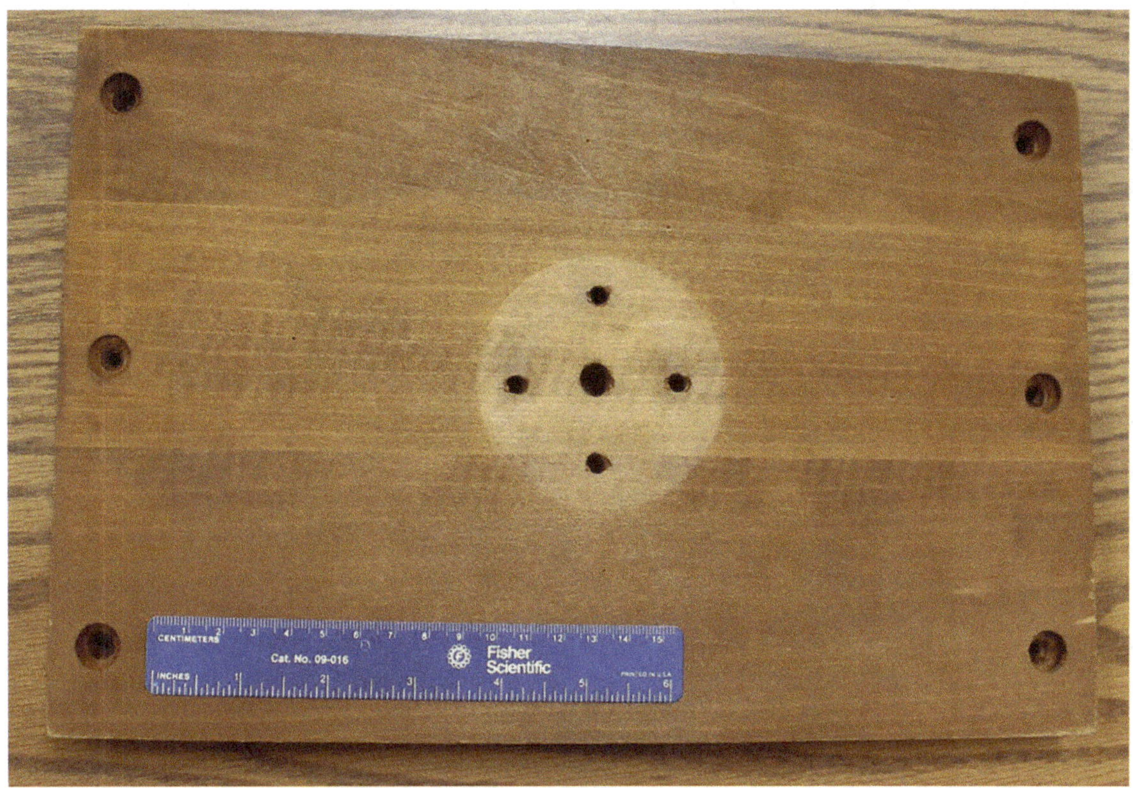

Figure 17G6.3: Bottom of the Brace.

The four holes around the center hole, that allow for four screws to hold the brace onto the top of the pedestal, were drilled on a small angle through the brace.

I'll label the four holes around the center hole as 1-4. We can measure the distance from the center hole to the four surrounding hole centers on the brace, using the method we employed earlier. I also measured the hole distances on the back (verso) side of each letter, starting with the outermost hole being #1, measuring inside to inside and outside to outside of the holes to calculate the distance between the hole centers, d12 and d23. Here are the measurements:

Table 17G.6.1: Distances between holes 1&2 and 2&3 on the Ransom Letters, mm

	Data				Results	
	x1o	x1i	x2o	x2i	d12	d23
Letter #1:	22.5	28	31	25	25.3	28
Letter #2:	29	21	32.4	24.5	25	28.5
Letter #3:				no singnature		
Letter #4:	29	21	25.3	32.5	25	27
Letter #5:				no singnature		
Letter #6:	28.5	20	33.5	25	24.2	29.2
Letter #7	21.5	28.4	25	32	25	28.5
Letter #8				no singnature		
Letter #9	30	23	30	23.5	26.5	26.7

Letter #10	29	23	30	24	26	27
Letter #11	23	30	23.5	30.5	26.5	27
Letter #12	30	22	31.5	23	26	27.2
Letter #13	29	22.5	30.5	24.8	25.7	27.7
Letter #14	30	25	28	23	27	25.5
Letter #15				no singnature		
Averages:					25.65	26.57 mm
Average of averages =					26.56 mm = 1.04 inches	

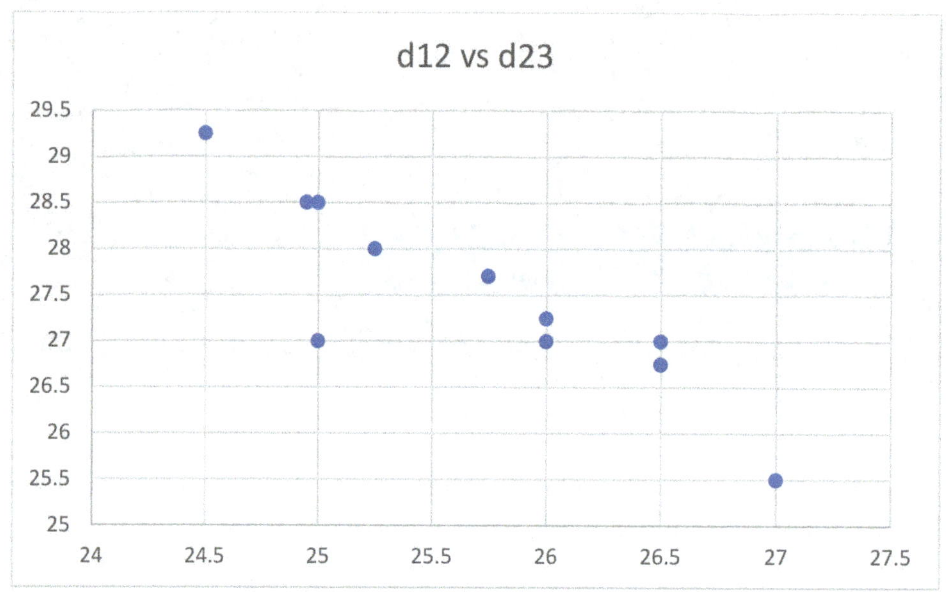

Figure 17G.6.4: Graph of d12 vs. d23 for the Ransom Letter Holes

They are not all the same, but it seemed like there was a pattern to the numbers, so I decided to construct a graph of d12 vs. d23. The data points fall on what is very close to a straight line. The slope of the curve (line) is negative with a slope of approximately -1. The largest value for one variable on a letter correlates with the smallest value for the other. So, for example, the first point on the left side of the graph has a high value of d23, 29.5 mm. It has a very low value for d12, 24.5. If you consider the last point on the right side, it has the lowest value for d23 and the highest value for d12. While they vary, the sum of the two is essentially constant, as seen in Figure 17G.6.5. I'm sharing this observation, but I have no idea why it would be significant.

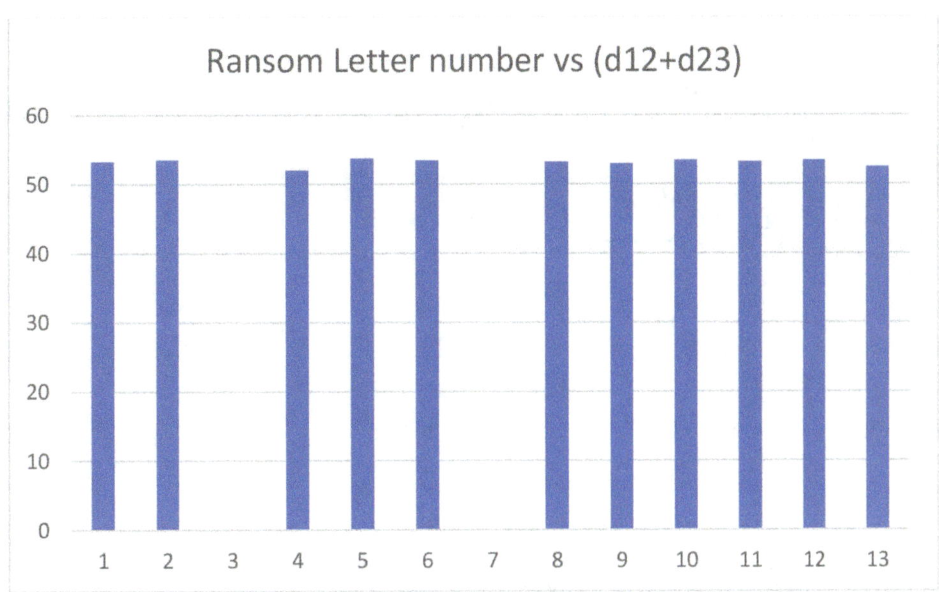

Figure 17G.6.5: The sums of the distances between pairs of holes on ransom letters are essentially constant.

So, concerning the distances between the holes on the ransom notes, looking at them from the backside of the page and numbering them 1,2,3 from left to right, the average distance between 1 and 2 is 25.65 mm and the average distance between 2 and 3 is 26.57 mm. The average of the averages is 26.5 mm. Converting to inches, on average, the holes are 1.04 inches apart.

As I've explained earlier, I've done all the measurements and calculations multiple times, at the mm level, and results can differ by as much as 1.5 mm because of the width of the lines I draw in making the measurements, and the fact that dimensions on the ransom letters vary, depending on where they are measured. A second set of measurements (not shown) gave an average d12 of 27.2 mm and an average d23 of 26.9 mm, with the average of the averages being 27.05 mm (the holes averaged being 1.06 inches apart).

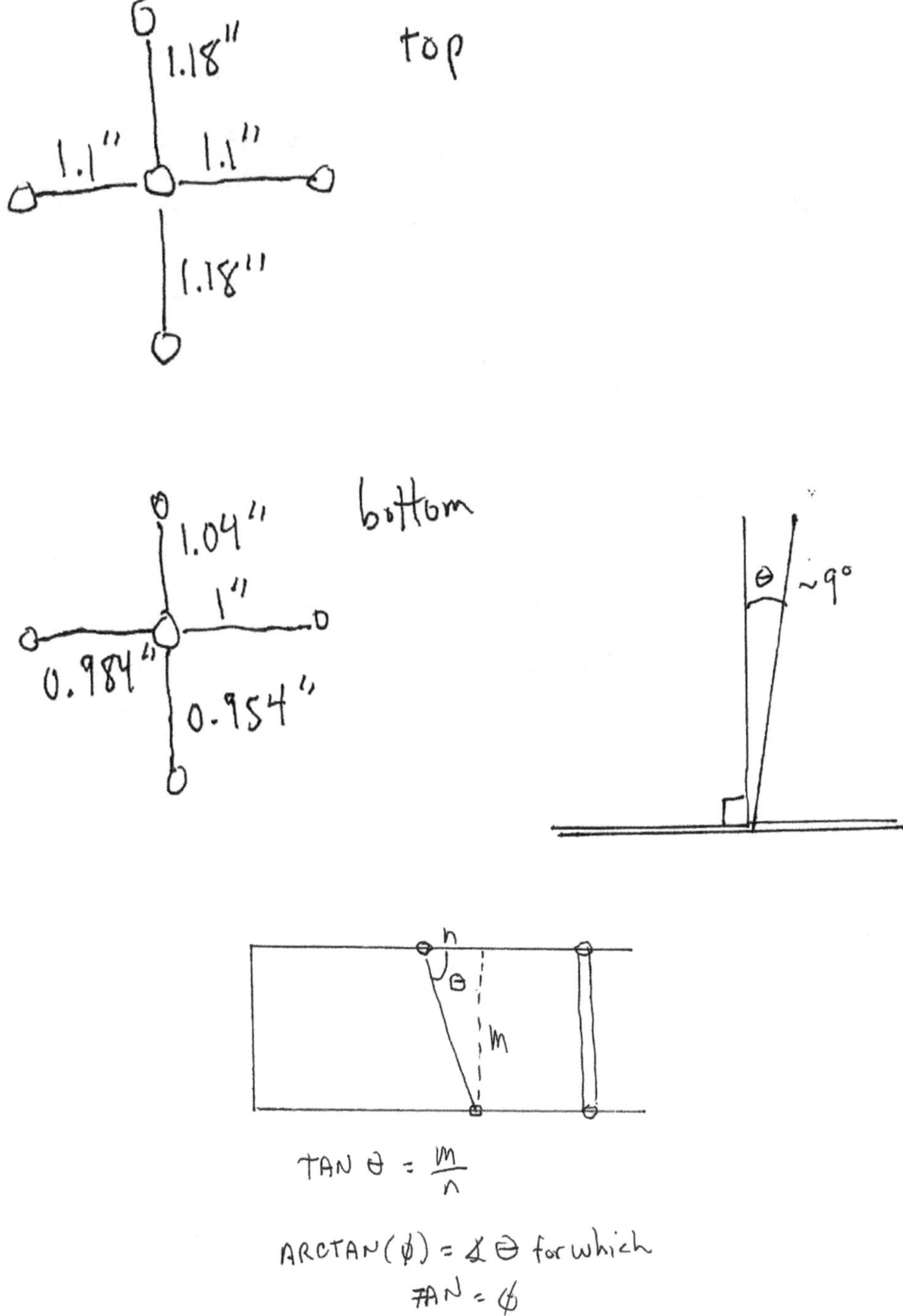

Figure 17G.6.5: All holes through the brace are cut on an angle relative to the center hole; spacing between the holes is larger on the top of the brace than on the bottom.

Figure 17G.6.5 shows that the distances from the center to each of the four holes on the top of the brace (where the writing is) are all larger than the other end of each hole to center, so all the holes are cut on a small angle pointing into the center. From the distances measured and 9th grade geometry class, I determined that the holes are drilled on a small angle varying from 7 to 13 degrees with an average value of 9 degrees. Figure 17G.6.5 also shows you what an angle of 9 degrees looks like. It's small but measurable. The trick is to take the angle shown and measure the length of the leg of the triangle opposite to it and the length of the leg adjacent to the angle. The ratio of those two lengths, opposite/adjacent, is defined as the tangent of the angle. There are tables that let you look up the arctangent of that value, the angle that would have that value for a tangent, so you can determine the angle.

We also measured a, and b as shown in Figure 16C.4. Recall, a is the distance between the lower edge of the page to the row of holes, and b is the distance from the right edge of the letter to the center of the nearest hole (both on the front side).

Summary:
Top of brace, hole spacings (between adjacent holes)
1.1 inch, 1.18 inch, 1.1 inch, 1.18 inch
Bottom of brace, hole spacings between adjacent holes
0.98 inch, 0.98 inch, 1.04 inch, 0.96 inch
Letter hole spacing (average)
hole1-hole2 1.04 inch hole2-hole3 0.9 inch

Where exactly are the holes on the page? Two additional measurements were made earlier, the distance from the hole center to the nearest edge of the page (b), and the distance from the holes (specifically the center hole) above the bottom edge, (a). These were measured and are reported below:

The Data

	a	b (in mm)
Ransom Letter #1	35.5	6
Ransom Letter #2	36	5
Ransom Letter #3	no singnature	
Ransom Letter #4	35.5	6
Ransom Letter #5	no singnature	
Ransom Letter #6	34.5	5.5
Ransom Letter #7	35.5	5
Ransom Letter #8	no singnature	
Ransom Letter #9	34	6.5
Ransom Letter #10	34.5	7
Ransom Letter #11	34	6
Ransom Letter #12	34	6
Ransom Letter #13	34	6
Ransom Letter #14	32.5	6.5
Ransom Letter #15	no singnature	
Average values	34.5	5.95 in mm
	1.35	0.23 in inches
	1 23/64	15/64 in fractional inches.

The average value of a is 34.5 mm and the average for b is 5.95 mm.

Again, I redid all of the measurements and calculations of all the a's and b's and my second set of measurements averaged a = 33.4 mm, b = 6.04 mm.

Mark Falzini is smart. He pointed out that the spacing on the letter holes matches those on the table brace holes. The implication was that the brace could have been used to make the holes, but he did not focus on that issue.

17G.7. The Table Brace as a Template – Making the Holes.

I got a piece of wood and drilled some holes in it to approximate the five holes, and their spacing relative to each other. Now I'm ready to make some letter signature holes. The problem is I don't know where to put the paper. I could sit it on top of the board, perhaps illuminate it from below to find out where the holes are, picking one set of three holes, or another.

My other choice is to put the paper *below* the brace holes and make the holes that way.

No matter how I do it, the holes in the brace will put them roughly in the same place relative to each other, but not in some absolute position relative to the letter. For this I need a *template*, something that will put the holes at a specific place on each letter, so we get the correct values of a and b.

The brace is not a template. However, what we have just learned here is that the spacing between the holes is essentially 1.0 inch. If the hole separation was 0.744 inches and the holes on the letters matched that value, it would be highly unlikely, making the letters/brace correlation of higher significance. However, for a dimension as common as one inch, well, there are many things that could be used as a template.

17G.8. A Possible Template for the Singnature Holes.

We need to find a template that will put three holes, *one inch apart*, at a precise location on a piece of paper that is usually 157 mm wide. Hobbyists have suggested many things for making three holes, one inch apart – from shoes to belts, with fellow hobbyists criticizing them because they didn't know dimensions to make such a decision. But we do.

I was thinking about the fact that the New Jersey State Police had been accused of interfering with the case in many ways, altering evidence, etc. That led me to think about the belts of State Police Uniforms. How could I ever hope to find any information about the evolution of NJ State Police Uniforms? Well, of course, Mark Falzini wrote the book on the subject. (*Trooper Togs: A History of the New Jersey State Police Uniform,* Mark W. Falzini, 2010). The first person to design a uniform for the State Police was Herbert Norman Schwarzkopf, their first superintendent. Part of the uniform was a brown leather Sam Browne belt. A Sam Browne belt was a wide leather belt that was accompanied by a narrower strap that was worn diagonally across the right shoulder. It was initially designed in the 1800s to hold a sword, or later, a pistol in a flap-holster. They are now rarely used in police and security uniforms because of the risk of strangulation if an opponent grabs the strap; however, it was long recognized as a benefit since it allowed police officers to carry more (heavy) equipment on their belts. I started to read about belts and how they were made and was surprised to find that belts are most often made with a one inch spacing between the holes.

Not only did Mark write a book on State Police uniforms, but part of the display at the State Police Museum is dedicated to that topic.

I shared the idea with Mark. In the NJ State Police Museum, there is almost always an officer there, assigned to the location. I was surprised (and embarrassed) when Mark called the officer over and asked him to take off his belt and hand it to me. I thanked him, and told him it wasn't necessary, but at that point, I already had it in my hand as well as a ransom letter. The holes in the two matched up. I had a second possibility in addition to the brace, but it wasn't (yet) a template, either.

Figure 17G.8.1: Wide leather Sam Brown belt and accompanying narrow diagonal strap

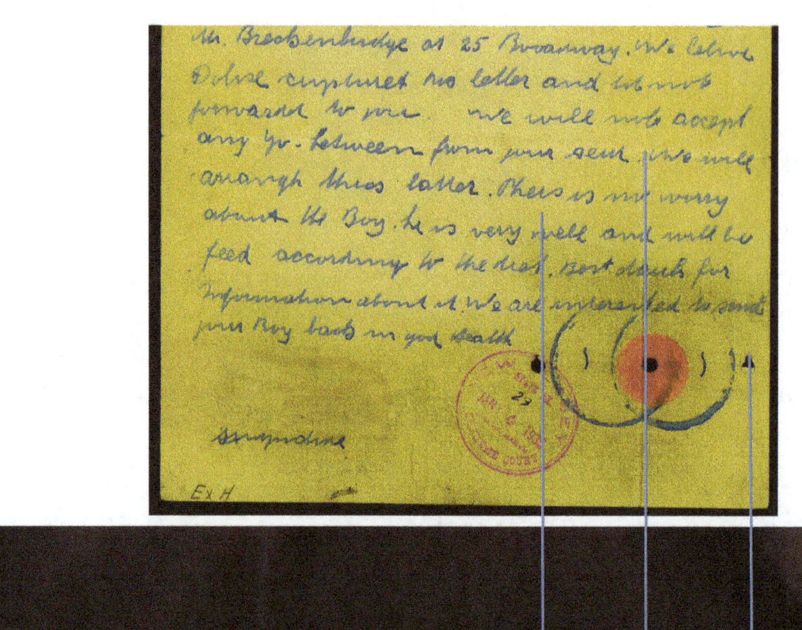

Mr. Breckenbridge at 25 Broadway. We belive Polise captured his letter and let not forward to you. we will not accept any go-between from your send. we will arrangh theis latter. There is no worry about the Boy. he is very well and will be feed according to the diat. Best thanks for Information about it. We are interested to send your Boy back in gut health.

Singnature

Ex H

Figure 18G8.2: Singnature hole spacing matches belt spacing – one inch.

I noticed that, on the cover of *The Aviator's Wife,* the woman on the cover was wearing an outfit with a wide belt.

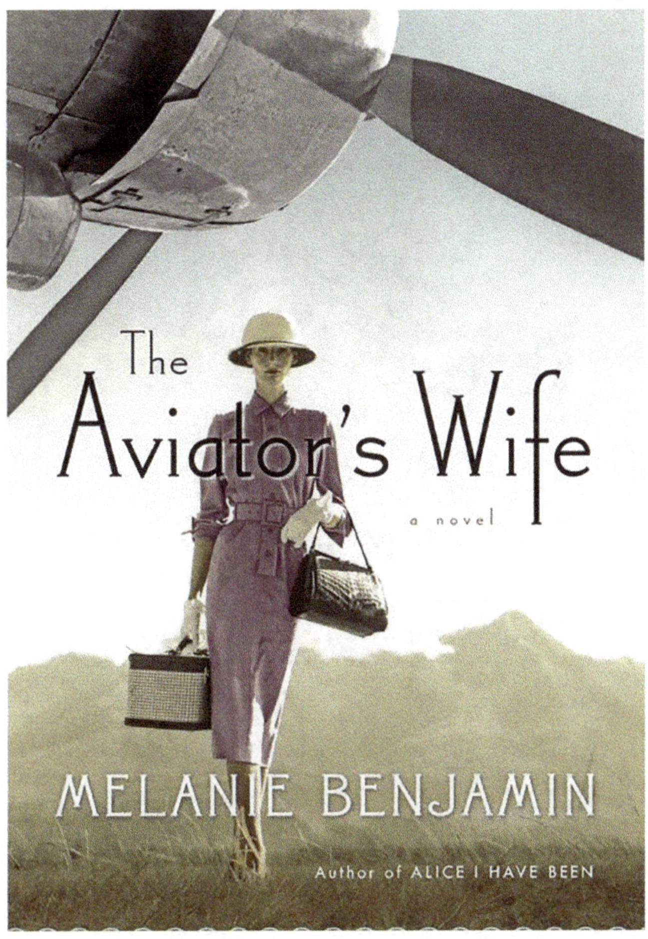

Figure 17G.8.3: Book Cover

Apparently, due to the fascination of America with Lindbergh and Earhart, aviation influenced fashion in the 20s and the 30s, especially women's fashion. Also, women's waistlines returned in the 1930s. The "Flappers" of the 1920s wore straight dresses; women didn't have waistlines during that time. But with the approach of the 1930s, and the Depression, when everyone was trying to save money, they often wore older dresses, but accessorized to make them look fresh.

Belts became a popular accessory.

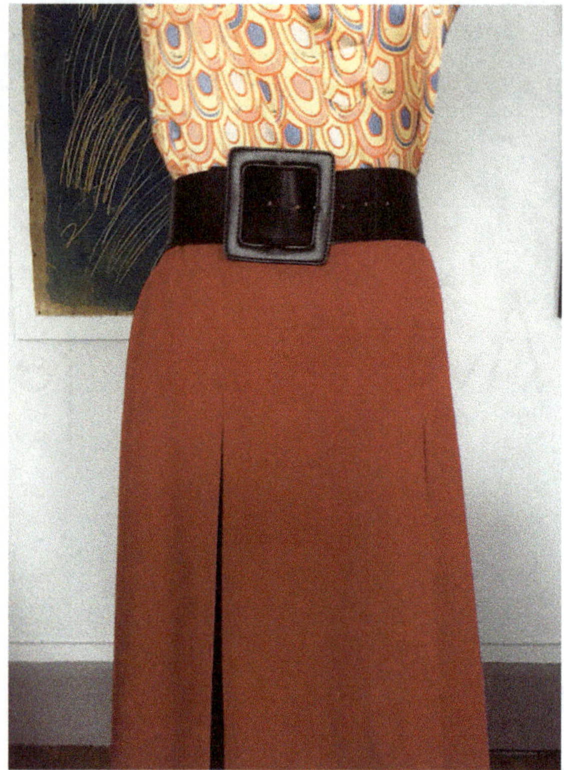

Figure 17G8.4: A wide leather woman's belt from the 1930s

I found the idea of using a belt as the template for the ransom note holes and their positions intriguing. The College people who handled mail were already curious when my purchase of the book *Everyday Fashions of the Thirties* by Stella Blum arrived; their curiosity increased when I ordered a reproduction of a woman's alligator belt from the 1930s that I found on E-Bay.

The belt was 2 ¾ " wide, three feet long, with five holes. The end was flat, and the first hole was four inches away from that flat end. Shown below is the end of the belt that didn't have the buckle.

Figure 18G.8.5: End of my belt

Here is what I did with my new belt. I cut a piece of paper 157 x 177 mm, the most popular dimensions of a ransom letter.

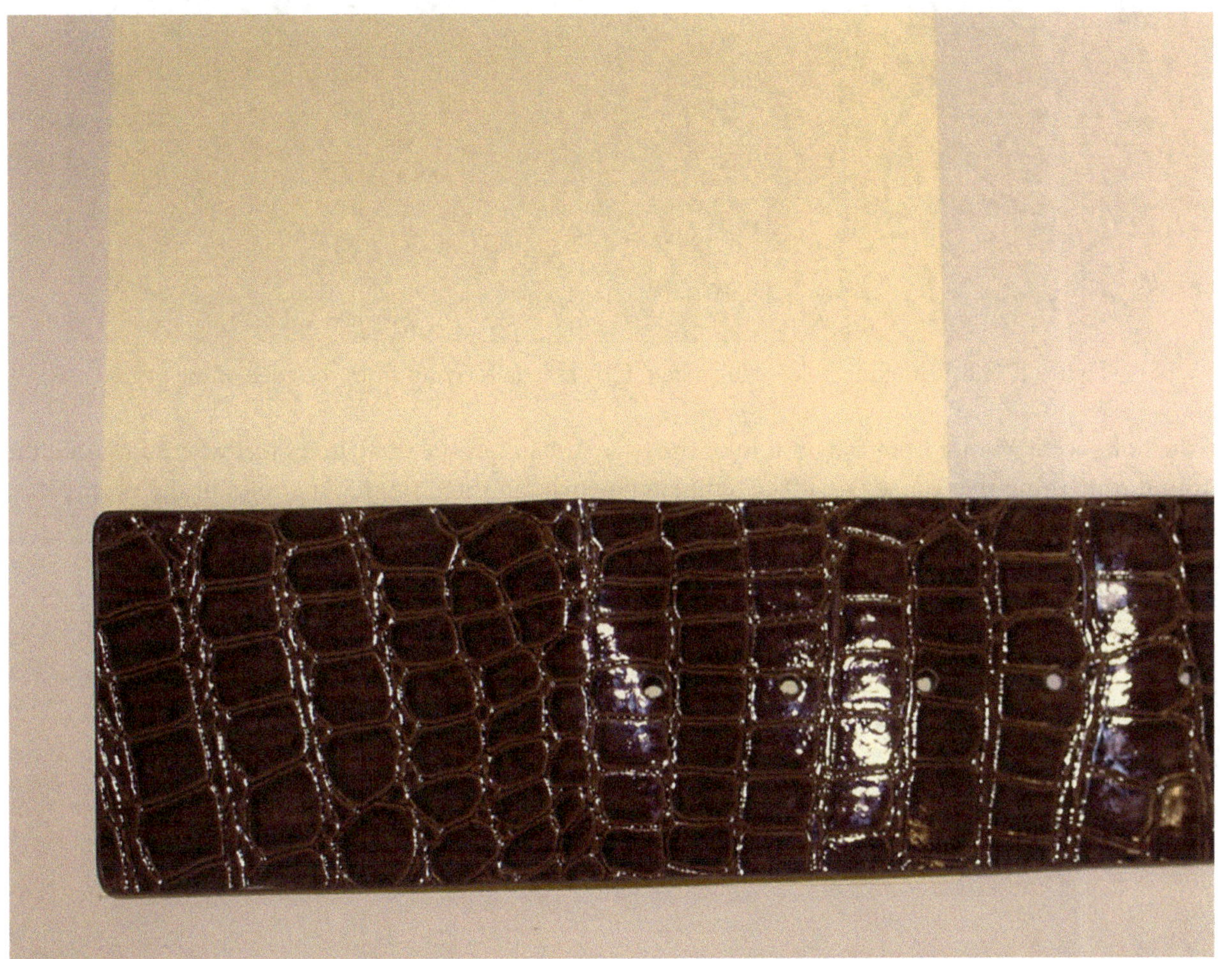

Figure 17G.8.6: Lining up the belt and a blank ransom letter.

I put one edge of the paper against the bottom of the belt and the flat belt end against the left side of the paper. I stuck a pen through the first three belt holes and then took the belt off the paper. The right-most dot/hole was about 6 mm away from the edge of the page,

Figure 17G.8.7: Making holes using a belt. One hole falls 6 mm from the edge of the page.

and the holes were 35 mm from the bottom of the page. It had put the three holes just where I wanted them! I'd found something that can act as a true template for making three signature holes in the exact place on the page where all of them should be.

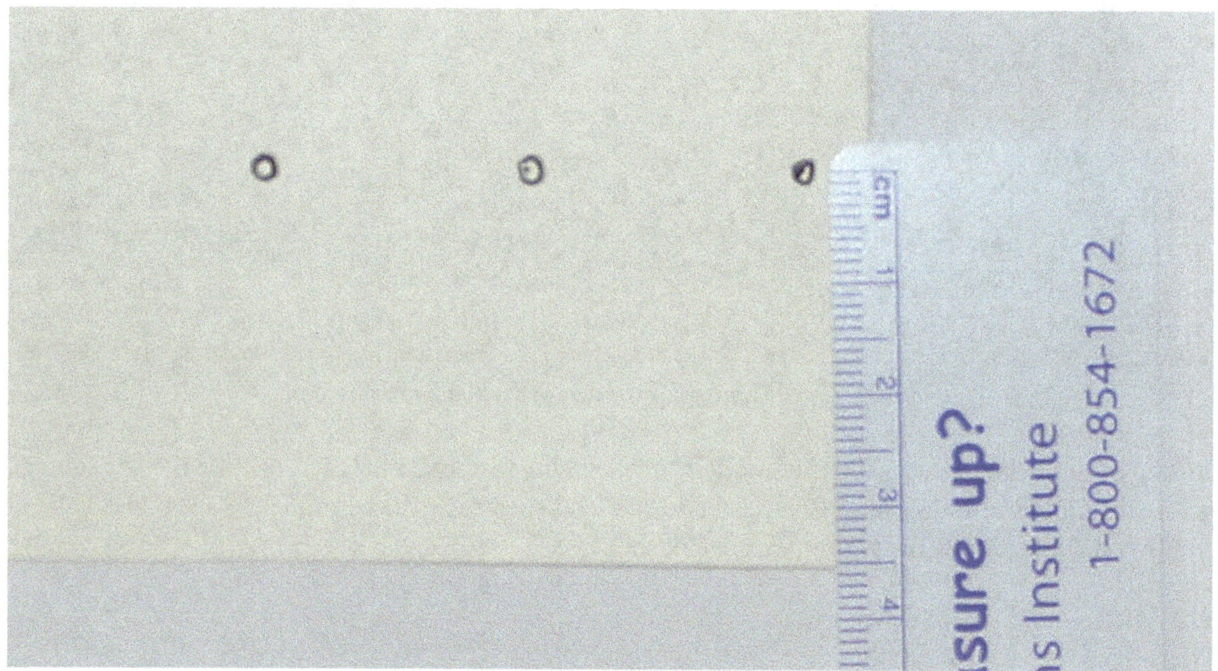

Figure 17G.8.8: My three holes are 35 mm from the bottom of the page.

I think it would be much easier to use a belt than a big slab of wood and not only are the holes separated by an inch, but they're put in the correct place on the page – not bad for my first woman's belt! I'm not prepared to present this as proof that a belt was used, but the exercise does show how simple it is to find something that satisfied all the requirements of a hole positioner and a template. There must be many others.

You should be suspicious at this point. I showed you how a belt could be used as a template for a ransom letter's holes, but I reported to you that there were three different letter sizes. Did I pick the one page size that I knew this would work with? Well, no, but if it works with the first size paper, you couldn't do the same thing with that belt for the other two paper sizes. So, is this useful at all? I propose that it is because they could have made several size A pages with a belt and used some of *those* as templates to punch holes in the size B and C pages. Simple as that.

Since we are discussing belts, this might be a good place to briefly comment on how belts are made. If you're interested, you could begin here:

> http://www.styleforum.net/t/260644/equus-leather-bridle-leather-belts-official-affiliate-thread/765

There is also a good tutorial on belt-making at

> www.the spruce.com/how-to-make-a-belt/1106110

The best part about this website is that it also provides instructions for making a Gryffindor robe. (If you don't know what that is, ask someone younger.)

The holes in a high-quality belt are usually an inch apart, although sometimes it is ¾ inches for smaller belts. Typically, the belt extends for four inches past the last hole.

If you purchase, for example, a 34" belt, that number corresponds to the distance from the buckle to the third hole, as shown in the figure.

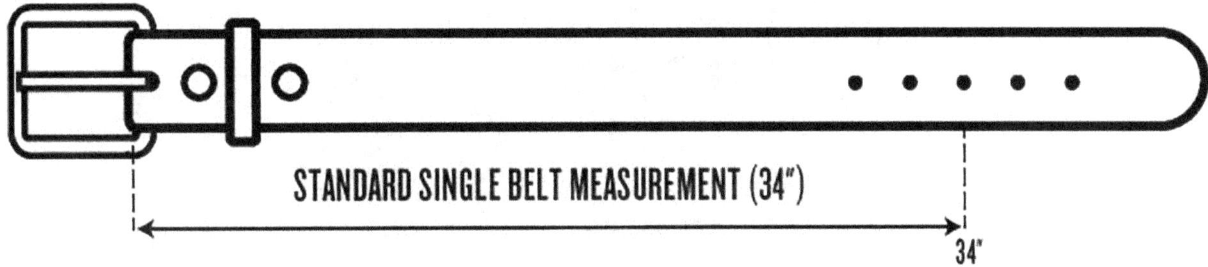

Figure 17G.8.9: Standard Belt Dimensions

If you start with a blank leather belt, a common approach is to put masking tape on the belt and mark where the holes will go on the tape.

Making the holes can be as simple as using a nail and a hammer. An alternative is to use an actual belt hole punch.

There are punches that make round holes and ones that make oval holes. The following figure shows a punch that makes oval holes.

Figure 17G.8.10: A belt hole punch, oval.

Figure 17G.8.10 above shows a Tandy Leather Craftool Oval Punch #9. This item 3778-09 measures 5/16" x 7/32" (7.9 mm x 5.5 mm) and is used for belts, straps and anything that has a buckle.

Here is another type of leather hole punch for making round holes in belts.

Figure 17G.8.11: A leather hole punch

One can even use a drill.

Figure 17G.8.12: Making belt holes with a drill

17G.9: Making The Holes.

I had one of my classes try to poke some holes for me. You tried earlier. We looked through the variety of hole types – some appear "trilobal," some are round, some are round but have a part of the paper hole still attached, some appear square. I brought into class some paper towels to put under the paper to make it easier for students to push something through, and then I had a collection of possibilities – nails, screws, pencils, punches, square floor nails, an ice pick, etc. I had students start making holes with these things. It was difficult, and, from the standpoint of the paper, very messy. So, I asked them for suggestions on how we could make a hole.

I was reminded that there are more things we can do. Question everything. I had this belt explanation all wrapped up, except I never actually punched holes with the method. Now that I saw how hard it was to make holes in paper, I needed to determine whether a belt could be used. I'd never actually *measured* the size of the holes on the letters, or the holes on the belt. I have no idea if they're even similar, but they need to be. I can't make a 40 mm hole by pushing anything through a 30 mm belt hole! It's time to make a few more measurements.

I picked a few ransom letters that had signatures and measured the heights and widths of the six holes. Here are my results, in mm.

Typical Ransom Letter Hole Sizes (heights or widths, mm)

2.5	3.0	3.0	3.0
2.5	2.9	3.0	2.5
3.5	4.0	3.0	3.0

The average is 35.9/12 = 3.0 mm

Next, I measured the hole dimensions on my ladies' belt (front and back). (Five holes, two sides, that should be ten measurements, but I only made nine – my bad.) I was tired that day.

Typical Belt Hole Dimensions, mm (front and back of belt)

3.5	3.0	3.5
3.0	3.8	3.0
3.0	3.0	3.0

The average is 28.8/9 = 3.2 mm

Those are two good numbers –close to each other, but the belt holes are just slightly larger, so we should be able to make a 3 mm letter hole by pushing something through a 3.2 mm belt hole.

After many failed attempts, I remembered that when I was discussing how to make a belt, one of the options for making the holes was to use a drill, so I tried that. It turns out that a drill works well. I want to make a 3 mm hole. If I use a 1/8" drill bit (a popular size), 1/8" is equal to 0.125", and there are 25.4 mm in an inch, so 1/8" is 3.2 mm.

Because your innate curiosity about everything has probably intensified, I'm guessing that you are interested in the history of power tools. A good place to start is Jeff Griffin's 2016 article in *Electrical Contractor Magazine* (*100 Years of Innovation: History of the Electric Drill*). You can find it at:

https://www.ecmag.com/section/your-business/100-years-innovation-history-electric-drill

Drills have been around for a long time. Apparently, early man realized the application of rotary tools more than 30,000 years ago. This, of course, eventually led to the hand drill.

The invention of modern hand-held drills couldn't occur until we invented electric motors. Some say this was the work of Arthur Arnot, an Australian who patented the first electric drill in 1889.

Figure 17G.9.1: An old hand drill called an "eggbeater" drill.

Pistol-grip, electric (corded), right-angle drills have been the most common drill for most of the 20th century.

In 1910, S. Duncan Black and Alonzo Decker built a machine shop in a Baltimore warehouse. One of their clients was Colt, the maker of firearms. As history tells it, they were designing an electric drill, trying to figure out how to hold it and control its drilling function. Near them, as they talked, was a Colt handgun. The trigger and pistol grip inspired them. In 1917, Black and Decker opened a plant in Maryland where they made things like hand-held drills. Black and Decker put a full-page ad in *The Saturday Evening Post* introducing people to this new technology. They started selling drills around 1923.

Figure 17G9.2: The first hand-held drill from Black and Decker (Note gun handle)

The first portable drill, built in 1916, can be found in the Washington, D.C. National Museum of American History. There had been electric drills before that, but they were often large stationary tools such as drill presses.

In the 1920s, electricians and others were using Black and Decker tools, but the competition was not far behind. The *hole shooter* was developed by A.H. Pearson in 1924. It was a portable drill that could be used with one hand.

To recap, the concept of using a belt as both a jig and a pattern for the holes is an attractive one. We looked even further into the ransom notes and the belts and found that the size of the ransom note holes were a fraction of a mm smaller, and when we used a small drill to cut the paper below the belt, the holes very much resembled those on the ransom notes.

We started with a low power, hand-held, rechargeable drill.

Figure 17G.9.3: A small Ryobi drill

In the Ryobi tool kit that accompanied the drill was an 1/8" Drill bit

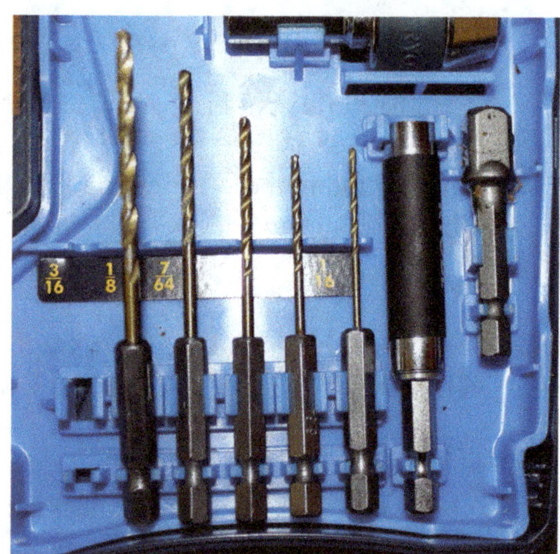

Figure 17G9.4: Drill bits for the Ryobi Drill

We cut a piece of paper to match the size of the ransom notes (7" x 6 7/64") and drilled through the belt holes …

Figure 17G9.5: Drilling Through my Belt Template

The three holes drilled are precisely the distance from the lower and right edges of the letter as is observed on the ransom letters.

Figure 17G9.6: My Holes Made Using a Belt and a Drill.

And, if you look at the other side, this is where much of the paper ends up.

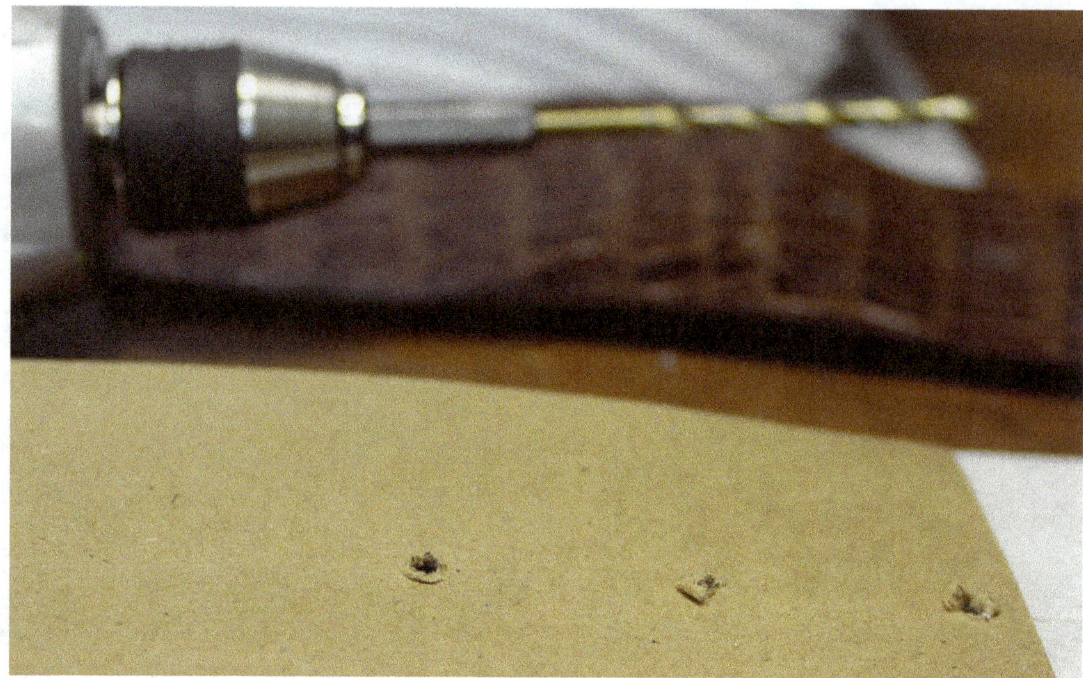

Figure 17G9.7: Drilled paper holes (verso)

While the holes are nice and neat from the top, a drill is not a punch, so there are "hanging chads" on the other side. Surely, over 80 years much of these small pieces of paper have worn/fallen off the original letters, but several of the holes have small paper fragments still hanging on to the back. The drill is an attractive method for making the holes, using a belt template.

I will leave it to you, my friend, to try and make decisions on the method for making the holes.

Yes, I'd like you to give it a try. Use any old belt for now. Our goal is to make holes in paper that resemble the holes on the ransom notes. There appears to be more than one shape. There are specific, repeating hole patterns, I believe. As far as I can tell, all the B letters have three holes that are round, round, round. Add to that, the fact that the very first letter has three circular holes. The second pattern is that the first hole is "trilobal," the middle hole looks square, and the third hole is round. Most of the A letters have that same pattern, except for Letter #2. Try again to make holes that look most like the holes in the actual ransom notes.

Some questions to ponder/questions that you can investigate:

1. What was the weapon of choice? A screw? A nail? What kind of nail? (My father left me with many jars of random screws and nails, and some of the older ones are square.) Also, at my local Home Depot I found some very nice, hardened steel "cut Flooring Nails" that have rectangular cross-sections and were three inches long. Many choices! I think for some of the letters a drill was used, and for others, perhaps a set of three punches was used.
2. How does the result depend on the number of sheets you punch at one time? Many have suggested that the holes were made in paper two sheets at a time. Is there an advantage to that? Is it true?
3. If you use a belt as a template on top of the paper, how do the results vary according to what you put on the other side? Cardboard? Perhaps a nice soft sponge or maybe something firmer?

4. How does the appearance of the holes depend on how deep you press it into the paper? (I had one big nail, and if I just pushed it a little bit, I got the star shape of the nail's tip. However, if I push the nail in further, the hole eventually becomes round to match the shape of the nail body.)

I just have to say…. This is one aspect of the story that continues to bother me – It's not very important but my many verification attempts have not been satisfying.

The table is called the Mersman table, because the owner of the store that sold it said (told a reporter?) it was from the Mersman company. We have a good photo of the table (minus the top). I have never been able to find a picture of the same table identifying it as a Mersman product. Can you?

It appears to be black, possibly a table that requires some assembly. It is almost unique in its simplicity relative to comparable tables of this type.

A 1978 Mercer County Ohio History Book contains the story of Mersman Tables.

https://mersmantable.com/Mersman%20Furniture2.htm

J.B. Mersman was a midwestern sawmill operator. He decided to start making products rather than dealing with lumber, and began making headboards, footboards, and slats for beds.

Around 1900 the city of Celina, OH approached Mersman to create a furniture factory there, and he did. According to this history, the company made beds, library tables and dining room tables. In 1906, the factory employed 125 workers, 10 travelling salesmen, and sold medium and high-grade dining room tables nationally.

By the early 1930s, they sold bedroom suites, dining room tables, and radio cabinets. By World War II they were making desks for the federal government, mess tables with benches for the Navy, and mobile repair units for the Air Force.

Were there other tables they were selling that resembled the NJ State Police photo? There is a Mersman catalog gallery showing images from their 1911 and 1918 products at

MersmanFurniture.com

and images from their 1930 and 1933 catalogs at

https://mersmantable.com/MersmanHistory/Mersman-1933-gallery.html.

They made very nice furniture, none resembling the table in question.

There is a 'Borough of South Plainfield' website

http://southplainfieldnj.com/spnj/Police/_zumu_sidebar/Police%20Home/Police%20DepamMrtment%20History/#NOTEWORTHY%20INVESTIGATIONS)

that contains a section entitled 'History of the South Plainfield Police Department'.
This contains a subsection entitled 'Noteworthy Investigations,' with one being 'The Lindbergh Kidnapping, 1932'.

Probably the best-known newspaper article on the table is Figure 18G.3.1, which makes the Mersman identification. In fact, several newspaper articles appeared locally on the brace. (most of them relating the found message to a wobbly table leg), which are discussed in the South Plainfield Police Department History. It includes:

1. LINDBERGH KIDNAPPING "CONFESSION" FOUND IN SOUTH PLAINFIELD TABLE. THE DAILY HOME NEWS, November 22, 1948

2. KIDNAP "CONFESSION" NOTE IS INVESTIGATED. PERTH AMBOY EVENING NEWS, November 22, 1948

3. LINDY KIDNAP NOTE WRITER HUNTED HERE. November 22, 1948 (Newspaper Source Unknown)

4. LINDBERGH KIDNAP NOTE CALLED HOAX/PAPER FOUND IN LEG OF TABLE PURCHASED 10 YEARS AGO. BERGEN EVENING RECORD. November 22, 1948

5. POLICE CONTINUE HUNT FOR KIDNAP NOTE AUTHOR [sic]. November 1948 (Newspaper source unknown)

The texts for all these news articles can be found in THE HISTORY OF THE SOUTH PLAINFIELD POLICE DEPARTMENT. None of them mention the word Mersman.

CHAPTER 18
ENDINGS

18A. What Ever Happened to Jafsie?

John Condon, a.k.a. Jafsie was well known in the Bronx, having saved several lives. Nationally he was recognized for his record in coaching the Fordham Football Team. But he was a strange guy, often seen hanging out with Al, his friend, a former Boxer. Al was Jafsie's driver since he didn't have a car or a license to drive. We'll never know why Condon jumped into the fray when the newspapers first got the story of the kidnapping, but he put an ad in a local Bronx paper, offered to help, and the kidnappers saw the article and agreed to work with him as the go-between with the Lindberghs. And so, he was at the center of the kidnapping investigation. He made two visits to cemeteries, and on both occasions talked with the man called known as Cemetery John. Many facts in the kidnapping story came from John through Jafsie. No one got a good look of John except for Jafsie. He apparently felt he became an indispensable assistant to the Lindberghs and while he never asked for, nor was never offered, any payment at the end of the trial, he always felt it would have been appropriate and expressed some disappointment that no payment appeared.

He wrote a book (*I Am Jafsie*) and went on a Vaudeville tour selling his book and telling his story. He wrote a letter to the President introducing himself and offering to work for the President in whatever capacity he felt suitable. The President apparently did not get a good impression from this aging self-proclaimed hero and had to decide how he would respond to Jafsie's offer to work for him. He didn't want to do anything to encourage Jafsie, so he had his secretary send him a glossy photo of the President (a common response to letters from citizens), but without any message written on it. At some point in his life, he was also accused of molesting girls who were in the college athletic program.

18B. Who is Mac?

If you buy a book on Amazon, particularly a used book, they often give information on its status – is it like new? Did someone take notes in the book? Was it signed by the author? I have an assignment for you. At least I did when I first wrote this. I wanted you to track down someone. First let me tell you that Sidney B. Whipple was a reporter and journalist who, as a reporter for the United Press, covered the Lindbergh case and wrote about a half-million words about it in two books. He wrote *The Lindbergh Case* (Blue Ribbon books, NY 1935) shortly after the trial. Now a good reporter has and makes lots of good contacts, and to keep them, knows when to keep a secret. I bought a copy of this book (used, of course) that had a dedication on the inside cover, from Whipple to MAC. MAC may have had a hand in the case in some way that is not common knowledge. So, who was he? If you can figure this out, let me know. Now I know to buy old books with writing and the author's signature within. Perhaps Whipple wrote something very personal, assuming it would never be seen. We're looking for a Scott, possibly another reporter who learned something important and only shared it with a few others. Is the name McKeurghan? This could be a significant find!

Well, it is very curious that I made this a challenge to a class I teach at TCNJ on the Lindbergh Kidnapping, and somehow it appeared on two of the Lindbergh discussion boards! I'm not sure if one of my students initiated the "threads" by writing that their professor challenged them to investigate a dedication found in one of Sidney S. Whipple's books to "Mac". It could have been one of my students or the information could have somehow drifted over to someone else, but as far as I know, I have this one book, and a student asked for discussion board help, and I'm not very happy about that.

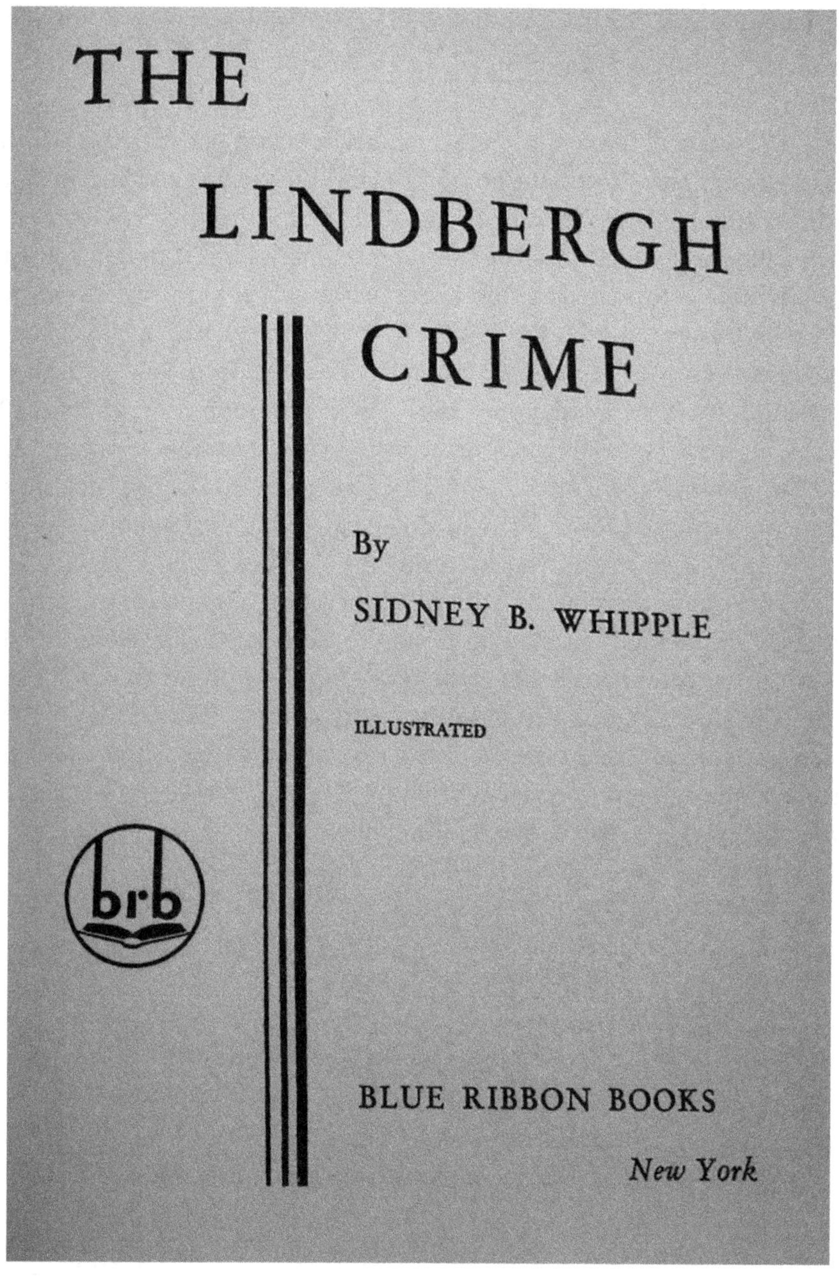
THE LINDBERGH CRIME

By

SIDNEY B. WHIPPLE

ILLUSTRATED

BLUE RIBBON BOOKS

New York

Figure 18B.1. The Book

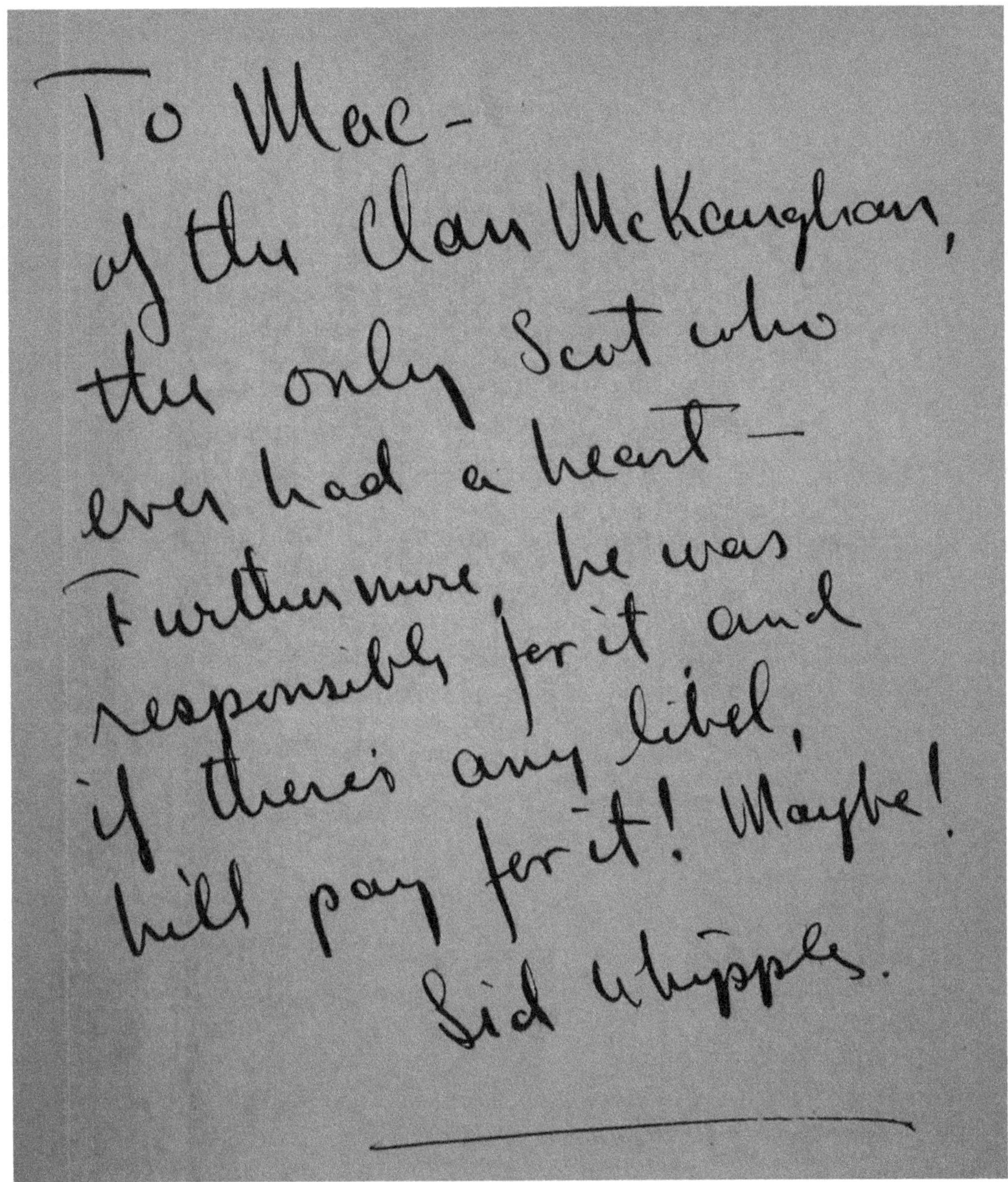

To Mac-
of the Clan McKaughan,
the only Scot who
ever had a heart—
Furthermore, he was
responsible for it and
if there's any libel,
he'll pay for it! Maybe!
Sid Whipple.

Figure 18B.2. Inside Message

However, my students did come up with some interesting things, like Whipple usually signed his name as Sidney Whipple, so the whole message, signed by Sid Whipple, could have been a fake, written for someone's personal benefit, or as a joke. Fortunately, the discussion board folks were extremely active, and *they* found some interesting possibilities.

Fortunately, the student stated that the Mac name was found in a dedication to Whipple's book. That didn't indicate which book (It was from *The Lindbergh Crime*, 1935), and for people who know what a dedication is and where it is found in a book, the dedication was actually "To My Mother and Father".

Let me share with you some things that came out of the hobbyist's discussions.

In 1934 there was a big airmail scandal, (the "Air Mail Fiasco") related to a Congressional investigation involving airmail. Only select airlines were given contracts to carry airmail, and at the same time, President Roosevelt decided that the US Army Air Corps should oversee airmail. (Side note: the first airmail flights were from New York to D.C. with a stop-over in Philadelphia)

It is a long and involved story, but there was a Senate Investigation, and William P. MacCracken Jr. was cited for Contempt of Congress. MacCracken was the first federal regulator of commercial aviation, and he was named the first Assistant Secretary of Commerce for Aeronautics in 1926. In 1929 he left the position, returning to his law practice, and represented several major airlines. So, there is a possible "Mac" for you – William MacCracken. Certainly, a person of interest to Lindbergh, but not related to the case and no obvious connections to Whipple.

If the comments were really some sort of message from Lindbergh (through Whipple, if they ever even met), then also relevant is a 1970 book entitled *Mr. Mac: William P. MacCracken Jr., a Biography on Aviation, Law, Optometry* by Michael Osborn, Joseph Riggs, with introductions by Charles Lindbergh and Hugo Black. Apparently, Mr. Mac was very influential on the early days of air travel. Could MAC be William MacCracken Jr.?

The discussion boards also dug up and proposed the following (keep in mind that Whipple wrote two Lindbergh books, both published by 1938). Apparently, NJ Governor Hoffman wrote "His Part 6 Liberty" article in 1938. In this article, he cited Sidney Whipple for writing:

> "The Governor succeeded in interesting a noted New York criminal attorney, Samual Liebowitz, in the case."

According to Hoffman, he was not involved in bringing Liebowitz into the Hauptmann case, and that this was one of *several* errors that appear in Whipple's books on the case. So, Whipple was the one who committed libel with the statement above.

Accusations of libel occurred in 1938. Whipple's *The Trial of Bruno Richard Hauptmann* was published in 1937, so Whipple could have been out doing book signings. It pulls libel into the discussion, but there was no obvious "MAC" involved.

The best explanation, I believe, that makes the most sense of the words used is related to Betty MacDonald, who wrote *The Egg and I*. She and her husband and the book's publisher (J. B. Lippincott Company, where J.A. McKaughan was their Director of Advertising) had a lawsuit brought against them over the book, by the Albert Bishop Family – Albert Bishop and his six sons, two daughters and one daughter-in-law, living in Washington. The Bishops (Albert and his deceased wife Suzanne) claimed that they were depicted by Betty MacDonald as the Kettle Family (as in Ma and Pa Kettle). The book was a non-fiction best seller. The Bishops stated that they were the object of shame and humiliation because they were identified with these characters in the book. The book was a best seller – more than a million copies were sold in less than a year, and in 1947 a film was made based on the book, *Egg*. When the movies began, the motion picture company hired attorneys to look for potential libel suits in the script, and some chapters were eliminated to avoid such lawsuits.

The book, *The Egg and I* has a secondary title *Life on a wilderness chicken ranch told with wit and high humor.*

In addition to Betty being a Mac (although not a he), J.A. "Mac" McKaughan was the distribution director for Lippincott's.

The trial began on 5 February 1951 in Seattle. The basis of the trial was libel. The trial lasted two weeks. It has been suggested that Whipple was out selling his books and met someone associated with that Libel case and wrote that note in one of his older books, specifically to distinguish between a bad Scott and a good one: Betty MacDonald and Lippincott's J. A. McKaughan. In 1951 Whipple was still alive. He could have met J.A. McKaughan at a book talk or signing that year, and that could have initiated the inscription that Whipple wrote. It could have had nothing to do with the Hauptmann case at all, just a convenient place to acknowledge his opinion of a situation involving an ongoing libel case.

I still encourage you to figure out for me who MAC really is. I'm not convinced we know the story yet.

18C. Who Killed Little Charlie?

There are now multiple books out there that provide a good argument that the entire plan was designed by Little Charlie's Daddy. Those who knew Charles felt he was a very strange person, not well-adjusted at all socially. When little Charlie started to walk, Lindbergh would throw pillows at him and knock him over. He "stole" the baby once and hid him in the house, then told everyone in the house that the baby was missing. Eventually they found him in a trash closet. He was very supportive of the concept of Eugenics, and the possibility of having a sick child as his son was an embarrassment to him. Some have suggested that he wanted to send the boy away to be adopted by someone else, somewhere else. Even though both he and Anne were probably not very ideal parents, and enjoyed flying around the world, gone for months at a time from their son, he couldn't take the chance of telling Anne his plan, so he found some people to help him to stage a kidnapping. No one planned on an accident occurring somewhere along the way, but one probably did, and the boy died.

From the second that they saw the empty crib, Charles was in total charge. No one initially saw a ransom letter anywhere, although he eventually pointed out that it was on the windowsill of the window that was presumably used for the kidnapping. What would you do? If you were kidnapping a baby, and wanted to leave a ransom note, where would you put it? I think a good place would be in the crib. But to climb in and out using a ladder, and on the way out of the window, baby in tow, to try to close the window and shutter, and to somehow leave the letter on the windowsill (without it blowing onto the floor), just makes no sense. Lindbergh had a strange set of explanations for his unusual evening schedule for that evening, and very few people would have even known the baby was at this house that evening, except for close family and employees. Lindbergh was a cold man, possibly cold enough to just want his flawed son to be gone.

Lindbergh was also, of course, a creative person. He'd built a small ladder to allow Ann to get on their plane, over pontoons on the bottom (for landing on water), while she was pregnant. He built a unique ladder that folded up and could be kept under the seat of their plane. Perhaps he was just the kind of person who could build a three-piece ladder, made of nesting parts. He was constantly thinking of aerodynamics and efficiency. On the Spirit of Saint Louis, he even cut the edges off maps to save a few ounces of the load.

The thoughts of Little Charlie being kidnapped and purposely or accidentally killed, seems impossible for anyone, but unfortunately most likely may have been by the country's hero.

CHAPTER 19
IN CLOSING

I enjoyed spending time with you learning about the Lindbergh Baby Kidnapping. It's quite an important piece of New Jersey history, although we may not know much of what really happened.

I've tried to give you some idea of how an investigator may think. You must question everything. You shouldn't hesitate to get out a pencil and paper and sometimes even a calculator. Investigate! Don't hesitate to look up information. This is particularly vital in a cold case like this, where everything happened in the 1930s. The world was a different place. Don't hesitate to learn new things. They will only help you again in the future.

Along the way you've hopefully learned something about topics of Science and Forensics. We discussed fingerprinting, making meaningful measurements, handwriting analysis and spectroscopy. We've used a ruler and digital images to make measurements, because numbers often tell an interesting story. And once you have a set of numbers, question them, step back and ask if they are reasonable, graph them!

The effort that you put into a project will always come back and assist you. Don't ever hesitate to look deeper. It's fun (or it should be if you want to be in this business). I've tried to share with you my thoughts, and I hope you learned by watching me at work. And, by the way, many of my suggestions work for more than just these kinds of investigations. Whatever you do in life – get involved, don't be afraid to learn new things.

Investigate everything! Good luck.

APPENDIX I. ALLISONweb

Welcome to ALLISONweb, your source of information even when you don't have your computer. It's the internet of choice for information on Lindbergh People, Lindbergh Places, and Lindbergh Things.

APPENDIX I. ALLISONweb

A. Batteries and Flashlights

Carl Gassner obtained a patent for what we now call the dry cell in 1886 (German Patent). Typical was a zinc-carbon dry cell. They were easy to make, easy to package and ship around the country, provided a potential of 1.5 Volts, and were first sold by the National Carbon Company in 1896.

Flashlights were soon available, first sold starting in 1900.

B. Betty Gow

Betty Gow joined the family in Feb. 1931, as caregiver for Little Charlie, when he was less than a year old. She came to the US from Scotland.

Anne called Betty on March 1, 1932, a Tuesday, and asked Betty to come down from her parents' house in Englewood to their house in Hopewell to take care of Little Charlie, who was sick. The Lindberghs always returned to Englewood on the Monday morning after the weekend, but they delayed the trip because Little Charlie has a bad cold. Betty had planned to go on a date with her boyfriend, Henry (Red) Johnson, but instead went to Little Charlie. When she got there, she called Red to tell him she had to cancel their date. The Police suspected that the call was part of a message to Red, signaling him to come to the house and kidnap the baby.

Some believed that the kidnapping was an inside job, and Betty Gow was a suspect initially, but eventually the Police believed that she was innocent.

She was unprepared when Charles and Anne left her alone with Little Charlie, and flew off, such as in his first summer, on their pioneering voyage across the Bearing Sea to Asia.

C. Cemetery John

Dr. Condon, the person who exchanged mail between the Lindberghs and the kidnappers, twice went into a cemetery and talked to a kidnapper and, according to Condon, met the same man both times. Jafsie called him Cemetery John. There is much information about John. Unfortunately, no one ever saw him except for Condon. So, Condon either provided useful information for identifying one of the kidnappers (who quickly became the kidnapper), or got the description and much information completely wrong, or just made it all up.

D. Condon, Dr. John F.

Dr. John F. Condon," Jafsie," thought very highly of his country and of himself. He wrote patriotic stories and poems for local Bronx newspapers, signing them as P.A. Triot, J.U. Stice, L.O. Nestar, etc. For communicating with the kidnappers through the newspapers, he used a name he had used before, Jafsie, which represents, we are told, how one would pronounce JFC, his initials. We are told that he created the Jafsie name, to keep anonymous during the process, although some of his school students indicated that he had used it in some classes when he taught.

Dr. Condon was married and lived in the Bronx. When he first heard of the kidnapping, he was outraged that someone would do this to an international hero. He had about $1,000 in the bank, his life savings, and he offered to add it to the ransom, because he felt he needed to do something, and wanted to be able to, someday, hand Little Charlie back into his mother's arms.

Dr. Condon was a hero and a football coach with a national reputation. He had taught at P.S. #12 in New York City and became an administrator. He completed a Ph.D. from Fordham University where he later served as an instructor. At the time of the kidnapping, he was retired. By placing ads in local (Bronx) newspapers, he managed to communicate with the kidnappers. It seems very unlikely that he would have been successful in this regard, since the Bronx Home News had a circulation of 150,000, compared to New York City newspapers that had national circulations of roughly 6 million. And who would have even guessed that a kidnapping in New Jersey would have been pulled off by a gang in New York? Through the paper he managed to convince the kidnappers that they should accept him as an intermediary between them and the Lindbergh family and everyone agreed to this. The first time Jafsie received a ransom letter, he contacted

Lindbergh and went to his home to deliver it. He accepted an offer to stay overnight, and he slept in the baby's empty nursery on the floor.

When the time came to hand over the $70,000 ransom money, Jafsie went alone to a Bronx cemetery to negotiate. He had two cemetery meetings. He met the same person both times, who was either German or Scandinavian. His name was John. He probably spent two hours talking with John. At one point, as a test, Jafsie spoke to John in German, but he didn't appear to understand, establishing that John was not German. Condon wrote down every word that he remembered that was said during his encounters with Cemetery John and worked with the FBI to make an oral record by recording his voice onto phonograph records. Condon had even imitated John's dialect. These very valuable records were never used in the trial. While Jafsie reported having no luck speaking German with John, he later went to visit him in jail, where they did have a conversation in German, or so Condon reported.

Jafsie supposedly covered many topics with Cemetery John. He had access to $70,000 to be used for the ransom money – the original request was for $50,000 but since the negotiations were taking so long and since Lindbergh involved the police as he was asked not to do, the kidnappers had to pay two women who were taking care of Little Charlie more than initially negotiated, an extra $20,000.

Jafsie was always coming up with theories and going places to look at photos of convicts trying to identify Cemetery John. Jafsie claimed that, looking in the baby's bed, it was the bottom of the blankets that were disturbed, suggesting to him that the baby was pulled out from under the covers by his feet. (The covers were safety-pinned to the bed near Little Charlie's shoulders.) It seemed to many as the least likely maneuver, one that would surely wake a sleeping baby. He then provided several explanations such as "a drugged baby, a strangled baby, and a dead baby."

One of the ransom notes specified how the ransom was to be delivered in terms of denominations of the currency and sent specific plans as to the size of the package in which the money would be delivered. It was supposed to be a 6 x 7 x 14 -inch package. Somehow along the way between getting measurements and delivering the ransom, "package" had become "box", which Condon provided.

When the kidnapper(s) asked for an additional $20K, they requested the extra in $50 bills. Jafsie seemed to have a hard time keeping his story straight over the building of the box for the ransom money. Ralph Hacker, Jafsie's German son-in-law, drew up plans for a 6 x 7 x 14 wooden box. Condon took the plans to Fran Peremi, a local cabinet maker, to have the box built. Also, Jafsie purchased several kinds of wood for the box's construction (white pine, poplar, and boxwood), since these would make the box unique. He didn't like the price he was given from Peremi so didn't use him. In 1933 Condon informed an FBI agent that he had used a box that was a family heirloom. It even had a lock on it. Jafsie's story often changed. He explained that the heirloom box he had in his family was an old voting box, and that he eventually went back to Frank Peremi, who was willing to make a copy of that box for $3.25.

Jafsie would often hang out with his boxer friend and driver, Al Reich. Al would often spend long evening hours in Jafsie's home in Brooklyn. On one night, Lindbergh drove Jafsie to his appointment with Cemetery John. Jafsie decided he would try to convince John to accept $50,000, the original price, because no one, including Charles Lindbergh, had money during the Great Depression. John accepted that, so Jafsie saved Lindbergh $20,000.

During one cemetery visit, Jafsie had a hard time finding anyone to talk to until suddenly, someone behind a bush waved a handkerchief at him, saying "Doctor, over here!" As the story goes, Lindbergh, sitting in the street in his car, heard the words and the person, and identified that person based on his voice/accent two years later! In the time that Jafsie and John were together, they seemed to freely speak of many things. John told Jafsie that he lived nearby with "father" and said that there were 5 people in the gang, and many of the suspects (such as Violet Sharpe), were not involved in any way. It was curious that John knew so many of their names as he listed off innocent suspects, since many of them worked for either the Lindberghs or the Morrow Family. When Jafsie showed John two large safety pins that he had taken from Little Charlie's Crib, he correctly identified them, essentially proving that he was in the house at the time of the kidnapping. (Or Jafsie made that story up.)

After Jafsie convinced John to accept $50,000, he insisted on receiving some sort of receipt (it is not clear whether this was typical in kidnappings or not). John then left Jafsie for a few moments and came back with a letter explaining where Little Charlie could be found – on a boat with two women who were not part of the plot, a boat called Nellie. Jafsie had gone back to the car to talk to Lindbergh, explained that he talked John into taking just the original $50,000. Lindbergh and Condon packed the box with $50,000 in bills as specified and found that they could not close the box. Lindbergh put additional pressure on it to close it and cracked it in his attempt.

Jafsie had been told to be at his home evenings, in case someone from the gang needed to contact him. One evening a caller with a strong accent called and asked for Jafsie. In addition to some discussions over where to find the boy, there were a few side conversations. The caller apparently was requested by someone else on the "gang" end of the call to ask a question. The caller asked, "Doktor Condon, do you sometimes write articles for the papers?" to which Jafsie replied, "yes". The voice on the other side became muffled as the speaker turned to a companion to explain: "He said sometimes he writes pieces for the papers." Then he heard another voice in the background say "Statti citto!" Which is Italian for "shut up". (Apparently Jafsie spoke German and Italian!)

Statti citto is NOT Italian for 'shut up"; the actual phrase is sta'zitto. But he was close. Question Everything.

Perhaps Jafsie (who spent so much of his life telling stories about himself saving lives and being an all-around hero) knew that stories could be "enhanced" – possibly even more enhanced every time they were told. He would often spend time with two officers from two different agencies, who became concerned that his stories of the case and his involvement were inconsistent, so one day they took him to headquarters. Jafsie assumed it was to look at more photographs of criminals, but this time it was because their boss wanted to talk to Jafsie as a possible suspect. They found nothing.

It was not uncommon for the police or FBI to write a summary of a conversation with a suspect. Leon Hoage apparently wrote the report on Jafsie. It was 24 pages long, and the title was The Story of Doctor John F. Condon: "Egoist" Extraordinary.

After the trial, Jafsie wrote a book, "Jafsie Tells All", which he sold as he traveled around the country telling his story, in a kind of one-man vaudeville show.

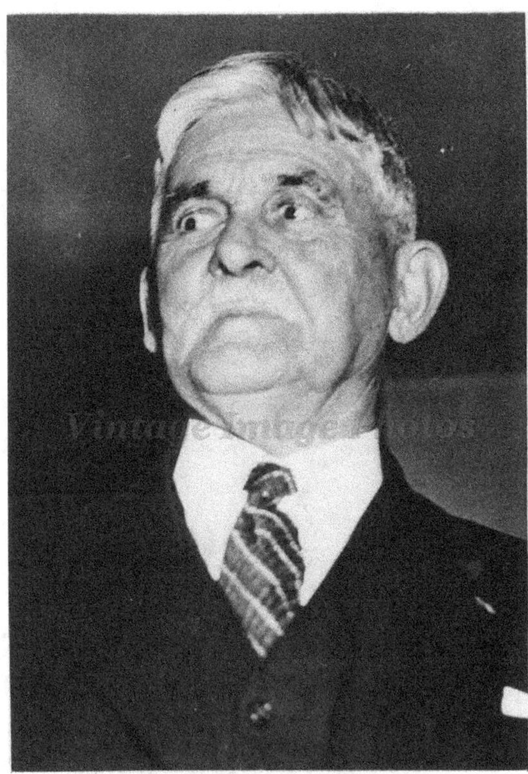

Jafsie, Dr. John F. Condon

E. Cork

Did you ever wonder where you wine bottle cork came from? Sadly, some are synthetic these days but there are still many natural corks out there, cork board, etc. If you guessed that cork grows on trees, you're essentially right. In Africa and Europe there lives Quercus suber, the cork oak tree. The trees live for about 300 years. When they are 25 years old, the first cork can be harvested. It is the bark of the tree that is stripped off, which is the natural cork (under the bark). Nine years later they do it again, and again until the tree is 300 years old. Then they replace the old tree with two new ones. Because cork was at one time a living thing, it has a "cellular structure", which contributes to its compressibility, which is why it can be easily inserted into wine bottles, which can vary somewhat concerning neck size.

Many debate whether a cork is actually a good choice as a stopper for wine bottles; some now use screw tops or plastic corks. The biggest problem is that gases can pass through, both around the sides of the cork and through the cork body. However, movement of oxygen into the bottle can improve a wine as it ages. Some cheap wines use an inert center clad with a real cork veneer. Now that sounds like a lot of work!

F. Eugenics

Francis Galton (b. 1822) was an English scientist and explorer. One of his areas of study was eugenics and human intelligence. Eugenics involved the concept that certain characteristics could be selected in humans, and "more suitable races or strains of blood could be given a better chance of prevailing over the less suitable." It ultimately failed as a science when the Nazis used the concept as a reason for exterminating entire races. Charles Lindbergh was a supporter of the concept of Eugenics. Some believe that it was difficult to support the concept while having a young child who was clearly "flawed" physically in many ways.

G. FBI/FOB

An agency capable of identifying known criminals nationally, the National Bureau of Crime Identification, was created in 1896. In 1908, President Roosevelt created another investigative service that would only report to the Attorney General. This group in the federal government became a formal Bureau of Investigation (BOI) in 1908. Eventually they became an independent service within the Department of Justice, and in 1935 it became the Federal Bureau of Investigation (FBI). J. Edgar Hoover, who served as the FBI director from 1924 to 1972 had served in both the BOI and FBI.

H. Hanging Chads

It was the year 2000, George Bush the Younger vs. Al Gore, former Vice President. The race for the Presidency was close. It ended up being another one of those races where the person with the most popular votes did not win because their competition won in the electoral college. It all came down to how Florida voted (where it just so happened that the Governor was Jeb Bush, George the Younger's brother.)

They used a relatively old system of voting at the polls. You slid a card into a frame that had pages of questions on it, and you used a little punch that you would stick through a hole to vote for someone. There were pre-perforated ("pre-scored") squares in the card, and your little punch would knock them out and that would be your selection, on your voting card. You would make your selections then turn the page and make a second set of punches indicating more of your choices.

The problem was, sometimes these little pieces of paper, the small squares called chads, didn't fall off completely (were left hanging). So, did the person really intend to punch that square out or not? The safest thing to do was to not count ballots that had hanging chads.

If the punch was still hanging on by one corner, it was called a hanging chad (a.k.a. dangling chad). If it was still attached at two corners – it was a swinging chad (trapdoor chad). Holding on at three corners - it was a tri-chad. And if it appeared that it was selected but none of the four corners broke, it was just pushed in, that was a dimpled or a pregnant chad.

They started to do a recount of the hanging chad ballots, attempting to determine each voter's intention. Different counties in Florida had different rules on recounts and deadlines, and Gore v Bush did go to the Supreme Court, twice, then was headed back to the Florida Supreme Court. People were hand "evaluating" each chad on each of the voting cards that were not included in the election. Eventually, Gore stopped fighting and let the vote stand as it was, but many Floridians did not have their vote counted. The vote was close; Bush the younger won. Then he went on to accuse Iran of having weapons of mass destruction, we were at war, and all hell broke loose. To many, our enemy was our President! But that's just my humble opinion.

A card with precut punchouts, registering someone's many votes (mostly swinging chads in the figure).

You may wonder why there were so many hanging chads in this election. Some have suggested that there was a good voter turnout in the state. The voting boxes would quickly get filled up with chads that were correctly pushed off each voting card, and if the box got too full, there wasn't any place for your potential chads to go. Chads were pushing back on your chad wanna-be's.

I. Hearst (William Randolph Hearst)

William Randolph Hearst (1863-1951) was an American newspaper publisher. He built the nation's largest newspaper chain and media company, Hearst Communications Inc. (often just referred to as Hearst). They were known for their sensational stories and crime stories. Hearst created a chain of about 30 newspapers in major cities, later expanding to magazines. When Bruno Hauptmann was charged with the kidnapping and murder of Little Charlie Lindbergh, the Hurst newspaper chain paid his attorney fees in exchange for rights to interview Hauptmann's wife during the trial.

J. ISO

ISO stands for the International Organization for Standardization. They have developed over 22,000 international standards on many aspects of business and technology. The group has 164 countries represented. The bad news is that the first ISO meeting was in 1946, years after the kidnapping. The ISO paper sizes are used in most countries in the world today, but not in the US. Three standards are relevant to us, ISO 216, ISO 217, and ISO 269. A key part of the standard is that the paper sizes have the same aspect ratio (square root of 2):1. According to Wikipedia, the first discussion of the advantage of this aspect ratio was found in a letter from a German scientist in 1786. ISO paper sizes such as A2, A3, B3 and B4 were developed in France and listed in a 1798 law on taxation of publications. It was Wilhelm Ostwald who, in 1911, proposed using the square root of 2:1 format for paper sizes.

Before ISO, many countries had a committee in place to set standards such as Germany's Deutsches Institut fur Normung (the Standardization Committee of German Industry). They were important contributors to the ISO standards. So, while the standards were set years after the Lindbergh Baby Kidnapping, many were in place in many countries in the 1920s, with the Germans leading the way in paper size standards.

K. The Lindbergh Family

They were a small family of only three – Colonel Lindbergh, Anne Morrow Lindbergh, and their child Little Charlie (b. June 22, 1930). Their staff included Betty Gow, nurse to Little Charlie, Marie Cummings, a registered nurse for the child, and Elizabeth Sheets, secretary to Lindbergh. Ollie Whateley served as butler, caretaker, and chauffeur. He and his wife Elsie acted as caretakers of the Hopewell estate and lived there. He often acted as a guide to tourists and the curious when the Lindberghs were not there. Betty Gow often came to assist with Little Charlie.

L. The Metric System – Units of Length

The unit of length for this system is the meter(m), although the centimeter (cm) and the millimeter (mm) are also frequently used. A meter is roughly equal to a yard, 3 feet.

If you know how big an inch is, 1 inch = 2.54 cm = 25.4 mm

Mostly, my measurements in this book are done in mm. This is a small distance so if we're off by only a mm it could be due to human (gasp) error.

One mm is small. A sharp pencil point is about 1 mm and a new pencil eraser is about 5 mm.

A one carat diamond has a diameter of about 6 mm.

In US currency, the diameter of a dime is 17.9 mm, and a quarter has a diameter of 24.3 mm (almost an inch).

An iPhone 6 is about 7 mm thick (7 mm thin!).

The Durex Comfort XL condom is 215 mm (8.5") long with a width of 56 mm (2.20 ") at the base.

Some, when they describe the singnature on the ransom notes, compare the size of the large blue circles to being about the size of a silver dollar (about 37 mm in diameter). See below.

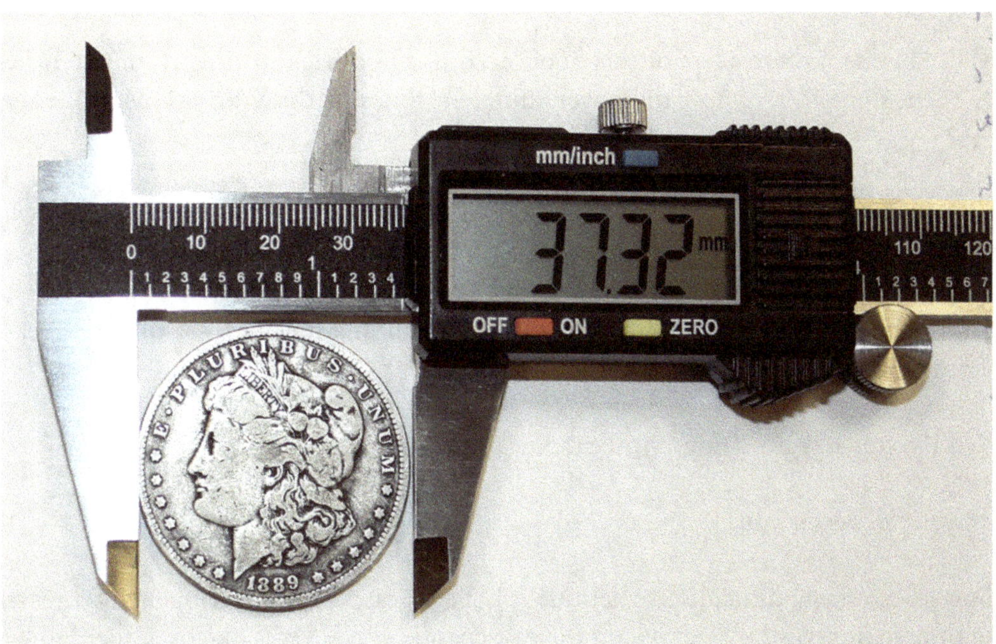

M. The Morrow Family

The parents of the family were U.S. Senator Dwight Morrow and his wife Anna Morrow. They resided in Englewood, NJ. Elizabeth, the oldest child, operated a kindergarten school. Anne was a few years younger. There was also a son, Dwight Morrow Jr. One additional child, Constance, was the youngest in the family. Senator Morrow passed away before his grandson, Little Charlie, was born.

Elizabeth was often considered as a possible accomplice to the kidnapper, with a motive being that Lindbergh "overlooked her" and instead dated her younger sister Anne. It had been suggested that one day when she was at Highfield, she threw the baby out the window in a fit of jealousy. At times both Elizabeth and Dwight were considered as suspects. Each had reportedly suffered emotional problems.

In 1929, when Constance Morrow was 15 and attending private school in Massachusetts, her father received a letter demanding $50,000 (an interesting choice) to prevent harm to Constance. Many find it interesting that in this instance, only $50,000 was requested, since much larger ransoms were not uncommon.

Dwight Morrow Jr., the only son, was at one time in a sanitarium in New York, although the exact illness he had is not known. Elizabeth was also considered unstable, but her medical problem was that she had a heart condition and was constantly fatigued (Berg, 1998), so those suspicions may be unfounded.

The "FBI Files on the Lindbergh Baby Kidnapping" lists 20 staff in the Morrow home. Some assisted Lindbergh and Anne in taking care of Little Charlie as well. Names that appear in this story include Septimus Banks (butler), Violet Sharpe ("waitress"), Mary Beattie (personal maid to Elizabeth), and Mary Smith (dressmaker and travelling companion of Elizabeth).

N. Mr. Peabody and Sherman. (Going Back in Time)

> "Well, Sherman, the readers of this book need us to go back in time to the 1930s and give them some idea of how those were different times. Is the Wayback Machine ready to go?"
>
> "I'm just cleaning the MacDonald's bags out of the back seat, Mr. Peabody. Ready when you are. What do they want to know?"
>
> "Oh, I have a list somewhere. It really was poor planning for dogs not to have pockets, you know?"
>
> "Well I'm not actually a dog, Mr. Peabody."
>
> "Ah, yes. So sad for you."

We are tackling an extremely difficult case because it is a cold case, one that happened 85 years ago, and we must take the time to understand what life on the east coast of the US was like back then, so we can put the events that have been recorded into context. But first, for those of you who don't know Mr. Peabody and Sherman, I am going to briefly indulge myself and educate you.

When I was young, every Saturday morning I watched on TV the cartoon series The Adventure of Rocky [a flying squirrel] and Bullwinkle and Friends. This was the late 1950s and early 1960s. Each week one of the five-minute, five-second shows was "Mr. Peabody and Sherman."

> (https://www.youtube.com/watch?v=Lj61eUqDuP4)

Mr. Peabody is a very intelligent and accomplished dog, having been everything from an inventor and Nobel Laureate to an Olympic medalist. Mr. Peabody encountered a boy, in the process of being beaten up, in an alleyway. The boy was named Sherman, who just happened to be an orphan. Mr. Peabody decided to adopt him. As a birthday present for Sherman, Peabody invented the WABAC (pronounced way-back) time machine, and he and Sherman go on trips back in time as part of Sherman's education.

The Rocky and Bullwinkle Show brought to us a dizzying collection of characters, and if you know them, you will enjoy hearing their names again – Rocky (Rocket J. Squirrel), Bullwinkle J. Moose, Boris Badenov, Natasha Fatale, Dudley Do-Right, and Snidely Whiplash. It was filmed in some very exotic locations including Frostbite Falls and Moosylvania.

Sherman and Peabody entering the WABAC machine

Some sources indicate that the meaning of WABAC is unknown but apparently the name is related to the names of early computers such as UNIVAC and ENIAC, and it stands for the WORMHOLE ACTIVATING AND BRIDGING AUTOMATIC COMPUTER. Now you know.

The last piece of irrelevant information for you: Every one of their cartoon shows ended with Mr. Peabody making a pun. After visiting Marie Antoinette, Peabody explains to his boy son that she "should have issued an edict giving every citizen a loaf of bread. The problem was that she couldn't have her cake and Edict too."

An animated feature film on Mr. Peabody and Sherman was released in 2014, and there is also a cartoon series they starred in, that premiered in 2015 on Netflix. It is a talk show where Peabody and Sherman host guests of historical interest.

O. Ratios. A Tutorial

Burj Khalifa in Dubai (United Arab Emirates) is usually ranked as the #1 tallest building, with a height of 828 meters (2,717 feet). This is it's "roof height", excluding any antennas. It is taller than the Chrysler Building in Manhattan, which has a total height of 318.9 meters (1,046 feet).

Let's consider some of these numbers, and their ratios. The basic concept is that the Ratio of the heights of the two buildings is a constant.

Q#1. How big is the Chrysler Building Relative to the Burj Khalifa?

A#1. If we take the ratio of the two numbers,

Ratio = 318.9 meters /828 meters

And if you divide those two numbers

218.9/828 = 0.26= Ratio

You have their ratio.

If you want the number in %, multiply the ratio by 100 (per cent literally means per hundred).

Ratio x 100 = 26%

The Chrysler Building is only 26% as high as the Burj Khalifa!

Conversion factors are also ratios. For example, to convert from meters to feet, we know what we need from the data above. We know that the Chrysler Building is 318.9 meters tall, also reported as 1064 feet. Obviously these two numbers must be equal.

1064 feet = 318.9 meters

Someone must have used the feet-to-meters conversion factor to get from one to the other. We can rewrite these two numbers as

$$\frac{318.9 \text{ meters}}{1064 \text{ feet}} = \frac{0.2997 \text{ meters}}{\text{foot}} = 1$$

We could also multiply this conversion factor by another, since all conversion factors are equal to one, and multiplying a number by 1 never changes its real value, only it's dimensions.

Or we could have written them the other way

1064 feet/318.9 meters = 3.33 feet/meter (read as 3.33 feet per meter)

The ratio of the heights is a constant.

Could this be correct? Well, we used to have yard sticks or meter sticks in classrooms. Sometimes a single stick will be printed as a yard stick on one side and a meter stick on the other side of the same stick, so a meter is roughly a yard, and a yard is three feet, so a first approximation is that 3 feet is roughly equal to 1 meter, so 3 feet/1 meter is a good conversion factor.

Getting back to the two buildings, suppose you wanted to make models of these two buildings with popsicle sticks. You build a replica of BK that is 12 inches tall. How tall would the Chrysler building model be if you want them to represent the relative heights of one to the other?

0.26 (ratio of Chrysler/BK) x 12 inches (BK) = 3.12 inches for Chrysler model

Sometimes you may get confused on how to use a ratio. Just be sure you can define it correctly. The 0.26 ratio is (Chrysler/BK) ratio. You could write

$$\frac{0.26}{1} = \frac{\text{Chrysler}}{\text{BK}} = \frac{\text{? inches (Chrysler)}}{\text{12 inches (BK)}}$$

To solve for ? you can cross multiply – the top of the first ratio times the bottom of the second equals the bottom of the first times the top of the second.

0.26/1 = ?/12 so, 0.26 x 12 = 1 x ? = ? ? = 3.12 inches = height of Chrysler model

We are safest using the metric system when doing such calculations. They do not work with feet and inches, for example. Six feet, four inches is not equal to 6.4 feet. You must convert it into a decimal equivalent.

4 inches x 1 foot/12 inches = 4/12 feet = 0.33 feet

so, six feet four inches is not equal to 6.4 feet, but 6.33 feet.

Now you know. Ready to tackle Hillary?

P. Sig Figs and the Q Test

You're either the kind of person who understands this as second nature, or you've never heard of them before. The concept is Significant Figures, and you need to have some appreciation for them as we work with numbers.

First, just so you can sound like you know what you're talking about, consider the following question:

Q. You are measuring the height of corn stalks at a farm. This particular farmer claims that all his corn grows to exactly the same height, so they are no hazard for low-flying aircraft. You measure seven stalks, and the heights are:

7.2 feet
7.1 feet
7.2 feet
7.1 feet
7.0 feet
7.0 feet
7.0 feet
4.2 feet

A. You add the seven values up and divide by 7 to get an average. The sum of the seven values is

7.2+7.1+7.2+7.1+7.0+7.0+7.0= 49.6 feet

Average = 49.6/7 = 7.08571429 feet

First, you probably noticed that I didn't include the 4.2 feet in my calculations. I didn't just throw it away, but I first determined whether it should be included with my other calculations using what is called the Q test. To do this I first put the values in order from high to low.

7.2, 7.2, 7.1, 7.1, 7.0, 7.0, 7.0, 4.2

The difference between 4.2 and its nearest neighbor,7.0, is

difference = 7.0 - 4.2 = 2.8

The spread, from the smallest to largest number (including the questioned number since we haven't ruled it out yet) is calculated next.

Spread = 7.2-4.2 = 3.0

Q is the ratio of the difference divided by the spread

Q exp = (real) difference/spread = 2.8/3.0 = .9333333

For 8 measurements, the theoretical cutoff value for Q, called Q(crit) is 0.47.

The experimental value of Q is larger than the theoretical critical value. When this occurs, the point is rejected and not used. It's just, statistically, so far away from the other values that it is likely not a part of the set of values but was probably measured incorrectly or is an oddity.

Critical values for obtaining a 90% confidence in the questioned number depends on the number of measurements you have. Here are the critical Q values for rejection of a data point with a 90% confidence level.

Number of Measurements	Qcrit (@90% confidence)
2	-
3	0.94
4	0.76
5	0.64
6	0.56
7	0.51
8	0.47
9	0.44
10	0.41

So, on this basis I decided that the point was not to be included, not representative of the set. It doesn't mean that I made a measuring error, just that the number in question was too far away from all the other points. You have to think about using the Q test and if you even want to question a value or just include it in with the other calculations. This was a small set of numbers so one must be careful to reject anything.

Most of my numbers were around 7, so what can I say about those values. Was I accurate? Or was I precise? Precision is used to describe how reproducible my results were. How close they are to each other. I may be good at getting close to the same value every time, but they could all be far from the real value. The term accuracy is used to indicate the nearness of measurements to an accepted value, the real value. So, if the farmer knows that all his corn stalks will grow to a height of 9.00 feet, my numbers were fairly precise, but not accurate.

Now you know at least a few terms and concepts from statistics. Let's get back to the one I wanted to discuss, significant figures. I added up my values (minus the questioned value, which I decided to reject based on the Q test). The sum of the seven values was 49.6. The average was 49.6 divided by the number of measurements (7) = 7.08571429. Can you guess if I used a calculator to do the division? Of course I did! All my values had two digits, two "significant figures". The average can't have more significant figures than the value with the least number of digits. When you enter numbers into a calculator, it handles 7.2 as 7.20000000 when it tries to do a calculation. But we were unable to measure the number to 9 places. We're probably not even sure about the 2 of 7.2. It is the least significant of the digits.

When I was measuring the ransom notes, a millimeter is a small value, and sometimes I thought a value matched. If the letter height or width clearly fell between two marks on my ruler, I would try to estimate the last value such as 176.4. I then rounded the value. My rule for rounding is that, if I have a number such as 176.5, I round it up to 177, and if I have a value of 176.4, I round it down to 176. That is what I did.

Bottom line, you obviously have no mathematical basis for taking numbers with three significant figures (e.g. 177) and reporting an average with more significant figures. You can't know the average more precisely than you know the individual values. It is best to not write down calculator values. So, all my ransom letter height values were:

177
177
177
177
165
177
177
177
178
178
178
177
172
178

(And I didn't include the last height, 127 – that was just a different size of paper)

So, I have 14 values. Their sum is 2,465. The average is 2,465/14 = 176.071429. I'd round that to 176.1, and to have a result with no more significant figures than the original values, I'd round that to 176.

I still have some concerns since almost all the values were 177 or 178; it's only the 165 and 172 that pulls the average down to 176. But again, on the scale we are using, 1 mm compared to the typical value of 177 mm only makes a difference of 1/177 x 100 = 0.56%. Half of a percent -a very small difference.

Q. The Triskelion story and the Singnature

At some point in the original investigation, someone "explained" to authorities that the singnature on the ransom letters was the triskelion, the symbol of the Italian Mafia. OK, fine, thank you, glad someone knew that! End of story. Apparently, nobody looked up what a triskelion was. It is apparently a three-legged symbol, not seemingly related to the singnature at all. So, let's not accept a random guess as fact. Let's investigate it. It could be useful to know if the Italian or Sicilian mafia were responsible for the kidnapping!

Let me share a little of what I learned about the three legs symbol, since one evening on Jeopardy I was half watching and saw it and learned that "it" was on the flag of the Isle of Mann (Man).

Wikipedia states that "this version" has the triskelion centered as a whole rather than based upon the imaginary circles created by the prongs of each leg."

It is also on the coat of arms of this "self-governing British Crown dependency in the Irish Sea between the islands of Great Britain and Ireland."

Even though it has, apparently, nothing to do with the singnature, it is important to go back in time to determine whether the symbol even existed in the 1930s. Apparently, the island's symbol, the triskelion (3 legs joined at the thigh) has existed for centuries, at least back to the late 13th century, although its origin is unknown.

The Flag of Sicily.

APPENDIX II. REFERENCES

These are the key sources of information that I used in writing this book. When a reference is cited within, it will be in a shortened form – (last name, year of publication). With that, you should find the complete listing here. The references are in alphabetical order, author first (author last name, first initials, *Book Title* Publisher & Location, Publication Date). For publications in scientific journals, the references are listed as (author(s), "Title of Paper", *Title of Journal*, volume number: issue number, year, page number(s)). The facts provided, especially in Chapters 5 and 6 came from these sources:

Ahlgren, G. & Monier, S. *Crime of the Century/The Lindbergh Kidnapping Hoax*, Branden Books, Boston 1993.

Axelrod, A., Antionozzi, G. *The Complete Idiot's Guide to Forensics* 2nd Ed. Alpha Publishing 2009

Bahm, Jim. *Beneath the Winter Sycamores*, 2010

Berg, A. Scott, *Lindbergh*, Berkley Books, New York 1998

Blum, Stella, *Everyday Fashions of the Thirties (As Pictured in Sears Catalogs)*, Dover Publications, Inc. New York, 1986

Brant, J & Renaud, E, *True Story of The Lindbergh Kidnapping/The incredible, the impossible, the utter absurdity, had actually happened!* Kroy Wen Publishers, Inc. New York 1932

Burns, Cathy, Dr. *Masonic and Occult Symbols Illustrated* Sharing Publishing, Mt. Carmel PA, 1998

Cahill, Richard T. Jr. *Hauptmann's Ladder* Kent State University Press, Kent, OH 2014

Cha, S.-H., Yoon, S. & Tappert, C.C. "Handwriting Copybook Style Identification for Questioned Document Examination" *Journal of Forensic Document Examination* 2006, available at www.csis.pace.edu/ctappert/papers/2006JFDE.pdf

Cooper, J.C. *An Illustrated Encyclopedia of Traditional Symbols,* Thames & Hudson, London 1978

Condon, J.F. (Dr.) *Jafsie Tells All!* Jonathan Lee Publishing Corp. New York 1936

Cooke, T.G. "New Method Now Develops Fingerprints Left on Cloth and Other Substances / Dr. E.M. Hudson of Lindbuergh-Hauptmann Trial Fame is Credited as the Inventor" Fingerprint and Identification Magazine, 3:17 Sept. 1935 (explains how it works and how to do it)

Croatto, Pauo *Case Authority, Mark Falzini is one of the Foremost Experts on the Lindbergh Kidnapping Case* TCNJ Magazine 16:3 March 2012

Encyclopedia.com. Bruno Richard Hauptmann Trial: 1935 www.encyclopedia.com/people/social-sciences-and-law/crime-and-law-enforcement-biographies/bruno-richard-hauptmann

Crown, D.A. "The Development of Latent Fingerprints with Ninhydrin" *J. Crim. Law, Criminology and Police Science* 60(2) 258-64; 1969

Falzini, M. *Studying the Lindbergh Case: A Guide to the Files and Resources Available at the New Jersey State Police Museum* 2007

Falzini, M.W. *Their Fifteen Minutes*, iUniverse Inc. New York 2008

Falzini, M.W. & Davidson, J. *(Images of America Series) New Jersey's Lindbergh Kidnapping and Trial*, Arcadia Publishing, Charleston 2012

Fensch, Thomas, Ed., *Top Secret: FBI Files on the Lindbergh Baby Kidnapping,* New Century Books, The Woodlands, TX. 2001

Fitchett, Bev. *Bev Fitchett's Guns Magazine; Gunshot Wounds* www.bevfitchett.us/gunshot-wounds/gunshot-wounds-of-the-brain.html

Fisher, James *The Ghosts of Hopewell* 1999

Gardner, Lloyd C. *The Case that Never Dies: The Lindbergh Kidnapping.* Rutgers University Press, New Brunswick 2012

Geary, R. *The Lindbergh Child.* ABM Comics, Lit. Nantier, Beall, Minoustchie Publishing Inc, New York 2008

…, Goldspot, *Goldspot writing and fine Luxury Gifts Annual 2015 Catalog* 6, issue 1, 2015 www.goldspotpens.com

Great Idea Finder, www.ideafinder.com/history/Inventions/flashlight.htm

Green, Floyd J. *The Sigma-Aldrich Handbook of Stains, Dyes and Indicators*, Aldrich Chemical Co. Inc. Milwaukee 1990

Gunshots, biology.nkeyon,.edu/slone/bio3/2001 Projects/Bone/gunshots
Or
Slone/bio3/2001projects/Bone/gunshots.html

Harding, JV *The Hand of Hauptmann,* The Hamer Publishing Co., Plainsfield, NJ 1937.

Harrison, B.G. *Italian Days* 1998.

Harrison, D., Burkes, T.M., Seigler, D.P. "Handwriting Examination: Meeting the Challenges of Science in the Law" *Forensic Science Communications* 11(4) 2009.

Hicks, R.W. *Ballistics vs. the Lindbergh Case,* Police Research Bureau 1934.

Houck, M.M. *Forensic Anthropology* Elsevier Science 2017

Houck, M.M. & Siegel, J.A. *Fundamentals of Forensic Science, 2nd Ed.*, Academic Press, New York 2010

Kennedy, L. *The Airman and the Carpenter/The Lindbergh Kidnapping and the Framing of Richard Hauptmann* Viking Penguin Inc. New York 1985

Kent, T. *Fingerprint Development Handbook,* Heanor Gate Printing, Ltd. Heanor, UK 2000

Koch, R. *The Book of Signs,* Dover Publications, New York 2015 (first published 1930)

Koehler, A. "Technique used in tracing the Lindbergh kidnapping ladder", *Police Science, pp 712-724*

Lehner, E. *Symbols, Signs and Signets/ A Pictorial Treasury with over 1350 Illustrations,* Dover Pictorial Archive Series, Dover Publications Inc. New York, 1950

Lindbergh, A.M. *Hour of Gold, Hour of Lead,* Harcourt, New York 1973

Lindbergh, R. *Under A Wing,* Delta Trade Paperbacks, New York 1998

Linden, D.O. Famous Trials, *www.famoustrials.com/hauptmann/1398-ransom*

Lyle, D.P. (M.D.) *Forensics for Dummies, 2nd Ed.* Wiley 2016.

Martin-Gil, J. Ramos-Sanchez, M.C., Martin-Gil, F.J., Jose-Yacaman, M. "Chemical Composition of a Fountain Pen Ink" *J. Chem. Ed.* 83(10) p. 1477; 1906.

McLean, A.J. & Anderson R.W.G. "Biomechanics of Closed Head Injury" in *Head Injury,* Reilly P. & Bullock, Rose Chapman and Hall, London 1997

Melsky, M. *The Dark Corners of the Lindbergh Kidnapping, Volume 1,* Infinity Publishing (2016) and Volume 2, iUniverse, Bloomington (2018)

Monroe, Judy *The Lindbergh Baby Kidnapping Trial/ A Headline Court Case,* Enslow Publishers, Inc. Berkeley Heights NJ 2000

Morris, R.N. *Forensic Handwriting Identification, Fundamental Concepts and Principles,* Academic Press, New York 2000

nexusilluminati.blogspot.com/2014/09/the-enigma-of-prehistoric-skulls-with.html "The Enigma of the Prehistoric Skulls with Bullet-Like Holes"

O'Brien, P.J. *The Lindberghs/The Story of a Distinguished Family*, Universal, Book and Bible House, Philadelphia 1935

Osborn, M. & Riggs, J. *Mr. Mac,* Southern College of Optometry 1970.

Osbourne, Ozzie, "Mr. Crowley" on the record album *Blizzard of Ozz*, Jet Records UK 1985, reissued 2002.

Patterson, Mary Jo, Newhouse News Service, San Francisco Examiner, July 11, 1999, p. 6

Rowland, D. (author) &Harris, N. (illustrator), *The Ladder of Truth: Forensic Detectives at Work* McGraw Hill, New York (no year given)

Scaduto, A. *Bruno Hauptmann was Innocent* in New York mag. Nov. 22, 1976, p. 60

Scaduto, A *Scapegoat/ The Lonesome Death of Bruno Richard Hauptmann*, G.P. Putnam's Sons, New York 1976

Schrager, A.J. *The Sixteenth Rail/The Evidence, the Scientist, and the Lindbergh Kidnapping,* Fulcrum Publishing, Golden, CO. 2013

Spencerian Authors, *Theory of Spencerian Penmanship (for School and Private Learners)*, Mott Media, Fenton, MI 1985 (copyrighted 1874).

Stratton, S.W., Director *Inks – Their Composition, Manufacture, and Methods of Testing*, U.S. Bureau of Standards, 1920.

ULINE, "One Piece Corrugated Shoe Boxes", www.uline.com/BL_5647/One-Piece-Corregated-Shoe-Boxes

Web, FERA (Forensic Evidence Review (Australia). The Lindberg Case – A Short Case Study http://forensic-review.com.au/the-Lindbergh-case-a-short-case-study/

Web, Encyclopedia.com. Bruno Richard Hauptmann Trial, 1935, https://www.encyclopedia.com/people/social-sciences-and-law/crime-and-law-enforcement-biographies/bruno-richard-hauptmann

Web, FACT monster, www.factmonster.com/math/money/facts-about-us-money

Web,Littlecoin, https://www.littletoncoin.com/webapp/wcs/stores/servlet/Display%7C10001%7C10001%7C-1%7C%7CLearnNav%7CLarge-Size-US-Paper-Money.html

Westcott, T. "The Vesica Piscis Connection/Jack the Ripper, Jesus Christ and the Lindbergh Tragedy" *Ripper Notes/ The American Journal for Ripper Studies*, Oct. 2004 p. 49

Whipple, S.B. *The Lindbergh Crime*, Blue Ribbon Books, New York 1935

Whipple, S.B. (Ed.) *The Trial of Bruno Richard Hauptmann*, The Notable Trials Library, Gryphon Editions, Inc. 1989

Wikipedia, Roscoe Turner

Wikipedia, Great Lakes Aircraft Company

Wikipedia, National Air Transport

Young, L. Rule, G.T., Bocchiori, T., Walilko, T.J., Burns, J. M. & Ling, G. "When Physics Meets Biology: Low and High Velocity Penetration, Blunt Impact and Blast Injuries to the Brain". *Frontiers in Neurology,* 6:84 2015

Zorn, R. *Cemetery John/ The Undiscovered Mastermind of the Lindbergh Kidnapping,* The Overlook Press, New York 2012

Websites/ blogs:

The Lindbergh Kidnapping Site – the Real Story!
www.lindytruth.org and their Lindy Kidnap Discussion Group

Lindberghkidnap.proboards.com/thread/528/reexamining-bullet-theory
Lindberghkidnap.proboards.com/thread/896/Lilliput-charlie?

Web, M.W. Falzini Archival Ramblings, njspmuseum.blogspot/co /2008/03/one-of-the-most-facinating-areas-of-study.html

Web, FBI. History. Famous Cases and Criminals, Lindbergh kidnapping, https://www.fbi.gov/history/famous-cases/lindbergh-kidnapping

Web, LKH. www.lindberghkidnappinghoax.com/MISS.html

(JF). Jim Fisher The Official Web Site, Jimfisher.edinboro.edu/Lindbergh/a1988_1.html

(LKDB) Lindbergh Kidnapping Discussion Board, Lindberghkidnap.proboards.com

If you ever feel the urge to read more about this case, I highly recommend:

1. *The Lindbergh Kidnapping Case,* part of the Notable Trial Library, (inside title – The Trial of Bruno Richard Hauptmann.). Yes, it's the actual transcript of the trial with a historical commentary by Sid Whipple.
2. Anne Morrow Lindbergh's *Hour of Gold, Hour of Lead* - an informative collection of letters and diary entries written in the period 1929-32.

APPENDIX III. LIST OF FIGURES

A comment on figures/images: Category 1: Photos taken and figures drawn by myself or assembled are copyrighted here (©johnallison2021). Category 2: Images from other sources are used based on the Fair Use Policy, as discussed in the Digital Media Law Project (www.dmlp.org/legal-guide/fair-use).

Category 1: Figures 7E.1, 7E.2, 7N.1.1, 7N.1.3, 9.1, 11C.4, 12.1, 12.2, 12.3, 12.4, 12.5, 12.6, 12.7, 12.8, 12.9, 14.3, 14.4, 14A.1,15A.2,16C.1, 16C.2, 16C.3, 16C.4, 16C.5, 16D.1, 16D.2, 16D.3,16F2.1, 16F3.1, 16F5.1, 16F5.2, 16F5.3, 16F5.4, 16F5.5, 16F5.6, 16F6.2, 16F6.3, 16H.1, 16H.2, 16H.3, 16H.4, 16H.5, 16H.6, 16H.7, 16K.1, 16K.2, 16K.3, 16K.4, 16K.5, 16K.6, 16K.7, 16K.8, 17A.5, 17C.1, 17D1.1, 17D1.2, 17D1.3, 17D2.1,17D2.2, 17D3.1, 17D4.1, 17D4.2, 17D4.3. 17D4.4, 17D4.5, 17D4.6, 17D5.1, 17D5.2, 17E2.1, 17E3.1, 17E3.2, 17E3.3,17E5.2, 17E5.3, 17E5.4, 17E5.5, 17E5.6, 17E5.7, 17E5.8, 17E5,9, 17E5.10, 17E5.11, 17E5.12, 17E5.13, 17E5.14, 17E5.15, 17E5.16, 17E5.18, 17E5.19,17E5.20, 17F3.2, 17F3.3, 17F4.1, 17F4.2, 17F4.3, 17F4.5, 17F5.1,17F5.2, 17F5.3, 17F5.4, 17F5.5, 17F5.6, 17F5.7, 17F5.8, 17F5.9, 17F5.10, 17F5.11, 17F5.12, 17F5.13, 17G2.1, 17G3.2, 17G3.3, 17G3.4, 17G6.1, 17G6.2, 17G6.3, 17G6.4, 17G6.5, 17G6.6,17G8.2, 17G8.4, 17G8.5, 17G8.6, 17G8.7, 17G8.8, 17G8.9, 18D.1, 18D.2

CATEGORY 2: Figures 7J.1, 7J.2, 7J.3, 7N.1.2, 7N.3.1, 7N.3.2, 7N.3.3, 8N.3.4, 8N.3.5, 11C.1, 11C.2, 11C.3, 11C.5, 14.1, 14.2, 15A.1, 15A.3,15A.4, 15A.5,15A.6, 15A.7, 15A.8, 15A.9, 16F3.1, 16F6.1, 16I.1, 16I.2, 16K.9, 16K.10, 16K.11, 16K.12, 17A.1, 17A.2, 17A.3, 17A.4, 17A.5, 17A.6, 17A.7, 17A.8, 17A.9, 17A.10, 17A.11, 17A.12, 17A.13, 17E2.2, 17E2.3, 17E2.4, 17F2.1, 17F2.2, 17F2.3, 17F3.1, 17G1.1,17G1.2, 17G1.3, 17G2.2, 17G3.1, 17G8.1, 17G8.10, 17G8.11, 17G8.12, 17G9.1, 17G9.2, 17G9.3, 17G9.4, 17G9.5, 17G9,6, 17G9.7,

APPENDIX IV. SUPPLEMENTAL MATERIALS. – EXPERIMENTS

I occasionally propose that you do an experiment. Additional information you need for each is listed here. If you may need to purchase something, I'll try to give Amazon ordering information (just a suggestion) based on the Amazon website of March, 2022.

In **Section 2D** I discuss using a small pocket balance. It is useful for you to know things such as the weight of a paperclip or a pin or a penny. Amazon sells inexpensive balances such as the GOSONO Digital Pocket Balance Weight. Scale measuring tool. It can measure up to 200 grams, accurate to 0.01 grams. It can report results in units of grams or ounces. $6.99 rated 4.1out of 5 stars

CHAPTER 9. How many bills can you put in a shoebox?
Supplies needed
- Scissors
- Tape
- Cardboard/cardstock
- Paper

Safety Considerations: Don't run with scissors

CHAPTER 12. Fingerprinting
Dusting for fingerprints
- An inexpensive alternative to a squirrel hair brush:
  - Safariland disposable latent print brush
  - $9.49
  - Rating: 4.7 out of 5 stars
- Dusting powder:
  - Lightning powder black latent fingerprint powder, 2 ounces
  - $11.74
  - Rating: 4.3 out of 5 stars

- Silver nitrate crystals/powder
  - 5 grams. 99.99% pure
  - $29.99
  - Rating: 4.5 out of 5 stars
- Iodine crystals
  - 1 gram
  - Luciteria Science
  - $7.50

All in one makeup kit

20 eyeshadows, 3 blushes, 1 concealer, mirror, brush
for teens, beginners
$8.99
Rating: 4.3 out of 5 stars

Safety Precautions: When you buy a chemical compound it should come with an MSDS (Material Safety Data Sheet). These include all safety considerations you need to know. There are many free collections of MSDS's on the web. See, for example:

Iodine. https://www.labchem.com/tools/msds/msds/LC15590.pdf
Silver nitrate. www.silvernitrate.org/info/MSDS-AgNO3.PDF

Always work in a well-ventilated area, wear safety glasses, and avoid getting any compounds on your skin, as the MSDS will recommend.

APPENDIX V. FOR YOUR (POSSIBLE) ENTERTAINMENT: A SHORT STORY

Did I ever tell you that I write short stories (and occasional plays and monologues)? Well, I do. Here's one for free. I hope you find it entertaining. Only someone at the end of this book could appreciate it. My short story is called *He Said his Name was John T.A. …*, presented here for the first time. Considering some of the more recent "Lindbergh books" out there, it presents an equally likely explanation to it all.

Title: *He Said his Name was John T.A. …*
By John Allison

Aliens … yes, aliens. They are a very interesting group, at least most of the species we've met so far. They can project their own image so you can see them where they're not. They seem to smile a lot (and they do) and communicate telepathically. You'll know it when you do it. "If you've never seen Spielberg's *Close Encounters of the Third Kind*, rent it," John T.A. once told Lindbergh. John The Alien (T.A.) is in the movie, although hard to pick out of the crowd. He walks out of the alien posse as the first to interact with a human. Although you'd think it hard to see into the future, John T.A. apparently can, so when he told Lindbergh to rent a movie that hadn't yet been made, Charles has no idea what that meant.

The very first time Lindbergh flew without someone else training him, he climbed and climbed, addicted to the view of the countryside below. He spotted a strange, cigar-shaped aircraft flying alongside. John appeared to him, floating along just outside the trainer biplane, smiling and calmly, gently speaking to Lindbergh. Charles had no choice but to believe what he was hearing and seeing, although of course, he didn't appreciate the joke of the Alien calling himself John at the time. They bonded that day, and years later John T.A. helped him win the Orteig Prize. Lindy never stated that he didn't actually cross the Atlantic without assistance.

John would, over the next few decades, share some important technology with him. "They" wanted to help to transfer their technology to Earth through Lindbergh and he was an eager recipient. John T.A. would make Lindy famous and beyond. In return, John needed people for his work. For his studies, it would be ideal to have one young and one old human. No rush. John promised they'd be treated well and would eventually live back on John's planet. Lindbergh agreed.

When asked how he got the name John, he said that Jafsie gave it to him. Just another one of his little jokes where Lindbergh had no clue what it meant. John telepathically chuckled.

Lindbergh would often see John, usually when he was in the air, but John could project his image anywhere, and much of Lindbergh's adult life was influenced by the alien. He proposed many of the concepts that lead to the construction of the Spirit of St. Louis and kept his part of the deal by making Lindbergh rich and famous.

Lucky Lindy would not have completed that New York to Paris flight that made him an overnight sensation, were it not for John T.A. About 50 miles out of NY, Lindbergh was flying at a fairly high altitude when his single engine stopped. While this was very bad news for Lindbergh, he was also shocked when an old man, only known as Barbara Harrison's Uncle, crawled out from behind some canvas bags and said, "Dona worry Mr. Lindbergher, I'm here to help you." (His accent sounded like that of Lawrence Welk.). A stowaway on The Spirit! Then Lindbergh heard in his head the voice of John. "What can I do? How can I help?"

It seemed like the engine was not getting fuel, Lindbergh explained to John. John started to systematically look at every part of the engine, projecting the images into Charles' head. "There! I see it," Lindbergh said. There was a valve in the fuel line that is partially closed. How sloppy of him. He explained it to John, and John's projection reached in and turned the valve clockwise, opening it up. Lindbergh explained to John how he would have to spin the propeller once for it to restart, and John did as he was asked. The engine roared back to life. Barbara's Uncle didn't know what was going on when John introduced himself, and John didn't know that the second man in the cockpit was a stowaway.

After the fuel line was fixed, Lindbergh, still stunned that he had an old man on board, remembered his deal with John.

"John," he said, "I'd like to present you with part one of my promise, an older human. He's all yours and you may take him with you." John did and the man was never seen again on this planet.

So, because of John T.A.'s help, Lindbergh completed his flight to an awaiting Parisian crowd, and as all could see, it was a solo effort.

It was John T.A. who gently teased Lindbergh about being such a loner and pointed out shy, quiet, and smart Anne Morrow. "Pick her," John said. "You two will have some amazing adventures, I promise you." So, pick Anne he did. Lindbergh had learned that a suggestion by John always worked out well. John always offered a 10-year guarantee with his life-recommendations.

John T.A. disappeared from Lindbergh's life for a while, until Charles and his new wife started flying around New Jersey looking for land on which they would build their house. John appeared to Lindbergh one afternoon and pointed out a mountain top where they'd be very isolated and would also have enough room to build a runway and a small hangar. After it was built, John would occasionally use the runway to land his ride, which Lindbergh had dubbed The Cigar II. (No, there was no Cigar I). Lindy would occasionally agree on times when they could meet and talk there, in person. John T.A. was a hard secret to keep but the technology he kept sharing was so phenomenal, it was worth the silence.

Of course, the Whateleys saw the Cigar II land multiple times and watched the small alien with the skinny little body, big head and big almond-shaped eyes come into the house. They admired the little guy, but it was clear that their biggest strengths did not include keeping secrets, so at the end of each visit, John T.A. would have to wipe some memories from their brains (an idea he got from *The Men in Black*). To John, we were simple creatures, easy to manipulate, especially Lindbergh.

While John could project his image, and physically appear at that location as well, he had all sorts of other talents in addition to telepathy. He could essentially float in the air – one little trick that Charles greatly admired and wanted. "Maybe in 10,000 years," John T.A. replied.

Oh yes, on the topic of the kidnapping -- Charles and Anne had their first child. Weird little kid. Lindbergh never liked him much and Anne rarely had enough time to do that mother-son bonding thing. John T.A. would just look at Little Charlie. One time, he projected a picture of John T.A. with Little Charlie to Lindbergh. Lindbergh smiled realizing they both had unusually large heads. One day John T.A. said, "OK Charles, let me just say it. You still owe me a young human and I can see you've yet to bond with him, or as *you* call him, it. Anne does not seem to be connected enough to him either. Little Charlie is not wanted here, but he'd be loved back on my planet. I'll personally, what's the word you use, adopt him? I promise he'll be well cared for and loved and will see the Universe as few humans have. Charles, can I take him?"

Charles blurted out as fast as his lips could move, "Yes! Please! Yes!" But Anne is his mother, and Charles couldn't predict if she'd allow this. "We need to somehow just have Little Charlie disappear into the night," Lindbergh said.

"I'll take care of everything, Charles," John T.A. replied. "You know you can trust me."

It was a cold and rainy evening. John T.A. hovered outside Little Charlie's window, watching Anne and Betty putting him down for the night. He had what humans called a bad cold and was not happy. As soon as they left the room, John materialized next to the crib. He looked into it and touched Little Charlie's head, filling it with images of his new life with John. While Little Charlie could not yet express his feelings, he could feel John's adoration and his parent's coldness, and was happy to finally be loved. John T.A. took Little Charlie out of his crib and wrapped his arms around him as the two disappeared from the nursery, reappearing on the Cigar II, which hovered just above the house, above the low-lying clouds. So, no footprints, no fingerprints (John's race lost fingerprints millennia ago), no crying or noises (Little Charlie was more than ready for a change of scenery, although he wished he could have taken his dog, Sparky. Unfortunately, John T.A. was allergic to earth pets.)

Little Charlie vanished from the Lindberghs' life without even a wave good-bye. No sorrow, only relief. John T.A. was not impressed with human beings if most of them were like the Lindberghs.

John never had a chance to say goodbye to Lindbergh, but pictures would occasionally be injected into Charles' brain of Little Charlie (growing up fast) and John T.A. on a beautiful two-mooned planet, both with big smiles (the two guys, not the moons). New tech would also regularly pop into Lindbergh's mind, which he always pursued. Medical concepts, rocketry, exploration of Mexico by air – all John T.A.'s ideas, all making Lindbergh over and over, the hero of a planet.

John never sent any pictures of Barbara's Uncle. He didn't have the heart to tell Charles that the old man had died on the trip home, and John didn't ask for a replacement. Pity, he was a nice old man, but he never stopped talking! Charles sensed relief as well as sadness.

John T.A. would have been great as an earthling; sad that he chose not to stick around.

Oh, and if you're wondering about the ladder, it belonged to a construction worker who left it in the grass three months before the reported kidnapping. It was never up against the house for anything other than construction work.

So now you know how little Charlie was kidnapped. It wasn't an Alien Abduction, although all the signs were there if you can look at things from that perspective. It was just as John said, an alien adoption.

This story is completely true. Charles never told anyone except Ollie Whateley, one dark and stormy night, as they spent the evening drinking scotch and talking. It was the one-year anniversary of the night that Hauptmann was arrested. Neither Lindbergh nor his new associate, John Condon, seemed uneasy in picking a person out of the blue and ruining his life, just so Anne could keep thinking it was a kidnapping. Hauptmann was also an alien, of a completely different order. He agreed to participate in this little charade as a favor to Condon. He pretended that the thousands of volts sent through his body affected him, but they didn't. Now you know. No one else has been able to put together a reasonable explanation of it all, not like this. You should also be aware that John T.A. is the real hero of this crazy story.

Oh, and of course Spielberg was very appreciative of John T.A. and his work on *Close Encounters*. It's all there for us to see when we want it to.

In the Cigar II on the ride home, Little Charlie was playing a game with John. Charlie giggled, something which Lindbergh had never heard, and it really is very infectious. Too bad.

You should know that Little Charlie spent much of his young life visiting other worlds. He became an interstellar celebrity, much like Daddy was back on earth.

OK, I'll let you ask one question. Yes, uh huh, ok. If Little Charlie left with John, how do we explain a child's body found near the house? John T.A. found a dying boy similar in stature to Little Charlie (in South Dakota- it was a fiery car crash in Rapid City (the gateway to Mt. Rushmore)). The child and both parents died, and John T.A. brought the child's body back to New Jersey – a child that Charles could swear was his son, and he did, as the alien ship circled earth once and then sped out past the moon's orbit.

John Allison
Manhattan, NY
1 April 1935.

I just heard you roll your eyes. If you want to know more about Lindbergh and Aliens, consult the creators of The History channel (History.com). They maintain a website called "10 Fascinating Facts About Charles Lindbergh." Fact #4 discusses Lindbergh and John, focusing on Lindy's hallucinations during his New York – Paris flight.

Lindbergh had been up for 22 hours before his famous 33 hour flight, and the sleep deprivation was said to be the cause of hallucinations.

Of course, Lindbergh couldn't really talk about John T.A., but the medical community asked questions about the effects of sleep deprivation, so Lindbergh reported "vaguely outlined forms, transparent, moving, riding weightless with me in the plane."

"Lindbergh even claimed the apparitions spoke to him and offered words of wisdom for his journey."

Printed in the USA
CPSIA information can be obtained
at www.ICGtesting.com
LVHW081140150524
780224LV00010B/254